KT-477-114

MY FAVOURITE WIFE

Hot shot young lawyer Bill Holden and his wife Becca move with their four-year-old daughter to the booming, gold-rush city of Shanghai.

Bill's law firm houses the family in a luxury mansion block full of 'second wives': beautiful young women like their neighbour JinJin Li. After Becca witnesses a near-tragedy, she returns to London with Holly—and Bill and JinJin are thrown together.

Bill wants to be a better man than the millionaire who keeps JinJin Li as a second wife. But can he give JinJin anything different—can he give her the love she deserves? And can he love his wife too?

WITHDRAWN FROM LIBRARY

MY FAVOURITE WIFE

Tony Parsons

WINDSOR
PARAGON

First published 2008
by HarperCollins
This Large Print edition published 2008
by BBC Audiobooks Ltd
by arrangement with
HarperCollins Publishers

Hardcover   ISBN: 978 1 405 64915 5
Softcover   ISBN: 978 1 405 64916 2

Copyright © Tony Parsons 2008

Tony Parsons asserts the moral right to be
identified as the author of this work.

This novel is entirely a work of fiction. The names,
characters and incidents portrayed in it are the
work of the author's imagination. Any
resemblance to actual persons, living or dead,
events or localities is entirely coincidental.

All rights reserved.

British Library Cataloguing in Publication Data available

City of Liverpool College

Acc No.	Date Cat
6582117	10·10·17
DDC	RFID
FIC PAR	£18.99

Printed and bound in Great Britain by
CPI Antony Rowe, Chippenham, Wiltshire

For Yuriko, MFW

You see, I loved her.
It was love at first sight,
at last sight,
at ever and ever sight.

Lolita

A man with two houses loses his mind.
A man with two women loses his soul.

Chinese proverb

PART ONE:

BE THE PRINCE

ONE

Bill must have fallen asleep for a moment. He was jolted awake by the limo hitting a pothole and suddenly there was Shanghai. The towers of Pudong split the night. He rubbed his eyes, and turned to look at his wife and daughter in the back seat.

Holly, their four-year-old, was sleeping with her head in her mother's lap, blonde curls tumbling across her face, dressed like some sort of Disney princess. He wasn't sure which one.

'She can't be comfortable in that,' he said, keeping his voice down. Holly had been awake, or sleeping fitfully, for most of the flight.

Becca, his wife, carefully removed the child's tiara. 'She's fine,' she said.

'Foreigners are very jealous they see this,' said the driver, whose name was Tiger. He indicated the Pudong skyline. 'Fifteen year ago—all swampland.' Tiger was young, barely in his twenties, wearing a half-hearted sort of uniform with three gold stripes on his cuff. The young man bobbed his head with emphatic pride. 'New, boss—all new.'

Bill nodded politely. But it wasn't the newness of Shanghai that overwhelmed him. It was the sheer scale of the place. They were crossing a river much wider than anything he had expected and on the far side he could see the golden glow of the Bund, the colonial buildings of the pre-war city staring across at Pudong's skyscrapers. Shanghai past facing Shanghai future.

3

The car came off the bridge and down a ramp, picking up speed as the traffic thinned. Three men, filthy and black, their clothes in tatters, all perched on one ancient bicycle with no lights, slowly wobbled up the ramp towards the oncoming traffic. One was squatting on the handlebars, another was leaning back in the seat and the third was standing up and pumping on the pedals. They visibly shook as the car shot past. Then they were gone.

Neither Becca nor the driver seemed to notice them and it crossed Bill's mind that they had been a vision brought on by the exhaustion and excitement. Three men in rags on a dead bicycle, moving far too slow in the fast lane, and going in completely the wrong direction.

'Daddy?' His daughter was stirring from deep inside her ball gown.

Becca pulled her closer. 'Mummy's here,' she said.

Holly sighed, a four-year-old whose patience was wearing thin.

She kicked the back of the passenger seat.

'I need both of you,' the child said.

*   *   *

Bill let them into the apartment and they gawped at the splendour of it all, like tourists in their own home.

He thought of their Victorian terrace in London, the dark staircase and crumbling bay window and musty basement, holding the dead air of a hundred years. There was nothing shabby and old here. He turned the key and it was like stepping into a new century.

There were gifts waiting for them. A bouquet of white lilies in cellophane. Champagne in a bucket of melted ice. The biggest basket of fruit in the world.

> *For Bill Holden and family—welcome to Shanghai—from all your colleagues at Butterfield, Hunt and West.*

He picked up the bottle and looked at the shield-shaped label.

Dom Pérignon, he thought. Dom Pérignon in China.

Bill went to the door of the master bedroom and watched Becca gently getting the sleeping child into her pyjamas. She was quietly snoring.

'Sleeping Beauty,' he smiled.

'She's Belle,' Becca corrected. 'From *Beauty and the Beast*. You know—like us.'

'You're too hard on yourself, Bec.'

Becca eased Holly into her pyjamas. 'She can come in with us tonight,' she whispered. 'In case she wakes up. And doesn't know where she is.'

He nodded, and came over to the bed to kiss his daughter goodnight, feeling a surge of tenderness as his lips brushed her cheek. Then he left Becca to it, and went off to explore the apartment. He was bone tired but very happy, switching lights on and off, playing with the remote of the big plasma TV, opening and shutting cupboards, unable to believe the size of the place, feeling like a lucky man. Even full of the crates they had had shipped ahead from London, the glossy apartment was impressive. Flat 31, Block B, Paradise Mansions,

5

Hongqiao Road, Gubei New Area, Shanghai, People's Republic of China. It was in a different league to anywhere they had ever lived back home.

If they stayed on at the end of his two-year contract then they were promised a step up the Shanghai property ladder to an ex-pat compound with its own golf course, spa and pool. But Bill liked it here. What could be better than this? He thought of his father and wondered what the old man would say about this place. The old man would go crazy.

The suitcases could wait until tomorrow to be unpacked. He carried the bottle into the kitchen and rummaged around until he found two glasses. When he came back Becca was at the window. 'You should see this,' she said.

Bill handed his wife a glass and looked down ten storeys to the courtyard below. Paradise Mansions was four blocks of flats surrounding a central courtyard. There was a mother-and-child fountain at its centre, lights glinting below the water.

The courtyard was clogged with brand-new cars, their engines purring. BMWs, Audis, Mercs, the odd Porsche Boxster and two 911s. At the wheel, or lounging by the open driver's door, were sleek-looking Chinese men. They looked as if they came from a different world to the three men on the bicycle. The porter was moving between the cars, gesturing, trying to regain control. Nobody seemed to be taking any notice of him.

'Because it's Saturday night,' Bill said, sipping his champagne.

'That's not it,' Becca said. 'Cheers.' They clinked glasses and she nodded at the window. 'Watch.'

So he watched, and he saw young women begin

to emerge from Paradise Mansions. They were all dressed up, and like the female leads in some wildlife documentary about mating rituals, each joined one of the men waiting in the cars. They did not kiss.

One of them caught his eye. A tall girl with a flower in her hair. An orchid, he thought. Maybe an orchid.

She came out of the block opposite, and headed for one of the 911s. She raised her face to their window and Becca waved, but the young woman did not respond. She slid her long body into the passenger seat of the Porsche, struggling with her legs and her skirt. The man at the wheel turned his face and said something to her. He was older by about ten years. The girl pulled the door shut, and the Porsche moved away.

Bill and Becca looked at each other and laughed.

'What is this place?' she smiled, shaking her head. 'Is this place a . . . what *is* this place?'

But he had no idea.

So they drank their champagne and watched the beautiful girls of Paradise Mansions pairing off with the men in their fancy cars, and by the time they had drained their glasses they were both dumbstruck by weariness.

So they took a shower together, soaping each other with tender familiarity and then they got in bed with Holly between them. They smiled at each other over the child's face.

*   *   *

He slept until first light and then abruptly he was wide-awake.

7

He counted the things stopping him from going back to sleep. His body clock was pining for London time. Tomorrow morning at 8 a.m. the driver—Tiger—would take him to the Pudong offices of Butterfield, Hunt and West, and he would start his new job. He was curious to know where they were, and what their new life looked like in daylight. How could he possibly sleep with his head so full? As quietly as he could, Bill got up, got dressed and slipped out of the apartment.

The courtyard where the men in cars had waited for the girls was empty apart from Tiger. He was sleeping with his bare feet on the dashboard of the limo, his legs either side of the steering wheel. He jumped to attention when Bill walked past.

'Where to, boss?' he said, pulling on his shoes.

'It's Sunday,' Bill said. 'Don't they give you the day off on Sunday?'

Tiger looked blank. And then hurt. 'Where we going, boss?'

'I'm walking,' Bill said. 'And stop calling me boss.'

The Sabbath may have meant nothing to Tiger but out on the streets of Gubei New Area it felt almost like Sunday morning back home, with nobody around apart from the odd jogger and dog walker, the neighbourhood shuttered and still. It was early June, and the heat was already starting to build.

Bill walked. He was hungry to see what he thought of as *the real China*, the China that was nothing to do with plasma televisions and Dom Pérignon. The real China was somewhere nearby. It had to be. There were blocks of flats as far as he could see in a bewildering jumble of styles, but broken up with patches of manicured green and oversized statues. There were strips of restaurants—he could see Thai, Italian, everything but Chinese—a Carrefour supermarket, and a couple of international schools, including the one that Holly would go to in the morning. Little parks. A nice neighbourhood. Gubei was greener and cleaner than the grimy, crime-ridden patch of London they had left behind. His family could live here. His wife and daughter could be happy here. He felt a quiet satisfaction, mixed with relief.

He glanced at his watch and decided he had time to explore before Becca and Holly stirred. So he walked towards the rising sun and as he left Gubei New Area behind, the streets quickly filled. Women selling bruised fruit stared through him from shaded side streets. Someone bumped into him. Someone else spat at his feet. There were men in filthy, dirt-encrusted two-piece suits working on a building site. On a Sunday. And in the streets there were people. A tide of people. Suddenly there were people everywhere.

He stopped, trying to get his bearings. The roads were wide and traffic flew by, horns mindlessly beeping, ignoring red lights and pedestrians and the rest of the traffic. He saw a chic girl in sunglasses with her hair up behind the wheel of a silver Buick Excelle. There were flocks of VW Santana taxis. A muddy truck piled high with junk and men. And more trucks, lots of them, with their strange cargo of cardboard or orange traffic cones or pigs or yet more cars, so new they still shone with the showroom wax.

As the sun got higher, and Bill continued to walk east, the city got noisier, adding to his sense of

9

dislocation. A woman on a scooter mounted the pavement and just missed him, beeping her horn furiously. Schools of cyclists with giant black visors over their faces swarmed past. Suddenly he was aware of the time difference, the light-headedness that follows a long-haul flight, the sweat of exhaustion. But he kept walking. He wanted to know something about this place.

He walked down alleys where thin men shaved over ancient metal bowls and fat babies were fed, and where ramshackle buildings with red-tile roofs were draped with drying laundry and satellite dishes. Then abruptly the jumbled blocks with their red-tile roofs suddenly gave way to the new shining towers and shopping malls.

Outside Prada men with their skin darkened by sun and grime tried to sell him fake Rolex watches and DVDs of the latest Tom Cruise movie. Young women hid from the sun under umbrellas. Naked Western models advertised skin-lightening products on giant billboards.

And as Bill walked on, he felt something that he had never felt in his life, and it was an awareness of the sheer mass of humanity. All those people in the world, all those lives. It was as if he truly believed in their existence for the first time. Shanghai gave him no choice.

Bill hailed one of the Santana taxis, impatient to see the Bund, but the driver didn't understand a word he said and dropped him by the river, glad to get rid of him. He got out next to a wharf with a ferry; not a sightseeing ferry but some kind of local public transport.

Bill handed over his smallest note, received some filthy RMB in return, and joined the milling mob waiting to cross to the other side. He tried to work out where the queue began. Then he realised that it didn't begin anywhere.

And as the ferry filled with people, and then continued to fill even more until Bill was hemmed in on every side, and fighting back the feeling that the ferry was overloaded, he saw that here, at last, was the real China.

The numbers.

It was all about the numbers.

He knew that the numbers were why he would be starting his new job in the morning, why his family's future would be decided in this city, and why all the money problems of the past would soon be over. They filled the dreams of businessmen from Sydney to San Francisco—the one billion customers, the one billion new capitalists, the one billion market place.

He struggled to move his arms and glanced at his watch, wondering if he could make it back home to his girls before they woke up.

The ferry began to move.

*   *   *

That afternoon they did the tourist thing.

The three of them joined the queues and took the lift to the top of the Oriental Pearl TV Tower where they stared down at the boats on the Huangpu River and saw that the city seemed to be without end.

On the other side of the tower they looked down at a park that was full of brides, hundreds of them, all in white, looking like a flock of swans as they surrounded the lakes, feeding confetti-coloured

11

fish food to koi carp.

Bill lifted his daughter so she could see.

'New school tomorrow,' he said.

Holly said nothing, her eyes wide at the sight of all those brides.

'You're going to make lots of new friends,' Becca said, gripping one of Holly's ankles, and shaking it with encouragement.

Holly thought about it, chewing her bottom lip.

'I'm going to be very busy,' she said.

Although foreigners were a common sight in Shanghai now, Bill and Becca and Holly were the only non-Chinese at the top of the Oriental Pearl TV Tower that afternoon, and people stared at them.

The child and the woman were so blonde, their skin so pale, and their eyes so blue they looked like weather. The man holding his little girl and the child with her arms circling her father's neck and the woman with her arm draped around her husband's shoulders.

That's what was noticed about them—those gestures of child-like affection, the little family holding on to each other in their new home, as if the three of them could not exist without that physical contact, or without each other.

Everybody knew that Westerners didn't care about family in the same way that the Chinese did, especially not Westerners in Shanghai. But this man and woman and child seemed different.

TWO

He was gone by the time she woke up.

Letting Holly sleep on, Becca padded through the flat, edging around the stacks of crates. There was the sign of a shower, the smell of after-shave, a tie that had been considered and discarded on the back of a chair. She pictured Bill at his desk on the first day of his new job, working hard, the earnest face frowning, and felt a stab of the old feeling, the feeling you get at the start.

She picked one of the crates at random and prised it open. It was full of baby stuff. A pink high chair in three pieces. A bassinet. A cot mattress. Assorted blankets, sterilisers and stuffed rabbits. All of Holly's old things. She had kept them, and shipped them across the world, not for sentimental reasons. Becca had kept them for the next one. Their marriage, seven years old now, was at the stage where neither of them doubted that there would be another child.

Becca went back to the bedroom and watched Holly sleeping. Then she pushed back the sheets and held her daughter's feet until the child began to stir. Holly stretched, moaned and tried to curl up into sleep.

'Wakey-wakey, rise and shaky,' Becca said. She stood listening to her daughter's laboured breathing, a wheezing more than a snoring, caused by Holly's asthma. 'Come on now, darling. You've got school.'

While Holly came round, Becca banged about in the strange new kitchen, preparing breakfast.

Yawning, Holly came and sat at the table.

'I'm a bit worried,' she said, with her spoon poised halfway to her mouth. Becca touched her daughter's face, curled a tendril of hair behind her tiny sticky-out ears.

'What are you worried about, darling?' Becca said.

'I'm a bit worried about dead people,' Holly said solemnly, the corners of her mouth turning down.

Becca sat back. 'Dead people?'

The child nodded. 'I'm afraid they're not going to get better.'

Becca sighed, tapping the table. 'Don't worry about dead people,' she said. 'Worry about your Coco-Pops.'

After breakfast Becca set up the breathing machine. It was routine now. The thing had a mouthpiece to make it easy for Holly to inhale her medication, and her blue eyes were wide above it.

Just before nine, Becca and Holly walked hand in hand to the Gubei International School. The children seemed to be from every nation on earth. There was that awkward moment when it was time to part and Holly clung to the belt of her mother's jeans. But then a small, plump girl of about four who looked like she was from Korea or Japan took Holly's hand and led her into the class, where the Australian teacher was taking registration, and Becca was the one who was reluctant to leave.

Everyone else was rushing off. Some of them were dressed for the office, some of them were dressed for the gym, but all of them acted like they had somewhere very important to go. Then there was a woman by her side, smiling, wheeling a fat toddler in a pushchair. The mother of the child

14

who had taken Holly's hand.

'First day,' she said in an American accent. 'Tough, right?'

Becca nodded. 'You know what it's like. The trembling chin. Fighting back the tears. Trying to be brave.' She looked at the woman. 'And that's just me.'

The woman laughed. 'Kyoko Smith,' she said, offering her hand. Becca shook it. Kyoko said she was a lawyer from Yokohama, not practising, married to an attorney from New York. They had been in Shanghai for almost two years. Becca said she was a journalist, currently resting, and she was married to yet another lawyer, whose name was Bill. They had been in Shanghai for two days.

'You want to get coffee sometime?' Kyoko asked Becca. 'Tomorrow, maybe? I've got to run right now.'

'Oh, me too,' Becca said. 'I have to run too.'

'Well, that's Shanghai,' Kyoko Smith smiled. 'Everybody always has to run.'

As Becca walked slowly back to Paradise Mansions she called Bill on his mobile.

'She go off okay?' Someone was with him. Becca could tell. She could also tell he had been thinking about Holly on her first day.

'Oh, she was fine,' she said, far breezier than she felt.

'She'll be okay, Bec,' he said, knowing how hard it was for her to leave their daughter. 'It will be good for her to be with kids her own age. We have to let her go sooner or later, don't we?'

The silence hummed between them and she made no attempt to fill it. She fought back the sudden tears, angry with herself for feeling like a

15

mad housewife.

'Try not to worry too much,' he said. 'Listen, I'll see you later, okay?'

Becca still said nothing. She was thinking, wondering if the best thing for Holly wasn't to stay with her, just keep her close, weighing it all up. Then she finally said, 'Good luck up there, Bill,' releasing him to get on with his job.

She couldn't face the flat and all that unpacking. Not yet. So she caught a taxi to Xintiandi, the new area they always talked about in the guidebooks, the place she had been looking forward to seeing, where they said you could see the oldest and newest parts of the city. The flat could wait.

> *Suddenly a puff of wind, a puff faint and tepid and laden with strange odours of blossoms, of aromatic wood, comes out of the still night— the first sigh of the East on my face. That I can never forget. It was impalpable and enslaving, like a charm, like a whispered promise of mysterious delight.*

Becca sipped a skinny latte on a stool by the window and read her Joseph Conrad paperback. That was what she was seeking in Xintiandi. The first sigh of the East on her face. On a side street away from the cafés and restaurants, she found the place she was seeking.

The modest little museum on Huangpi Lu was where the Chinese Communist Party had first met. She paid 3 RMB to go in, a sum so small she couldn't calculate it in pounds. The place was deserted. The only other visitor was a serious female student in thick glasses taking notes by a

16

tableau of dummies plotting to overthrow the foreigners and free the masses. All eyes were on the waxy features of the young Mao.

Becca drifted across to a small television displaying a propaganda film about China before the revolution. The film was grainy and ancient and only lasted a few minutes, but Becca watched it dumbfounded.

The starving faces of long-dead children stared back at her. She had never seen such poverty and misery, and as the images blurred behind a veil of tears she had to look away, telling herself, *Get a bloody grip, woman*, telling herself it was just the jet-lag and Holly's first day at school.

*   *   *

Shanghai was Becca's idea.

Bill would have been happy to stay in London and build a life together, and work hard, and watch their daughter grow. But life in London had disappointed her in a way that it had not disappointed him. Becca was ready for them to try something new. She saw Shanghai as a way out of their old life and their constant struggle for money. Shanghai was where they would turn it all around.

They had married young, both of them twenty-four, the first of their little group to settle down. They had never regretted it.

Becca had watched their single friends optimistically hooking up with someone they had just met in a bar, or a club, or a gym, only to grow unhappy, or bored, or trapped, or get their heart kicked around, and she was glad to say good riddance to all of that.

17

Marriage had seemed natural to them. They talked about it. If you find the right person, and you are both sure, then you can't be too young, can you? And even at twenty-four both of them had felt too old for the sad dance of the gym and the bar and the club.

Some things they didn't need to talk about. They had always taken it for granted that they would both work, and this didn't change when Holly was born just after their third anniversary. Because it couldn't change. Bill was a corporate lawyer at a firm in the City, Becca a financial journalist at a newspaper in Canary Wharf, and the mortgage payments on their little house in one of the leafier corners of North London demanded that they both keep earning. Every morning Bill would take Holly to nursery, and every afternoon Becca would pick her up.

And then one day everything changed.

Holly had just turned three and she had been at her nursery for a few hours when suddenly she was struggling to breathe. 'Just a cold,' said one of the carers, even when the child began to sob with terror and frustration. 'Just a very bad cold.'

By the time Becca came to collect her, Holly was ready to be rushed to the nearest Accident and Emergency. By the time Bill arrived at the hospital, the doctor had diagnosed asthma. Holly never went back to the nursery and Becca never went back to her newspaper.

'No stranger will ever look after her the way I will,' Becca said, choking back tears of rage, and he soothed her, and he understood, and he told her that of course she was right, and nothing was more important than Holly.

Holly's asthma was controlled with the help of a paediatrician in Great Ormond Street, who prescribed chewable tablets that she quite enjoyed and the breathing machine. She was brave and good-natured, never complaining, and Becca and Bill tried not to ask the question posed by every parent of a sick child—*Why her?* There were children far worse off than Holly. They saw them every time they came to Great Ormond Street.

But while Holly slept at night, sometimes making that strange sound at the back of her throat that they now recognised as a symptom of the asthma, Bill and Becca got out the calculators, applied for online overdrafts, thought about remortgaging, and wondered how long they could stay in their home.

They talked about moving to a cheaper, bleaker neighbourhood a few miles east. They talked about staying in the neighbourhood but selling their home and renting for a while. They talked about moving out to the suburbs. And everything they talked about depressed them.

Holly was well, and of course that was the main thing, but suddenly they were struggling just to get by. They loved their house. That was a problem. And they needed their house. That was another problem. Sometimes the senior partners at the firm invited them to dinner in their magnificent homes, these smooth-skinned old millionaires with their charming, hawk-eyed wives, and when you invited them back, you wanted them to come to a neighbourhood where they wouldn't necessarily get mugged at knife-point for the bottle of Margaux they were carrying.

'One of your senior partners had his wife's

19

fiftieth birthday party at the Sandy Lane,' Becca said. 'When they come over to our place, we can't open a six-pack in a bedsit.'

'We'll never have to open a six-pack in a bedsit,' Bill said, a note of resentment in his voice.

She put her arms around his neck. 'You know what I mean, darling,' she said.

He knew what she meant.

Some of the firm's younger lawyers were already in big flats or small houses in Notting Hill and Kensington and Islington, bankrolled by indulgent parents who stayed together, or guilty parents who didn't. Bill and Becca were doing it on their own. Nobody was giving them a thing.

Then suddenly there was a way to end all their money worries. Your life can change in a moment, Becca realised. You go through the years thinking you know what the future looks like and then one day it looks like something else.

Becca sat next to a man at the annual dinner of Bill's firm, and nothing was ever the same again.

*   *   *

Every January, Hunt, Butterfield and West rented one of those big soulless hangars in a posh Park Lane hotel and personnel from the firm's offices all over the world flew in to celebrate the anniversary of Robbie Burns' birth. Five hundred lawyers in black tie, or kilt, and their wives—or, more rarely, their husbands.

Bill found himself sitting between the wives of two senior partners from New York, who knew each other and were happily talking across him. Becca was at the next table and she smiled as he

20

rolled his eyes and mouthed three little words—
Kill me now. Then she looked up as two men sat
down either side of her. The men from Shanghai.

One of them was a big blond Australian in a
kilt—Shane Gale, he said. He looked like he had
been a surfer ten, fifteen years ago. Head of
Litigation in Shanghai, he said. Shane was
suffering from the effects of the champagne
reception, but the way he avoided eye contact
made Becca think that perhaps his real problem
was not drunkenness but shyness.

The man on the other side was a tall, thin
Englishman called Hugh Devlin, senior partner of
the Shanghai office. It was funny the way their job
titles tripped off their tongues as naturally as their
names, she thought, fighting back the urge to say
*Becca Holden—housewife, homemaker and former
financial hack*.

While Shane silently buried his face in the
Burgundy and started to get seriously rat-faced,
Devlin took the table in hand.

She smiled across at Bill, her handsome young
husband in his tuxedo, the American wives still
talking across him, and Devlin smiled at him too.
He had heard such good things about Bill, he said.
Nothing but good things. A real grafter, said
Devlin. Billed more hours than anyone in the
London office two years in a row. Devoted to his
family.

'Yes,' Becca said. 'That's my man.'

But, Devlin wanted to know, *what's your husband
doing wasting his time in London? If he's truly
ambitious, then why doesn't he come and try his luck
in the fastest-growing economy on the planet? It was
New York in the twentieth century and London in the*

21

nineteenth. And now it's Shanghai, Devlin said. *If you can make it there . . .*

He saw the doubt on her face. A move to the Third World? London was rough enough for her. *I mean it*, he said. *I'm serious. Lower taxes, higher salary. He'll make partner out there a lot faster than he will here.* And then he had her attention. A partner—it was what the young lawyers—and their wives—dreamed of. To escape the salaried life, and share the firm's profits. When you made partner you were no longer working for the firm. You *were* the firm.

Devlin was talking about a life of colonial splendour that Becca had imagined went out years ago. You would have a home with a maid and a cook and a nanny and a driver—these things were cheap over there. These things were *normal*. And it was almost as if Devlin sensed something that she had tried to keep buried, even from Bill—that their life in London had let her down, that she was bitterly disappointed with their lot, that her little family had to struggle when they deserved so much more . . .

But—they couldn't *really* do it, could they? Surely Shanghai was a place for a single man, Becca suggested. A man with no family ties?

No, said Devlin, not at all—Shanghai was actually a perfect posting for a man with a family. A man with stability, ambition, loved ones to work for. Shanghai had too many distractions for the single man, he said. Too many *distractions*. Later they would all become experts on the distractions of Shanghai.

Devlin was a family man himself—and he showed Becca a wallet photograph of a beautiful

22

middle-aged woman and three smiling boys. Devlin said he *liked* his staff to have families. It meant they had a stake in the future.

Becca turned to Shane, who had been listening to some of this with a lopsided grin, and asked him how his own wife liked Shanghai. But Shane said that he wasn't married, and they all laughed.

The pipers came into the room. They were playing 'Flower of Scotland'. And when the dinner started to break up, and Bill came over to their table, Becca could almost hear the invitation from Devlin to have breakfast, to talk about the future, all the coy small talk of the headhunter.

But as Bill took his wife's hand, happy and relieved to be back by her side, the man from Shanghai surprised both of them.

'I like it that you're married,' he told Bill.

*　　　*　　　*

Becca picked up Holly from the school at twelve sharp. She could have stayed until three, but Becca was afraid that her daughter might miss her.

'She's been fine, didn't miss Mummy at all,' the Australian teacher said, giving Becca a shrewd look that said, *Who's doing the missing around here?*

The pair of them held hands as they walked back through the peaceful streets of Gubei to the flat and, as Holly played with her Disney princess figures, Becca made a start on the unpacking.

'Where did Daddy went?' Holly asked.

'Where did Daddy *go*,' Becca said.

'That's just what I was wondered,' Holly said, stunned at this amazing coincidence.

23

Becca pulled open a case. Suits. Dark blue suits for the hot young lawyer. 'Your daddy's at work, darling.'

Holly banged Prince Charming's plastic head against the palm of her hand. 'I need to talk to him.'

'You can talk to him later,' Becca said, but she wondered if Bill would get home from work before their daughter went to bed. She knew he would try his best. She also knew it was unlikely.

When Becca stopped for a cup of English breakfast tea, she went to the window but the courtyard was empty. There was no sign of the young women they had seen on Saturday night.

It was only early afternoon and the girls of Paradise Mansions were still sleeping.

THREE

The firm occupied three floors in a Pudong skyscraper so new that he could still smell the paint. Bill sat with his back to the window. Behind him the financial district stretched off into the summer mist.

There were spiked Tolkien towers constructed from steel and gold and black glass, one of them built to look like a hundred-storey pagoda, another with a screen covering an entire side of the building where a smiling beauty advertised a phone network. Looming above it all like the true masters of the landscape were the giant cranes.

On Bill's desk there were neat stacks of draft contracts and a silver-framed photograph of his family—Bill and Becca and Holly standing in the surf on a beach in the Caribbean, Bill holding the then two-year-old Holly in his arms, Becca looking jaw-droppingly gorgeous in some kind of orange shift thing, the three of them wearing slightly shy grins as they gazed at the kind passing stranger who was taking the picture. It was the holiday they took before Becca gave up work and the money got tight. When his eyes drifted to the photograph in the course of his working day, Bill always found himself smiling.

He was going through the transactional documents of a new property development on the outskirts of the city. It was called Green Acres. When completed, it would be a gated community for the new rich of Shanghai. Butterfield, Hunt and West were representing the project's German investors, DeutscherMonde. Bill had already noticed that the firm were doing a lot of work for DeutscherMonde. He looked up as Shane appeared in the doorway.

'These Germans,' Bill said. 'Do they have a fixed cap?'

Shane shook his head and Bill looked suitably impressed. Clients often pressed law firms for a fixed cap on fees for any deal, knowing that if they were billed by the hour then the legal fees were potentially limitless.

'Sky's the limit,' Shane said. 'Limit's the sky. That's why they're so important.' The big Australian came into the room and leafed through some papers on Bill's desk. 'This place is going to be beautiful, mate. One hundred millionaires in one square mile. Gardens based on Versailles. Pools, saunas, panic rooms—all based on the actual pools, saunas and panic rooms that they had at Versailles. Twenty-four-hour armed security for the blokes who only just got used to using inside toilets. Lovely jubbly.'

Bill leaned back in his chair. He had building plans in one hand and a map of the area in the other. The development was being built in a place where right now there were only fields and a small village.

'It looks like it's being built on farmland,' he said, handing Shane the map.

'That's right. The village is called Yangdong. They've been pig farmers for generations.'

Bill thumbed through the file. 'So who owns the land?'

Shane put the map back on Bill's desk. 'The People,' he said.

Bill looked at the map and up at Shane. 'So the people of this village—the farmers—they own it?'

'Not the farmers,' Shane said. 'The People. In China, all farmland is owned collectively. Each family in the village has a long-term lease on its holding. Our clients are buying the land from the local government.'

'What happens to the farmers?' Bill said.

'They get a compensation package,' Shane said, 'and get to say so long and fare-thee-well to their pigs. Our clients build their two-million-US houses for people rich enough to afford them—and there are plenty of those. These places were all sold off the drawing board. And in a year there will be palaces where there used to be pig farms. And everybody will be happy.'

A man with fair, thinning hair appeared in the doorway. He was maybe ten years older than Bill, in his early forties. Bill had noticed him around the office because he seemed older than everyone else.

'Shane?' the man said. There was the north of England in his accent. 'Mr Devlin is looking for you.'

'Thanks, Mitch,' Shane said. 'I'm right there, mate.' Shane made no attempt to introduce the man to Bill, so the pair of them smiled awkwardly at each other for a moment, and then the man was gone.

'Who's that?' Bill said.

'Pete Mitchell,' Shane said. 'Mad Mitch, we call him.'

'What's mad about him?' Bill said. It would be hard to imagine a more quiet, self-effacing soul.

Shane glanced at the empty doorway. 'He's the wrong side of forty and he never made partner. Wouldn't you be mad?'

Bill frowned. 'Doesn't the firm's up-or-out policy apply here?'

An up-or-out policy was a law firm's way of staying lean and hungry, a money-making machine that carried no deadwood. If you lacked the stuff needed to make partner, then you were finished. The firm would not carry you to retirement. You moved up—or out.

'Sure,' Shane said. 'Most—I guess, oh, eighty-five per cent—of our associate lawyers make partner. The ones that don't are like a girl that gets left on the shelf. You know, the Bridget Jones lawyers— like an unmarried bird facing the change without her Hugh Grant.'

Bill shivered as though someone had stepped on his grave. 'Then what's he doing here?' he said. 'Mad Mitch, I mean.'

27

'Mad Mitch was in the Hong Kong office but he couldn't stand the pace after the hand-over. For years the Hong Kong boys made money hand over fist, but it got a lot tougher when the Brits shipped out. Mitch was posted out here back when Shanghai was still a soft option.' Shane sighed. 'Sad, innit, mate? Forty-odd years old and still a wage slave. And we can't go on forever, can we? Not the way we work. Lawyer years are like dog years—they run that bit faster than human years.' Shane picked up the photograph on Bill's desk. 'But great things are expected of you,' he said, nodding gravely. He studied the little family for a while and then gently replaced the photograph.

'You're a lucky man, Bill.'

'Yes,' Bill said, straightening the silver frame. 'I am.'

*   *   *

The Mercedes came out of the tunnel and on to the Bund.

The famous road curved off ahead of them, a great sweep of stout colonial buildings made of marble and granite, the architecture of Empire.

'The West is finished,' Devlin said, watching the Bund go by. 'The future belongs to the Chinese. They own it already.' He turned to look at Bill. 'Do you believe that?'

Bill smiled, shrugged, not wanting to disagree with his boss, but reluctant to concede the future to anyone. 'I don't know,' he said.

'Believe it,' Devlin told him. 'They work harder than we do. They put up with conditions that would make us call a human rights lawyer, or the

28

cops. They make us—the West, the developed world, all the twenty-first-century people—look lazy, soft, the pampered men of yesterday. We haven't seen anything yet, I promise you.'

There were four of them in the car, with Tiger at the wheel. He had taken off his toy soldier uniform and was wearing a business suit. Bill sat in the back seat wedged between Devlin and a lawyer called Nancy Deng, one of the firm's Chinese nationals. She had her briefcase open on her lap, examining some files, and she hadn't spoken since the journey began.

Shane sat up front, his wafer-thin mobile phone in his big meaty fist, talking in calm, fluent Chinese. The words didn't have the barking sound of Cantonese, or the rural, West Country burr of Mandarin, and so Bill guessed this must be what Shanghainese sounded like.

'What happens when the Chinese can make *everything* the West makes?' Devlin said, smiling back at Bill. 'Not just toys, clothes and dinky little Christmas decorations but computers, cars, telecommunications—when they can make all that stuff at one tenth of the cost it takes our fat lazy work force?'

'You want to pick up our Germans or meet them at the restaurant?' Shane said over his shoulder.

'We'll pick them up at their hotel,' Devlin said. 'I don't want our Germans getting lost.' He looked back at Bill. 'The Chinese are *united*,' Devlin said, his eyes shining. 'That's the thing that nobody gets. They're *united*. They have a unity of national vision that the West has lacked since, oh, World War Two. That's why they will win.'

Shane was telling the Germans that he would see

them in the lobby in ten minutes.

'I love the Chinese,' Devlin said simply, leaning back. 'I admire them. They believe that tomorrow will be a better day. And if you are going to believe in something, anything, then that's not a bad thing to believe in.'

Bill watched the Bund go by, and silently agreed with him.

*   *   *

The beggars saw them coming.

At first it seemed to Bill as though every single one of them had an oversized baby in her arms, as though begging without a toddler was forbidden by some local statute, but then he realised that there were also old people shambling along at the back of the mob, filthy hands outstretched, and solitary feral children who ducked and dived beneath the women with their toddlers in their arms, the toddlers carried as if they were babies.

But Bill had not noticed the old people and the big children. He had only noticed the toddlers being carted under the arms of their mothers.

Because they all seemed to be just a little bit younger than Holly.

Shane cursed. He had not wanted to walk to the restaurant. He had advised the two Germans that it was better to take the Mercedes and a cab, but they had insisted. They wanted to stroll along on the Bund, and now look what had happened. The beggars were on them, all over them, with their toothless, ingratiating smiles, the rank smell of their clothes and their bodies, all the bewildered faces of the children carried under one arm.

30

Shane shoved on ahead, shouting at them in Shanghainese, while Nancy pleaded with them and Devlin gave instructions to the clearly terrified Germans. Only Bill dawdled, stunned by a world where children the same age as Holly were begging in the street.

He reached for his wallet, and immediately realised his mistake. He had planned to give some money to the women with children but there were just so many of them, too many of them, and suddenly he was overwhelmed, the coins and notes falling from his fingers and the women with toddlers being trampled by the older children. Empty palms were thrust in Bill's face.

One of the bigger kids—a weasel-faced runt with a cropped head and the eyes of an old man—grabbed Bill's jacket and wouldn't let it go. The child clung on as Bill edged his way through the mob to the building where his colleagues and the Germans were waiting. A uniformed doorman prised the child from Bill's jacket.

'Better watch your wad around here, mate,' Shane said. 'They're not all driving BMWs and shopping at Cartier. There are still millions of the little bastards wiping their arses with their hands.'

'And nobody gets left behind in the West?' Devlin flared. Then he smiled easily. 'There's more upward mobility here than anywhere on the planet.'

Bill was embarrassed, shaken. The Germans were staring at him. One of them was balding and in a business suit, and the other had the long greying hair and the leather jacket of a wild youth. But they were both all business, and they could have been brothers. They murmured to each other

31

in their own language.

Bill wiped sweat from his face. As they went up to the restaurant in the lift, Nancy gave him a tissue for the smear of grime that the young beggar had left on his jacket. He thanked her, his face burning, and dabbed at the mark but saw that it would not budge.

The perfect black print of a child's hand.

*   *   *

Bill didn't understand.

Their clients, DeutscherMonde, were investing billions of RMB in the Yangdong project. The company had already built an identical development in the suburbs of Beijing. And yet, as the Germans sat with their expensive lawyers across the dinner table from the local government officials of Yangdong—five men with cheap suits and soft flesh and bad teeth, accompanied by their own lawyer, a bird-thin man of sixty with a shock of dyed black hair, and a slab-like stooge who looked like some kind of bodyguard—it was as if the Germans were the supplicants, the ones most desperate for the deal, the beggars at the feast.

Courses came and went. The Germans sipped their mineral water. The Chinese chain-smoked high-tar cigarettes and swilled soft drinks. The conversation ebbed and flowed from English to Shanghainese, much of it concentrating on the glory of the Green Acres development, and how it would enrich the community.

The oldest of the town's representatives said the least. With his hooded eyes, long upper lip and frog face, Bill thought he looked like a mini Mao.

They called him Chairman Sun. He smoked constantly, even when the chopsticks in his spare hand picked at a dish. Sun made no eye contact, yet still managed to convey the impression that he was mildly dissatisfied with everything, including the project, the food, the choice of restaurant, the presence of so many foreign devils, and possibly life itself.

Only Bill had turned off his phone, and tinny snatches of familiar tunes punctuated the lunch. The *Mission Impossible* theme, the opening chords of 'Brown Sugar', niggling soundbites from Beethoven and Oasis and Faye Wong. Shane pushed his plate to one side and placed his laptop on the table.

'What do you keep on that thing?' Bill asked him.

'The truth, mate,' Shane told him. 'The brutal truth.'

Chairman Sun called for the waiter and gave him his instructions. The waiter went away and came back with the wine list. Sun chose a bottle and Shane ingratiatingly smiled and mumbled his compliments in Shanghainese at the excellence of the choice.

Everyone fell silent as they watched the ritual of the waiter returning with the bottle of Burgundy, presenting it to Chairman Sun, who—after a tense moment—nodded his faint approval.

The waiter removed the cork and delicately poured a splash of red wine into Chairman Sun's glass. His frog face twitched with suspicion as he smelled the wine, tasted it and—after another breathless moment—nodded his approval.

The waiter half-filled Chairman Sun's glass with

Burgundy. Then the Chairman topped it up with the can of Sprite in front of him, took a long slurp and exhaled with pleasure.

Bill glanced across at Shane and Devlin and Nancy and the two Germans.

But they didn't even blink.

*   *   *

On Saturday afternoon he came home to an empty apartment.

He placed the stack of files he was carrying on the table, tore off his jacket and tie, and read the note Becca had stuck to the fridge. She had taken Holly to ride the bumper cars at Fuxing Park. He had promised to go with them, if he could get away in time. But Saturday was a work day at Butterfield, Hunt and West.

Bill had spent the afternoon going through paperwork with Shane and Nancy. The contract between the Germans and the Yangdong officials was in Chinese and drawn up under Chinese law, but the deal was structured so that all the important commercial rights were offshore, governed by Hong Kong law with documents in English.

'It makes the deal easier to enforce,' Nancy had explained.

'When someone steals all the money,' Shane added.

Bill took a bottle of Evian from the fridge and crossed to the window. The courtyard was empty apart from a silver Porsche 911. It looked like a shark waiting its prey on the bottom of the ocean. A 911, Bill thought, yawning as he stretched out on the sofa. A 911 in China . . .

He woke up with his daughter's face pressed close, and he could smell the sweetness of her breath as she laughed with delight. She held a brightly coloured plastic figurine in each tiny fist. A prince in one hand, and a princess in the other.

'Be the prince,' Holly urged. 'Come on, come on—be the prince, Daddy.'

He closed his eyes. He had never felt so tired. When he opened them, Holly was still offering him one of the little figurines. He stretched, groaned, and closed his eyes.

'Later, darling,' he heard Becca say from the kitchen. 'Your daddy's been working very hard for us.'

Bill felt relief as he heard small footsteps walking slowly away. When he opened his eyes he saw his daughter kneeling on the far side of the room, playing quietly by herself, and he felt unkind.

'Holly?' He was propped up on one elbow.

'Yes?' she said with that shy formality that always touched his heart, and then owned it forever.

He swung his legs round, ran his fingers through his hair.

'What do you want me to do?'

Holly looked up at him with her perfect face. 'Go on,' she said, advancing towards him with the figurines in her hand. She pushed a piece of plastic in his face. A little unsmiling man in a golden crown and trousers that were too tight. 'Go on, Daddy,' his daughter urged. 'Go on, Daddy—be Prince Charming.'

He did his best.

FOUR

He liked watching his wife get dressed. He especially liked it at times like this—when she was getting dressed to go out somewhere special, and he knew that soon men and women would turn their heads to look at her in any room she entered. But now, half-dressed and getting ready for the night, the way she looked belonged only to him.

Watching her face as she put on her lipstick, a blonde tendril of hair falling across her face as she leaned towards the mirror, the familiar lines of her body, the special dress waiting on the bed. He loved it. He could watch her forever.

'Who are you looking at?' she said, smiling at him in the mirror.

'I'm looking at you.'

They were in his room. He had his own room now, the second bedroom, so he could come home late from the office and leave early in the morning without disturbing Becca and Holly, who slept together in the master bedroom. The sleeping arrangements of the first night had become the sleeping arrangements of every night.

In many ways this was a drag. He missed the physical nearness of Becca, of sensing her the moment he woke up. He missed being able to reach out and touch her in the middle of the night, he missed the soft sound of her breathing when she slept, and he missed the warmth of her body beside him. And yet in many ways sleeping apart made her physical presence more of a treat, as if they were playing some kind of game, rationing intimacy, pretending to be strangers. And perhaps that was a part of the excitement he felt now. It wasn't every day that he saw his wife getting dressed.

She stood, her make-up done, dressed in her underwear and heels. The sight of the Caesarean scar on her stomach moved him, as it always did, although he never quite knew why.

He watched her slip into her dress and the label stuck out of the back. Koh Samui, it said, and he thought of the little shop in Covent Garden, and how much she loved it, and how they would linger there on Saturday afternoons before Holly was born. He zipped her up and deftly tucked in the label with the assured touch of the married man.

'How do I look?' she said, and he told her she looked great, and then he tried to touch his mouth against hers, but she turned away laughing, protecting her make-up, and he laughed too. Even though it felt as if he was never allowed to kiss her when he most wanted to.

It was their first night out in Shanghai, or at least their first night out without Holly. Their first grown-up night, they called it. They had been in Paradise Mansions for three weeks now, and the jet-lag was gone and so were the packing crates, but they had never felt comfortable leaving Holly. They still didn't, not really, but Bill could not get out of dinner invitations from Hugh Devlin forever, and Becca had to concede that the elderly Chinese ayi, Doris, who as far as Becca could tell had practically raised her own grandson, was at least as trustworthy as the string of East Europeans and Filipinas who had baby-sat for them in London.

Holly was sleeping, sprawled sideways, and Doris was sitting by the side of the bed watching her. The old ayi smiled reassuringly as Bill and Becca crept in. They stood by the bed, reluctant to leave.

Bill looked at the beauty of his daughter's face, and it made him think of the high chair that was parked in a corner of his bedroom, and of the second child that they had talked about trying for once they were settled. They both wanted more children. But Bill loved his daughter so much that a secret part of him felt that another child would somehow be a betrayal of Holly.

He understood why people had more than one child. Most of all it was because when you had just the one, you almost loved them too much. You were sometimes paralysed with love. That wasn't good, the constant fear. That wasn't the way to be. But with a second child, how could you ever again spend as much time with the first? Already he felt that he wasn't spending nearly enough time with his daughter.

If he had to find space in his life, and his heart, and his weekends, for a second child, then surely that would mean there was even less for Holly. Or didn't it work that way? Did you love the first one in the same old way and just as much, but discover a new store of love for the second child? Did the heart just keep expanding?

Yes, that's the way it must work, Bill thought, as they left their daughter with the ayi.

The heart just gets bigger.

You don't love the first one any less. The heart can always find room for the ones that it loves.

*　　　*　　　*

38

A red Mini Cooper with a Chinese flag painted on the roof was blocking the exit to the courtyard.

Tiger leaned on his horn as George the porter excitedly conferred with the driver of the Mini. A number of women were gathered around the car, offering advice to the driver. George had to push his way through them. He came and stuck his head in the window.

'Hello, lady. Hello, boss,' he said to Becca and Bill, before releasing a stream of Shanghainese at Tiger.

'Keys stuck,' Tiger translated, looking at Bill in his rear-view mirror. 'Keys stuck in car.'

Becca winced as Tiger put his hand on the horn and left it there. 'Bill?' she said, so Bill touched Tiger on the shoulder, requesting silence, then got out of the car and walked up to the Mini. George followed him. The women around the car watched him coming. From the window on Saturday night they had looked as similar as sisters, but up close they could not have been more different. There was a woman in her middle thirties, by far the oldest, who had the lithe body of a dancer. A much younger woman in thick glasses who could have been a librarian from central casting. There was one who was plain and slightly overweight who wore no make-up and carried a pack of disposable nappies. And there was one who clutched a Louis Vuitton bag and wore a mini-kilt that just about covered her sporran.

'Excuse me,' Bill said, and the little crowd parted without expression or complaint. He leaned in the window of the Mini with the Chinese flag on the roof. The tall girl with the orchid in her hair was in the driver's seat, her long limbs everywhere as she yanked desperately at the ignition keys.

'My goodness,' she was saying, interspersed with torrents of Chinese. 'Oh my goodness.'

'Car broke,' George said over Bill's shoulder. 'Brand-new car and broke.'

Bill sighed, shaking his head, glancing from the gearbox to the girl's face. She was a good few years younger than him. Middle twenties, he guessed. But it was hard to tell out here. She could have been anything.

'Miss? You have to put it in *park*,' Bill told her patiently. 'You'll not get the keys out until you've got it in park. It's designed that way so the thing doesn't drive off by itself and kill someone.'

She shot him a fierce look. A leg emerged from the slit in her dress, a *qipao*, which back then he still thought of as a cheongsam. Her skin was an almost milky white. He thought, *Why are they supposed to be yellow? Where did that myth come from? She's paler than I am.* He had never seen skin so white. It was like alabaster.

'Do you mind?' she said, glaring at him like a rich man's wife putting a stroppy tradesman in his place. She had the biggest eyes he had ever seen. 'My husband will address the problem.'

Bill stared at her, momentarily stunned by the formality of her English. Then he laughed. She dressed like Suzie Wong but she talked like a member of the Women's Institute.

'No, I don't mind,' he said. 'Fine.' He turned to George. 'She's got the car in drive and she needs to put it in park before it will let her remove the key.' George looked confused. 'It's the way they make them,' Bill explained, not quite as patient now.

George thought about it, and understanding slowly dawned on his round face.

'Ahhh,' George said. 'Very clever safety device.'

'My husband will be here soon,' the tall girl insisted, still struggling desperately with the key. She unleashed some Chinese and then slapped the steering wheel with her open palm. 'Oh, my goodness!'

Bill looked at her, said nothing, and after nodding in acknowledgement at the women gathered around the car, walked back to the limo. Tiger leaned on the horn again, that promiscuous use of the horn that Bill had already realised was endemic in China. He frowned, shook his head and Tiger stopped.

Bill settled himself next to Becca. He could see the back of the girl's head, and the white orchid she had pinned there. George was leaning into the Mini, giving her careful instructions, as though it were all very complicated. The flower moved as she shook her head.

'What's the problem?' Becca said.

'Got it in the wrong gear,' Bill explained to his wife. 'She's not going anywhere like that.'

*   *   *

They stood holding hands on the balcony of the private members' club and the city surrounded them in all its money, mystery and pride. It was wild. It was like nothing they had ever seen.

They looked out over the floodlit rooftops of the Bund and saw the mighty river shimmer with fragments of reflected neon, the barges invisible now but their foghorns blaring as they moved

41

through the darkness, and all the shining peaks of Pudong beyond.

In the daylight Shanghai was hot, cruel, overcrowded, but at night Bill thought that it was always beautiful, undeniably beautiful; at night it looked as it had looked the very first time he had seen it, coming across the bridge from the airport, still punch-drunk from the flight.

He squeezed Becca's hand and she smiled at him.

Devlin came out on to the balcony and stood beside them, drink in hand, shaking his head at the sight.

'There was never a city like this before,' he said quietly, and Becca thought it was as if he was talking to himself as much as them. He was like some old Empire builder, she thought, he had that mad passion about him. She could imagine him on a farm in the Ngong Hills in Africa, or suffocating in the heat of Satipur, or being carried on a sedan chair up Victoria Peak. But of course there was no Empire left.

'Never,' he said. 'Not in the history of humanity.' He looked at her and smiled, and he had enormous charm, and she could do nothing but share his wonder. He filled his lungs with the thick air of the Shanghai night. 'To be living in this place at this time—I tell you, future generations will envy us.'

Becca smiled at him. What she liked about Devlin most of all was that he talked about the Chinese with genuine affection. She had grown up on the move, her father a reporter for Reuters, and until they finally returned to England when she was eleven her childhood had been measured out

42

in extended postings in Johannesburg, Frankfurt and Melbourne. Becca knew that the default expat reaction to the country he or she lived in was usually a kind of amused contempt. But Devlin was not like that. He loved the Chinese, and now he stared out at the night talking about how China's economy was already bigger than the UK's, how it would be bigger than Germany's by 2010, bigger than America's by 2020, and he seemed awed, not resentful, as if it was only what the Chinese deserved. There was something wonderful about him, Becca thought, feeling that their lives would get better and keep on getting better if only they stayed close to Hugh Devlin. He made her feel that this was a good move for her family, and that the coming years would be all they dreamed.

And there was another reason for Becca to like Devlin—he didn't patronise her, he didn't treat her the way the firm's senior partners in London had treated her. As a wife and nothing but a wife, she thought. As a mother and nothing before or after she was a mother. *A homemaker*, they would say, *hardest job in the bloody world,* and she knew they didn't believe it for a second, and she saw the buried mockery.

With Devlin, she didn't feel as though she had to establish her credentials as a former career woman, the lapsed financial journalist, and she knew that Devlin realised that rising young hotshot Bill Holden would not be here without her.

A thin, blonde woman of about forty wobbled on to the balcony with a drink in one hand and a cigarette in the other. She looked as though she should have switched to Perrier an hour ago. It was the woman that Becca had first seen in Devlin's wallet in London. Tess Devlin held out her hand and Becca shook it.

'I want your husband to give me a child before it's too late,' she told Becca.

'That's fine,' Becca said. 'Can he finish his drink first?'

'Oh, come inside, you two lovebirds,' Mrs Devlin said, kissing Bill on both cheeks, and taking him by the arm. She shot a look at her husband. 'It's so hot out here.'

Mrs Devlin allowed Bill to dawdle behind, talking to her husband, but she didn't let go of Becca until she had steered her to the seat next to her own. It was a table for twelve, all lawyers at the firm and a smattering of the wives, although quite a few of the men seemed to be single, or at least alone.

Becca could guess the identity of some of them from the shoptalk that Bill had brought home. The Asian woman instructing the waiters in Shanghainese must be Nancy Deng. The tired-looking Englishman sitting by himself and staring sadly into the middle distance had to be Mad Mitch, who apparently was not long for this firm. She only recognised Shane, and he grinned at her and said her name, and she was touched that he remembered, as he raised a glass of Tsingtao in his meaty fist.

'Where did they put you, dear?' Mrs Devlin said, as an assortment of languages buzzed over the steaming bowls of shark's fin soup.

'Gubei New Area,' Becca said, smiling across at Mad Mitch, who had accidentally made eye contact. He looked startled at this gesture of warmth.

44

'Gubei?' Mrs Devlin smiled her approval, and Becca saw that she had been a beauty. And she still was, if you got past the hard, glossy veneer and the professional charm and the effects of the booze. 'Lovely, isn't it? Good schools. We were in Gubei for the first two years when we came over.' A drink was placed before Mrs Devlin and she turned viciously on the waitress. 'I said Amaretto with no ice. This is Amaretto with ice. Americans and Germans may drink Amaretto with ice, but I am neither an American nor a bloody German. I am English. And we do not need to have every drink so full of ice that we can't taste it. Take this away and bring me what I ordered.' Mrs Devlin turned back to Becca, all smiles again. 'So how is it? Have you settled in yet?'

Lost for words, Becca watched the young waitress walk away with the offending Amaretto. Then she looked back at Tess Devlin, and tried to put it into words. 'It's different. I was expecting—I don't even know what I was expecting. Temples and teahouses, I suppose. Conrad and Kipling. I had this romantic image of Shanghai. I have it still, I guess. The taste of the East on my face . . . Silly, really.'

Mrs Devlin patted her hand, as if to say that it was not silly at all.

'I lived abroad as a child,' Becca said. 'I love London, but England is hardly my home, not the way it is for Bill. So I can't be one of those expats that tries to recreate the old country. You know—ordering Marmite online and buying the latest comedy DVDs and obsessing about football results.' She picked up her big white soup spoon and contemplated it. 'We have a beautiful apartment, a wonderful ayi, and Holly loves her school.'

Mrs Devlin pushed away her shark's fin soup and lit a cigarette. 'And the money's good, isn't it?' she said, just the hint of a smile, the smoke streaming from her nostrils. 'And it's forty per cent tax for high earners in the UK, and only sixteen per cent in Hong Kong, where we cough up.'

'The money's very good indeed,' Becca said, keen to show that she was sensitive to the realities of the working world. Sometimes she felt that she should keep Kipling and Conrad to herself.

Becca couldn't tell this woman she had just met—this powerful, volatile, half-cut woman—the real problem. And the real problem was that she no longer saw her husband as much as she had in London, or as much as she would have liked, or as much as she needed. She missed him, and she couldn't even mention it to Bill, because that would only be more pressure, and what could he possibly do about it? So Becca smiled brightly, the game younger wife. 'I guess it just takes time to adjust,' she said.

'It's not an equal opportunity city,' Mrs Devlin said thoughtfully. She sucked her cigarette, exhaled through her mouth now, her green eyes squinting in the Marlboro mist. 'It's very different for men and women. You'll see that. Perhaps you've seen it already.'

Becca thought of the girls of Paradise Mansions coming out to meet the cars, and she wondered if Mrs Devlin had seen them too.

Tess Devlin leaned close to Becca. She smelled of Amaretto and cigarettes and Giorgio Armani. 'I know it's hard sometimes, but look at it this way,' she continued. 'A few years out here and the pair of you will be set up for life.'

A drink was placed before Mrs Devlin. Amaretto, no ice. Without acknowledging the waitress—taking what she had wanted all along as nothing more than her right, Becca thought—she cradled the glass in the palm of her hand, checking the temperature, shooting the waitress a withering look that said, *Oh yes, I know that old trick, where you just fish the ice out and don't bring me a fresh drink.* Then she slowly sipped her drink, her genuinely fresh drink, giving Becca a conspiratorial look that said, *They can't fool me.* The waitress vanished.

'Oh yes, Gubei New Area is lovely,' Mrs Devlin said thoughtfully. 'Dear old Gubei. You hardly know you're in China at all.'

*   *   *

There was something wrong with the rest room. Bill felt it the moment he walked in. It appeared to be empty but—why was there a bucket and a mop in the corner? And what was that sound? What was going on in here?

He advanced with caution, his gaze shifting to the short row of cubicles. And that was strange too, because the doors were all ajar. But he could definitely hear someone. Someone who sounded as if they were trying to give birth.

Then Bill saw him. The old cleaner with his tattered trousers and filthy drawers around his ankles, sitting on the throne with the door flung open, grunting and groaning and straining, as if there wasn't enough fibre in the world to free his

47

strangled bowels.

He was in the furthest cubicle from the entrance, and perhaps that was his only nod towards decorum. For he considered Bill without a trace of embarrassment.

In fact Bill thought the man looked at him as though he was fresh off a British Airways flight from Heathrow, while he had been sitting there for a thousand years.

FIVE

Bill stood at the window and watched the courtyard, waiting for Tiger to appear. A large black BMW with an elderly man at the wheel stood by with its engine running. A young woman in glasses came out of the opposite block and walked smiling towards the car and the man, who could only be her father. I recognise her, Bill thought. The librarian. So we are not the only ones. There are other regular people here, too.

'Daddy? Daddy?' His daughter's voice, high and demanding. 'Do you know what planet we're on, Daddy?'

Bill had worked out that the silver Porsche came for the tall girl on Wednesday and Friday nights. It was there most Sunday afternoons. There were also sporadic visits during the week, delivering her back to Paradise Mansions early in the morning, or collecting her at strange hours. Her husband, he thought. Yeah, right.

Bill wondered what excuses the man told his wife. Maybe he didn't tell her anything. Maybe he didn't need to make excuses. Maybe that was the way it worked out here.

'Daddy?' Tugging at his sleeve now. He looked down at Holly and smiled, his fingertips touching her face. 'Do you know what planet we're on, Daddy?'

She was holding up a complicated contraption of string and wool and balls and cardboard for his inspection. Doris the ayi stood behind her, smiling proudly.

'Made at school,' the ayi said. 'Very clever. Very genius.'

Bill looked carefully at the dangling strings and balls.

'It's the planets,' Holly explained.

'It's really beautiful, angel,' Bill said, studying the contraption more closely. In her matchstick fingers, his daughter held a champagne cork. Blue wool came from the cork and passed through a paper plate that had been painted black and embellished with sticky gold stars. Below the plate, which he now recognised represented the night sky, or perhaps infinite space, the wool dropped to hold a collection of different-sized painted balls revolving around a large orange cardboard sun.

One little finger pointed to a yellow ball with a wavering purple ring daubed around it. 'That's Saturn,' Holly said confidently. She touched the smallest ball. 'Pluto—furthest from the sun.' A larger red ball. 'Mars, of course.' She turned her shining blue eyes up at her father. 'I was going to use yellow cardboard for the sun but . . . um . . . I used orange instead.'

'Personally, I think orange is even better,' Bill said. 'That's just my opinion.'

49

'And this is us,' Holly said, touching a green-and-blue ball. 'That's earth. That's where we are . . . and guess what, Daddy.'

'What, darling?' Did he know that much about the planets when he was four? He didn't think so. In fact, he didn't know that much about the planets at thirty-one.

'The brightest stars you can see are already dead,' she said confidently. 'We see their image, and they look nice and lovely, but they died a long time ago.'

The brightest stars were dead already? Could this possibly be true? He didn't know if he should correct her or not. She knew far more than he did.

'It's just something I learned,' Holly said.

The ayi ushered her off to brush her teeth before going to school, and Bill heard Becca in the bedroom on the phone to her father. He glanced at his watch. Breakfast time in Shanghai meant that it was around midnight back home.

Becca called her father almost every day. Bill felt a pang of guilt, because he hadn't phoned his own father since they'd arrived.

Perhaps he should give the old man a call, he thought, and immediately dismissed the idea. They wouldn't have anything to talk about. Or they would get into one of their pointless rows about nothing, hang up angry, and that would be even worse.

It was different when his mother was still alive. They were a real family then. But they had stopped being a real family fifteen years ago. Bill and his father tried hard, but they both knew that it was doomed to failure. Two men couldn't be a family. There were just not enough of them, there was no centre, no heart, and there were too many rough edges. Too much testosterone, too many rows. Everything and nothing proved reason for an argument, and then Bill was out of the house and off to university, working in the holidays and weekends because he had to, it was the only way he could afford to stick it, and because he didn't want to go home. It made him feel desperately sad to admit it.

Get the old man out here, Bill thought as down in the courtyard the limo appeared and Tiger pulled up behind the silver Porsche. Yes, get the old man out here for a few weeks. Show him the sights. Let him spend some quality time with his granddaughter, who he loved to bits. That would work.

His feeling that family life had ended forever didn't change until he met Becca six years later. It was Becca who made him believe that he had a chance to belong to another family. He fell in love with her the night he met her, and it was like starting all over again.

Bill turned as Holly and the ayi came back into the room. His daughter still had the home-made universe in her hands and he smiled at her and got down on his knees to better admire the intricate design.

That's what love is, he thought, as down in the courtyard came the sound of a Porsche 911 pulling away.

A chance to start again.

*   *   *

For five years, between the age of eleven and

51

sixteen, Becca and Alice Greene had been best friends.

It was one of those delirious all-consuming friendships of childhood, gloriously isolationist, a time of shared secrets and energetic recklessness— one night Alice had pierced Becca's ears with a needle that she had heated over a candle, and it was a bloodbath that they laughed about for years. But it was the kind of friendship that was always slightly out of whack.

They were both boarders at a school in Buckinghamshire, a grim Gothic building surrounded by lush wooded hills, like a setting from a fairy tale. When their friendship began they had dressed the same, and wore their hair in the same fashion, and both said they wanted to be journalists when they grew up. Naturally they loved it when their schoolmates and their teachers said that they looked like twins. Yet they were not twins.

Becca's father made a decent living at Reuters, but the school would have been out of reach without a scholarship, while Alice's family owned a string of restaurants on Boat Quay in Singapore, and Alice had that easy confidence that comes from growing up with money that you haven't earned.

The largesse was one-sided—Becca enjoyed family holidays in Bali with Alice and her parents, shopping sprees in Hong Kong courtesy of Alice's credit card, first-class flights to Singapore during the long summer break. Singy, Alice called it, and before she was twelve years old, Becca was calling it Singy too. *Coming down to Singy, Bec?* So when Becca learned that Alice was working as a freelance journalist in Shanghai, it felt like the best news in the world.

Alice turned up just before Holly's bedtime and when the two women embraced, fifteen years fell away.

The pair of them bathed Holly together, the child chatting excitedly at this admiring stranger, Alice making awestruck cooing sounds at Holly's beauty and newness, and Becca couldn't help feeling happy that perhaps she had restored some of the balance in their friendship. Now she had a child, a husband and a home, it felt like Alice wasn't the one who held a majority share in the good life.

When Holly was sleeping, Becca fetched a bottle of white wine from the fridge and carried it to where Alice was standing by the window.

'You're not writing any more?' Alice said, quite casually, although Becca felt the words press against some sensitive nerve.

'No. I'm looking after Holly, mostly.' She started telling the story of Holly's asthma attack in London, and Alice nodded and looked concerned, but Becca cut it short and poured their wine. It sounded like an excuse, and it wasn't. It was a reason. 'Anyway, there's lots to do around here,' she said. Why the hell should she apologise for giving up work? 'What brought you to Shanghai, Al? I thought you'd be in Hong Kong or Singy.'

Alice grimaced, and Becca smiled. She could see the ghost of the girl Alice had been at eleven, twelve, thirteen. Spoilt, generous, dead easy to love.

'You know what it's like for stringers,' Alice said. They clinked glasses and grinned at each other.

53

'Cheers. We have to follow the story.' Alice sighed. 'And the story they all want these days is the China dream. You know the thing—*How China is reshaping our world. One billion new capitalists. The great China gold rush.*' Alice looked out of the window. 'They—all the Western news outlets—want you to report the miracle.' She shook her head. 'But it's not all banana daiquiris at M on the Bund.'

'How do you mean?' Becca sipped her wine and felt a pang of foreboding. She really wanted them to have a good time tonight. Just get a bit drunk and talk for hours and feel that nothing had changed.

'I mean the principal reason the economy keeps growing is because foreign idiots want to invest here,' Alice said, and Becca recalled how impatient her friend could be with slowness and stupidity. There were girls at their school who were terrified of her. 'No Western CEO wants to go down as the man who missed China,' Alice said. 'But how can it be an economic miracle when five hundred million Chinese are living on less than a dollar a day? By the middle of the century China will have a bigger economy than the US. And you know what? They will still have five hundred million people getting by on a dollar a day. It stinks. The whole thing.' She sipped her drink. 'Nice wine,' she said.

'But a lot of them are leaving poverty behind, aren't they?' Becca said gently. 'I mean, that's what Bill's boss always says.'

'Some of them,' Alice conceded. 'A few million or so. But the Chinese deserve an affluence that's worth having—clean water, not empty skyscrapers; rule of law, not back-handers; uncensored news,

54

not broadband porn. They need education, democracy, a free press—not propaganda and Prada bags and traffic jams full of local-made Audis.'

'I thought it would be more like Hong Kong,' Becca admitted. 'Or Hong Kong the way we knew it. You know—day trips out to the islands, weekends on somebody's junk, Sunday lunch at Aberdeen.'

Alice laughed. 'You make it sound idyllic.'

'Well, it was, wasn't it?' Becca said defiantly.

'But it's not Hong Kong,' Alice said, her smile fading. 'Shanghai has always been mainland China. You can forget all that Paris-of-the-Orient stuff. The Anglos never made Shanghai their own the way they did Hong Kong.'

'Anyway,' Becca said, feeling that she had been too sentimental and revealed too much, and that Alice must think she was some sad old housewife dreaming of better days. 'I'm sure we'll be fine. Another drink?' she asked her old friend.

The two of them looked down at the courtyard. Gleaming cars were waiting with their engines running. The traffic was sparser than at the weekend, but there was a steady stream of young women getting into very new cars with older men at the wheel.

'It's very exciting,' Becca said brightly, wanting to lighten the mood. She was so glad to see her friend. She wanted them to have a great time, just like the old days. 'I think we've moved into some kind of knocking shop.'

'Not a knocking shop.' Alice smiled, and Becca saw she was happy for the chance to show off her local knowledge, eager to keep all the power for herself. 'Becca, Paradise Mansions is a *niaolong*—a birdcage. There are a lot of them here in Gubei. Maybe even more of them in Hongqiao. The girls are called *jinseniao*—canaries.'

Becca's blue eyes were wide. 'So it's true, then? These girls are all . . . prostitutes?'

Alice shook her head emphatically.

'No—they only sleep with one guy. It's all quite moral, in a twisted sort of way.'

Becca stared down at the courtyard.

'I get it,' she said. 'They are all some rich man's mistress.'

'They're not even really mistresses,' Alice said. 'It's closer to second wives. I wrote a story about it. These women fall in love. Have children. Do a lot of laundry, if the guy is from out of town. It's not a glamour profession, Bec. They live a normal, domestic life while waiting for the man to dump the number one wife. Which invariably he doesn't—although I suppose it has happened. It can be quite a chaotic existence. Status can change overnight. The guy gets bored. Or his wife finds out. Or the canary gets caught enjoying her own bit on the side. Or the guy takes one too many Viagra and dies on the job.'

Becca nearly choked on her Chablis.

'Don't laugh, you heartless cow, it happens!' Alice said. 'These women are the modern concubines. The man is often from out of town— Hong Kong, Singy, Taiwan. A lot of overseas Chinese. They set the woman up in a flat, stay there when they're in Shanghai. A lot of Taiwanese. *Taibazi*, the girls call them—which sort of means Taiwanese hicks from the Taiwanese sticks. They badmouth the Taiwanese, but most of the girls prefer the out-of-towners.'

Becca cradled her drink. 'Why's that?'

'Because they stay the night,' Alice said, looking down at the courtyard. 'Makes them feel more like a real wife, I guess.' She smiled at her old friend. 'You tell me, Bec. What does a real wife feel like?'

Becca just smiled.

Alice gestured at the courtyard with her glass. 'Most of these guys all look like locals. Nobody in Taiwan or Hong Kong dresses as badly as that. But think about it. The man is spared the agony of looking for company in the bars, and the woman— who invariably grew up in unimaginable poverty— gets security. For herself and her family. At least for as long as it lasts, which can be years.'

'A marriage of convenience,' Becca said.

'More like a meaningful relationship between sex and economics,' Alice said.

'I guess it goes on everywhere,' Becca said, trying to sound worldly, trying not to look alarmed. Somehow prostitution would have been easier to understand.

'These women can make a few thousand RMB a month in a normal job, if they're lucky,' Alice said. 'Or they can live next door to you and Bill. Using what they've got to get what they want. Very pragmatic. Very Chinese. And this city is full of them.'

Buzzing between the larger cars was the red Mini Cooper. Of course, Becca thought. The tall girl stuck in the wrong gear.

'There's money here, all right,' Alice said. 'But Shanghai is a distorting mirror. Go to the countryside. Half of the kids there have never seen the inside of a school.'

Out of the child monitor came the sound of crying, and Becca left Alice brooding at the window. Perhaps she was trying much too hard to recapture their old friendship. Perhaps she should enjoy her own company a bit more, Becca thought as she took the half-sleeping Holly in her arms. And the company of her child in the hours between school and bed, and the company of her husband on Sunday and sometimes part of Saturday. Married people shouldn't have this desperate need for friends, Becca thought.

But when Holly had settled Becca went back to the living room and found Alice smiling as if something had just come back to her.

'Hey Bec,' she said. 'Remember when I pierced your ears?'

*   *   *

They couldn't practise law in China.

That was the joke played on the Western lawyer in Shanghai, and Shane liked to mention it whenever the clock was creeping close to midnight and the lights were going out all over Pudong and they were sipping their cold coffee at desks still crowded with paperwork.

It said *Foreign Lawyer* on their business cards, because it was different for foreigners. If you were a foreign lawyer working for a foreign firm in Shanghai, the People's Republic of China restricted you to the role of legal representative and kept you in your place. Even a Chinese lawyer like Nancy Deng could not practise PRC law at a foreign firm and was designated *PRC lawyer, non-practising*. Butterfield, Hunt and West had to get

58

all their Chinese contracts rubber-stamped by some tame local lawyer.

But despite not being real lawyers in the eyes of the PRC, most nights the endless bureaucracy of doing business in China kept Bill in the office until he was too tired to see straight, and too full of caffeine to contemplate sleep.

'For blokes who can't practise law here,' Shane said, 'we sure are busy little buggers.' He yawned and stretched, and sat on Bill's desk, squashing a stack of files marked Department of Land and Resources. 'Enough for one night, mate. More than enough. Let's get a beer.'

A beer sounded good. Bill knew that Becca and Holly would have gone to bed hours ago. Now that he was sleeping in the second bedroom so as not to disturb them when he came back late, and when he left for work early, it didn't really matter when he got home. A little unwinding sounded like just what he needed.

*   *   *

'I'm going to tell you how it works out here,' Shane shouted, raising his voice above a song that Bill couldn't quite place. Something about making things more complicated. 'I'm going to tell you what we call the Kai Tak rules, okay?'

'The what?'

'The *Kai Tak* rules. Pay attention. The Kai Tak rules are very important.'

They were in a place called Suzy Too. 'Everybody comes to Suzy Too,' Shane said. It was loud, smoky, crowded beyond belief. There was a dance floor in one corner, although people were

59

dancing all over the place, including on the bars.

There were young Chinese men with dyed blond hair and Western women in jeans and T-shirts and Western men in stained polo shirts or business suits with their ties hanging off and Chinese women in short skirts or *qipao* or jeans that said Juicy on the back. Lots of them.

A woman pulled at Bill's sleeve. She looked hungry. She tapped in some numbers on her mobile phone and showed it to him. It said *1 0 0 0.*

'One thousand RMB,' Shane said, taking Bill's other sleeve. 'That's about £70.'

'But eight hundred is okay,' the woman said. She blinked, dazed by the smoke and exhaustion.

Bill stared at the handset, trying to understand.

'Are you looking for a permanent girlfriend?' she asked him.

Bill had pushed his face close to her, just to hear what she was saying. Now he reared back. 'I'm married.'

The woman took this in her stride. 'Yes, but are you looking for a permanent girlfriend?'

'No thank you,' Bill said, aware that he sounded as though he was declining a second cucumber sandwich at the vicar's tea party.

Shane put a cold bottle of Tsingtao in his hand.

'You know Kai Tak?' the Australian said. 'No? Kai Tak was the old airport in Hong Kong. Kowloon side. Your missus said she visited the Big Noodle as a kid. She would remember it. Before your time, mate.' Shane's free hand, the one that wasn't holding a Tsingtao, impersonated a plane making an erratic landing. 'Where you came in through the blocks of flats hanging their laundry on the balconies and you would often land with someone's pants wrapped around your neck. Sometimes your own.' He winked, clinking bottles with Bill. 'And that's the point.'

The woman with the mobile phone said something in Chinese as she draped an arm around Bill's shoulders, an act more of weariness than desire.

'You're beautiful,' Shane told Bill.

'Who says that?' Bill asked. 'You or her?'

'Her,' Shane said. 'To me, you're just about cute.'

The woman turned to Bill and said something, her eyes half-closed.

'She loves you,' Shane said.

Bill stared at her. 'But we just met,' he said.

'Doesn't matter,' the woman said in English, leaning against him. 'I have financial issues.'

Shane laughed, said something in Shanghainese and she turned away with a shrug. Then he looked quickly at Bill. 'You didn't want her, did you?'

Bill just stared at him. He managed to shake his head. Shane leaned in. This was important. This was crucial.

'Kai Tak rules means that we never talk about what happens when we are on an adventure, okay?' he continued. 'Kai Tak rules mean *omerta*. It means loose lips sink ships.' Shane gently prodded a thick finger against Bill's heart. 'Kai Tak rules means keep your cakehole shut, mate. You do not talk about it with your wife, your girlfriend, or the married stiff in the office. Whatever we get up to, you do not confess to Devlin, you do not boast to Mad Mitch. It's the first rule of Fight Club. You do not talk about Fight Club—right? What happens on tour stays on tour.'

'I've got no idea what you're talking about,' Bill

61

said. But he sort of knew. Already there was the first glimmer of understanding.

It was different out here.

There was an eruption on the dance floor. Notes had started to fall from the sky. They looked up and saw one of their German clients—not the old rock and roller but the other one, Jurgen, the conservative-looking one—grinning foolishly from the DJ box. He was throwing his cash away with both hands, making a Papal gesture every time he released a fistful of RMB, as though he was blessing the crowd.

'This will all end in tears,' Shane predicted, as the dancers fought each other to get at the cash, which drifted slowly to the dance floor before it was seized upon by leggy Chinese girls in *qipao* and sweating Western businessmen.

Two women wrapped their arms around Bill's waist, laughing and sighing and smiling as if they had mistaken him for Brad Pitt on an off night. Shane made a slight motion with his head and they went and did exactly the same thing to a small bald Frenchman who was slumped at the bar. He was about sixty-five and they acted like they had mistaken him for George Clooney. Bill stared at Suzy Too with appalled wonder.

'Does this go on every night?'

Shane nodded. 'And some say that Shanghai's commitment to late nights shows just how few people in this city really have serious business in the morning,' he said. He swigged Tsingtao. 'They may well be right.'

A woman with wild eyes and a Louis Vuitton handbag was dancing on a table, slowly moving her narrow hips, looking at the mirror on the wall, lost in herself. Another woman, all sinewy length and hardened flesh, no waste, was out on the floor, laughing as she eased herself into a scrum of businessmen clumping their feet to some thirty-year-old rock song.

Bill was certain that he had seen both of them at Paradise Mansions in the scrum of women who had gathered around the stalled red Mini. And, now he came to think of it, the one with the mobile phone looked familiar too. But it was not easy to tell who was touting for trade and who was just out on the town.

'Are these women all prostitutes?' Bill said.

Shane thought about it. 'It's prostitution with Chinese characteristics,' he said, looking up at Jurgen the German in the DJ box. The money was all gone but Jurgen was still standing up there with that foolish grin, as if he had made some kind of point. 'There goes Jurgen's profit margin for the last fiscal quarter,' Shane said. 'Prat.' He nodded at the laughing girls at the bar. They were stroking the Frenchman's head and cackling. 'I know those two. They're teachers. Mathematics and Chinese. They're just making a little money on the side for their designer handbags and glad-rags. Prostitutes? That seems a little harsh, mate. That seems a little brutal. Some of them are just here to dance the night away. They're as innocent as you and me. Well—you. The Paradise Mansions girls are saving themselves for the right man—even if he is married to someone else. That's the theory—at Paradise Mansions they are all good little second wives—although of course they do have a lot of lonely nights. The others, they just want their small taste of the economic miracle that they've seen on

TV, and they can't get that on what a bloody teacher earns, which is, oh, a few peanuts above nothing.' He thoughtfully chugged down his Tsingtao.

'And the authorities just condone all this, do they?' said Bill. He knew he sounded like a prude. He knew the tone was all wrong. He liked Shane. He wanted to understand. But the world was turned upside down. Commercial sex was not morally reprehensible out here. It was a career option, or a part-time job, or something a teacher did when she should have been marking homework.

'Not at all,' Shane said. 'When they hear about it the authorities are shocked—shocked! Let's see— year before last we were all in Julu Lu. Last year we were all in Maoming Nan Lu. Now we're in— where are we now? Oh yeah—Tong Ren Lu. Next year we'll be somewhere else. Every now and again, the authorities get tough and move us a block down the road. That's China.'

A skinny woman in her middle thirties danced herself between Bill and Shane, her arms above her head, a smile splitting her face. She was ten years older than most of the women in here, but in better shape. It was the one who looked like a dancer. She was a beauty, Bill could see that, but the beauty had been worn down by time and disappointment. You would not mind growing old with a woman who looked like that, just as long as you met her early enough. For he could not help believing that some man or some men long gone had had the best of her, and he thought that was a terrible thing to believe about anyone. But he could not help it. She was smiling in his face.

64

'This one won't dance,' Shane told her. 'Please don't ask as refusal can cause offence.'

'I teach,' she said. 'I give lessons.' She had an improbable French accent. *Teech*, she said. I *geeff*. She actually spoke English with a French accent. How did that happen? Shane said something in Chinese and she shrugged and danced away, giving Bill a little wave. He watched her go, with a pang of regret. Shane laughed.

'Forget about that one if you're looking to get your end away,' he said. 'You get all sorts in here, mate. That one's a taxi dancer who'll boogie all night but that's it. She dances with men for money and then goes home alone to Paradise Mansions. A taxi dancer in the twenty-first century! Strange but true. Then there are the pro-ams.' He gestured his empty beer bottle towards the teachers. 'Shanghai is completely unregulated. It's not like other parts of Asia. Not like Manila. Not like Bangkok. Not like Tokyo. The women in here don't work for the bar. They're punters, like you and me. They work for themselves. Like the great Deng Xiaoping said, "To get rich is glorious." But don't think they're promiscuous. It's not that. They're just *practical*, it's just too hard a place to not be practical. Hard for them, that is—not hard for the likes of us. China's not a hardship posting for you and me, mate. Don't listen to what those whining expats tell you—mostly Poms, mate. No offence intended.'

'None taken,' Bill said, sipping his beer. Maybe he should be getting back. Maybe he should have gone straight home. His suit was going to reek of cigarette smoke.

'China is an easy place to live because *everything is on a clear financial basis*,' Shane said. 'It's only

65

complicated if you choose to make it so.'

Then the woman with the mobile phone was back, yanking at Bill's sleeve, giving him a gentle shove and as he turned to her he saw that peculiarly Shanghainese gesture for the very first time—the thumb and the index finger rubbed together, followed by the open palm.

Give me money, mister.

He would see that gesture a thousand times before he left this city. They might have four thousand years of civilisation behind them, but they weren't too big on *please* and *thank you*.

In her free hand the woman was holding a photograph of a small, unsmiling boy. He was about the same age as Holly.

Bill fumbled with his wallet and gave her a 50-RMB note. She stared at it for a moment and then turned away with a disgusted snort.

'They don't take fifties,' Shane laughed, putting an arm around him. 'There's a minimum payment of one hundred, even if you're just being nice.'

'How the hell can there be a minimum payment for being nice?' Bill said.

'Because their motto is "Haven't you got anything bigger?"' Shane said. He slapped Bill on the back. He was happy that Bill was here. Bill had the sense that despite living on a beauty mountain, his colleague had been lonely. 'You'll get the hang of it,' Shane said. 'And then you'll find you're in the closest place to heaven.'

'Yeah,' Bill said bleakly. 'Poverty is a great aphrodisiac.' He watched the woman with the son and the mobile phone being ignored by a group of young tourists.

'That's right,' Shane happily agreed. 'And don't

forget—Kai Tak rules.'

'Don't worry about me,' Bill said, suddenly irritated by Shane's assumptions, and by all of the big Australian's unearned intimacy. 'I can keep my mouth shut. But I've got a wife and kid at home.'

Shane frowned, genuinely perplexed. 'But what's that got to do with anything?'

Bill looked at the skinny dancer. She waved at him. She was too old to be in here, he thought. But then everybody in here was the wrong age. Too young, too old. He looked away. 'So I'm not going to be playing around,' he said, not caring what he sounded like.

But Shane just studied the golden glow of his Tsingtao and said nothing.

And then Jurgen was asking them for cab fare, because he had thrown all his cash away, the stupid bastard, and Bill was looking at his watch and Shane was shouting for just one more round, *just one more, come on, Bill, you're not like the rest of those miserable Poms*, and Bill agreed, he wasn't like the rest of them, those pampered private school wankers, and then suddenly it was three o'clock in the morning and they were having one absolutely last drink, a nightcap, *you have to have a fucking nightcap, mate*, in a dive Shane knew where a Filippino band did songs by Pink and Avril Lavigne, and some other girl was showing Bill a picture of her daughter and Bill was pulling out his wallet to show her a picture of Holly, and giving her a 100-RMB note, and then giving her another one, and then another, and wishing her luck and telling her that she was a wonderful mother, and Shane was singing along to 'Complicated' in his hearty Melbourne baritone and then huddling with

67

Bill in a cramped red leather booth somewhere else and saying, *But there are just so many of them, Bill, just so many women in the world—how can you ever choose the special one, how can you ever really know?* just before the two teachers turned up, bombed out of their brains and calling loudly for more mojitos all round, and they stumbled off into what was left of the night with Shane sandwiched between them, all laughing happily, as though it was the most innocent thing in the world.

Then Bill was all alone in the tree-lined streets of the French Concession in the soft milky light that precedes dawn in Shanghai, unable to find a cab in the city where they say you can always find a cab, and one solitary street hawker was going to work, setting up his sad little display of cigarettes on the pavement, and on the far side of the street Bill saw a small hotel with a lone taxi parked outside, the driver asleep at the wheel.

Bill paused to let a tow truck rumble past, and on the back of it he saw there was a red Mini Cooper, and although the front half of it was smashed like a broken accordion, the guts of its ruined engine spilling out and the windscreen shattered, the front wheels just ragged strips of mangled metal and rubber, he could clearly make out the undamaged roof with its flag of the People's Republic of China, the red and yellow glinting in the light of the new day.

SIX

Most days he didn't bother with lunch.

The only excuse for lunch was entertaining clients. Otherwise there was no real need to ever leave his desk. There was an old ayi who wheeled a trolley through the office, the Shanghai equivalent of a tea lady, and she sold sandwiches and noodles, coffee and green *cha*. But Bill liked to get out of the building in the middle of the day, just so he could stretch limbs that had been still for too long and breathe some air that wasn't chilled by air conditioning, even if it was just for fifteen minutes.

There was a coffee shop near their building and at noon he headed towards it, inhaling the weather, smelling the river, when suddenly a hand reached out and grabbed his tie.

'Off to lunch?' Becca said, pulling him into a doorway. She pressed her mouth against his face, a recklessly aimed kiss that he felt on his lips and cheek.

'Lunch?' he said, as if he had never heard of such a thing. She kissed him again, full on the mouth this time. 'I thought I might get a sandwich.'

'Oh,' she laughed, pressing herself against him, feeling his instant response and loving it. 'That doesn't sound like much for a growing boy like you. Let me tell you about today's specials.'

She pulled him deeper into the doorway, kissing him harder, fingers in his hair. It was cool and dark. He looked around and was vaguely aware that they were in the entrance to a condemned building that was being torn down to make way for

69

more office space. Men in white shirts and dark ties passed by with their briefcases and their coffee cups, giving them the occasional glance. Bill swung her around so that she was pinned against the wall and he had his back to the street.

'You're nuts,' he said, and he looked at her face, so close that he could feel her breath. 'I missed you,' he said, and hugged her as hard as he dared.

It had been three days since the firm's dinner on the Bund and they hadn't seen each other since. Too many late nights when he had arrived home after Becca and Holly had gone to bed, and too many early mornings when he had quietly let himself out of the apartment while they were still sleeping.

'Do we know each other?' Becca said, her hands on his arms, squeezing, her eyes half-closed, her mouth smiling. He pulled her close and kissed her, holding her as if he would never let her get away.

'Oh,' she said, and she could feel how much he had missed her. 'I remember you.'

And he remembered her too.

*   *   *

Shane squinted at Bill through a ferocious hangover. 'How am I looking, mate?'

They were in the show home on the Green Acres site in Yangdong, sitting by a fountain in the shape of a dragon's head that wasn't working yet. On the drive north Tiger had stopped the car three times so that Shane could stumble off into some scrubby bushes.

'You look better,' Bill said. 'You're getting some colour back in your face.'

Shane exhaled. 'That's good.'

'But the colour is green,' Bill said.

'That's not so good,' Shane said. 'Bad thing about a threesome is that one of them always ends up staring out the window. Puts you right off your stroke, mate.' He brightened slightly, his beefy face turning a lighter shade of green. 'But the *good* thing about a threesome is that even if one drops out, then you're still having sex with someone.'

Bill had got back to the office to find that Devlin was sending a team to Yangdong. Chairman Sun had called a snap press conference and their clients at DeutscherMonde were nervous. Who knew what he might say if the Burgundy and Sprite started to flow? Bill looked up as Nancy Deng came through the front door with one of the Germans, the long-haired one in a leather jacket, Wolfgang, the one who looked like a mechanic who had won the Lottery.

'Here he comes,' Nancy said.

Shane and Bill stood up as Chairman Sun entered the show home, flanked by a delegation from the local government and a dozen members of the media.

At a discreet distance, Bill, Shane and Nancy Deng followed with their anxious German as Sun led the press pack through gleaming rooms, down sweeping staircases, under crystal chandeliers and round an Olympian swimming pool, talking in Shanghainese all the while. His bodyguard, Ho, that slab of a man, was never far from his side.

At that lunch Bill had pegged the Chairman as one of those men who rise to the top by keeping their mouths shut, but clearly when he did open up, he was a man who was accustomed to being listened to, even without the presence of a translator.

The journalists were all Chinese apart from two Shanghai-based Westerners. One of them was a razor-thin American woman in Jimmy Choos, and the other was Alice Greene. She smiled at Bill, whom she had not seen since his wedding day, and he nodded back.

In his experience journalists were rarely good news for lawyers.

They were going outside. Chairman Sun led the way out of the show home and Bill thought it was like stepping out of a Las Vegas hotel on to the surface of the moon.

As far as the eye could see, the bleak landscape was mud, churned by construction work and the summer rain. The farms had long been bulldozed and the barren fields where the new houses would stand were already partitioned, ropes staking out the plots of land, parcelling out the future. There was a cop on the door of the show home, a young Public Security Bureau policewoman with a fading love bite on her neck. As they filed outside Bill saw that there was security everywhere, although it was not easy to tell where the private guards ended and the PSB state police began.

There was something curiously martial about the site. Inside the wire that staked out the development there was a long, orderly line of snout-nosed trucks with red flags fluttering on their bonnets. Men in bright yellow hard hats swarmed between orange diggers adding to the piles of earth, their lights flashing in the mist. Everywhere there were patches of water with an oily, rainbow-coloured sheen, and on the far side of the wire, like a defeated army corralled into a POW camp, the farmers and their families stood watching.

The lawn had yet to be laid outside the show home and the woman in Jimmy Choos began to topple backwards as her heels sank into the mud. Bill caught her and she flashed him a professional smile.

'I'm from *Shanghai Chic*,' she said, holding on to him for support. 'Where are you from? Isn't this hilarious? We're doing a big piece.'

On the far side of the wire, a few bored-looking security men were attempting to move the villagers on. But they didn't want to move and began to argue with the guards. Then the dispute suddenly erupted into fury, the kind of hysterical, almost tearful scene that Bill had seen break out without warning on the streets of Shanghai. Press the wrong nerve, he thought, and all at once these people go ballistic.

He watched as a grubby-faced boy of about twelve drew back from the wire, and picked up something from the ground. He hefted it in his hand—a broken brick, discarded by the builders—and then threw it high and hard in the direction of the palace that had appeared on their land. The brick fell short, but they all turned to look as it clattered against the show home's cast-iron gates.

Orders were barked and the villagers took off across the field with the security guards on their tail. Bill saw that Ho had disconnected himself from Chairman Sun's side and was with them.

'Hilarious,' said the woman from *Shanghai Chic*. 'Isn't this hilarious?'

The boy who had thrown the brick paused by a

73

neat stack of fresh bricks and began hurling them at the chasing pack. An old man joined him, one of those wiry old Chinese men without a gram of fat on his body, and Ho and the security guards hid behind a bulldozer as the bricks rained down. Then they started throwing the bricks back.

Bill shook his head. 'It's like a medieval battle,' he said.

'China is a medieval country,' Shane said. 'A medieval country with broadband.' He looked across at the press delegation. 'We should put a stop to this, mate,' he said. 'It's not good in front of journalists. Even tame journalists.'

'I'll deal with it,' Bill said. 'You get Tiger.' He began walking towards the press pack. 'Ladies and gentlemen, if you would care to step back inside, Chairman Sun will take questions.'

But nobody was listening. They were watching the guards chasing the old man and the boy across the open mud flats. The old man was too slow, and when he fell the guards were immediately on him, lifting him by his arms. The boy had stopped, uncertain if he should run or fight, and then they had him too. As Ho barked instructions, the guards began hauling them back to the show home.

'Hello, Bill,' Alice smiled. 'Going to get rich in China?'

Bill smiled along with her. 'That's the plan,' he said, watching the security guards. They were taking the old man and the boy to the PSB. That's what they were going to do, he saw. Turn them over to the law. The cops had gone to the gates to meet them.

'You know who's going to get rich here?' Alice said. 'The Chinese. A few of them, anyway.

74

Chairman Sun, for example. And some of his pals. You comfortable with that, Bill?'

He looked at her and said nothing. She was still holding her notepad in her hands. She may have been at his wedding, and she may have been his wife's best friend when they were growing up, but she still looked like trouble. He began walking towards the gates. Alice followed him.

'You're an intelligent man,' she said. 'And I'm just curious to know what you think is happening here. Off the record.'

'And what do you think is happening?' he said, not breaking his stride. 'On the record.'

Alice shrugged. 'Looks like a standard land-grab to me. The new rich get their mansions. The local politicians get their cut. And the farmers get shafted.'

He stopped and stared at her. 'You think these people are going to be robbed?' he said, genuinely outraged. 'Is that what you think is going to happen? I've seen the details of their compensation package.'

She laughed at him.

'Just think about it,' Alice said. They had all arrived at the gates at the same time. Ho and the guards were handing over the old man and the boy to the PSB. The old man looked resigned to his fate but the child looked terrified. 'Until the mid-nineties all the land in China was owned by the People,' Alice said. 'And then suddenly it wasn't. One day you woke up and the land your family had farmed for generations was owned by someone you had never met. And he wanted you out.'

'These people are going to receive generous compensation packages,' Bill said, watching one of the security guards shove the old man. That wasn't right. They shouldn't do that.

'Don't buy that, Bill. We both know that the money goes to the local government. Your friend Chairman Sun—is he going to see the farmers right, Bill?'

He ignored her. The security guards were conferring with the PSB cops as they gripped the arms of the old man and the boy. They were working out what to do with them. Bill hesitated, unsure if he should stick his nose in here.

'Every foreigner who works in China has to learn the ostrich trick,' Alice said. 'You know what the ostrich trick is, Bill? It's when you ignore what's going on right in front of you.'

Ho suddenly got tired of all the chit-chat and punched the boy full in the face. The child went flying backwards and Bill watched him sprawl in the mud. For a moment Bill could not believe what he had seen. Then he was on Ho, pushing the larger man as hard as he could and not budging him, screaming in his face, telling him to leave the boy alone, let the police deal with it.

Bill helped the boy to his feet, trembling with shock and rage, and discovered that he had to keep holding him because the punch had knocked him senseless. There was blood on the boy's lips and chin from a broken nose. Bill searched in his pockets for something to wipe it with and found nothing. Two of the PSB officers took the boy's arms and eased him from Bill's grip.

'This is intolerable,' Bill said, even though he knew they didn't understand a word. His voice was shaking with emotion. 'My company will not be a party to this, do you hear me?'

The PSB led the boy and the old man away. Ho chuckled and gestured at Bill with real amusement. The guards gawped at him with their infinite blankness. Bill looked up and saw Alice Greene offering him a Kleenex.

For the blood on his hands.

*   *   *

On the road back to Shanghai, Tiger had to swerve to miss a blue Ferrari coming in the opposite direction on the wrong side of the road. As Tiger wrestled the limo across pockmarked gravel, Bill caught a glimpse of a boy and girl laughing behind their sunglasses.

'Look at that,' Shane said, placing a grateful hand on Tiger's shoulder as the Ferrari weaved off in a cloud of dust. 'There's about fifty million of them driving around who were on bicycles last year.'

Tiger revved the engine, trying to ease the car out of a pothole. A family of peasant farmers, their skin black from the sun, sullenly watched them.

'Very low,' Tiger said. 'Very low people.'

Nancy looked up. 'I am from Yangdong,' she said in English, but Tiger was fiddling with his climate control, and gave no sign that he had heard her.

Bill looked at Nancy and tried to remember her file. She had gone to two of the top colleges in the country—Tsinghua University Law School, then the University of Political Science and Law in Beijing. To get that kind of education, to become a lawyer after growing up in this dreary landscape— it told him that Alice Greene was wrong, and that Chinese ingenuity and hard work and intelligence would ultimately triumph over Chinese cruelty and corruption and stupidity.

That's what it told him.

But he didn't quite believe it.

*   *   *

Back at the firm, Devlin came into his office. 'Are you all right?' he asked Bill.

'I'm fine,' Bill said.

'I heard what happened. The boy and the old man.' He shook his head. 'Ugly business.'

'Yes.'

'But we can't get squeamish here,' Devlin said. Bill looked up at him and Devlin touched his arm. 'I mean it. It's better now than it's ever been. You know that, don't you? And it will get better. Change will come. Because of people like us.'

They stared out at the view. There were red lights on the peaks of the skyscrapers, and they seemed to wink in secret fraternity at the red lights of the discreet CCTV cameras in Bill's office.

'Do you know what I liked about you?' Devlin said. 'When we first met.'

'My wife,' Bill said, and Devlin laughed. 'That's what everyone likes best about me.'

'What I liked about you was that you're a lawyer, not a technician,' Devlin said. 'Lawyers solve problems. Lawyers can reason. Technicians—their mummy and daddy wanted them to be lawyers, so that's what they do for forty years. Technicians know a snapshot of the law, from when they qualified. But they don't feel it in their bones. They're not real lawyers. They're technicians. But you're a lawyer. You see the law as social lubricant

78

and not as a club. But you're coming from a land where the law is used to protect rights, and you are living in a place where essentially the people have no rights. We've done nothing wrong here, you know that, don't you?'

'But those villagers,' Bill said. 'That boy . . .'

'His family will be taken care of,' Devlin insisted. 'Look, Bill, you have to choose what you see here. You know what the China price is?'

'Sure.'

The China price was the key to everything, even more important than the numbers. When foreign manufacturers had looked at every price offered by their suppliers, they demanded the China price—which was always the lowest price of all.

'It means you can move any kind of operation to China, and get it all done cheaper.'

Devlin shook his head.

'The *real* China price,' Devlin said. 'The *real* China price is the compromises we have to make to work here. Forget all that stuff about ancient civilisations. Forget all that propaganda about four thousand years of history. This country is still growing up. And some diseases it's best to get when you are young.'

They stood together at the window and watched the sun set quickly. In the gathering darkness it suddenly seemed as if all of Pudong lit up at once, and the two men stared silently at the lights shining before them like the conqueror's reward.

* * *

He was ready for home.

The trip to Yangdong had left him with dirt on

79

his shoes and stains on his suit and the urgent need to crawl into bed next to Becca and just hold her for a while. Or perhaps she could come to his bed and then they would not have to worry about waking Holly and they could do more than just cuddle.

But Jurgen and Wolfgang were in Shane's office when Bill was leaving, clearly agitated, expressing some concern in streams of German to each other, and broken English to their lawyer. Shane came out of his office and took Bill to one side.

'They're getting their lederhosen in a twist,' Shane sighed. 'Worried about what the hacks might write after today. Let's buy them a couple of drinks and calm their nerves, mate. Tell them we're all going to live happily ever after.'

'I've really got to get home,' Bill said. 'I don't see my wife. I don't see my kid.'

'One drink,' Shane said. 'They're your Germans too, mate.'

'All right,' Bill said. 'But just the one.'

There was an Irish bar on Tongren Lu called BB's—Bejeebers-Bejaybers—run by a large Swede with absolutely no Irish blood whatsoever.

BB's was always mobbed because you could get English football with Cantonese commentators from Star TV, Guinness on tap and live music by a band from Manila.

'You see them all over Asia,' Shane said, recovered from his hangover and ready for the night. 'These Filippino bands with singers who can really sing and musicians who can really play. Maybe in the West they would have a record deal, or at least appear on some television talent show. Out here they play dives for the likes of us.' He chugged down his Guinness and called for another. 'You see it all the time.'

Bill stared at him. Because what you didn't see all the time was Shane looking at a woman the way he was looking at the tiny Filippina singer who was leaning against her keyboard player's back and giving a pitch-perfect rendition of 'We've Only Just Begun' by the Carpenters. She tossed back her waist-length hair, jet black but shot through with blonde highlights, and when she smiled it seemed to light up every dark corner of Bejeebers-Bejaybers. A little further down the bar, Wolfgang and Jurgen sipped their Guinnesses and stared up at her, the press forgotten.

'Who is she?' Bill said.

'Rosalita,' Shane said with real tenderness. 'Rosalita and the Roxas Boulevard Boys.'

'You know her?' Bill asked. Shane looked as though he had thought about her a lot.

Shane looked at him. 'I see you with your wife,' he said, taking Bill by surprise. 'I see you with Becca. Saw you together at that dinner. And I envy you, Bill.' He turned his gaze back to the stage. 'It can't go on forever, can it? This life.'

Rosalita was doing an upbeat number now. She shook her hair, she flashed her luminous teeth, and she jiggled her tiny rump. The top of a lemon thong peeked above the waistband of her trousers, which were as tight as a wet suit. The Germans licked their lips.

'She's got a tattoo,' Shane confessed, watching Bill warily to see how he would react to this news.

Bill shrugged. 'Well, a lot of women have tattoos these days.'

'Yeah, but her tattoo says *Tom*.'

Bill thought about it. 'Who's Tom?'

'Some asshole,' Shane said, and a cloud of depression seemed to pass across his face. 'She says Tom was just some asshole.'

The Roxas Boulevard Boys brought it back to a more romantic gear—Lionel Ritchie's 'Penny Lover'—and Rosalita tipped forward as if with an unendurable melancholy, her hair falling over her face. Shane sighed. And then, over the mournful minor chords, Bill heard the sound of expatriate whooping and jeering, the sound of men urging a woman on. He turned to look.

There were five of them, white boys in suits, surrounding her, the one, the tall girl he had seen with the orchid in her hair outside Paradise Mansions, although the flower was gone now, and they were all out on the tiny BB's dance floor.

She seemed to be in a daze, dancing alone to some song in her head, her eyes closed and her arms held high above her head, and their hands were all over her. The tall girl, with a scrape high on one cheekbone, as if she had been struck.

'Come on, darling,' one of the men said, tugging at the button of her trousers. 'Show us what you got.'

Another one was behind her. A young man, but already run to fat. His hands on her buttocks, her breasts, biting his bottom lip as he mimed taking her from behind, to the huge amusement of his laughing friends.

They moved in closer, getting bolder now, one of them pulling down the zip of his trousers, and then the zip of her trousers, another yanking up her cut-off top so that you saw a glimpse of a black bra. The girl didn't notice or she was too far gone to care. Then Bill was wading among them, shoving off the fat boy behind her, and then getting between the girl and the suit who had pulled down her zip, and their expressions changed from leering delight to bewilderment, then apoplectic rage.

As Bill took the tall girl by the arm and led her from the dance floor, one of them threw a punch at the back of his head. He caught it just below the base of the skull, turned and took another one on his ear. He threw a couple of punches but they were all over him, pushing each other out of the way for the chance to lash out at him.

But then Shane was there, meaty fists flying, and then there were Wolfgang and Jurgen doing these surprisingly authentic-looking side-kicks, and then the Swedish owner and a lad from Belfast who worked behind the bar were joining in, putting themselves between Bill and the girl and the five drunken suits. A full-scale brawl broke out for about five seconds and then it was over as quickly as it had begun and the suits were running to the back of BB's, throwing around a few bar stools as they retreated.

Bill held the tall girl's hand as Shane got them out of the club and into the back of a Santana taxi. 'Just go,' he said. The cab pulled away and she still hadn't opened her eyes. He saw that the wound on her cheekbone was livid and fresh.

'Did they do that to you?' he said. 'The mark on your face. Did those bastards do that to you?'

She leaned forward, touching her face. Then she sat back up, fighting back the sickness. Bill realised he had never seen anyone so hopelessly drunk.

'Airbag,' she said. 'The airbag from my Mini.'

Then they had to stop by the side of the road so

83

that she could be sick. She bent double out of the open back door, dry heaving because there was nothing left to bring up. The driver watched Bill in his rear-view mirror with barely concealed contempt.

Fucking Westerners, his eyes seemed to say. *Ruining our lovely girls.*

'Can't stop throwing out,' she said when they were on the road again. 'Please excuse me. I am throwing out all the time.'

Her English was almost perfect. Too clearly learned in a classroom, perhaps. Too painfully formal. But she got almost everything right, he realised, and when she did get something wrong, he still had no trouble understanding her. Didn't *throwing out* make more sense than *throwing up*? It was an improvement on the original.

'You had an accident,' Bill said. 'What happened?'

She exhaled, shivering with grief.

'My husband is very angry with me,' she said. 'Very angry with me for breaking the new car.'

He took off his jacket and wrapped it around her thin shoulders. She burrowed down inside it, trying to hide from the world, and he patted her gently, the way he might try to reassure Holly if she had a bad dream. And then she fell asleep. Leaning against him. He patted her again.

He looked at her asleep in his jacket and he saw that it was the one that still bore the ghost of a handprint.

That's never going to come out now, he thought.

*   *   *

84

It was the apartment of a single girl.

Something about it, Bill thought as he carried her inside, something about it said that here was a life lived alone. A fruit bowl containing a lonely brown banana. A magazine turned to a TV page with favourite programmes circled in red. A book of crossword puzzles, opened to one that was half-finished. She doesn't look like the kind of girl who does crossword puzzles, he thought. And then, *Well, what do you know about her?*

The flat was immaculately decorated but a much smaller apartment than the one he lived in. He found the only bedroom and laid her down on top of the duvet, still wearing his jacket. In the movies, he thought, in the movies I would undress her and put her to bed and in the morning she wouldn't remember a thing. But he couldn't bring himself to do anything except leave her sleeping on the bed, and turn the light off on his way out. Her voice reached him as he went to close the door behind him.

'He has nobody but his wife and me,' she said, unmoving in the darkness. 'I am quite sure of that.'

'He sounds like quite a catch,' Bill said with a contempt that surprised him, and he let himself out of the flat as quietly as he could.

*   *   *

Becca could tell there was something wrong. She could tell immediately. It wasn't the kind of crying she was used to—the crying of a child having a bad dream, or who was too cold or too warm, or who needed a glass of water or a cuddle.

Holly's crying came through the monitor as

85

Becca was nodding off in front of BBC World, and she knew immediately that it was her breathing.

It was bad. Very bad. And Holly was frightened.

Becca remained ludicrously cheerful and upbeat as she set up the nebuliser, the breathing machine, and placed the mouthpiece over Holly's face.

'Deep . . . deep . . . deep,' Becca said, miming inhalation with one hand as she desperately dialled Bill's phone with the other. 'Good, baby. Very good.'

No reply.

The nebuliser took the edge off the asthma attack but it wasn't enough. Becca had never seen her as bad as this, not since that first awful day. Holly's breathing was shallow and laboured and it scared the life out of Becca. It scared the life out of both of them. She needed a doctor. She needed a hospital. She needed it now.

No numbers, Becca thought, furious. I have no numbers. She had no idea what number to call for an ambulance. How could she be so stupid? How could she have been so certain that nothing bad would ever happen?

Becca quickly wrapped Holly in her dressing gown and grabbed her coat and her keys and dialled Bill's number again.

And again and again and again.

No answer.

Then Becca was out of the flat with Holly in her arms, the child surprisingly heavy, and trying to remain as upbeat as a game show host as they went out to the night in search of a taxi.

She saw one the moment she stepped outside Paradise Mansions, a beat-up red Santana, but it didn't stop for her and she shouted angrily at its taillights.

Holly began to cry and Becca held her tight and rocked her, while her eyes scanned the empty streets for another taxi. She tried calling Bill and there was still no signal and after that she didn't try again. After that she knew she was going to have to do it alone.

SEVEN

There was something wrong with his home.

It should have been still and dark and both of them sleeping, with just a nightlight left on in the kitchen. But all the lights were blazing. The television was on and BBC World was playing its theme tune. The door to the master bedroom was flung open.

And they were gone.

Bed empty. Duvet on the floor. Lights on.

And Becca and Holly were gone.

He flew through the apartment, throwing open doors, calling their names, and the panic was a physical sickness he could feel in his throat and in his gut.

Calling their names, even though he knew they were not there. Shouting their names over the bloody theme tune to BBC World. He didn't understand what was happening. It made no sense at all. He wanted them back. He looked at his watch and covered it with his hand. It was so late. He wanted to throw up.

'Becca!'

He walked to the table and picked up the

mouthpiece to his daughter's respirator.

His phone began to ring.

*　　　*　　　*

This was what she was good at. This was what she could do. She could look after her child. She could do that. And as long as she could do that, the rest of the world could go hang.

Holly was sitting up in bed in a private room at the International Family Hospital and Clinic on Xian Xia Lu being examined by a young doctor with an Indian face and a Liverpool accent.

'Have you heard of a man called Beethoven?' Dr Khan asked Holly, his fingers lightly feeling her ribs.

'No,' said Holly warily.

'Beethoven had asthma,' the doctor smiled.

Becca laughed, the tears springing. Devlin was standing by her side and he placed a hand on her shoulder. She touched his hand, sick with relief. Holly was going to be all right.

'How about Charles Dickens, Augustus Caesar and John F. Kennedy?' Dr Khan asked Holly. 'Have you heard of any of them?'

'I haven't heard of *nobody*,' Holly said, wide-eyed and looking at her mother for prompting. Becca was smiling at her now. 'Why are you crying, Mummy?'

'Because I'm happy, sweetheart. You make me happy. That's all.'

'That's a funny old reason to cry. Grown-ups don't cry.'

'Well,' Dr Khan said. 'Those people all had asthma.' He pulled down her top. 'All the best people have had asthma.' He turned to Becca and nodded. 'She's going to be fine.'

Becca nodded, overcome with gratitude. 'Thank you. Thank you.'

'Are you a doctor?' Holly asked him.

'I'm what they call a Senior Medical Registrar,' he said. 'It's a fancy name for a doctor.' He sat on the bed, holding Holly's hand as he spoke to Becca. 'She's had a trigger reaction that could have been caused by almost anything. If she's not around tobacco smoke, then air pollution is most likely. Shanghai is better than Beijing, but it's still a Chinese city. We have some of the worst car pollution in the country. Then there are all the factories and power plants in the northern suburbs, up in Baoshan.'

'Thank goodness they're starting to control that,' Devlin said. 'Ten years ago you often couldn't see Pudong from Puxi.'

'Asthma is not a disease that we cure,' the doctor said. 'But it's a condition we can control.' He stood up. 'But of course you know that already.'

Becca loved this hospital. Outside its glass doors the Changning District was as grubby and down-at-heel as anywhere in Shanghai, but the International Family Hospital and Clinic looked newer, cleaner and more modern than anything she had ever seen back home.

'All my boys have been in here at some stage,' Devlin said, as if reading her thoughts and trying to keep the mood merry. 'The youngest two were born here. And I think we have had—what?—two broken arms, one undescended testicle and a hyper-active thyroid gland.' He beamed at Dr Khan but Becca knew the words were meant to reassure her. And they did.

It was reassuring to know that this oasis of Western-trained, English-speaking doctors in their clean blue uniforms was available twenty-four hours a day.

Unlike her husband.

*   *   *

Devlin and Dr Khan were gone by the time Bill arrived. Holly was sleeping. Becca was almost asleep herself. Bill stood sweating and panting in the doorway.

'What happened? What happened?' he said, coming into the room. 'Is she okay?'

Becca stirred in her chair. 'She woke up struggling to breathe,' she said, her voice sounding mechanical and drained. She wanted to tell him, she really did, but it all seemed a long time ago, and it was all right now, and she really did feel tired. But he wanted more. He wanted to know everything.

'I tried calling you,' she said. She looked from her daughter to her husband, and couldn't keep the resentment out of her eyes. 'Lots of times. No answer. I couldn't even get your voice-mail.'

'I'm sorry,' he said, sinking to his knees next to her. He kissed her hands, kissed her face, put his arms around her. It was like holding a statue.

'I didn't know what to do,' she said. 'I didn't have the numbers. You know—emergency numbers. It's not 999, is it?'

'We'll get all the numbers,' he said, shaking his head. 'I'll get all the numbers for us.'

'I couldn't even get a taxi. So I called Tess

Devlin. She was fantastic. Then things started to happen. Then I had help. Devlin came with Tiger and they brought us here. Holly and me. And Dr Khan—he's been . . .'

Bill was on his feet, looking at Holly's face, and for a second Becca wondered if he was even listening to her.

'Where were you?' she said, very calm.

'I went for a drink with Shane,' he said, and it wasn't a good moment. He knew how it sounded. 'The Germans were flipping out. There have been some incidents. At the Green Acres site in Yangdong.' He shook his head. 'The security is out of control. They were hitting this little kid. I had to stop them, Bec.'

'Jesus,' Becca said, turning her face away. 'Oh, Jesus Christ, Bill.' Looking back at him now. 'Your daughter is being rushed to hospital and you're in some *bar*?'

Bill stared at her helplessly, feeling useless. He wanted so many things from this world. There was quite a list. But more than anything he wanted his wife and daughter to be happy, safe and proud of him. And he had let them down because he went for a drink with clients and got into a fight over a girl he didn't know. When it was his family who needed him, when it was his family he should have been with all along.

Maybe he could have explained it better. He had wanted to come home. He really did. But it was work. He wanted her to understand. He wanted her to get it. Surely she knew that there was nothing more important to him than her and Holly? He wanted to tell her everything.

But he couldn't tell her about the girl.

91

Devlin had told Tiger to wait for them. As they drove back to Gubei, Becca held Holly on her lap and the child slept in her arms. Bill touched his daughter's hair.

'She's okay,' he said. 'She's doing really well—'

Becca's anger exploded. 'What do you know about it, Bill? You're never around. How dare you? And she's not okay. She's not okay at school because she started in the middle of a term and the other kids already have their friends so she plays alone in the playground.' It was all pouring out now, even things she had decided not to share with him because she didn't want to worry him, because there was enough pressure already, he had enough on his plate at work. 'Did you know that? Of course you didn't. And her breathing's not okay because the air here is filthy. All right? So don't ever tell me she's okay, because you know absolutely nothing about it.'

They stared out at the elevated Ya'an Freeway. The lights of the city seemed to be glowing somewhere far below them.

'I'm sorry, Bec,' he said. 'It will get better. I'll make it better.'

Tears sprang to her eyes. This was a good thing about him. He would always reach out a hand to her. It had always been that way when they argued. He wouldn't allow them to go to sleep angry and hurt. He always tried to make it better. And he didn't say what he could have said, what most men would have said—*Coming here was* your *idea.* But this life wasn't what she had expected.

92

'I wanted us to see the jazz band at the Peace Hotel,' she said, almost laughing, it sounded so absurd. 'And I wanted us to buy propaganda posters and Mao badges in the Dongtai Lu antique market. All these places that I read about, all the great places they say you should go.'

He put his arm around her.

'And I wanted us,' she said, snuggling down, adjusting Holly on her lap. 'I wanted us to drink cocktails in hotels where in the thirties you could get opium on room service. I want to support you, Bill. And I want to be a good sport. And I want to muck in and I don't want to whine. But why isn't it like that?'

'We'll do all those things,' he said, and he touched her face, that face he loved so much, and determined to see her happy again.

'But *when*?'

'Starting tomorrow, Bec.' He nodded, and she smiled, because she knew that he meant it.

Her unhappiness, and her loneliness, and all the panic of tonight were things he would address with the dogged determination that he brought to everything. My husband, she thought. The professional problem-solver.

*   *   *

He could never understand why people felt sentimental about when they were young. Being young meant being poor. Being young was a long, hard grind. Being young meant doing jobs that sucked the life out of you.

Being young was overrated. Or maybe it was just him. For in his teens and twenties Bill had endured

93

eight years of feeling like he was the only young person in the world who wasn't really young at all.

At weekends and holidays, he had worked his way through two years of A-levels, four years at UCL, six months of his Law Society final exams and his two years' traineeship with Butterfield, Hunt and West.

Over eight years of stacking shelves, carrying hods, pulling pints and ferrying around everything from takeaway pizzas (on a scooter) to Saturday-night drunks (in a mini cab) and cases of wine (in a Majestic Wine Warehouse white van).

The worst job was in a Fulham Road pub called the Rat and Trumpet. It wasn't as back-breaking as lugging bricks on a building site, and it wasn't as dangerous as delivering pizza to a sink estate after midnight, and it didn't numb your brain quite like filling shelves under the midnight sun of the supermarket strip lighting.

But the Rat and Trumpet was the worst job of the lot because that was where all the people his own age didn't even notice that privilege had been given to them on a plate. They had a sense of entitlement that Bill Holden would never have, the boys with their ripped jeans and pastel-coloured jumpers and their Hugh Grant fringes, the girls all coltish limbs and blonde tresses and laughter full of daddy's money.

He had come across the type at university, but they had not been the dominant group, not at UCL, where the braying voices were drowned out by other accents from other towns and other types of lives. But this was their world, and Bill just served drinks in it.

Kids whose mothers and fathers had never got

sick, or broke up, or divorced, or died. At least that's the way he thought of them. They all looked as though nothing bad had ever happened to them, or ever would.

They stared straight through him, or bellowed their orders from the far end of the bar, and he had no trouble at all in hating every one of the fucking bastards.

The Rat and Trumpet had no bouncer, and sometimes Bill had to throw one of them out. The landlord slipped him an extra fiver at the end of the night for every chinless troublemaker Bill had to escort to the Fulham Road—they called it the Half-Cut Hooray allowance.

The extra money was greatly appreciated. But Bill—twenty-two years old and furious with the Fates—would cheerfully have done it for nothing. *Hilarious*, they always said. Like the woman from *Shanghai Chic*. Everything was *hilarious*. It was all so fucking hilarious that it made you puke.

One night some idiot was practising his fast bowling with the Scotch eggs and splattering yolk and breadcrumbs all over the customers in the snug. *Howzat? Hilarious, darling*. The Scotch-egg bowler was a strapping lad in a pink cashmere sweater and carefully distressed Levi's. They could be big lads, these Hoorays. They weren't selling off the playing fields at the kind of school his mummy and daddy sent him to.

There was a girl with him—one of those girls, Bill thought, one of those Fulham Broadway blondes—who was trying to get him to stop. She seemed halfway to being a human being. Bill gave her credit for looking upset. For not finding it absolutely *hilarious*. That was the first time he saw

95

Becca.

Bill politely asked the Scotch-egg bowler to leave. He told Bill to fuck off and get him a pint of Fosters. So Bill asked him less politely. Same response. Fuck off and a pint of Fosters. So Bill got him in an arm lock before his brain had registered what was happening and marched him to the door. It toughed you up on those building sites. It didn't matter how much sport they played at their private schools, it just wasn't the same as manual labour.

A meaty lad but soft inside, Bill thought. He gave him a push at the door—slightly harder than was strictly necessary—in fact a lot harder than was strictly necessary—and the fast Scotch-egg bowler skidded and fell into the gutter.

At the outside tables, people laughed.

'One day you'll bring drinks to my children,' he told Bill, getting up, his face red for all sorts of reasons.

'Can't wait,' Bill said. They must have been about the same age, he thought. Bill bet his mum wasn't gone.

'And you'll be a toothless old git with snot on his chin and your rotten life will be gone and you will still be waiting on the likes of me.'

Bill laughed and looked at the blonde girl. 'I hope your kids look like their mother,' he said, turning away, and never expecting to see her again.

But Becca came back inside to apologise on behalf of her boyfriend and offer to pay for the Scotch eggs and all the mess, and she was just in time to see the landlord fire Bill, who didn't like it that Bill had used more force than necessary to throw out the fast Scotch-egg bowler; he wasn't here to rough up the paying customers, he was here to stop trouble, not to start it, and Bill was saying that he couldn't possibly be fired, because he was fucking well quitting, okay?

Becca followed him outside and said, 'Don't go.'

And Bill said, 'Three quid an hour to be insulted by dickheads? Why not?'

But that wasn't what she meant.

She apologised again and said that he was a nice guy really, Guy was, and Bill got a bit confused there, because the boyfriend's name was Guy, and they had a little laugh about that, and that was good, because she had such a beautiful face when she laughed, and then she said that Bill shouldn't think they were all idiots and Bill said ah, don't worry about it, he had no objection to spoilt rich kids with no manners, they had to drink somewhere, and she said that was not her, and he didn't know her at all, getting angry now, and he said, *Well, prove it—let me have your phone number and I might give you a call sometime,* because he really didn't give a fuck any more and he was sick of not having a girlfriend who looked like her and sick of being lonely and sick of feeling that he had never had the chance to suck all the juice out of being young.

So she wrote her number on the palm of his hand and by the time he got back to his rented room on the other side of town his heart fell to his boots because the eight digits had almost worn off.

But he still had the number. Just.

And that was how he met Becca. She was the first one in that place, the very first, who didn't look straight through him, or look at him as if he was dirt, and he would always love her for that.

And he got scared sometimes. Because his

life was unthinkable without her. Because he wondered what would have happened to him if he had not met Becca. He thought—what then?

Who would have loved me?

*   *   *

The three of them walked hand in hand through a warehouse full of old masters.

There was Picasso's *Weeping Woman*, Van Gogh's *Starry Night* and Edward Hopper's *Nighthawks*. There were Degas dancers, Monet waterlilies and haystacks, Cézanne apples and mountains. There were Lichtenstein's comic-book lovers, Jasper Johns' flags and Warhol's Marilyn and Elvis and soup cans. There were canvases stacked everywhere, and on many of them the paint was still wet.

'Do one-two-three,' Holly commanded, happy to have a parent on each hand, so Bill and Becca went, 'One-two-*three*!' and swung their daughter up between them, her thin legs flying as they walked past Gauguin native girls, a pile of *Last Suppers* and *Mona Lisas* by the score.

'One-two-three!' they chanted, and Holly laughed wildly as they walked past Hockney swimming pools, Jackson Pollock splatter paintings and sailboats by Matisse.

They stopped at the end of an aisle where a girl in her late teens was painting half a dozen *Sunflowers* all at once. She worked quickly, occasionally glancing at a dog-eared *History of Modern Art*.

'It looks absolutely like the picture in the book,' Holly said.

'It looks exactly like the picture in the book,' Becca said.

'Is it really real, Daddy?' Holly said.

The girl artist smiled. 'Everything is fake except your mother,' she said. 'Old Shanghai saying.'

Becca ordered four *Sunflowers* to go with the *Starry Night* and *The Sower* that she had already bought. She laughed happily, in a way that she hadn't laughed for a long time. Vincent Van Gogh was going to fill the walls of their new home.

They caught a cab to the Bund, which by now Bill had learned to called the Waitan, 'above the sea', and finally they saw the jazz band in the bar of the Peace Hotel.

The six musicians were in their eighties now, the very same bunch of swing-obsessed Chinese boys who had been playing when the Japanese army marched into Shanghai a lifetime ago, and as the waitress fussed over Holly's hair and Bill and Becca sipped their Tsingtaos while the band swaggered through Glenn Miller's 'String of Pearls', for a few sweet dreaming minutes Becca thought it truly seemed as though the old world had never been pulled apart.

*   *   *

The next day Bill came back from work early and joined his daughter at the window. Devlin had packed him off home. He wanted Bill's family to be happy. He wanted them to stay.

'That's my favourite one,' Holly said, indicating a half-starved ginger kitten that was patrolling the perimeter of the fountain. 'That's the best one.'

There were no pets allowed in Paradise

99

Mansions but from their window Holly would watch the stray cats who haunted the courtyard— emaciated creatures that preened themselves in the shade of the straggly flower beds, or lapped delicately from the pools of water created by the mother-and-child fountain, or gnawed at bones they had foraged from the rows of huge black rubbish bins in an alleyway behind the main building.

Bill laughed. 'So why do you like her best?'

Holly thought about it. 'She's the smallest.'

'Shall we feed her, angel?'

Holly's eyes lit up. 'Shall we feed her? Shall we, Daddy?'

Holly hopped around with excitement while Bill got a carton of milk from the fridge and a saucer from the cupboard. Becca, in the bedroom getting ready to go out, frowned doubtfully, called something about fleas, but Bill and Holly were out of the apartment before she really had time to object.

Down in the courtyard, they watched from a respectful distance while the ginger waif lapped up its saucer of semi-skimmed and then took itself off to a flower bed where it collapsed with contentment in the dirt. Bill and Holly approached tentatively. The ginger kitten permitted Holly to stroke its back. Then Bill was suddenly aware that they were not alone.

The tall girl was standing there watching them with the cat. She was wearing a green *qipao* that made her long, slim body look even longer and her hair was hanging down. She was dressed to go out.

'Hello there,' she said, smiling at Holly, and Bill saw that she was holding his jacket. She had had it dry cleaned, and it was still in a cellophane wrapper that said Da Zhong American Laundry. He could see that they had not managed to remove the handprint.

'*Tse-tse*,' she said, holding out his jacket. 'Thank you so much.'

'*Bu ke-qi*,' he said.

'That means "you are welcome",' Holly told her, and they both laughed and the tall girl touched Holly's hair. 'So fair,' she said, 'I adore her,' and that was the first time he really heard her English, and the strange weight that she put on certain words, and the unfathomable choices she made with the language. *I adore her*. It somehow clanged. And yet it wasn't wrong. He could not say that it was wrong.

He held out his hand and she shook it lightly and awkwardly and quickly, as though she had never shaken hands with anyone in her life. Her hand was small and cool.

'Bill Holden,' he said, and he touched his daughter's head. 'And this one is Holly.'

'Li JinJin,' she said, and he knew that she was putting her family name first, in the Chinese fashion, the family coming before everything, the family name forever inseparable from the first name. 'Hello, Holly,' she said. Holding the slit of her *qipao* together with a modest gesture, she crouched down so that their eyes were on the same level. 'What are you up to with your daddy?'

Holly squinted at her. 'We're look aftering this cat,' she said, and the woman and the child silently contemplated the mangy ginger cat as it lolled in the flower bed. Bill sensed that JinJin didn't know quite what to say about the stray moggy. The

Chinese were not sentimental about animals.

Bill looked at JinJin when she stood up. The mark on her face looked better in the daylight. Not so raw. Or maybe he was just prepared for it now. And now he could see that it was from an airbag. He could tell that a human hand hadn't made it. But even with that mark on her face, there was still something about her, Bill thought. She wasn't the most beautiful woman he had seen in Shanghai. She wasn't even the most beautiful woman he had seen in Paradise Mansions—that would have to be his wife. But when JinJin Li smiled, she seemed to have this inner light. He had never seen her smile before.

'Have a good day in Shanghai,' she said, and now it was his turn to be lost for words as he struggled for something to say about the other night, to put it in its rightful place, but nothing came, and it did not matter because at that moment the silver Porsche pulled into the courtyard and she gave him one last smile before she started off to where the car was waiting for her, its powerful engine still running, ready to take Li JinJin off to her life.

*   *   *

Becca's night on the town had been fun, although she enjoyed it more in retrospect than she did at the time.

Alice had taken her to a bar on the Bund, plied her with ludicrously potent mojitos, and Becca had spent the evening with her mobile phone in her hand, just in case there was some problem with Holly. But Bill never called and they were both sleeping when she got home. Becca moved quietly through the apartment, checking on her family, and free at last to savour the evening, now that she knew everything was fine.

Holly was in the middle of the king-size bed, looking tiny. Breathing normally. And Bill in the spare room. His feet sticking out the bottom of the single bed. Looking comically big for it. Becca took off her clothes. He gasped and tried to sit up as she slid in beside him. She placed a soothing hand on his chest and kissed his face.

'She okay?' Becca said.

'Fine,' Bill said sleepily. 'She's been fine. What time is it?'

Then he felt her hands on him. She said his name. Not much more than a whisper. Her mouth touched his mouth. She felt his hands lightly run down her ribcage, the swell of her hip, the long flank of her thigh. Soft kisses in the darkness.

'Bill?'

'What?'

'Don't make love to me,' she said. 'Not tonight. Just fuck me, okay? You can do that, can't you?'

He could do that.

EIGHT

Bill's father came through the arrivals gate at Pudong, his tough old face lighting up at the sight of his granddaughter.

'Granddad Will,' Holly said, squirming out of Bill's arms and running to him.

Picasso, Becca had said the first time she met the old man. That's exactly what Picasso looked like.

Bald, broad-shouldered, eyes that stared straight at you and never looked away. Bill didn't know about Picasso. He thought his father looked like a bull. Old and strong. A tough old bull.

He had a suitcase in one hand—the only suitcase Bill had ever known him to own, the old man was very monogamous when it came to luggage—and tucked under his free arm was an inappropriately gigantic teddy bear.

'Dad,' Bill said, 'they have trolleys, you know,' and the old man said, 'Do I look like I need a trolley?' and so they nearly had a row before they had even said hello, which would have been some kind of record.

'Please be nice,' Becca murmured to Bill as Tiger led them to the car, and the old man listened patiently to one of Holly's meaningless monologues about a character she called her 'third-favourite princess'. Bill didn't remember that kind of patience when he had been growing up. Maybe everything was different with grandchildren.

Becca's father had been scheduled to be the first one to come out to visit, but a heart murmur and endless tests had kept him confined to London. It felt like more than ill health. For someone who had spent his life on the move with Reuters, Bill thought that Becca's father seemed very reluctant to stray far from home. But Bill's old man was hard as nails. He blinked back the effects of a ten-hour flight as if he had just woken from an afternoon nap.

'So what do you want to do?' Becca said as they drove to Gubei. The Bund was passing by the window. But the old man didn't take his eyes from his granddaughter. Bill felt he couldn't look at her without smiling.

'Well,' he said. 'I want to see the Great Wall, of course.'

Bill and Becca looked at each other.

'That's Beijing, Dad,' Bill said. 'The Great Wall is near Beijing.'

Becca was looking concerned. 'We could fly up there at the weekend,' she said to Bill. 'If you could get off work on Saturday . . .'

Bill shook his head impatiently. Silly old sod. He probably hadn't even looked at a guide book. 'What else, Dad?'

'How about the Forbidden City? That looks nice.'

'It's very nice,' Bill said. 'But the Forbidden City is right in the middle of Beijing.'

The old man looked at him. 'I don't want to be any trouble. If it's too difficult . . .'

'Oh, it's not too difficult at all,' Becca said happily.

'Granddad, Granddad,' Holly said, disappointed that his attention had been diverted. She kicked the back of the seat and Becca told her to please not do that.

'It's not too difficult, if that's what you want to see, Dad,' Bill said, with the exasperated impatience he knew so well. 'But it's like expecting the Tower of London when you're in Paris.' He felt his wife's restraining hand resting lightly on his shoulder and said no more.

*   *   *

They were all up early the next morning. As Holly

105

played with her grandfather, Becca took Bill to one side.

'Make the most of it,' she said, and Bill thought that she was thinking about her own father. 'He's not going to be around forever.'

'No,' Bill said, watching his father down on the carpet, doing one-arm push-ups with his granddaughter on his back. Holly squealed with pleasure. The old man's thick builder's hand pressed into the freshly cleaned carpet of the company flat. 'It just feels like forever.'

Holly lost her balance but righted herself by gripping what was left of her grandfather's hair. They both laughed. Holly held on tight and the old man changed hands and continued with his one-arm push-ups.

Bill made a move towards them but Becca stopped him. 'Leave them,' she said.

'But it's *dangerous*,' Bill said.

His wife shook her head, and he went to work before anything started.

*   *   *

Becca was making tea and toast when Bill's father came into the kitchen with Holly in his arms.

'His Lordship gone off to work?' he said, settling the child on the floor. She clambered up into her special chair.

Becca smiled and nodded. 'The pair of you were having such fun, he didn't want to disturb you.'

'Bill has an early start,' he noted, spooning three sugars into his tea.

'He has to work to get money,' Holly said, repeating the party line. She took a sip of her juice and half of it failed to go inside her mouth.

'Early starts and late nights,' Becca said, mopping the juice off the child's face with a piece of kitchen towel. Then she sat back in her chair and smiled at the unusual sight of three people sitting down for a meal. 'This is so nice,' she laughed.

'Long days,' the old man observed as Becca lavished butter on to a slice of toast, cut it into four triangles and placed them on a plate featuring the Little Mermaid.

'Well, he's either working late at the office or he's out with clients,' she said, placing the plate in front of Holly. 'So yes—they're very long days.'

The old man frowned with disapproval. 'He should slow down a bit. There's no end to that kind of life.'

Becca felt the need to gently defend her husband. 'He just wants a good life for us,' she said, buttering more toast for everyone. 'That's all. That's why we're here.' She picked up a tissue and wiped a greasy smear from her daughter's chin. 'That's what everyone wants, isn't it?'

The old man chewed his toast. 'Suppose so,' he conceded. 'I think Bill always thought I was a bit of a stick-in-the-mud.' He looked almost shy. 'That I shouldn't have been satisfied with our little house. My little job. My little life.'

Becca placed a hand on his arm. 'I'm sure he never thought that,' she said.

'Oh, he did,' insisted the old man, warming to his theme. 'And he still thinks it.' He looked defiant, a slice of toast poised halfway to his mouth. 'But that's the difference between me and His Lordship, Bec. He wants it all. And I only wanted enough.'

'But it was my idea,' she said. 'Coming out here. I pushed him. And he'll do anything I ask him to do. Because he loves me.' Now it was her turn to look embarrassed. She felt her face turning red. 'Because he loves *us*,' she amended. 'And he'll make it work,' she said, lightening the tone. 'He will. He's like you—a grafter.'

'Never got his hands dirty in his life,' the old man said, but with a rueful grin.

And Becca could see the pride that the father felt for the son, although she felt like she was the only person in the world who did.

*   *   *

At first Shane took it for a burn. But it was some sort of birthmark, a light brown stain on her darker brown skin, a birthmark the size of a hand mirror that she could never quite hide, no matter how hard she tried, or how carefully she adjusted her ponytail.

Rosalita had a waterfall of jet-black hair that she wore tied back and tossed in a thick ponytail over one shoulder. When she was on stage at Bejeebers-Bejaybers she sometimes tugged at the ponytail, as if making sure it was still in place.

Shane had watched her sing often enough to know that she did it to hide the mark on her neck and something about that birthmark, and the way she tried in vain to hide it, undid Shane, and filled him with unbearable feelings of tenderness. There was no real pleasure in the feeling, just a kind of tormented rapture.

Rosalita and her band, the Roxas Boulevard

Boys, finished their set with a spirited 'Bad Moon Rising' and she came off stage smiling and shining with sweat. Shane watched with hypnotised misery as the tiny Filippina joined a party of Portuguese businessmen, the small curvy figure surrounded by tall men in suits, clinking glasses and laughing. Every once in a while she looked down the bar and flashed Shane one of those merciless bone-white smiles. He turned away.

There was a woman sitting further down the bar who looked as though she had just got off the bus. She was glancing around Bejeebers-Bcjaybers nervously, clutching her fake Gucci bag, as though anybody in here would bother to steal it.

There was an untouched fruit juice in front of her. Shane ran expert eyes over her. Seeking her fortune in the big bad city, Shane reflected. Ah, aren't we all, mate? he thought, surrendering to his philosophical tendencies.

So he bought her a fruit juice. And then another fruit juice. And although he couldn't quite get a handle on her Fujianese dialect, they shared enough *putonghua*—literally common language, meaning Mandarin—for Shane to work out that she had not long arrived in the city from Fuzhou, her accommodation was conveniently close to BB's, and she thought that friendly old Shane was potential boyfriend material.

That would show Rosalita, he thought. Show her bloody good, mate. But when he looked up, Rosalita was leaving the club, with the paw of a Portuguese businessman acting as a rudder on her round Filippina rear.

So then Shane got stinking, stonking drunk on Tsingtao, while his quiet, doe-eyed companion knocked back cranberry juice after cranberry juice, and when Shane was starting to sing along to songs that had ended hours ago, and all the cranberry juice in Bejeebers-Bejaybers had gone, they decided to go. Shane was so rat-faced that he almost left his laptop on the bar stool, which would have been a major disaster for all concerned, but he tucked it under his arm and they went back to her place, where she insisted that he took his shoes off at the door and kept silent until they were in her cosy little room.

Shane did as he was instructed, and when they were alone and he lay on her touching little single bed watching her get undressed, he thought—you can't care too much about them. Care too much and they will just kick you from here to kingdom come. The trouble was, everything felt stronger when you cared too much.

In the morning, while the woman from Fuzhou slept on, heavily sedated by a couple of injections from Dr Love, Shane got out of bed buck naked and strolled into the kitchen, yawning widely and scratching his scrotum. Then he stopped dead. And so did the Chinese family eating their breakfast at the kitchen table. They froze with a sharp intake of appalled breath, brown eyes widening with horror and disbelief, spoonfuls of congee and cornflakes halfway to their mouths.

The family were all there. The middle-aged man in glasses, already dressed in a shirt and tie, ready for the office. His wife, the plump housewife with an unfortunate perm and those ridiculous mini stockings they wore in Shanghai that only covered the ankles. And their two children—a podgy crop-haired boy of about eleven and a long-haired

110

girl in her mid-teens with her hands on her mouth and her sickened eyes on Shane.

And as Shane covered himself with a carton of orange juice and the mother covered her daughter's eyes with a packet of Cheerios, Shane understood two things with blinding clarity.

The woman from Fuzhou was an ayi who was unclear about her terms of employment.

And it was time for him to settle down.

*   *   *

The old man didn't really want to see anything. That was the truth. Bill stood at the window watching him smoking a roll-up down in the courtyard of Paradise Mansions and he knew that his father could live quite happily without ever seeing the Great Wall or the Forbidden City or the entire contents of Shanghai, just as long as he could spend some time with his granddaughter.

As the old man smoked his cigarette, Holly capered and gambolled around the mother-and-child fountain with her favourite stray cat. A car entered the courtyard, and the old man took a protective step towards Holly, gesturing with his cigarette, although the car was nowhere near her.

'They love each other so much,' Becca said, squeezing Bill's arm, as though the visit was a great success.

Bill nodded, watching his father lift his daughter and hold her above his head. His hands, Bill thought. Those builder's hands. My father's hands.

That had been the big thing when Bill was growing up, the summit of his old man's parental wisdom—the difference between men who worked with their hands and men who worked with their minds.

'The hands wear out before the mind,' he told Bill endlessly. 'That's why your exams are important. So you never have to work with your hands.'

How poor we were, Bill thought. His adult world had been full of old men that looked like a different species to his father. He had seen them in law firms in the City of London, he had seen them on beaches in the Caribbean, and he saw them in the restaurants of Shanghai.

Old men with open-neck blue shirts, tanned from sun and ski slopes, their women still somehow youthful. Bill's mother had been beautiful, but he didn't remember her ever possessing that frozen youthful quality that you saw among the people with money. And Bill's father had never looked like the old men in open-neck blue shirts. They had that soft, spoilt look of men who had never done physically demanding work, who had never worked with their hands.

So Bill had to study hard at school. He had to sail through exams. He had to be a straight-A student—and it was a big thing, a terrible thing, if he ever slipped. All so that one day he would work with his mind and not his hands and enjoy the soft life, the easy life, the good life. The life his father had never known.

Oh, Dad, Bill thought sadly, watching the old man roll another cigarette. *What the fuck would you know about the good life?*

Not that Bill Holden would ever have said *fuck* in front of his father.

112

Rosalita stepped out of BB's and its air thick with beer and sweat and smoke and she smelled the flowers immediately. The scent of roses, dozens and dozens of them, cloaking the night-time stink of the traffic.

The band had gone on ahead of her while she had engaged in some playful goodnight arse-slapping with the owner, just a bit of fun, she was good at that sort of thing, and now the musicians stood in front of the van, its back door open and ready, their instruments cased and in their hands as they all grinned back at her.

And as the band grinned at Rosalita, she slowly looked down at her feet where her size-four spike heels rested on . . . roses, the start of a trail of roses, a hand-made road of roses that led from the door of the club and away from the band's van to a stretch limo—an unnecessarily, ridiculously stretched limo—with its back door open, where Shane sat on the nearside, an iced bucket of champagne resting precariously between his beefy legs.

Without warning a man began to sing loudly in the shadows. Rosalita jumped back in alarm.

'O Sole Mio' it was, delivered pitch-perfect by a fat young Italian engineer who Shane had discovered singing Elvis ballads at the Funky Fox karaoke bar on Tong Ren Lu. The young engineer sang with a hand on his heart, as if pleading the sincerity of the man who had hired him for an hour.

The Roxas Boulevard Boys grinned and chortled at the sheer brazen corniness of the scene, and

113

Rosalita laughed too, although there was a hint of flattered delight in her amusement. Shane smiled bashfully, and glanced quickly from the tiny singer to the boys in the band.

The drummer angrily jabbered something in Tagalog, and Rosalita angrily jabbered something back at him, and for a moment it could have gone either way.

The choice was hers—get in the van or go with the man.

And then Rosalita walked on the flowers of romance, as if the decision had never been in any doubt, her high heels clicking on the crushed petals underfoot, and her grin bone-white in the moonlight.

*   *   *

'Let me help you with that,' Bill said.

He knelt before his daughter and tightened the silver buckle on her roller skates. Holly held her foot out for him like a princess trying on a glass slipper, lifting her face to the deafening sound of the skating rink. Bill's father grinned down at her, holding on to the rail for balance, a pair of prehistoric roller skates already strapped to his feet.

'We have lift-off,' the old man said, and launched himself into the flow of skating Chinese teenagers. Arms flapping, he struggled for his balance, controlled it, and then skated off with surprising poise, waving back at his son and granddaughter.

Roller skates in China, Bill thought, as the metallic pounding of wheels on wood roared behind him. Who would have thought the city would have a place for such ancient pleasures? But that was Shanghai, where old-fashioned and even extinct entertainments still lurked in hidden corners of the ferociously modern city. 'Let me do the other one,' Bill said, and Holly offered him her skateless foot.

'Actually, it's a bit difficult for a small person like myself,' she said.

He smiled at her serious face as she frowned at her foot and then back at the rink, anxious to be out there with her grandfather and all the big children, and Bill felt an overwhelming surge of love.

Sometimes he felt that Holly was more Becca's child than his own. He fought the feeling, but he couldn't help it. When they spent time together alone he always felt as if he was staking his claim on her. *She's my child too.*

'There's our friend,' Holly said.

He looked up and saw JinJin Li laughing at the head of a pack of children. She was good on roller skates, her thin arms held out like a tightrope walker, as delicate as wings. Sometimes it seemed as though she had never really got used to the length of her limbs, but not when she was skating. There must have been about a dozen children following her, boys and girls, all around twelve years of age, and they were playing some kind of game where they held on to the person in front of them. JinJin was leading them. She had her hair pulled back. He had never seen her laughing like that before. Incredible, he thought. Not only can she smile, but she can laugh too. Whatever next? You could see her face better when she wore her hair like that, he thought. And that was a good

115

thing.

Holly waved and JinJin saw them, her eyes widened with surprise, and she swung towards them, breaking away from the child behind her. Bill felt himself lurch backwards on his skates, and quickly righted himself. Suddenly JinJin was there, holding on to the rail and panting for breath. She seemed to shine with life.

'You like skating, Holly,' JinJin said. A few of the children followed her, their laughter subsiding, suddenly shy in the presence of big-nosed pinkies.

'It's my first go,' Holly said.

'You'll be fine,' Bill said, looking up as the old man expertly skated to a halt. Bill tried to place her in his world. 'Dad, this is JinJin. Our neighbour.'

'Ah,' she said, shaking the old man's hand. She didn't seem so awkward this time. 'You take care of your father. Very good.'

The old man shot her a wicked grin. 'Him take care of me? That'll be the day, love,' he said.

'And these are my children!' JinJin said, indicating the boys and girls standing self-consciously behind her, struggling to keep up their good mood.

'You have a lot of children,' the old man said.

'From when I was a teacher!' JinJin said. She was hot and happy. Bill had never seen anyone so happy. 'I bring them here once a month.' She searched for the correct idiom. 'We stay in touch.'

Bill was taken aback. 'You were a teacher?'

'Number 251 Middle School, Shanghai,' she said, as if he might want to check up. She ruffled the hair of a large boy standing near her. The boy blushed furiously. The kid had a crush on her, Bill saw. A crush that would probably last a lifetime. But he guessed that they were all in love with her. Why wouldn't they be? A teacher who looked like that. And who took you roller-skating.

'Well,' she said, rolling backwards from the barrier. 'We must press on.'

'Yes,' Bill said. 'You press on. Have fun.'

She nodded politely at the old man as she rolled away. 'Nice to make your acquaintance, sir,' she said.

Nobody in the world ever really spoke English the way she did. It should have been obvious to Bill that she had been an English teacher.

'You too, sweetheart,' the old man said.

JinJin smiled at Holly. Not the polite smile in the courtyard but big and wide and unrestrained. It was a toothy sort of smile, just the wrong side of goofy, a little heavy on the overbite, but Bill liked it. And then he realised there was something he needed to ask her.

'Didn't you like teaching?' he called, and JinJin Li laughed happily.

'I loved it!' she said, just before she was gone.

And Bill was glad that he wasn't quite dumb enough to ask the obvious question—*Then why did you give it up?* Because he knew.

'Come on, slow coach, we'll race you,' the old man suddenly said, and he took off holding Holly in front of him, wheeling her between his legs, the pair of them laughing wildly over their shoulders at the sight of Bill lumbering behind, his face creased with effort, losing ground all the time, and aware that he could try as hard as he liked but he would never catch up.

NINE

'Let the healing begin,' Bill said, clapping his hands.

The old man lay flat on his back wearing a T-shirt and swimming trunks, lifting his head as the acupuncturist prepared the needles. The table he was lying on took up most of the little room, and Bill pressed himself flat against the wall, smiling at the worried look on his father's face.

'I'm not sure about this,' the old man said. He winced as the acupuncturist slipped the first needle into his big toe.

'Relax,' Bill said. 'The Chinese have believed in this stuff for thousands of years.' The needles were deftly slipped into his father's calf, thigh and hand. It seemed as though the acupuncturist hardly punctured the old man's skin. 'Mind you,' Bill said, unable to resist it, 'they also believe that eating the testicles of a tiger will make you more virile.'

The old man shot him a doubtful look, and Bill laughed.

The acupuncture had been Becca's idea.

She had seen the aches and pains of Bill's father, seen how his body had been worn down by a lifetime of manual work. His back, his knees, the joints in his hands—she had seen the grimaces of pain on his face when he was playing with Holly, seen him flinching when he swung her above his head, or bent down to play on the floor, and she knew that he intended to put up with these pains for the rest of his life.

But Doris the ayi had her rheumatoid arthritis

cured by this acupuncturist and so here they were, in a small room in a Chinese medical centre in the old French Concession while Becca and Holly went shopping in the Xiangyang market, and Bill chuckled with amusement as a needle was slipped into the top of his father's head and, finally, the old man cried out.

'Now that hurts,' he told the acupuncturist and the doctor nodded with academic interest. They had been assured by Doris that acupuncture was a gloriously relaxing experience, but to Bill it looked about as relaxing as root-canal treatment.

'And could you describe the pain?' said the acupuncturist in perfect English.

'I'll try,' the old man said. 'It feels like someone just stuck a needle in my head.' He craned his neck and looked at the needles rising from his body. 'I hope you're going to take them all out again.'

The acupuncturist lifted a hand, asking for patience. 'Must leave for thirty minutes,' he said, gently rotating the needles.

'Or I'll be picking up Radio Two,' said the old man.

Bill leaned back against the wall, laughing harder, and then the acupuncturist left the old man with the needles settled in the meridians of his body, and soon Bill could hear him through the thin wall in the next room, speaking Chinese to another patient.

The old man lay perfectly still, his eyes closed, his breathing steady, and Bill's smile slowly faded as he contemplated the thin needles in that hard, scarred old body, and made a silent wish that, in a city full of fakes, this might be the real thing.

*   *   *

They went to see the brides.

They had not seen the brides since that first Sunday, when they had watched them in the park from the top of the Oriental Pearl TV Tower. Now they were in the park, among the brides and their grooms, and there were all sorts of brides. Young and old and plump and pretty. Loud and subdued and flat-bellied and pregnant. As different as snowflakes, Bill thought, and he wondered how anyone could ever believe that the Chinese all looked the same.

Bill and Becca held hands and smiled at the brides and the grooms and each other as the multi-coloured fish food was thrown on the water and bright flashes of orange splashed and shimmered to the surface. The young men in their suits held the arms of their new wives as they lifted the hem of their wedding dresses and fed the carp.

The old man held his granddaughter in his arms and Bill wondered if the brides made the old man think of his own bride, Bill's mother, while Holly solemnly contemplated the dozens upon dozens of young women in their white wedding dresses, her eyes wide with awe and wonder, as if every last one of them was a real-life Disney princess, and as if every one of their stories would surely end with a happy ever after.

*   *   *

That was a good day, Becca thought, as she stepped back to admire her *Sunflowers*. The muted yellows and burnished gold of the painting made her remember walking through the art market with her husband and daughter, Bill and Becca hand-in-hand with Holly, playing the game they called one-two-three, swinging her up between them on the count of three, as people stared and smiled at the little family.

Becca knew what they had looked like, that perfect picture, and it made her feel better than anything in the world. The handsome husband. The beautiful wife. And the adorable child, shrieking with pleasure as she swung between them, her thin legs flying. That's what she wanted, Becca realised, hearing the soft voices of Bill and his father coming from the second bedroom. She wanted them to always be that perfect picture.

As Doris the ayi made up Bill's bed on the sofa, Becca slowly turned full circle, and there was a *Sunflowers* on every wall of the living room. She had a moment of doubt. Did all these fake Van Goghs look ridiculous? Too camp, too ironic—as if they were trying to say, *Look at what they do in this crazy place? Isn't it hilarious, darling?*

No, she decided, they looked lovely. And the *Sunflowers*, with *The Sower* in the spare bedroom, and the *Starry Night* in the master bedroom, made her hold on to the day just gone, as if it was something she could keep.

There was packaging all over the floor, all the thick protective cardboard and thin wood that the paintings had been packed in. With the help of Doris, Becca gathered it all up and stuffed it into two large green rubbish bags.

'I'll take this down, ma'am,' the ayi said, but Becca shook her head.

'No, Doris, they're not heavy,' she said. She

121

didn't want to become one of those expat wives who treated the ayi like a pack mule. 'You listen out for Holly. But I don't think she's going to wake up.'

With a rubbish bag in each hand, Becca caught the lift down to the basement. A car was pulling out of the underground car park, and for a moment its lights dazzled her, making her shield her eyes. Then the car was gone, and the basement was silent apart from the soft tread of Becca's footsteps as she walked across to the long line of giant black rubbish bins.

She threw in the first sack and had just lifted the second when she heard the noise.

A thin, mewing sound that made her smile.

I bet it's that mangy old ginger cat, she thought. The one that Holly is always following around.

It seemed to be close but she couldn't see it.

'No milk tonight, puss,' Becca said aloud, and her voice echoed strangely in the basement.

She lifted the second sack, and was about to throw it into a bin when she heard the sound again.

And she froze.

She walked slowly along the line of giant black bins and the sound seemed suddenly closer, and Becca swallowed hard because the mewing was recognisably crying, horribly and undeniably human, and she knew in a terrible second that it wasn't an animal that was in one of these rubbish bins.

Then Becca was tearing desperately at the black bins, pulling out sacks and ripping them open, clawing through the trash, her fingernails breaking and blood on her hands from somewhere, one bin turning over banging hard against her hip, and she

122

was almost screaming now, still scrabbling through rubbish in front of the overturned bin, on her hands and knees, the stinking cans and the unwanted food and the broken bottles spilling out, until finally she saw the fragile white living flesh of the baby, an exposed limb that her fingers closed around and refused to let go.

Then the baby was in her arms and Becca was desperately patting her pockets with her hand and, there it was, thank God, she had brought her phone with her, and the numbers were there, all the numbers you would need if the worst happened: 110 for the police; 119 for the fire brigade. And 120 for an ambulance.

She speed-dialled 120 and the woman came on the line immediately with a questioning, '*Wei?*' and Becca was explaining and pleading and slowly spelling out the address of Paradise Mansions, but the woman at the other end of the phone just said, '*Wei?*' and then there were a few phrases of impatient Mandarin before the woman hung up, and Becca was running for home with the baby in her arms, skidding in the trash, heading back towards the lift, and she wondered why she had been so stupid, why she had believed she could just store the numbers and everything would be fine, why she had ever assumed that when the worst happened she could call the emergency services and the person on the other end of the line would be able to speak English.

*   *   *

She had forgotten what it felt like to hold a newborn baby, she had forgotten the milky smell,

123

she had forgotten the weight in her arms.

It is next to nothing, Becca thought. So light that it is hardly there at all.

Then Bill was stuffing money into the hands of the taxi driver and they were running through the lobby of the International Family Hospital and Clinic on Xian Xia Lu, and there were nurses around them immediately, taking the baby from her arms and then Becca saw the best sight of all, Dr Sarfraz Khan, taking charge, issuing orders, asking Becca questions about the when and where of finding the baby, all the while moving down that over-lit hospital corridor, leaving Becca and Bill behind as he pushed through a door marked ICU.

An hour later he came to see them, when Becca was feeling sick to the stomach with the coffee that Bill kept bringing her because he had to do something. And sick to the stomach with the thought of what would have happened.

'She's a healthy little baby,' Dr Khan said. 'Although that's thanks to you, not me.'

Becca shook her head. She was so tired. 'I feel like I bother you all the time.'

Khan laughed. 'You're not bothering me. You bring me sick children to look after. That's what I do.'

'Thank you,' Becca said, her face in her hands. 'Oh God. Thanks, Sarfraz.'

She burst into tears.

And Bill looked at his wife, stroked her arm and thought—*Sarfraz?*

*   *   *

124

It was almost time for the old man to go home.

The next morning, leaving Becca in bed, Bill and his father took Holly and her bike to the park and only had one minor row about when was the right time for a child to dispense with stabilisers. When they arrived back at Paradise Mansions there were voices on the child monitor.

They had forgotten to turn it off when they came back from the hospital, sent the ayi home, and crawled into bed exhausted, Holly between them and sleeping through it all. The monitor must have been on all night because now the little lights glowed green with indistinct murmurs coming from the master bedroom. Like the sound of lovers in another world, Bill thought. The old man was holding Holly. He kissed her cheek, put her down and went into the spare room.

'What's Granddad Will doing?' Holly said.

'Granddad has to pack,' Bill said.

She turned her face to her father. 'Is goodbye?' she said sadly.

As the ayi whisked Holly away, all good cheer and agreement, Bill hesitated in the living room, listening to the sound of Dr Khan talking to Becca, and understanding none of it. The monitor wasn't built to pick up the sound of a man and woman talking.

He paused for a moment, then went into the bedroom. Becca was in pyjamas, sitting up in bed but on the edge of sleep. One sleeve was rolled up and she was pressing a plaster against her arm. Dr Khan was standing by the side of the bed. He had just given her a shot of something and Bill flinched at the sight of the syringe. She said Bill's name and he went to the bed and wrapped his

arms around her and kissed her face and squeezed
her until he thought perhaps he was hurting her.
Her eyes were sore and puffy and it was clearly an
effort to keep them open.

'I've given your wife a small dose of Diazepam,'
Dr Khan said. 'It will help her sleep.'

'But I *can't* sleep,' Becca said, closing her eyes.
She exhaled once, twice, and her head seemed to
settle on the pillow. Bill and Dr Khan stood there
silently for a minute. When they were certain she
was sleeping they quietly left the room. They could
hear Holly giving the ayi instructions for a game of
Princesses.

'When she's up to it,' Dr Khan said, 'bring your
wife to the hospital. I think she'll cope better if she
sees the baby.'

Bill nodded. 'Where did it come from?' That
wasn't what he meant.

What he meant was—*How can this happen?*

Dr Khan shrugged. They had drifted across to
the window. There were already a few cars waiting
for the girls of Paradise Mansions.

'There are around 300,000 abortions in this city
every year,' Dr Khan said. 'It's easier than having a
tooth out. This baby . . .' He inhaled, and released
it as a sigh. 'I don't know. Maybe they were
expecting a son. That happens. Or maybe the
mother thought the father would leave his current
family.' He looked from the cars in the courtyard
to Bill. He obviously knew all about Paradise
Mansions, and the places just like it.

'Sometimes these girls get their hopes too high,'
Dr Khan said. 'Some of the girls are led to believe
that their boyfriend is going to leave his wife. And
then—he doesn't. Incredible, I know.' He smiled,

126

shook his head. 'What are the odds of that? That's if the mother is one of the girls from this apartment block. But my guess is that she is probably some poor little *dagongmei*—what the Chinese call a migrant worker sister.' He looked down at the courtyard. 'It's just about possible, but I think the mother is unlikely to be a resident of this place. The girls here are too tough and too smart for this kind of mess.' He looked at Bill. 'They don't go to term with babies that they don't want.'

They watched an old VW Santana taxi pull into the courtyard and park behind the waiting cars looking like a poor relation. Alice Greene got out of the taxi. Dr Khan said he had to get back to the hospital and Bill thanked him and shook his hand. He walked Khan to the lift, saw him off, and he was still waiting there when Alice emerged a few minutes later.

Bill didn't want her inside their home. Not today.

'For Becca,' she said, passing the package in her hand to Bill, and he felt loose tea inside thick brown paper. 'It's Dragon Well tea from Hangzhou,' she said, almost apologetically. 'Most famous tea in China. From the Longjing spring.'

Bill looked at the package of tea. 'You know what happened?' he said.

She nodded. 'Becca called me. When you got back this morning. I don't think she has that many people who she can call.' Alice looked abashed, as if afraid this sounded like a criticism.

Bill kept staring at the tea in his hand. 'Thanks for coming. Really, I appreciate it. But she's sleeping now.' Then he looked at Alice evenly. 'Are you going to write about this?' he asked.

Alice shook her head.

'Oh no,' she said, and her smile was full of an almost physical pain. 'A baby girl getting abandoned? A baby girl left out with the trash? No. My paper doesn't want that. You see, it's not news.'

*   *   *

The next day Bill saw his father off.

Tiger drove them to Pudong and they joined the long line for economy check-in. That's the worst thing about being poor, Bill thought. It is so time-consuming.

'Dad, I can get you upgraded to first,' he said, looking at the long line. Already there were starting to be more Chinese faces than Anglos on their way to Europe. 'Or at least business class.'

The old man shook his big, bull-like head. 'No point,' he said, placing his suitcase on the floor, settling in for a long wait. 'It's a waste. I'm just going to sleep until Heathrow anyway.'

Bill had made the offer without impatience, and the old man had declined without resentment. This was some kind of first.

'Hope Becca feels better,' his father said awkwardly and Bill nodded. Something had shifted between the pair of them. Something long frozen had started to thaw.

My daughter, Bill thought. Holly did that. Yet he could not deny that when the old man turned and waved from the departure gate, Bill was still relieved to see him go.

*   *   *

Bill got into bed and put his arms around his wife. She murmured and moved against him, although she was still sleeping or drugged or both.

On the other side of the door he could hear Holly chattering as the ayi undressed her for her bath. She was going to sleep in Daddy's bed tonight, with Daddy, because Mummy wasn't well.

Bill was slipping into sleep when he heard Becca say his name. He propped himself up on an elbow. She still had her eyes closed.

'What is it, angel?'

'Remember when I used to come and wait for you outside your office? When you were doing your training? And you could only take an hour so we had to eat lunch in places where the waiters were quick? Remember that, Bill?'

He buried his face in her hair, inhaled deeply, then kissed her bare neck, and kissed her shoulder blade through her pyjamas.

'I remember everything,' he said. 'Why don't you sleep for a little bit more?'

She turned her head and he saw her smile in the darkness. 'That was a good time, wasn't it?' She was waiting for a reply, and he stroked her arm, encouraging her to rest.

'It was a really good time,' he agreed.

'I can't really do that now, can I?'

He was silent.

Her voice was soft, understanding. He felt his fingers on her ribcage. 'It's not that kind of job, is it, Bill?'

'No,' he said. 'It's not that kind of job, angel.'

She was silent for a few minutes. He could hear her breathing.

'Bill?'

'What?'

He could feel her searching for the words. She didn't know how to say it. He heard her take a breath in the dark. From somewhere else in the flat there was the sound of their daughter's bath being run.

'I might go back for a while,' she said.

It lay there between them until the statement—offered tentatively, as though it had just occurred to her—seemed to fill the room.

'Go back?' he said, dumbfounded, unable to comprehend what this meant. For him. For them. For their little family.

'My dad's not well,' she said quickly, playing the trump card at once. 'He's not like your dad. He's not fit. Independent. He can't make it without my mum. He's a different sort of old man.' She patted his arm, wanting him to be all right about this. 'And I just think it might be good for me and Holly to go back for a while,' she said, happy to get it out in the open at last.

He didn't know what to say. 'How long would you go back for?'

'I don't know,' she said. 'Until I feel better about things.'

Something about her shoulders told him that she was filling up with tears. He held her fiercely, as if the strength of his feeling could change a mind that was already made up.

'I'm not asking you to leave,' she said. 'This was all my idea. Coming out here. I really think Devlin means it—you could be a partner in a few years. It could never happen that fast back home.'

'But what about us?'

'Well, there will always be us.' She patted his arm. 'Of course there will.'

'Or you could stay,' he said. He could hear the sound of splashing, and Holly laughing. 'Or you could stay and we could try for a second one.'

'What?' She genuinely seemed to not get it. How could she fail to get it? Didn't she think about this all the time? The baby who had yet to be born.

'A brother or sister for Holly,' he said. It was his own trump card, the only one he had to play.

'No,' she said wistfully. 'No, I don't think so. I think the best thing is if we go back for a while.'

'That baby will be okay,' he said, wondering if he truly believed it. 'That baby you found.'

'But it's still a cruel place. It's still a hard place. How different is it from the days when it said *No Chinese, no dogs* outside the parks? How different is it really?'

'God, Bec, it's really different. It's better than it's ever been. That's what you have to remember. It's better for more people than it's ever been. And we could have a good life here. You know we could.'

'Yes, but how many things do we have to ignore for our good life?'

Then she was silent and he didn't have the heart to argue with her. She had already decided. When she was sleeping he went back to his own room where Holly was sprawled across the single bed. The ayi had left a nightlight on, and Bill calculated where he could sleep and then turned it off and squeezed into the small sliver of bed that was still vacant.

He carefully put an arm across his daughter, amazed at the smallness of her, barely thirty pounds of life, a fragile and precarious presence in

131

the world, and he held her as tightly as he dared in the darkness.

But sleep did not come here either, and sleep would not come, and so he left this second bedroom and went to the window, staring down at the empty courtyard of Paradise Mansions.

TEN

The elevated freeway of Chengdu Lu runs right above St Peter's, the Catholic church in Chongqing Nanlu. As the bride and groom stepped out into the sunshine the cheers of the congregation mixed with the buzzsaw of the traffic flowing high above the church spire.

Holly was in Becca's arms, throwing confetti with her eyes screwed up, as if she was the one being bombarded. Most of it went over Bill. He looked at his wife. She looked beautiful today. And he wasn't the only one who noticed. When they had entered the church, it seemed to Bill that men on both sides of the aisle, the neat little Filippinos and the big affable Australians, all looked at his wife with a certain hunger. And now it seemed to Bill that, despite the two thousand or so nights they had spent together, he looked at her in exactly the same way.

Yet he knew that only he saw the fragility there, only he saw how the woman he loved was struggling to hold it together and put on a good front. They all look at her, he thought. But I'm the only one who really sees her.

He watched Becca smile at the sight of Shane

and Rosalita, and it made him smile too. The happy couple were a study in opposites. The groom as big and blond as his bride was tiny and dark. Shane grinning like an idiot, bashful in the glare of all this attention, Rosalita laughing and waving to her friends in the crowd, centre stage at last, happy to be top of the bill.

'He gets youth and beauty, and she gets affluence and security,' Mrs Devlin said, suddenly appearing at Bill's side. She lazily threw a fistful of confetti. 'At least that's the plan, I suppose.' She sighed wearily, as if she had seen it all many times before. 'What could possibly go wrong?'

The three Devlin boys were running wild, dodging in and out of legs, assaulting each other with confetti mixed with gravel that they had scooped up from the ground. The smallest one got caught in the eyes by one of his brothers and began crying.

Holly eyed them warily and Bill picked her up. She didn't much care for boys. She took Bill by his ears. It was her new way of getting his attention. He felt her sweet breath on his face.

'We're going back for a while,' she whispered. 'But you're staying in your home.'

He felt the panic fly up in him. 'My home is with you,' Bill whispered. 'Always. Wherever you are, that's my home. Okay?'

She thought about it, staring at her father with the solemn blue eyes of her mother.

'Okay, Daddy,' she quietly agreed, and they held each other as they stood there in their wedding clothes, and the chatter went on around them.

*   *   *

133

'We must do something with our children,' Mrs Devlin was telling Becca. Bill thought she meant some kind of military discipline, but apparently it was a play date with their daughter that she had in mind. 'Does Holly like pandas?' Tess said, baring her teeth at Holly. 'Do you like pandas, dear?'

'I like cows,' Holly said.

'We found this place near Renmin Square with a giant panda,' Mrs Devlin said, straightening up, ignoring Holly's affection for cows. 'A sort of Chinese circus. Well, their version of a circus. And the panda—he drives a car!'

Devlin grimaced. 'They *do* have a taste for the grotesque,' he murmured.

One of his sons crashed against his legs.

Becca smiled apologetically, and said nothing.

'They're going back for a while,' Bill said, and Mr and Mrs Devlin took it in and quickly looked away with frozen smiles, as if embarrassed to intrude upon a marriage more fragile than their own.

*   *   *

On the first floor of the Portman Ritz-Carlton, Becca and Holly joined the queue to congratulate the bride and groom.

Bill drifted off in search of a rest room and then he saw them coming—a group of casually dressed Chinese men and young women making their way down a spiral staircase.

The girls all had the look, that Shanghai look.

The look that summer was a tall slim girl in heels

and tight white trousers. Straight shoulder-length hair, worn its natural jet black. In the chic, self-confident Shanghai of the new century there was a lot less of the highlighting and lightening than you saw among women in other parts of Asia. And the Shanghai look was no make-up, except maybe a little lipstick, and a short-sleeved or capped top to show off long, slender arms.

Everything about the look accentuated height and length and a willowy beauty that was specifically Chinese. The Shanghai look could make a young woman of quite average height appear over six feet tall.

It took him a moment to see that one of the young women with the look was JinJin Li.

He stood transfixed as the group walked past him as if he wasn't there.

If she saw him, she gave no sign.

And he knew that she saw him.

And he wondered, how did it work? Her unknowable life. Her unimaginable nights. How was it played? Bill saw that the man was about forty, big and fit but balding, the high school jock running to seed, too old for her by far.

How did the arrangement work? Did she get a certain amount of money paid directly into her bank every month? It had to be. Was the apartment in his or her name? How many times a week did they meet? Did he fuck her every time? Did his wife suspect a thing?

And did he love her?

Bill felt a ridiculous anger towards her, and towards the man. But what did he expect? What would he prefer? That she would stay as a teacher in Number 251 Middle School and meet some nice boy who would want to marry her? Yes, that was exactly what he wanted, that was exactly what he would have preferred.

*   *   *

There was a live band at the reception and after they had played their opening number Rosalita climbed on stage to sing 'Right Here Waiting for You', a beautiful power ballad about longing and loyalty that she supplemented with much slow grinding and wicked grinning.

'Ah, the unblushing bride,' Mrs Devlin said. 'In her element at last.'

Becca and Holly hit the dance floor and Bill made his way to the end of the queue for the buffet, his head swimming with the lights and the candles and the smell of orchids, and the hole in his future as he wondered what his life here would be like without them.

He steeled himself when Devlin approached him with a sympathetic smile, but his boss said nothing, just patted him twice on the back and let his hand linger for a moment on Bill's shoulder.

Then Devlin was gone, moving off into the chatter of the guests and the muffled battery of champagne corks, and Bill stared after him with gratitude.

Bill could see what Becca would never see—the good that was in this city, and the kindness and generosity of these people.

His wife was immune to something that increasingly had Bill in its grip—the glory of this place and time, the magic of what was happening here.

Everyone's life would be better, eventually. He could be a part of that, contribute something, and make a difference.

And his life would get better too. He would not be held back the way he would be held back in London, where in the end they always wanted to know what school you went to and what your father did and what your real accent was like. All that sad old bullshit that had been going on for centuries in England. They didn't really care how well you did your job back in England.

The thing that Alice Greene complained about— the educated elite lording it over the huge pool of cheap labour, driving the economy on and on— most of the people in this room saw that as a *good* thing. Of course it wasn't fair. But when had China ever been fair? Tell me when, he thought.

As he moved away from the buffet table he found he had loaded his plate with jam doughnuts and foie gras. Nothing else. Just two jam doughnuts and a sliver of foie gras. A ridiculous meal, he thought, smiling with embarrassment at his choices.

He hesitated for a moment and then he thought—but why not? Really—why not?

Why shouldn't you have whatever you want?

*　　　*　　　*

In the master bedroom Bill read Holly a story until she slept. When she had nodded off he closed the book and just sat there for a while, smoothing back a tumble of fair hair that fell across her face. His daughter was the one who had taught him about unconditional love. There was nothing she could

137

ever do in her life that could make him stop loving her.

Becca was packing things. She was being very selective. She was careful to make it seem as though they were not going for good. Things were being left behind.

Including me, he thought, fighting the bitterness and losing. And it wasn't my idea to come here.

'What's the book?' she said, her arms full of folded sweaters that seemed to belong to another world.

Bill looked at the book in his hands. He hadn't realised he was still holding it. '*Farm Friends*,' he said. 'Didn't we see the movie?'

Becca nodded seriously. 'That has to go back to the school,' she said. 'It's not one of ours.'

'Okay,' he said, opening the book. 'I'll get Tiger to run it over.'

There was a reading list at the back of the book, a little library card with DATE DUE—TITLE—DATE RETURNED at the top, followed by a list of all the books that Holly had personally chosen to take home from school. The list made him smile, and he pictured her earnest face as she made her selection.

5th June—*Bunny Cakes*
12th June—*Do Donkeys Dance?*
19th June—*The Treasure Sock*
26th June—*Favourite Rhymes*
3rd July—*But No Elephants*
10th July—*There Was an Old Lady*
17th July—*Christmas Can't Wait*
24th July—*Imagine You're a Princess*
31st July—*Happy and Sad*
7th August—*Sssh!*

A Christmas book in July? And another one in August? Something about the list seemed to capture his daughter's sweet, funny essence.

He slipped the reading list into his pocket and went over to where Becca stood at the window silently watching the rain hammer down on the empty courtyard of Paradise Mansions.

'Did she go down okay?' she asked him.

'She's worn out,' he said. 'Two hours of dancing the Macarena.'

What would they talk about if they didn't have their daughter?

'Bloody weather,' he said, feeling ridiculous in the presence of English small talk. But the subject animated her.

'I think this must be the start of the Plum Rain season,' she said. 'Doesn't that sound just lovely? *The Plum Rain season*. I read about it before we came over. I wanted to see it. More than almost anything, really.'

They stared out at the courtyard, and he felt her take his hand. The Plum Rain season, the rains of summer, had turned Shanghai into a city of mist. They seemed to be floating in the clouds.

'How long does it last?' Bill said.

'I don't know,' Becca said. She gave him that sly, sleepy look, the one that said *you know me*. 'It doesn't last for ever, darling.'

He took her hand and they went to his little bedroom where he made love to his wife, her body warm and loved and familiar, that familiarity that you only get after years together, which is the good

139

side of knowing another human being so well, and she slept in his arms until their daughter began to cry in the hours just before dawn.

Then Becca went back to the master bedroom and he lay there for what was left of the night listening to his wife calm their child, smelling her perfume on his body, and thinking about the city his wife and daughter would soon be flying to, and remembering their old life in London when they were very young and very poor and very happy.

*   *   *

He came out of the departure gate of Pudong and looked at the mist and rain. Tiger beeped his horn from a no-parking zone. Bill dashed through the rain to the waiting limo.

'Where to, boss?' Tiger said.

'Home,' Bill said. 'Let's just go home.'

The car headed towards the city. Bill stared straight through sights that had once filled him with bemused awe. He didn't see the blue and red flashing lights all along the highway, meant to replicate the watching eyes of the *gong'an ju*, the cops of the PSB. He didn't see the ancient trucks, overloaded with animals, produce, junk and men who were wet to the bone. And he didn't see the girls with the Shanghai look in their brand-new BMWs.

He wasn't interested in seeing any of that.

Instead Bill pulled his daughter's crumpled reading list from his pocket and it seemed a far greater source of wonder than any of these things. It made him smile. That girl. His girl. That little girl, sitting on her mother's lap with her books and

140

her crayons, 35,000 feet above—oh, it had to be Inner Mongolia by now.

'Everything okay, boss?' Tiger said, slightly worried now. You never knew when these crazy *da bizi* would crack. The heat and the pressure and the stress. It got to all of them eventually.

'Yup,' Bill said, finishing the reading list and going right back to the start.

Outside, the Plum Rain season was at full pelt and although Tiger's windscreen wipers did their very best, they could not keep pace with Bill Holden's tears.

PART TWO:

THE PERMANENT GIRLFRIEND

ELEVEN

The Chinese did what they wanted to do. That was the strange thing. That was what caught him off guard.

Before they had ever come over, he had read all about the human rights violations, and dissidents arrested, and Falun Gong members setting fire to themselves on Tiananmen Square, but when Bill walked around the Old City on Saturday afternoon, when there was no more paperwork to keep him at the office and he didn't want to go home to an empty apartment, it felt like the Chinese were the freest people in the world. Or perhaps what they had was closer to anarchy than freedom.

Middle-aged women rode their motor scooters on the pavement. Businesses were set up in the street, and usually consisted of no more than a stool and a cardboard box and a couple of tools— the proprietors shaving old men, or helping clients to try on spectacles from a selection of hundreds, or cutting their hair. And in a pink-lit barbershop, where hairdressing was low on the agenda, two young women beckoned to him from the doorway.

Bill shook his head. One of them feigned disappointment. The other immediately turned to the next passing man. And in his loneliness Bill was so happy about the one who was pretending to be disappointed that he kept looking at her until he banged his shin against the bumper of a car parked on the pavement.

When he looked up it was a red Mini with a

Chinese flag painted on the roof.

Looking more closely, he could see that the car was about seven different shades of red. The vehicle had clearly been pulled apart, and patched back together.

JinJin Li got out of the car. She had two ways of wearing her hair, he realised. She wore it down when she was out on the town with the man she called her husband, and pulled back in a ponytail for the rest of her life. Today she had it pulled back, the ponytail dragged through the back of a yellow baseball cap that said LA Lakers on the front, and he realised he preferred it that way because it meant you could really see her face.

She was a pretty girl with troubled skin. Later, when he saw the attention she lavished on keeping her skin under control, when he saw all the lotions and potions and pills and special soaps, he came to believe that the troubled skin was a manifestation of some inner turmoil. Later still, he didn't think about it—that was just who she was, and she was always beautiful. But that day in the Old City he thought that she was just a bit too old to have such troubled skin.

'Ah,' she said, as the central locking flashed orange behind her. 'You have come to the Old City. In the past no foreigners dared to come to Old City. Oh my gosh. They very afraid to come here.'

He watched her tugging the Lakers cap down over her eyes. What did she know about the Lakers? 'Is that right?' he said.

She nodded curtly. 'How about you? Are you afraid to come here?'

'Only if you're driving.'

146

She nodded. 'English joke,' she said, dead serious. 'I'm going to the market. Yu Gardens.' She smiled encouragingly. 'You want?'

'Sure,' he said, and she took his arm, and he was absurdly pleased. He felt his face reddening. He hadn't blushed for years. But he knew it didn't mean anything. He told himself that possibly she was lonely too.

The Yu Gardens market was the usual collection of everything. In ramshackle wooden buildings untouched by time and developers, Mao memorabilia was stacked up next to bootleg Disney merchandise and the latest software from Microsoft.

'For your daughter,' JinJin smiled, holding up a strangely familiar costume inside a sealed plastic package. A yellow skirt, a blue top with red piping, puffy short sleeves. There was a picture of a girl with the face of a glacial brunette, like the young Elizabeth Taylor. And Bill thought—but where are the seven dwarves? *Snow Girl,* it said on the wrapping. Snow Girl? It was a counterfeit Disney princess.

He smiled, as if impressed but unwilling to commit himself—Holly would spot a bootleg princess a mile off—as the woman squatting in front of the stall spread her arms indicating that if he wasn't in the market for a genuine fake Snow Girl costume, then how about an opium pipe, or a Little Red Book, or a Deng Xiaoping watch, or a green coat from the People's Liberation Army, or a propaganda poster of heroic factory workers?

They kept moving. An old woman and her fat little Buddha of a grandson walked hand in hand, neither of them too steady on their feet, both eating courgettes as though they were ice cream cones.

'Look at those two,' Bill said, nodding at them as they paused to solemnly consider a badly scarred mechanical rabbit.

JinJin smiled. 'Fat little boy,' she agreed. 'Very nice child.'

For JinJin Li, this was the real world. What was strange to his eyes was normal to hers.

They emerged from the tumbledown maze of the Yu Gardens bazaar and there before them was a teahouse on a small lake. A wooden bridge zigzagged crazily across the water.

'The Bridge of Nine Turnings,' she said as they stepped on to it. Below them the water bubbled and exploded with hundreds of golden carp. 'Because evil spirits can't turn corners.'

He looked at her face. She was perfectly serious. He felt her hand in his, small and cool, and she led him across the twisting bridge to the teahouse on the lake. They stepped inside a wooden room and Bill looked up at a photograph of the last American president grinning widely over a cup of green tea.

'Huxinting teahouse,' JinJin said. 'It is very famous. Many VIPs come here.' She indicated the former president. 'And some V-VIPs. Do you know?'

Suddenly he did know it. Of course—the Huxinting teahouse was the great symbol of the city's past, a photo opportunity for every big shot that passed through Shanghai and wanted to show that they were in touch with the real China.

He had always meant to come here with Becca, but somehow they had never got around to it.

JinJin spoke to a woman in Mandarin as Bill looked up at the pictures of movie stars and presidents and royalty. But although the bazaar was teeming with people, the Huxinting was almost empty.

'We shall drink tea now,' JinJin informed him, and they sat opposite each other at a wooden table in a narrow room.

JinJin took off her Lakers baseball cap. Cups were placed before them. A tiny pot. Three small glass jars with leaves and assorted plant life were filled with boiling water. He wondered how much of this was genuine historic ritual and how much of it was for the tourists. But then the thought left him because he was enjoying himself, and he liked having some company, and he was happy to make it to the Huxinting teahouse at last.

A couple of funky young Japanese men with blond hair sat at the next table. Bill and JinJin smiled at each other, then looked away. He didn't know what to say. He felt there were huge areas of her life that he couldn't approach. She saw him staring at the long queue outside a shop on the other side of the lake.

'Nan Xiang,' JinJin said. 'Very famous dumplings. Do you want?'

'Sounds good,' he said, and he realised that he was free, and had nowhere to go and nothing to do and no one to meet. Then JinJin was looking up at someone standing beside him.

'Bill?' Tess Devlin was touching his shoulder. 'How are you getting on without them?'

Then he was stuttering a reply with his face flushing hot—*no blushing for fifteen years and then twice in the space of minutes,* he thought, *good*

149

going, Bill—feeling as if he had been caught out. JinJin sipped her tea, and set down her cup. The water was still boiling hot.

He noticed a Taiwanese client and his wife gawking up at the pictures on the wall, and Devlin smiling as he stepped around his wife to introduce himself and shake hands with JinJin Li. He does it so well, Bill thought, with a flash of admiration. He sees the situation and just takes control. JinJin shook hands with Bill's boss as if it was a custom as alien to her as rubbing noses.

Then Tess Devlin turned her beady all-seeing eyes on JinJin and Bill's heart sank as they all joined them at the table.

The Taiwanese stared blankly at Bill, even though they had been introduced at the office, and then smirked as he ran his eyes over JinJin Li. Bill tried to remember what this hideous little man was in town for. Something to do with a joint-venture dispute with a Chinese telecom operator. His small, bespectacled wife, along for the shopping, began unloading strange painted figurines on to the table. They were ornamental torture scenes depicting old men having their heads shaved, and women in glasses having their arms bent behind their backs, their tormentors angry figures in green, holding up their little red books as though they were the truth and the light.

'Look what Mr and Mrs Wang found in Dongtai Lu market,' chuckled Tess. 'Isn't that hilarious? Souvenirs of the Cultural Revolution. Why on earth do they make things like that?'

'Because they know some mad tourist will buy it,' Devlin said, smiling sweetly at the Taiwanese client's wife.

Tess was thoughtful. 'Oh, yes, money, of course,' she said. 'There's always that.'

Orders were placed for more tea. Bill thought that the logical thing would be to ask JinJin to do it, but Tess Devlin chose to instruct the waitress herself, slowly and loudly, in broken English.

'And where are you from, dear?' Tess said, staring at JinJin's features as if examining important forensic evidence. 'You don't look typical Shanghainese.'

'My mother is from Changchun,' JinJin said. Bill had never heard of Changchun. She must have sensed it. She turned to him. 'Big city in the Dongbei—the north-east. Near the border with Korea.' She turned back to Mrs Devlin. 'My father is from Guilin. Down south. But I grew up in Changchun.'

Tess looked delighted. 'So you're—what do they say? A *Dongbei ho . . .*'

JinJin smiled and nodded. *'Dongbei ho*—north-east tiger . . .'

The Taiwanese gasped and jumped up having scalded his tongue with boiling tea. His wife looked around, sighing with boredom until she saw a picture on the wall of a famous Buddhist Hollywood star sipping tea in the Huxinting. She got up to examine it, bumping the table with her behind, and making her torture sculptures rattle precariously.

'I thought so,' Tess continued. 'Your face—not really typically Chinese, even, let alone Shanghainese.' She narrowed her eyes, making her judgement. 'Hmmm—got a touch of the Manchu about you.'

JinJin frowned, and Bill was reminded of the first

151

time he had met her, when he had tried to tell her that she would never remove the ignition key while she had it in drive.

'Changchun,' her husband was saying. 'They've had it tough up there. Did all right during the planned economy. Bit of an industrial powerhouse. Coal. Cars. Heavy machinery. Missed out on the big payday, though. What is it up there?' This to Bill, as if he would know. 'About fifty per cent unemployment?'

Both Devlin and his wife seemed to have a genuine academic interest in JinJin. Bill wasn't certain if he should be offended or not.

'There are many people no job,' JinJin confirmed, rising from the table. Her English seemed to crack under stress. It became a pared down, spartan language, largely pruned of personal pronouns and the archaic idioms that he found so enchanting. He saw that it wasn't the mass unemployment in her hometown that concerned her. 'I'm *not* Manchu,' she informed Mrs Devlin.

The two women stared at each other.

'Of course you're not, dear,' said Tess. 'Silly of me to think so.'

'Need rest room now,' JinJin said, her way barred by the Taiwanese, who was still standing up, dabbing his scalded mouth. JinJin squeezed past him. He twinkled, leered, licked his burning lips. JinJin left without looking at Bill.

'What a lovely girl,' Tess said. 'Where on earth did you find her?'

'She's a neighbour,' Bill said. 'Just a neighbour.'

Hugh Devlin looked disturbed. 'Places like Changchun—breaks your heart when you think about it.' He carefully sipped his Jasmine tea.

152

'China's rust belt, Bill, that's what it is. Reminds us that it's not just rural peasants that have been left behind, it's entire cities, entire *regions*.' He stared thoughtfully at his tea. 'Changchun is a city of twenty million people, and they are bloody desperate up there. We have to acknowledge that, and do something about it.' He rose from the table. 'Excuse us. I must give them the grand tour before they head to the airport.'

He took the Taiwanese off to see the view from the top of the teahouse, and Bill was left alone with Tess Devlin. She smiled and sighed into the silence.

'Bill, Bill, Bill,' she laughed.

He forced himself to meet her eye. 'What?'

'Oh, do be careful there, Bill.'

He shook his head and laughed. 'I told you, she's a neighbour.'

'Really? I could have sworn you were about to start holding hands. I said to Devlin—good God, Bill's about to start holding hands with that Chinese girl . . . what's her name? You do know her name, Bill? You didn't introduce us and I didn't like to ask. We've been through all this with Shane, of course. Many times.'

He took a breath. 'Her name is JinJin Li.'

Tess Devlin looked hugely amused. He couldn't tell if it was genuine or not. 'And do you know how many JinJin Lis there are in the PRC? About, oh, one hundred million of them.'

'Really?' She was getting on his nerves. 'Who counted?'

Tess nodded. A serious woman now. 'I don't have to tell you to think about your wife and child, because I know you'll do that. But think about

153

yourself. I'm very lucky with Hugh, I know—he's not into the bamboo. Never has been. One of the few good men out here that doesn't like Asian girls. Don't know why.' She nodded, as if it was all a mystery. 'Some of them are lovely when they're young.'

Bill warmed his palms on his teacup. It wasn't so hot now. He took a gulp. 'They probably say the same thing about us, Tess—*Oh, those big-nose pinkies, they're lovely when they're little.*'

'No doubt,' she said briskly. 'But what I never understand is how a man can get serious about a girl like that. Ask yourself—do you really want to be with a little old Chinese lady? What would you talk about? All I'm trying to do is give you some sound advice.'

'Thanks so much, Tess.'

'For your sake. For Becca's sake. For the sake of the firm—do be careful there.'

Bill sighed. 'I had the lecture when I arrived. How does it go? *Hard as nails, these Chinese girls. Gold diggers, the lot of them. They don't see a man—they see a cash-point machine.* But I wonder, Tess—what do we see when we look at them?'

She laughed and poured him some more tea.

'Oh dear—you sound quite keen,' she said, and he felt his face burning. He was really going to have to stop doing that. 'A mistress is a great idea in theory, Bill.'

'She's not my bloody—' He stopped, shook his head. 'I don't want a mistress, Tess,' he said, and he truly meant it. The idea sickened him. It didn't fit with his idea of himself, or what he wanted from his marriage. He loved his wife, he missed his wife, and he didn't want to be like one of those men who

154

drove their cars into the courtyard of Paradise Mansions. He wanted to be a better man than that. He didn't want to believe that he was just like everybody else.

'Good,' said Tess Devlin, as if they had come to some agreement. She lowered her voice a notch. 'Because you don't fall for a girl like that, Bill—you just fuck her. That's *what she's for.* And if you really get stuck on her—and I can see how you might, she's such a hot little Manchu slut—then you set her up in a nice little flat and then make your excuses and look for the exit sign.' She laughed. 'Don't you know anything?'

'No, I'm fresh off the banana boat, Tess.' He found he was fiddling with a yellow baseball cap advertising the LA Lakers. 'I don't know a thing.'

Her husband was coming back with the Taiwanese. It took them a while to negotiate the tight wooden stairs.

'Just don't get carried away, that's all I'm saying,' Tess concluded, lightening the tone. 'These Chinese girls, Bill—they're just so *practical.* They are so practical that, if you let them, they will break your heart.'

Her husband was grinning with pleasure. 'Any more of that tea?' he said.

Bill stared out at the queue for Nan Xiang's dumplings and was just in time to see JinJin step off the far side of the zigzag bridge, designed so that no evil spirits could ever get across.

TWELVE

Awards, Bill thought. Lawyers love awards.

Best new this. Most promising that. Most valuable the other. Any excuse to get pissed and pat ourselves on the back.

He was in a ballroom with hundreds of lawyers in dinner jackets, the dresses of the women splashes of colour in a sea of black tie, sitting at the firm's table between Nancy Deng and Tess Devlin.

Most of the firm's table consisted of identically dressed men. On the other side of Tess Devlin was Shane. Then came Devlin. Then Mad Mitch. And finally the two Germans, Wolfgang and Jurgen, with Rosalita laughing between them.

Too many men at this table, Bill thought, missing Becca, feeling her absence. He realised that for years these events had been made bearable because, no matter how long they dragged on, he could always look up and see her face, or share a silent private joke.

But the night crawled by in a blur of bad food, harassed waiters and too much drink, the glasses topped up quickly yet sloppily, a strange combination of the servile and the slapdash. A succession of men in tuxedos, and occasionally a woman in an evening dress, went on stage to collect a glass sculpture of a bird from a willowy Chinese woman with a professional smile that never wavered and a man in a dinner jacket who had something to do with one of the sponsors.

Then came the last award of the night, Foreign Lawyer of the Year, and when Shane's name was announced Bill was suddenly on his feet, cheering and clapping louder than anyone. 'Sit down,' someone shouted from behind him. A disappointed nominee, Bill thought, sitting down. But he got up again, clapping harder and laughing as Shane weaved his way to the stage with an embarrassed grin.

'Thank you, thank you,' the big Australian said, squinting at his award. 'I shall always treasure this, er, glass pigeon.' Laughter. 'You know, the public think that lawyers are a heartless, mercenary bunch,' he said, only slightly slurring his words. 'But of course we all know that's not true.'

Whoops of knowing, derisive laughter. Shane straightened himself up.

'I am reminded of the beautiful young woman who made an appointment to see a lawyer,' he continued, with inebriated gravitas. 'She said, "Please take my case. Unfortunately I have no money. However, I will give you the best blow-job in the world."'

More laughter, but now mixed with disapproving catcalls and the odd cry of 'Shame.' It was a conservative crowd. Bill looked at them. At the tables of rival firms, heads were being shaken, smiles fading. Shane had gone too far. These people didn't want blow-jobs with their after-dinner mints.

But Shane leaned on the podium, and it wobbled dangerously. 'The best blow-job in the world,' he repeated, with an edge of defiance, as if every word were true. He paused for effect, glaring at the crowd. 'And the lawyer said, "What's in it for me?"'

He had won them back. And as they all clapped

and cheered, even the rival firms who had feigned offence, it seemed to Bill that this was the very essence of his friend. Teetering on the edge of disaster, and then somehow stumbling to glory.

Shane came back to the table amid much backslapping and congratulations and Devlin sent the waiter off for champagne.

Bill looked at his watch. Knocking on for midnight. Back in London, Becca would have picked up Holly from nursery by now. If there was no ballet and no swimming lessons, then they would be home and he would be able to talk to both of them. He pulled his phone from his dinner jacket but saw there was no signal.

The night was breaking up. As the others got up to network and stretch their limbs, Bill was the only one who remained at the firm's table, the debris of empty wine bottles and coffee cups before him. A waiter appeared with a bucket bristling with champagne bottles and placed it on the abandoned table. Shane and Devlin looked over at Bill as he headed for the exit.

'I'll be right back,' he mouthed.

He didn't notice the four men at another table who got up and followed him out of the ballroom and into the hotel lobby. He was looking at his phone, waiting for the signal to appear, so he still didn't see them when he stepped out of the hotel and into the soft summer night. It was only when the signal appeared and he was speed-dialling Becca's number that he looked up and saw them standing there.

Four men he didn't recognise, staring at him as though he should know them.

'Hello?' Becca said, but Bill didn't hear her

because he was closing his phone, and knowing all at once that he had to get away from these men.

Because now he knew them. Now he remembered them. Now he could see them out on the dance floor of Suzy Too, laughing like lottery winners, with their hands all over JinJin Li.

Bill moved to walk past them but one of them threw his cigarette away and stepped in front of him.

'A piece of advice,' the man said.

They were like one person, Bill thought. Young but running to fat, with those closed, spiteful faces that he knew so well. His countrymen.

'Don't try to tell us what we can and can't do with some Chinese whore,' the man said, and then he punched Bill full in the face. His friends chortled their approval.

Bill had seen it coming but he was too shocked to move. He had stood there like an idiot as the blow struck the side of his mouth and the force knocked him backwards and he trod on someone in the queue for taxis and heard a girl scream. He was hit again, felt something hard and unbreakable split his lip—maybe a wedding ring, he thought—and crashed into something big and hard. He held on to it for support and saw it was one of the two Chinese lions protecting the entrance to the hotel. He had scuffed his hands on the lion but it broke his fall and kept him on his feet.

His fingers went to his mouth and came away wet and red. He felt he could smell the blood, rank and metallic. He half-turned and there were three of them in front of Bill now. Fists clenched, working themselves up, all wanting their crack at him. The lips taut on their mean, stupid faces. Oh, he knew

159

them now. The one that had hit him seemed keen to explain something.

'Where do you think you are? The school disco? She would have been happy to fuck the lot of us for five hundred RMB,' he said. 'You ignorant fucking tourist.'

Tourist was the worst thing you could call someone in Shanghai. *Tourist* made *motherfucker* seem like quite the compliment.

Another punch, but Bill had realised that he should possibly be making some effort to duck and this one skimmed off his forehead. Then someone he didn't see kicked him in the ribs and the wind went whoosh out of him and he was down on all fours, gasping with shock and fear, because the pain in his side was unbelievable. He wondered where this would end, and if they were going to kill him.

Then from somewhere far away he heard Shane's voice. Calling his name, calling them bastards, telling them to leave him alone. And at first it seemed as though they were doing just that.

The blows stopped and as Bill crawled across the pavement towards the lobby of the hotel, aware of the people in the taxi queue backing away from him as though he was carrying some dreadful disease, it felt like a miracle. But they had only turned their attention on his friend.

Bill lifted his head up and saw Shane going down with all of them around him. Bill held on to the stone lion and got up. Shane was lashing out and cursing, but one of the men dropped on top of his chest, fists moving like pistons, while the others were kneeling on him, pinning him down, making him roar. There were shouts in Chinese and

160

English. People were coming out of the hotel to watch.

Bill was back on his feet, holding his side as he staggered towards his friend. Something exploded in his ear like a red flash of light and he ducked, almost comically after the event. He saw the faces of two of the men, turning away from Shane, one of them with blood on his dress shirt. That might be mine, Bill thought.

The other two were still kicking Shane. In the head, between the legs, in the ribs. He curled up and they kept kicking him.

Bill was aware he should do something. But it was all happening too fast, and there were too many of them, and he didn't have the fury in him that he had had when he saw them with JinJin Li and felt his blood pumping with rage at the sight of that young, manhandled flesh. Tonight the rage was all in them.

The men who were stomping Shane were breathing heavily, sweating hard, slowing down. Their bow ties had come loose. Shane had stopped shouting. He was curled up on the pavement, not moving. Bill moved towards him but the talkative one was in Bill's face, bouncing on the balls of his feet, fists clenched by his sides. His trousers had those long satiny stripes that lawyers liked. That they were all wearing black tie somehow made the scene more grotesque, and made the men seem like a pack of psychopathic penguins.

'Protecting her honour, were you?' He had JinJin Li on the brain, this one. 'What do you think, you stupid bastard—that she doesn't fuck men for money?'

He punched Bill in the gut and it bent him

161

double, but then it was suddenly all over, because the hotel security were on the pavement and the men were walking off, in no hurry at all, giving each other high fives as though they had just won a basketball game, exulting and laughing and shouting obscenities over their shoulders. The hotel security stared after them, and then at Bill and Shane with equal hostility. Shane was sitting up now but bent forward and moaning with his hands cupped over his groin. He had been sick down the front of his dinner jacket.

Bill helped Shane to his feet and felt the full weight of his friend leaning on him. They staggered to the road where Tiger was scrambling out of the car and staring at them in horror. He was saying something but Bill couldn't hear him.

Yes, that's exactly what I believe, Bill was thinking, as the humiliation of taking a beating kicked in. *I really believe it, you pig.*

I believe with all my heart that she never fucked anyone for money.

*　　　*　　　*

When they were very young and starting out, Becca and Bill had talked endlessly, talked about their relationship, feelings, life, the world, jobs, friends, problems, fulfilment, parents and all the disappointments of the past.

And then they got married and had a baby, and after that they mostly talked about their daughter.

'She was looking for "YMCA",' Becca said on the phone. 'The CD with "YMCA" on it. By the Village People.'

'Yes,' Bill said, resisting the urge to say *I know*

162

who sings 'YMCA'. He absent-mindedly felt the mess they had made of his face, and smiled at the memory of Holly out on the floor at Shane and Rosalita's wedding, facing her mother as they sang and danced along to the Village People. Her thin white arms thrown flamboyantly wide for *Y*, fingertips touching her head for *M*, leaning sideways with her arms almost forming a circle for *C*—that was the funniest part, for some reason— and her hands making a quick triangle above her head for the *A*.

'It's on *Now That's What I Call Disco*,' he said. His voice sounded strange to his ears. It was his fat lips, and whatever they had done to his teeth.

'But it's not,' Becca insisted. 'That's what I thought, but it's not on *Now That's What I Call Disco*. "In the Navy" is on there. Their other hit. The Village People, I mean.'

Bill sighed. 'Then look on *Super Dance Party 1999*,' he suggested. 'Might be on there.'

'Okay,' Becca said doubtfully. If Holly wanted to dance to a certain song, it never occurred to either of her parents to do anything other than search through their entire CD collection until it was found. 'Hold on, Bill. She wants a word with you.'

There was the shuffling sound as Becca gave the phone to their daughter.

'Holly?'

And then her voice in his ear. Sweet and formal, infinitely more grown up than he was expecting, than he remembered.

'Hello?'

'Holly, it's Daddy.'

'I know.' A pause. 'I have a question.'

'Go ahead, darling.'

163

'Did you have a scary night last night?'

He stood up abruptly and recoiled as he caught sight of his face in the mirror. He was suddenly aware of what his cuts and bruises looked like, and not just what they felt like. He was a mess, and this would be an embarrassment in the office.

'A scary night, angel?' But how did she know what had happened? How could she possibly know about that? 'Why would I have a scary night?'

A long pause. Then a sigh, the kind of sigh that only an exasperated four-year-old girl can make.

'Because you were *alone*.'

He laughed. She made him laugh. She made him laugh more than anyone he had ever known.

'No, I'm okay,' he said, the relief filling him up. 'And you know why?'

Silence. She was probably shaking her head. 'No,' she said eventually.

He could hear her mother's voice in the background, pulling her away. *She's my child too*, he thought.

'Because if ever I'm down or scared, all I have to do is think of you and then I always feel better. Always. I remember that you're my little girl and that makes me feel so happy.' His blinked angrily. There was silence at the other end, not even the shuffling sound of the handset being passed like a baton in a relay.

'Holly?'

'I have to brush my teeth.' No note of apology, just a statement of fact. It was the way things were.

'Before you go—'

'Night-night,' she said briskly, and the panic flew up in him. This was no good.

'Wait, wait—before you go . . .' He stopped, not

knowing what to say to his faraway daughter. And then he knew. 'Just remember that I'm your daddy,' he said. 'And I will never stop loving you. And whatever happens, and wherever you are, and wherever I am, no matter how far apart, I love you now and I always will and I'm so glad that I'm your daddy. And I am so proud that you're my daughter. So proud. Remember my face. Remember my voice. Okay, Holly?' Nothing. 'Hello?'

'Okay, but I really do have to go now.' Sounding like his girl again. 'Night-night, Daddy.'

'Goodnight, angel.'

THIRTEEN

He paced the floor of his apartment with the counterfeit Lakers baseball cap in his hands, watching the light in her window.

Pathetic, he thought. Another married big nose eyeing the local talent when the wife has her back turned—what a cliché. Oh, you are such a cliché.

Just look at you. Calculating how long you should wait before you make the next move. What are you *doing*? What do you think you're *doing*? Nothing, he told himself, the cap in his hands. I'm not doing *anything*. I'm just working out the best time to give back her Lakers hat. And I'm lonely. It's okay to be lonely, isn't it? Being lonely doesn't break any of the wedding vows, does it?

It's all perfectly innocent, he lied to himself.

But he didn't go over there. He felt too shy, too nervous, too stupid. As far as he could remember,

165

those kinds of feelings always put a girl off.

So on Saturday night Bill just waited, and he watched the light in her window, and then it was too late anyway because the silver Porsche arrived and after a while the light went out in her apartment. He turned away from the window and went to look inside the refrigerator. He didn't watch her leave. He wasn't going to put himself through that.

He threw aside the Lakers hat and lay down on his single bed, the master bedroom abandoned now, and he felt ridiculous. He had imagined that JinJin Li was just like him, that most nights she was home alone, the table set for one and the phone not ringing. Missing someone. That's what he thought she did with her time—sat around missing someone. But perhaps he was wrong. Perhaps JinJin Li was just fine.

Perhaps it was the man's wife who was the lonely one.

*   *   *

The next night he went to her flat.

It still felt too soon, but when the weekend was over he would be working late or out with clients and the chance would be gone until next weekend. She would probably have a new baseball cap by next weekend. And what was the big deal anyway?

He was only returning a bloody hat.

He went over there, to the opposite block of Paradise Mansions, and caught the lift to her floor and then paused outside her door. He remembered the last time he was here—the girl drunk and sick, and him struggling to hold her up

166

as he fumbled for her keys.

That should have been the end of it. That should have been enough.

But he rang the doorbell anyway.

Nobody came. Thank God for that. He could hear music inside, but nobody came and Bill was about to escape back to his safe lonely life when the door suddenly flew open and there she was in all her wide-eyed beauty, and he knew that it was simply not true that the Asian face is unreadable because on those high-cheek-boned northern features, on that *Dongbei ho* face, he could see surprise, and a bit of pleasure and a lot of wonder. Her eyes seemed to shine when she looked at him. Maybe she liked him, he thought. Or maybe that was just the way she looked at the world.

Bill had never seen a face that was so expressive, a face where so much was happening, a face that said so much. And it said, *What is this big-nosed pinky doing at my door?*

He held out his yellow-and-purple excuse. 'You forgot your hat,' he said.

She took it from him. She had small hands. Extraordinarily small hands for such a tall woman. 'Oh,' she said. '*Tse-tse.*'

'*Bu ke-qi,*' he said. And then the awkward silence. He defensively struggled to fill it. 'What do you know about the Lakers anyway?'

She thought about it. 'NBA. Magic Johnson. Yellow shirts,' she said. 'The Lakers are basketball. Kobe Bryant. Shaquille O'Neal.'

'That's more than me,' he said. 'I don't know anything about the Lakers.'

'LA,' she said. 'LA, California.'

He really liked her. He felt as if she had just

167

opened up her eyes and seen the entire planet. 'You didn't have to leave, you know,' he said.

A flash of irritation in her eyes. 'That lady,' she said. 'That lady, she said I'm Manchu.'

He didn't know much about Manchuria. About as much as he knew about the LA Lakers. He knew Manchuria had been in the Dongbei, the north-eastern region she came from, and that it had been colonised by Mongols, Manchus and the Japanese. But although he didn't know much, he knew enough to know that Tess Devlin had a point.

JinJin's face was not typically Chinese. It was easy to believe she carried the blood of some high-cheekboned invader, and easy to understand why she was so touchy about it. It was like telling someone on a kibbutz that they looked like a cossack.

'I think she said you look a bit Manchu,' he said, playing it down.

Now he was really getting on her nerves. 'But I'm not Manchu.'

He held up his hands in surrender. This wasn't going great. But then she tossed her baseball cap on to the back of her head and smiled, a smile that somehow broke the enchantment cast by her looks. It was a bit of a goofy grin because her teeth stuck out slightly, and the dentists of the Dongbei had been careless with her, or maybe her parents had other things to worry about, like finding food for the table, but that smile was full of warmth and humour. And if that toothy, goofy grin took the edge off the classic beauty that resided on her face when she wasn't smiling, then it replaced it with something better—or at least something that Bill liked a lot more.

'Please come in,' she said, with the scrupulously polite formality she was capable of, stepping back to invite him into her apartment. And suddenly he felt very married. Did he really want this to happen?

He wasn't cut out for this game. That was the truth of it. All his plotting, all his calculating, all his watching from his window—when it came to the crunch, when it was time to go into her flat, he just didn't have the heart to go through with it. You see, he loved his wife.

'I've got to go.' He jerked his thumb over his shoulder. 'Early start tomorrow.'

But she had made her mind up.

'Please come in,' she insisted. 'I want you to try my dumplings.'

This was too much. Just too much.

'Oh no, I can't, I couldn't,' he said in a weak voice.

'Please,' she said, and he was struck again by her adherence to form, as though there was a strict code of etiquette here that had to be obeyed, and somehow it made her impossible to resist. In a daze, he found himself entering her apartment, and it took his brain a few moments to realise that when JinJin Li offered you dumplings, that really was all she was offering.

The smell of dumplings filled the air and the flat was full of people. All of them young women. Apart from a child, a tiny child, a sturdy crop-haired toddler who staggered between the legs of the girls of Paradise Mansions. There was a gap at the back of his trousers where his fat little bum stuck out to make it easy for him to do his business.

They were cooking dinner, which seemed to consist exclusively of dumplings, all these small packets of dough that were being filled with pork, fish or vegetables, and then fried or steamed.

Most of the faces he recognised. These women were not strangers. The tall taxi dancer from Suzy Too was at the stove, pulling dumplings from a steamer with one hand, and fast frying a pan of dumplings with the other. She waved at him.

The woman who had tapped a number into her mobile phone and offered herself for peanuts was playing on the floor with the small boy. She pointed at the child and laughed. She seemed a lot happier than the last time he had seen her, and he realised that he hadn't seen her smile or laugh when he met her before, surrounded by all that fun.

There was another one he thought he recognised but could not place, an alarmingly thin girl in a mini-kilt who was washing up dishes in the sink. Where was she from? And then he saw the monogrammed handbag nearby and got it. It was one of the Louis Vuitton-addicted teachers, who he guessed had perhaps found a sponsor since the last time they'd met. She glanced up at him, but gave no sign of recognition. Why would she? He had been just another guy in Suzy Too.

And there was someone else—not one of the young women he remembered from out in the night, but a face he had seen when she was putting the rubbish out, or chatting to the porter, or strolling the aisles of the local Carrefour supermarket, or when she was going off with her father. At least he had thought it was her father.

She was the plain girl in glasses that he had seen

leaving with the old man in his BMW, and she had seemed to be from a different world to the rest of them. She was knitting now, and it made her look more like a fifties housewife than a kept woman. But she wasn't from a different world to the rest of them. She was from the same world.

'Neighbours,' JinJin said, ever the perfect host. 'All the neighbours. Making *xiao long bao*. Shanghainese dumpling. And *jiaozi* dumpling from Changchun. Like ravioli. You know?'

He knew. 'I know.'

'Please to try.'

JinJin found him a seat between the girl in glasses and the woman with the kid and brought him a cold Tsingtao. The child held up a scratched metal car and Bill took it. 'Ferrari,' he said, 'very nice.'

The one in glasses was called Jenny Two. Jenny Two? Yes, Jenny Two. The one with the boy was Sugar. 'I think we met,' he said, unsure if mentioning it was the right thing to do. He was sure JinJin could have told him. 'How are you?' he asked Sugar, and unfortunately she told him.

'Sometimes I have to lock myself away from my family,' she said, quite matter-of-fact, watching Bill play with her child. 'My mother and father and son. I can't be with them. Because of my work.' She paused, taking a breath. This was what they did, he thought. They bottled everything up for so long that when they finally let go, it all came pouring out. 'Last night there was a man in Suzy Too,' said Sugar. 'An Australian. And when we left he wanted to go to casino. And I said—oh no, no casino, we just go to your hotel. But he wanted casino and he lost.'

171

Bill nodded. He lost at the casino. What were the chances of that?

'Then this morning he gave me ten US dollar,' Sugar said, and at first Bill thought he hadn't heard her right. Ten dollars? 'And he said, "What can I do? Everything else is gone." And I was good to him.' The tears came and she blinked them back. Her child looked up at her, the little metal car in his hand. 'It's not enough, is it?' she said.

'No,' Bill said quietly. 'It's not enough.'

She nodded. Her son held out his toy as if to comfort her. 'So sometimes I have to lock myself away from my family,' she said, taking the scratched toy Ferrari.

Jenny Two put a protective arm around her and Bill looked away, unwilling to intrude on this personal grief and unable to offer any words of comfort. Ten US dollars for your body. Sugar was the poor relation, he learned, bouncing between Jenny Two's spare room and her parents' apartment. The rest of them all had someone. The rest of them all had some kind of sponsor. And while the world he lived in would certainly disapprove, having some kind of sponsor was better than being paid ten US dollars for your body.

He looked over at JinJin and she smiled and he immediately felt better—he was getting used to it now, that toothy grin that revealed her soul in a way that the cool, poker-faced beauty she wore when climbing into a Porsche never did, and never could. He was getting used to her smile but he thought that he could never get tired of it.

He had been wrong about her, he realised, pulling a book of crossword puzzles from beneath

172

him. He had been wrong about all of these women, the *jinseniao* in the *niaolong* of Paradise Mansions. All the pretty canaries in their golden cage.

They might spend nights alone waiting for the call. And when they were back from the jewel-box of the Shanghai night, back from the restaurants and the cocktail bars and clubs of the Bund, back from it all and finally home alone, they might sometimes feel second best, and they might suffer all the indignities of being a married man's mistress, of going to bed with someone but usually waking up alone.

But they would never be lonely, not in the way that he was lonely. This was their city. And the girls of Paradise Mansions had each other.

*   *   *

It was a different kind of karaoke bar to what he was used to.

Bill had accompanied Shane and clients, all of them Asian, to glossy joints in the old French Concession, but the karaoke bar that the girls of Paradise Mansions favoured was just a warren of plain little boxes in a Gubei backstreet, and the neon sign above the door was not in English, and there were no pretty girls employed to applaud middle-aged Taiwanese businessmen for drunkenly murdering 'My Way' in Mandarin.

Bill and the girls crammed into a room the size of his wife's walk-in wardrobe and ordered fruit juice all round, and a Tsingtao for Bill.

Sugar had stayed home—she had a spare room in Jenny Two's place that she shared with her son—but the rest of them were there, studying the songbook menus in earnest silence, like famished souls who had unexpectedly found themselves in a five-star restaurant.

He leafed through the leather-bound book on his lap and understood none of it. There were hundreds of Mandopop and Cantopop standards, but nothing—he realised with profound relief—that would require him to sing.

Watching JinJin seize the microphone and stare intently at a screen where an Asian man and woman were walking hand in hand down a beach with tower blocks in the background, Bill at last understood the attraction of karaoke bars to the Chinese.

The karaoke bar offered privacy in a country where privacy was scarce, and freedom of expression in a culture where expressing yourself too freely could get you a bullet in the back of the head, and the bill for the bullet sent to the folks back home.

JinJin launched herself into a tearful Mandarin ballad, a song that he deduced could only be about undying love.

When the song was over, the taxi dancer—Jenny One—leapt up and tried to wrestle the microphone from JinJin, who refused to let it go. They barked at each other in Shanghainese. JinJin won, kept the microphone and began emoting her way through another overwrought ballad, flushed with delight, watching the little ball bounce across the Chinese characters as a woman on the TV screen gazed mournfully out of a window. JinJin's voice was not bad, but it had a tendency to crack at the big climax.

Jenny Two looked up from her knitting.

'She has a beautiful voice,' she murmured, her eyes gleaming behind her glasses. 'And a beautiful face.'

Bill nodded politely. He certainly agreed about the face.

'I have neither,' said Jenny Two, smiling happily. 'But my husband likes me anyway. I am very lucky. He is very old.'

Bill marvelled at his own naivety. 'North block, right?' he said, and she nodded, showing teeth that protruded beyond cute and into dental disaster.

Bill could see the 7-series black BMW parked in the courtyard of Paradise Mansions, and the well-groomed, sixty-something driver who never got out. He had seen Jenny Two running to the car, a look of innocent delight on her face, and had always assumed it was a wealthy old man taking his plain student daughter out for dinner on the Bund.

Jenny Two just didn't carry herself like the others. She didn't have the look. But Bill liked her a lot. There was a gentleness about Jenny Two, and she seemed to quite enjoy playing the ugly duckling of the group. And when she stood up to hold a formless length of blue wool against his chest, he saw that she had a hard, compact body, and that she was the only one of them with real curves. And she was nice. Bill could understand why some old *taipan* would take a shine to her.

'Eet eez always these way with JinJin and the karaoke,' sighed Jenny One, flopping on to the cracked sofa.

'Where'd you learn to speak English?' he asked her, already guessing the answer. The answer to almost every question in Paradise Mansions was 'a man'. *I met a man*. Or more than one man.

175

'I took language class,' Jenny One said. 'In bed. Best place to learn language, no? I have two French boyfriends. The first—he eez young and poor and I love him very much. But he eez young and poor so I finish.' Tears sprang to her eyes, undermining the casual harshness of her words, and she dabbed at them with a little paper napkin. They were boiling with emotion, these women. It was always laughter and tears with them, Bill realised, often in the same sentence. 'The second eez rich and married and then he go back to Paris.'

Bill guessed that the Paradise Mansions flat must have been a goodbye gift from the rich and married Frenchman. That's why Jenny One could afford to live there and yet still go home alone. She had a sponsor, even if he was long gone. 'He called for a year and then he didn't call any more.' She looked at Bill searchingly. 'Why do you think he stopped calling?'

Bill shook his head. 'I don't know.' He supposed the man's wife must have had something to do with it. Jenny One was crying openly now, and Bill saw that the girls of Paradise Mansions were regular young women. Back home they would have been accountants and teachers, girlfriends and wives. But not in Shanghai. Not in times like these. He watched JinJin, reluctantly surrendering the microphone to the Louis Vuitton addict in the mini-kilt.

'You know that girl?' Jenny One asked him. 'She is Annie—you know?' Bill shook his head.

'She is new,' Jenny Two said, her knitting needles clacking. She nodded knowingly at Annie as though they were gossiping over a garden fence. 'Man from Taiwan!'

Annie began screeching some awful Cantopop song.

'Big apartment in west block,' Jenny Two continued, her eyes wide, and magnified further by her milk-bottle spectacles. 'Three bedroom! And the man will be in Shanghai for two years! Long contract!'

'His family are here?' Jenny One asked, and when the other Jenny nodded, she pulled a philosophical *c'est-la-vie* face.

Annie finished slaughtering her song and came over to join them. She imperiously sipped her fruit juice, studying Bill.

'Have you been to Hawaii?' she asked him, crossing her legs. He shook his head. She seemed amazed, as if every self-respecting foreigner knew Hawaii inside out. 'You should go,' she advised him. 'I was living there with my American boyfriend.' She thought for a moment. 'Four months. He sold time share.'

Jenny One looked away, as if she had heard it all before. But Jenny Two put down her knitting. 'What happened with the American boyfriend in Hawaii?' she wanted to know. Bill noticed that they had slipped into English for his benefit, and he was touched.

'We didn't click,' Annie said, tugging at the hem of her kilt as Jenny Two looked sympathetic.

JinJin sat down beside Bill and smiled. 'Now I find you something,' she said, ignoring his protests as she searched the songbook. He reached for his drink, flustered, wondering why only Westerners were capable of being embarrassed by karaoke. Because we think it is a performance, he thought. Because we think we are expected to be good. And

177

karaoke has got nothing to do with being good.

JinJin was the only one of them who did not have an adopted Western name. She was the only one who had kept the Chinese name that she had been given at birth, and as he watched her looking for his karaoke song, he wondered what that said about her. It was as if there was something about JinJin that was unchangeable, untouchable, and out of reach. He liked it that she hadn't adopted a Western name.

JinJin finally found him something and they all applauded as he got up and awkwardly stood there in front of the TV set, and he was surprised when she joined him, a microphone in her hand. Maybe giving him his turn was just an excuse for her to reclaim the microphone.

It was a Carpenters song she had dug up from the furthest reaches of the songbook, 'Yesterday Once More', a chunk of unadulterated corn that had the girls of Paradise Mansions swaying from side to side with a faraway look in their moist brown eyes. JinJin's voice swooped and soared uncertainly, disintegrating on the high notes, a made-in-China Karen Carpenter, and Bill croaked along as best he could.

When the final chords were dying and the girls were all clapping, Bill reached across and squeezed one of JinJin's tiny hands.

She quickly pulled it away.

She didn't mind being set up in a flat by a married man who came round when he felt like it, but she wasn't going to start holding hands in a karaoke bar with some big-nosed pinky. The girls of Paradise Mansions held on to their dignity.

Then he had to do it alone. There was no escape.

He resisted at first, but they wouldn't hear of it. There was no way round it. Taking your turn at karaoke in China was as inevitable as death, and far more inevitable than paying your Chinese taxes.

'I understand,' JinJin said. 'You're too ashamed to sing.' There it was again, her arbitrary choice of word that in the end somehow seemed more fitting than the obvious choice. It was true. He wasn't embarrassed or bashful or shy. He was ashamed.

But they found him some classic Elvis and, Tsingtao in one hand and microphone in the other, he did his best to moan the lyrics as they came alight on the screen.

The girls from Paradise Mansions cheered what they thought was his shyness. But that wasn't the problem. The problem was that he knew the lyrics to this old Elvis song, he knew them well from all those nights out with Shane and the Asian clients, on all those other nights when the karaoke had been compulsory.

And what were being illuminated in front of him were not quite the words, just a rough Chinese imitation, a ham-fisted facsimile of the real thing.

But still Bill sang along to 'She's Not You' with JinJin Li smiling up at him, he sang along as best he could, he sang along although the words were all wrong.

FOURTEEN

By the time he got in he was feeling so good that calling his wife seemed like a sound idea. Her

179

voice echoed across six thousand miles, stone-cold sober and still in yesterday. 'Hello?'

'It's me.'

There was a pause while she weighed him up.

'Are you drunk, Bill?' she said in such a way that he couldn't tell if she was irritated or amused or a bit of both. More than anything, it was the sound of a pissed-off wife. 'I was just putting Holly to bed,' she said, and he heard the sigh in it, and was suddenly aware that she knew him so well.

That was the trouble with marriage, he thought. They got to know you so well.

'I just wanted to tell you something,' he said. It had seemed so important when the thought had occurred to him in the cab home from the karaoke bar, in the back seat between the two Jennys, with JinJin and Annie up front next to the driver, JinJin abruptly subdued after all those hours of singing about love that lasts for ever.

But now he felt the importance of what he had wanted to say draining away as he sensed the reality of their lives in London. 'I'm going to get her a copy of "YMCA",' he announced. 'Online, one-click buying.' Warmed up to the idea of singing at last, and thinking that perhaps his voice wasn't as bad as he had always believed, he launched into a snatch of the old Village People song. But he stopped when he heard his wife's deafening silence.

'And that's what you called about?' He felt he could hear her shaking her head. 'What time is it over there?'

He looked around for a clock. What had he done with that clock? 'It's late,' he confessed, sheepish now. 'It's like—four, I guess.'

'Is it like four or is it four, Bill? Well, it's bedtime here. And it's really sweet that you're thinking of Holly when you're out getting drunk with Shane, but she's forgotten all about that silly song. You know what it is this week? It's "Independent Women" by Destiny's Child. Do you know that one, Bill?'

He laughed. 'Independent Women' by Destiny's Child! Something about his daughter's choices, the things that captured her attention—they amused him greatly, and delighted him, and enchanted him, and somehow seemed to measure his love for her.

'Becca, can you put her on for a minute?'

Silence. He knew her many silences so well. 'She's already in bed, Bill. It's a school night—remember? If you had called a bit earlier . . .'

'It's all right,' he said quickly. 'Next time. Everything okay? With her breathing?'

'It's better in London,' she said.

'And how's your dad?' He should have asked her about her father sooner. He realised that now. And then came the longest silence of them all.

'It looks like he may have to have surgery,' she said, her voice flat and expressionless. A pause. 'Thanks for asking,' she added, and he winced at the hard sarcastic edge to it.

'Surgery? That's awful. What—you mean a bypass?'

'First he's got to have something called cardiac catheterisation,' she said, softening now, and he could hear her holding back the tears. 'They put a tube in his heart through a vein or an artery or something and inject a dye. After that, they decide if he needs to have surgery.' He heard her swallow.

181

'I'm scared, Bill.'

'I'm so sorry, Bec,' he said, and they were silent but not in a bad way. Just holding on to that connection, and both finding comfort in it.

'He'll be all right, Bec,' he said softly. 'I know he will.'

'Thanks, Bill.' Getting a grip on herself now, and he felt a flood of love. It couldn't be easy for her. 'Look, I've got to settle Holly down,' she said. 'I can hear her stirring.'

He could hear it too, hear his Holly's rising cry, filtered first through the child monitor and then across six thousand miles. A bad dream.

'Sure,' he said. 'I love you, Bec.'

'And I love you too.'

They didn't say it very often. They were not one of those married couples that felt the need to say it every day. But it came out when they realised what they had, and they were grateful, and they were wise enough to count their blessings.

He replaced the phone, feeling flat and tired, as if all the magic of the night was just an illusion brought on by Tsingtao, old Elvis songs and the face of JinJin Li. He went over to the last window in the master bedroom. Her light was still on. JinJin was still awake.

He decided that in the morning he was going to go out and buy some of those crossword books. He could see how much she liked them.

And then perhaps it wouldn't matter so much when her phone didn't ring.

*   *   *

Shane couldn't sleep. Every time he felt himself

slipping into oblivion, a current of pain pulled him back, and forced him awake.

As gently as he could he adjusted his large body, and the pain, which was located somewhere in the deepest regions of his groin, subsided to a dull ache. He remained motionless for several minutes, afraid to breathe in case he disturbed her again. But it was no good.

Rosalita exhaled wearily in the darkness. In one smooth move, she got out of bed, pulled on a thin robe and went into the living room. She left the door open and the darkness of the bedroom was broken when she switched on a light.

It had been this way ever since he had been beaten up with Bill—or, as Rosalita liked to call him, 'Your loser friend whose pretty wife left him.'

The pain sometimes went away, but it never went very far, and it never let Shane sleep the night. He rolled on his back and felt himself down there, cursing silently, and more scared than he had been in his life.

Something was wrong with him. He could sense it. Something was very wrong.

When he went into the living room Rosalita was sitting with her back to him, tapping away at the computer. He buried his face in her mass of black hair, his hand feeling her shoulders through the thin silk of the robe. He glanced at the window. It was still dark outside.

'Come back to bed,' he said, his voice rough after being pulled from sleep. 'It's too late for all that now.'

Her small brown hands flew across the keyboard. 'No sleep, no make love,' she said breezily. 'So check email.'

He looked over her shoulder at the screen, and his exhausted eyes suddenly blinked in disbelief.

My darling, how I miss your eyes, your lips, your big fat cock—

He jumped away from her, as if from an electric shock. 'What the fuck, Rosalita?'

'Old mail, old boyfriend,' she said dismissively. 'I was just deleting him.'

Shane stared at the screen but the message was gone. His wife swivelled in her chair and stared at him with eyes like huge brown headlamps. He winced with another shiver of pain.

'You should see a doctor,' she said angrily. 'If you sick, then you should go see a doctor.'

'Who was that?' he demanded. 'Who was it? I want to know.'

But she just smiled coldly up at him and he took a step back. There was a fierceness in her that you would never suspect when she was singing all those soppy love songs. 'Please, I want to know, Rosie.' His voice softer, pleading.

'No,' she said quietly. 'You don't want to know. You really don't want to know.'

She logged off and sprang from the chair, a little brown wild cat, lithe and tiny and capable of clawing your eyes out. Towering above her, Shane meekly followed her back to the bedroom. She shrugged off her robe and he caught his breath as she slipped naked between the sheets, turning her back towards him again.

He still wanted her. At least in theory. At least in his head. But his body hadn't really felt like sex since they had got their kicking, and all the pain had begun. That confused him. Shane had believed that he would want to fuck her forever, and already—so soon!—it had gone off the boil. Perhaps it would have been all right without the pain and the worry. Perhaps the pain and the worry were spoiling everything.

So Shane lay in the darkness, trying not to move, missing the physical life they had known before, that closencss in all its colours, but also pining for something that Shane and his wife had never really experienced, something that he saw in the marriage of his friend Bill, something that looked a lot like friendship.

*   *   *

In the morning Bill came to collect him.

They were going for brunch with a representative from a private health-care company from Switzerland. Rosalita slept on. Shane hoped that she would keep sleeping on. He didn't want his friend to see how bad it had got.

'This is going to be the next big growth market in China,' Bill said, watching Shane struggling to put his shoes on. 'Private health care. The new rich are going to go crazy for it.'

'Lot of money in that racket,' Shane agreed.

It was Shanghai's favourite subject—the next big new thing, the next killing to be made. The Swiss were in Shanghai to evaluate the potential of a private hospital in China, the kind of service offered to the expatriate community at the International Family Hospital where Becca had taken Holly, but serving an exclusively Chinese clientele. 'The Chinese are a nation

185

of hypochondriacs,' Shane said. 'The Great Unwashed get an itchy arse and they think it's cancer of the colon.' He tied the laces on his Church's brogues, the pain all over his face.

'You all right?' Bill said as Shane stood up, sweat beading his forehead.

'I'm fine, mate,' Shane said. He pushed a swathe of damp blond hair away and sat down again to catch his breath. He flipped open his laptop and withdrew a disk. 'Stick that away for me, will you? In the safe.'

Bill took the disk. It said SUN on the label. 'Behind the *Mona Lisa*,' Shane told him.

Above the plasma TV set there was a perfect reproduction of the *Mona Lisa*. Bill carefully placed the painting on the floor and, as Shane called out the six-digit combination, turned the dial of a small wall safe. The thick metal door came open with an electronic double beep. As Bill slipped the disk inside, he was aware of passports, jewellery boxes, and wads of foreign currency.

And then he saw it.

The gun looked like a toy. So small and simple and cheap looking. Almost harmless. Sitting there surrounded by the blue boxes from Tiffany and the wad of US bank notes and the passports of Australia and the Philippines.

Bill reached in his hand and pulled it out by the barrel, aware that his heart was pounding. It was heavy, much heavier than it looked, but quite not as heavy as a bag of sugar. It smelled of oil. Bill let it rest in the palm of his hand, and he held the gun out to Shane.

'What the fuck is this?'

'Kai Tak rules,' Shane said. 'Don't forget the Kai

Tak rules. Don't say a word to anyone. Now put it back.'

'Kai Tak rules?' Bill said. 'You're not banging some bar girl. This is not some little escapade that happened on tour. And who would I tell? What would I say? Our award-winning Head of Litigation is—what?—packing a piece? Is that the correct terminology?'

'I mean it, Bill. Put it back where you found it.'

'I want to know what it is, Shane.'

'All right.' Shane took it from him. He looked surprisingly expert with it. As if he knew that it wasn't going to suddenly go off, Bill thought.

'This is a PSM, often called a Makarov,' Shane said. 'It's Russian. A Russian knock-off of the Walther PP. You know—James Bond's gun. This is the cheapo Communist version. China's full of them. From the days when Stalin wanted Mao to do his fighting for him. Fifty years back, during the Korean War. When Mao was telling Stalin that he would sacrifice a million Chinese in a war with America, but he needed the firepower to do it. Mao wanted an arms industry, but Stalin only gave him weapons. Like this one. It's small, easy to carry, dead simple to fire. Any idiot can use it.'

Bill was speechless. He didn't know where to start.

'But what do you want a gun for? They'll throw you out of the country. They'll toss you in jail. They could kick out the firm.'

'Nobody's going to kick out the firm.'

Bill stared at the gun, dumbfounded. 'I can't imagine how you managed to buy this thing.' He looked sharply at Shane. 'And I don't want to know.'

'You can buy anything in China,' Shane said. 'Don't you know that yet? The place is full of guns. When Mao was arming the people, waiting for some foreign invasion, what do you think happened? Do you think they just gave them all back?'

'They will come down on you like a ton of bricks,' Bill said. 'If it doesn't blow your head off the first time you pull the trigger.'

Then he waited for an explanation. But Shane couldn't explain it. He didn't even try. He carefully put the Makarov back in the wall safe and locked the door.

Bill watched him replace the *Mona Lisa*, still waiting, but Shane shook his head. He couldn't find the words. It was beyond words. He knew that needing the gun had something to do with their beating, and something to do with the fear of what the pain might mean, and the overwhelming feeling that everything in his life was starting to fall apart.

But in the end Shane could not really explain to his friend why he needed a weapon in this city.

He knew it was somehow related to his jokes about the Great Unwashed, and his habit of getting drunk every night, and the need to see the money piling up, and the longing for something that felt like real love.

That's why he had a fifty-year-old gun in his home.

Anything to convince himself that this place could never hurt him.

*   *   *

188

Not every client wanted to be taken to Mao Ming Nan Lu. Not every businessman who engaged the services of Butterfield, Hunt and West wanted to see the girls in Suzy Too. But they all wanted to see what they thought of as the real Shanghai.

The city, in all its frenetic modernity, encouraged the belief that you were somehow always missing the real Shanghai. The self-consciously epic skyline of Pudong, the girls dancing on tables in Bejeebers-Bejaybers with a Guinness in their fist, the cappuccinos on every corner—this could not be the *real* Shanghai, could it?

The girls that came out at night on Mao Ming Nan Lu, or who lived in the apartments of Paradise Mansions, were no less citizens of Shanghai than a street barber on Fuyou Lu. These days, loving Starbucks was considered authentically Shanghainese—it was said that Shanghai now had more of the coffee shops than Miami—yet at the same time the city harboured a chippy need to show the developed world that China had not only caught them up but was about to pass them by and leave them for dead in the dust.

It was all the real Shanghai, if you wanted it to be.

Bill was happy when their client from the health-care company—a sickly-looking Miles Davis fan from Geneva—announced at brunch that what he really wanted was to see the jazz music at the Peace Hotel.

Bill knew that Shane secretly sneered at the Peace Hotel as a tourist trap, so he let his friend cry off, because he looked like hell, and anyway Bill always enjoyed sipping a Tsingtao and listening to those Glenn Miller standards being played for the millionth time. He sat there and thought of Becca and Holly, and how they must be walking home from school right now, as he watched the jazz band who had been teenagers when the Japanese marched in, now sprightly old cats in their eighties, and still banging out their spirited versions of 'In the Mood' and 'String of Pearls' and 'I Love My Wife'.

When the client had had his fill, and his jet-lag was kicking in hard, Bill got Tiger to drive his guest back to the hotel while he caught a cab home to Paradise Mansions. He let himself in, happy that he still had the Book City carrier bag with him.

He had been carrying the bag around for hours and had been afraid that he would leave it under the table in the bar of the Peace Hotel. It contained a wide selection of crossword puzzles. Every book of crossword puzzles that he could find in Book City.

His doorbell rang and he flew to it, expecting to see her face on the other side of the door. But it was Jenny One, holding a steaming takeaway container wrapped in a white linen napkin.

'Noodle soup,' she said, as if that explained everything. 'You need noodle soup.'

She came into his apartment and examined it with expert eyes. 'Company pay,' she observed, looking for somewhere to place the soup. 'You don't 'ave to pay.' She went into the kitchen and rattled around looking for pots and plates.

'You're very kind,' he said. 'But why do I need noodle soup?'

'Wife gone,' she said.

Did they all know? And what did they think? Did they think that Becca had gone for good?

'Only temporarily,' Bill muttered, watching the taxi dancer heating up the noodle soup.

The soup was good. Full of vegetables, thick noodles and juicy pieces of pork. She watched him wolf it down, declining his invitation to join him with a Gallic shrug.

'Good chopsteek technique,' she said, turning down the corners of her mouth with approval. The Book City bag caught her eye and she peered inside. 'Ah.' She looked at Bill with a knowing smile. 'Are these for Li JinJin?'

He shook his head, feeling his face redden. 'No,' he said. 'They're for me. I like crossword puzzles.'

She folded her arms, unconvinced. 'Is good soup?'

'It's very good. Thank you, Jenny One.'

'I think he love her very much.' She nodded. Bill kept eating, his eyes on his noodle soup. 'I think he does. I think he leave his wife for Li JinJin. In the end.'

He said nothing, but he saw that Jenny One wanted JinJin to have a happy ending, the ending that had eluded the taxi dancer with the French accent.

And Bill also saw that although the girls of Paradise Mansions scandalised and appalled the expat world he moved in, they all dreamed very conventional dreams—dreams of relationships that lasted, dreams of marriage, and monogamy, and children. At best they were kept women, there was no denying it, but what they really wanted, and what not one of them had, was someone who would stay the night.

'You love 'er,' Jenny One said, and he riled at the casual Chinese use of the word. The way they

191

tossed it around as though it meant nothing, or as though it meant you had a soft spot for someone.

'I love my wife,' Bill said, thinking of the song in the Peace Hotel, and Becca and Holly walking home from school. 'That's who I love.'

'And maybe Li JinJin love you,' Jenny One continued, ignoring him. She was serious now, and he saw that this was the real reason for the visit. It had nothing to do with noodle soup. She had to tell him something, something that he was just too dumb to realise. 'But she has to think about her future,' Jenny One said, and she counted off the strikes against him. 'Married . . . foreigner . . . no future.'

She got up to go. There was nothing else to discuss. Bill thanked her for the soup, saw her out and when Jenny One had gone he went to the last window of the master bedroom and looked down at the courtyard. The silver Porsche was parked and empty. The man had come round, but they were not going out tonight. And in his mind he saw with hideous clarity the image of the man fucking JinJin Li and her loving it, and moaning, and begging for more.

Bill watched the lights in her apartment until they all went out and when that finally happened he stuffed the Book City bag containing all the crossword puzzles into the bottom of the rubbish bin.

And that was the real Shanghai too.

*   *   *

They could walk from Holly's paediatrician in Great Portland Street all the way to Becca's sister's house in Primrose Hill and their feet touched nothing but grass almost all the way.

Becca bought two ice creams by the little lake in Regent's Park, the last ice creams of summer, smelling the zoo in the distance, and London felt like a city built on a human scale, a city where a child could breathe.

They came out of Regent's Park, walked past the zoo and across Prince Albert Road on to Primrose Hill. They were some distance from the zoo when two giraffes suddenly loomed out of nowhere.

'Look, Mummy!' Holly cried. 'The secret giraffes!'

This was what they thought of as one of their family secrets. The giraffes at London Zoo were kept on the far side of the road to the entrance, well away from the main body of the zoo, and it meant that the giraffes could suddenly appear as if by magic, their heads swaying above the trees as if they were free to roam the busy North London streets.

'We saw them with Daddy, didn't we?' Holly said excitedly. 'Remember? We saw the secret giraffes with Daddy.'

'That's right, darling,' Becca said, taking her daughter's hand as they looked up at the giraffes. 'We saw them with Daddy.'

THE CITY OF
LIVERPOOL COLLEGE
LRC

FIFTEEN

The next night the old man called.

The phone was ringing as Bill came through the door, worn down from twelve hours at the office and a few more taking clients down Mao Ming Nan Lu. His spirits sank when he heard the fury in his father's voice. He was too tired for an argument with the old man.

'You have to come back,' the old man told him. 'You have to be with your family.'

How long had he bottled this up? Days? Weeks? Bill could see the old man brooding as he went about his daily routine of shopping, telly and tea. The life of quiet domesticity that always had this great store of rage bubbling under the game shows and the cosy chats at the local supermarket. His father would be angry until the day he died.

'I can't come back, Dad,' Bill said. 'I have a contract. And this is my chance. My big chance to become a partner.'

'I don't understand,' the old man said, and Bill knew that was exactly the problem. The old man didn't understand and he would never understand. Because the old man had broken his back for peanuts all his life. 'Why is becoming a partner so important, Bill? What does that *mean*?'

Bill took a breath, let it go. 'Partners don't work for the firm, Dad,' he said. 'Partners *are* the firm. Partners are not salaried employees. They share in the firm's profits.'

The old man mulled this over. '*If* there are profits,' he said.

'What?'

'If there are profits,' the old man repeated. 'You can only share in profits if there are profits. You can't take a share of air pie and windy pudding, can you? You can't take a percentage of bugger all, can you?'

Bill laughed with disbelief. 'Technically that's

194

true,' he said. 'But it's not going to happen out here. Trust me, Dad. It's not going to happen in Shanghai. The economy is going through the roof over here. The firm has more work than it can handle.'

'I don't know anything about it,' the old man said, 'but I suppose a partner has to share costs as well as profits, doesn't he? I mean, you can't just share the good times, can you? But of course I don't know anything about it.'

How technical did Bill have to make it to show his father that he was a stupid old bastard? He was aware that his head was throbbing. From banging it against a brick wall, he thought. From banging it against the old man.

'You're right, Dad,' Bill said calmly, rubbing his temples. 'A partner is taking on the entire liability of the law firm. That's why there's what's known as a capital call when you become partner. You have to invest in the firm. About £250,000. The firm helps you take out a loan.'

There was a moment of stunned disbelief at the other end. 'You have to take out a loan of a quarter of a million quid when they make you a partner?'

It was more money than the old man had ever seen. It was more money than he could imagine. He lived in a little suburban house that had taken his entire working life to buy. You could buy four of those little houses with that kind of money.

'You invest in the firm so that you are in the same boat as the partners,' Bill said. 'For better or worse, for richer or poorer.'

'Like a marriage,' the old man said.

'Yes, Dad—just like a marriage.'

More silence. And then the real reason for the call.

'Come home,' the old man told him, his voice gruff with emotion. 'Come home now.' It wasn't a suggestion. It was an order. 'Walk away from it, Bill. Your baby needs you.'

'Holly? But she's doing well. Becca told me she's—'

The rage suddenly flared up in the old man, and for a moment Bill believed that his father truly hated him.

'You think you know everything, don't you?' the old man said. 'But you know nothing. Absolutely nothing. Holly's not even staying with her mother. Did you know that?'

Bill felt his stomach fall away. 'What?'

'That's right, Einstein. That's right, Mr bloody know-it-all. The poor little thing has been palmed off on Becca's sister. What do you think about that?'

Becca's sister? Holly was staying with Becca's mad sister? Everything changed every few years or so with the sister. Career, hair colour, man.

Fighting the panic and the anger, Bill got the old man off the line as quickly as he could and tried to call Becca. Engaged.

Probably at the hospital with her father, he thought bitterly. The excuse for everything.

He found the address book and tried calling the number he had for her sister. It was out of date. He called the old man back but he only had Becca's number and Bill hung up without bothering with goodbye.

Why didn't Bill have the sister's number? Because that was another thing that changed with

196

dazzling frequency. Her phone numbers. The mad sister was always changing her phone numbers to shake off her mad ex-boyfriends and sometimes their angry wives.

Bill pictured his daughter staying with her unstable Auntie Sara, and for the first time in this whole sorry mess he was angry with his wife.

What was happening in Sara's life right now? Whose marriage was she currently trying to destroy? What was she into this week—Tantric sex or an organic vegan diet or crack cocaine? It could be anything. Bill didn't care how sick Becca's father was, he didn't care how bad it was getting. There was no excuse to pack Holly off. How could she do such a thing? Somewhere on the other side of the world his daughter was being looked after by Becca's unstable, promiscuous, messed-up sister.

And whoever was living with her.

Bill flung the phone across the room and it came apart with a crash against a copy of Vincent van Gogh's *Sunflowers*.

*   *   *

In the morning he saw that someone had slipped a note under his door. A sheet of 'Hello Kitty' paper folded in half. *Please call me*, it said, and then JinJin's name in both English and Chinese characters and a mobile phone number.

He looked at it for a moment and then screwed it up and tossed it in the bin that still contained the crossword puzzles. This was all bullshit. He was tired of adolescent games, tired of being fed things he never asked for, tired of watching the light in her window.

197

He started getting ready for work. He couldn't call London yet. Too early here, too late there. Whatever way you looked at it, the timing was all wrong.

Then, late on Sunday afternoon, when he had nothing to do but wait for the working week to start, JinJin knocked on his door.

'You know how to work?'

She had a Sony Handycam, still boxed up. It was the latest version of the camera that he had used to record his daughter growing up.

'Any idiot can use one,' he told her.

She nodded happily, holding out the Handycam.

He was the idiot she had chosen.

They went back to her apartment and while Bill charged up the Handycam, she disappeared into the bedroom and eventually came out wearing an immaculate red *qipao* and far too much make-up— some hideous skin-whitening stuff that made her look like a ghost of herself, apple-red blusher, and some sort of sticky goo that made her mouth look all wet. He shook his head, hardly recognising her as the same young woman who never used cosmetics beyond the permanent lines of black mascara around her eyes.

'What do you think?' she said, her natural beauty buried under a thick layer of powder and paint.

'Very nice,' he lied.

JinJin Li had not built all her dreams around the man in the silver Porsche. More than anything, she dreamed of reading the evening news on China Central Television. That would solve all her problems. To sit solemnly behind that desk with a picture of the Shanghai night skyline behind her, reading an autocue that brought glad tidings of

China's latest triumph—she seemed to want this even more than a happy home.

She fussed around the flat until she found a spot for him to film her. They were both nervous. JinJin because she seemed to believe that this was her big chance to break into show business, and Bill because he couldn't work out how to turn on the Handycam. It had been a while since he had filmed his daughter.

When the little red light finally came on he gave JinJin the nod and she delivered a piece to camera about herself in formal Mandarin, while he attempted to keep the Sony Handycam steady. CCTV, the state TV channel, was looking for trainee presenters, and JinJin was looking for a change of career, another life, a way out of Paradise Mansions.

It was a touching and pathetic dream, Bill thought. It reminded him of seeing her refusing to let go of the microphone in the karaoke bar. It seemed a strangely juvenile fantasy, as though there was a neglected part of her that craved attention, that made her want the world to notice her.

But who was he to sneer at anyone's dreams? He felt a surge of unearned pride in her—why shouldn't she be reading the evening news on CCTV? She was more beautiful than the girls they had on CCTV. Or perhaps she just had more life in her.

He lifted the camera and her funny Valentine face filled the frame. Her mouth was too small. Her chin was a little weak. Her black-brown eyes were big and seemed even bigger in the small head that rested on the long lines of her body. Even without the teeth-filled smile she was not quite a classic beauty. Would someone hire her as a TV presenter? He did not know. But as he lowered the camera and kept looking at her, he could see very easily why someone would love her.

'Is there something wrong?' she said.

He shook his head. 'There's nothing wrong, JinJin.'

Her fingertips flew to her face. 'Is it my skin?'

'Your skin is fine,' he said. In truth her troubled skin was invisible to the naked eye under all that make-up.

'Do I look ugly?'

'No,' he said, and laughed shortly at the absurdity of the question. 'You could never look ugly.'

'I have very sensitive skin,' she said, staring at the fingers that had touched her face. 'You're lucky. You don't have sensitive skin.'

'That's true,' he said. 'I have very insensitive skin.' He lifted the camera and then brought it down again. 'But a sensitive heart.'

'Hah,' she said, and her buck-toothed smile came out like the sun. 'English joke.'

'You're lovely, JinJin,' he said. 'Don't you know that? Haven't a thousand guys told you that?'

'Ah,' she said, and he saw the uncertainty in her. 'Being told is not the same as knowing.'

'Is that a wise Chinese saying? Or did you just make it up?'

She grinned. 'It's a wise Chinese saying that I just made up.'

'Okay, take it from the top,' he laughed, framing her face once more. 'But try breathing this time. You're allowed to breathe.'

'Pardon?' She said *pardon* when she wanted something repeated. He didn't know anyone who said *Pardon?*

'Let's just do it again,' he said.

And they did, and his heart sank because he saw that perhaps she wouldn't be reading the evening news on CCTV. Because all her quirky grace and charm and humour and warmth and loveliness seemed to evaporate the moment the red light came on. And because she was too nervous, and the nerves did not diminish as they did take after take. And because her skin, like her ambitions of TV glory, was strangely adolescent—it was young, troubled skin that was prone to sudden rashes and eruptions.

Her nerves made him nervous too. When he gave her the nod, her smile—that lovely, natural toothy-goofy smile—became frozen in a cold rictus grin, and she stumbled over her words and couldn't keep the tremor of fear from her voice.

She wasn't good enough. That was the truth. But maybe she could improve, break through the fear barrier, do something about her difficult skin. For some reason he wanted to have faith in her.

When they had finished filming, she sat him at the table in the tiny kitchen and brought two steaming bowls of congee. She told him that congee, rice porridge, was all she ever ate when she was home alone.

'I go to many restaurants,' she said. 'But when I am in my home, I like simple food.'

'I know what you mean,' he said, watching her pour two cups of green tea. 'I go out to a lot of restaurants.'

'With your wife?' she said, not looking at him.

'Sometimes,' he said. He reached for the cup but it was too hot to hold and he quickly pulled his hand away. 'But mostly with clients.'

'It doesn't need to be rich all the time,' she said.

Then he heard the key in the door and the man came in. He was suddenly there with them. The unknown man in the silver Porsche.

He gawped dumbly at JinJin and Bill as if equally surprised to find them here. Bill stared back at him, wondering why he was shocked to discover the man had a key. Of course he had a key. This was his place and he owned it all, including fixtures and fittings.

JinJin flew to the man's side, and although she did not kiss him, she laughed and took his arm in a proprietorial way that somehow seemed more intimate than a kiss would have been, and far worse.

She babbled a happy explanation about what they had been doing, then showed the man an ad in a Chinese newspaper as if to prove she wasn't lying.

Bill watched JinJin fussing around the man— getting him settled on the sofa, giving him the Handycam so that he might examine it and give his approval, then going off to prepare fresh tea, all the while chatting away—and Bill fought back emotions he had no wish to feel.

He was disappointed in her. After those long moments watching the man make himself at home, he was bitterly disappointed in her. He did not want to feel this way, but he couldn't help it.

She gave up teaching for this guy? She left those children who adored her for him? She played the golden canary for somebody as ordinary as this?

This was the guy she gave her body to?

The two men nodded at each other, and Bill fought back the bile, his face seized with a disgusted grin of embarrassment and loathing. The man was around forty. No spring chicken, Bill thought. Prematurely grey-haired, but without the physical puffiness that a lot of successful Chinese businessmen toted around. He was a big man—Bill wasn't sure why that surprised him. Bill also wondered if he had disguised the fact that he despised the man on sight.

The man was dressed in the smart-casual style of the affluent Asian male. Polo shirt, grey flannel trousers, shoes so polished you could see your face in them—the off-duty-Japanese-salaryman look that all the new Chinese big shots were adopting as their own. He didn't speak English, and made no attempt to shake Bill's hand, but there was no hostility there. The man simply did not care. Bill Holden was nothing to him. Just a dumb big-nosed pinky neighbour who had been roped in to do a domestic chore.

No threat, no rival, no problem.

Without even being asked, JinJin had clearly offered the man an explanation of what they were doing and the man accepted it. It wasn't a big deal to him. Bill's meaningless presence in JinJin's flat had no impact whatsoever on his life, or his plans for the evening.

And Bill wondered what Becca would have thought if she had walked in on him pointing a brand-new Sony Handycam at the face of JinJin Li.

His wife would have seen right through him.

*　　　*　　　*

This is what he wondered. He wondered if every marriage in the world became less and less about the man and the woman and more and more about their child, or if that was just his marriage.

In the afternoon Becca called him at work.

Right in the middle of a crisis meeting, a meeting called because back in the UK the press had picked up on the soaring number of industrial accidents in the factories of China, all those men and women who were losing eyes, limbs and lives in the workshop of the world so that the West could have their cheap gadgets and trainers and rock-bottom underpants. Foreign investors in China were suddenly being made aware of the phrase *ethical shopping*, and up at the firm they knew that this could only be bad for business. Something had to be done.

But when Bill saw Becca's number on his phone, he stood up at the conference table with all of them there, Devlin and Shane and Nancy and Mad Mitch, and he did not care what it looked like. No meeting was more important than his daughter.

'Sorry, I have to take this,' he said, and stepped outside the conference room, and then kept walking, just to be moving, and to stop them from hearing.

'Bill?'

She sounded down, way down, and he unexpectedly felt a flood of the old love, the original love, the feeling that was there from the start. Just one word and he could read her mood. She said his name and he felt it, knew it with total certainty—it was her father.

'Your dad,' he said. 'What's happened, Bec?'

But it wasn't her father. He was wrong.

'My dad's actually doing okay,' Becca said, so breezy that Bill felt like a fool. 'He went to the hospital for his test, but they let him come back home until his cardiologist has looked at the results.'

Then there's no excuse, Bill thought. There is just no excuse.

'So what's happening with Holly?'

Becca laughed, and it infuriated him. 'She's fine. She's so grown up. She misses you, Bill. She misses her daddy. She misses it when you throw her around. I can't do that with her. Not the way you can.'

He had forgotten about the throwing around. How could he have forgotten that? His daughter would wrap her arms around his neck and he would let her go, and she would scream and squeal as her fingers slipped away and she started to fall, and then—just at the moment she let go—he would catch her and swing her up over his shoulder, and upside down, and into his arms, her eyes inches from his own.

'I talked to my old man,' he said, suddenly hoping that it wasn't true and that perhaps the old man had got his ancient wires crossed, the silly old bastard, perhaps Holly had just been shunted off to the mad sister for one night, while Becca's father had his tests. 'My old man said that Holly was staying with your sister.' It always seemed unnatural to call her by her name, as though nothing could fit her better than *mad sister*. 'With Sara,' he said.

'She is,' Becca said, brightening, as if this were nothing but good news. 'And Sara's with this new

205

guy, and he's just great with Sara's kids and with Holly.'

Some guy? Some fucking *guy*?

It got worse.

It got far worse than Bill had ever imagined. It got so bad that he could hardly contain his feelings.

'I'm coming back,' Bill said. 'Next flight. Give me Sara's address.'

'Why?'

'Because if you can't take care of her, then I will.'

'You're not coming back,' she said. 'You don't need to come back. Look, I know how you feel about Sara. And it's true she has had problems in the past. But she's calmed down so much over the last few years. Since she stopped drinking and the other stuff, she's so much nicer, so much more herself. Therapy has done wonders for her. And Holly is totally safe and happy, and I was going to tell you—really—but I knew you'd fret.'

Then he lost it. 'You knew I'd fret? I'm doing more than fret, Becca. When were you going to tell me? And let me know when I'm fretting too much for you.'

'But it's only until my dad is well enough to take care of himself.' Genuinely astounded that he should feel this way. It drove him crazy. 'And they're all really great with Holly. They love her so much. Sara. Her kids. All of them. Especially Sara's partner.'

Sara's partner.

Sara's fucking partner.

'It's temporary, Bill,' Becca said, very calm, and wanting him to be calm too. 'Until my dad is a little better. And Holly's very happy. Please believe me.'

'I don't like it.'

And then her sighing. Her sighing was driving him nuts. It would be wonderful if he never heard her sigh again.

'What don't you like?'

'I don't like Holly being with strangers.'

'My sister is not a stranger.'

'No, she's a flake. She's a lunatic. Always has been. One minute she's married, the next she's a lesbian—'

'Oh, that was just a phase after her first marriage broke up. She's settled down a lot, Bill. Do you think I'd put Holly somewhere there was any sort of danger? Sara's been a great help to me. You have to trust me on this.'

But he didn't trust her on this.

'I don't like it,' he said. 'She should be with you.'

'But I've been with my dad.'

'I still don't like it.'

Then her patience was gone, and she was sick and tired of him, and there was the coldness that was always waiting there to greet him when he stepped too far out of line.

'But you're not here, are you?' she said. 'So I'm the one who has to deal with it.'

'If anything happens to Holly,' he said quietly, 'I'll never forgive you.'

'Oh fuck you, Bill. How dare you suggest I would put my daughter in any kind of danger? If you want to know the truth, she's having a lovely time. More fun than she ever has with us. Sara's family eat their meals together, they spend time together—'

'And we don't? Why's that, Becca? Because I'm working twelve hours a day to give you a lifestyle of the rich and famous.'

'You think that because you make the money

207

you're excused all other duties.'

'You're always telling me what I think.'

'Does that annoy you?'

'No, I love it. Really. Truly. I fucking love it.' He looked up and saw Shane waiting at the other end of the corridor. Beyond him the others were waiting for him in the conference room. 'You should put Holly first,' Bill said, turning his back on Shane. 'You should put her before everything.'

'I do, Bill, and one day you'll realise that,' she said. 'What about you? What's your number one priority? Sara and I were discussing this last night. Some men clock off with their family as soon as they clock in at the office.'

'Don't you ever discuss me or my business with that crazy bitch,' he shouted, and heard the line go dead. A hand lightly touched his shoulder. He turned to look at Shane's face.

'Family all right, mate?' his friend said.

'Never been better, mate,' said Bill.

*   *   *

Becca watched Sarfraz Khan walking towards them down the corridor of the paediatric clinic with a big smile and for a long moment she thought she was seeing things.

'What are you doing here?' she said, thinking how rude that sounded.

'Seeing some friends,' he said. He crouched down to say hello to Holly. He was good at that, Becca thought. He always arranged himself so that he was on the same level as the child. 'I'm getting the train up to Liverpool tomorrow morning.' Something passed briefly across his face. 'My mother hasn't been well.'

He stood up and looked away, running a hand through his glossy black hair, and she recognised that feeling. The guilt of the absent adult child.

Becca was aware of her sister staring at her, and at Sarfraz Khan, and she hastily made the introductions. The doctor shook Sara's hand, his eyes flicking almost imperceptibly over her cropped orange hair.

'Everything all right?' he asked Becca, and she knew he was talking about Holly.

'Good,' Becca said. 'Very good. No more attacks. She likes being back in London. Misses her father, of course.'

'Of course,' he said, and he dropped into his professional squat again, smiling at Holly. 'How was that long plane journey?'

'I saw the cockpit,' she said.

'Did you?' he said.

'It's where the pilot goes,' she nodded. 'They invited me.'

'Wow,' he said, standing up and smiling at Becca. 'I wish I got invitations like that.' He hesitated for a moment, as if summoning up his courage. 'You're not free for a quick coffee, are you? It turns out my old friends here have other plans.' He tried to make a joke of it. 'How quickly they forget.' He looked at Holly and Sara. 'I mean—all of us. If you're free.'

Becca shook her head. 'Sorry, I can't.'

'Oh go on,' Sara said, nudging her, and Becca caught a glimpse of the old recklessness. 'I'll take Holly home and you have coffee with your friend.' She turned to Khan. 'She's hardly been out of the house since she came back, unless it's to see some kind of doctor.'

'Well, he's a doctor too, of course,' Becca said, but somehow it was settled. Becca and Sarfraz watched Sara and Holly walking up Great Portland Street until they disappeared into Regent's Park. Then he turned to her and clapped his hands. She didn't think she had ever seen an Indian blush before.

'Starbucks?' he said. 'There's one right across the street from my hotel.'

Becca grimaced. 'Don't we see enough of Starbucks in Shanghai?' she said.

'Then the café at my place,' he said, and she found herself accompanying him to his hotel. *Should have gone to Starbucks,* she thought.

He had a room at the Langham on Portland Place. There was a café in the lobby, full of tourists buttering scones and enjoying high tea. They ordered their coffee and she started to relax. Khan was so clearly a decent man, and he was so open about his guilt about his mother—struggling with the early stages of MS while her only son was on the other side of the world—that she found herself opening up and telling him how torn she also felt. Torn between their family life in Shanghai and her responsibility in London, between the roles of mother and daughter and wife.

'Sometimes I just don't know what to do,' Becca said. 'No, that's not true—I never really know what to do.' She stared at her coffee cup. 'Because the most important things in my life—my father, my husband, my daughter—are all pulling me in different directions.'

Khan stared at her thoughtfully, and she thought that mentioning Bill had subdued him somewhat.

And she was glad about that because she did not want him to confuse a coffee break with a date. But then she realised that he was just trying to remember something.

'This is what you shall do,' he said.

'Excuse me?'

'This is what you shall do,' he said again. 'Love the earth and the sun and the animals, despise riches, give alms to every one that asks, stand up for the stupid and crazy, devote your income and labour to others, hate tyrants, argue not concerning god, have patience and indulgence toward the people, take off your hat to nothing known or unknown or to any man or number of men.'

'Well, thanks for the advice,' Becca said. 'I'll certainly keep all that in mind.'

He was crestfallen. 'Don't you like it?' he said.

'I think it's one of the most beautiful things I've ever heard in my life,' she said. 'What is it? A poem?'

He nodded. 'Walt Whitman. Did you know he was a doctor of sorts? Cared for the injured and the dying during the Civil War. It was the defining experience of his life.'

He called for the bill and tried to put it on his room but Becca insisted on paying it. She was glad he didn't offer much of a fight. When they were in the lobby she said she hoped that things worked out with his mother and his trip up to Liverpool.

'Take good care of your mum,' she said.

'Go freely with powerful uneducated persons,' he said, stepping sideways to avoid a bellhop wheeling a stack of suitcases, 'and with the young and with mothers of families.'

211

And Becca thought—a doctor who quotes poetry.

'Read these leaves in the open air every season of every year of your life,' he said, as if she was no longer there, 're-examine all you have been told at school or church or in any book, dismiss whatever insults your own soul, and your very flesh shall be a great poem . . .'

She wasn't sure how it happened.

She told him that she was going to the little bookshop in Primrose Hill first thing in the morning to buy everything she could find by Walt Whitman. And Khan said he had a copy of the collected works in his hotel room and he wanted Becca to have it.

She said *oh really that's okay no thanks* but he insisted, and she didn't want to make a big deal out of it. That would have been even worse. So they walked through the gilded old lobby of the Langham because somehow it would have seemed inappropriate to wait in the lobby while he went off to fetch Walt Whitman and then they got into the mirrored lift and said nothing as the floor lights ascended and they went up to his room.

Khan let himself into the hotel room. Becca followed him. It was a suite, far larger than she had been expecting.

'They upgraded me,' he said, picking up the chocolate truffle that had been placed on his pillow. 'I always stay here when I get back from Shanghai on my way up to Liverpool. It's too far all in one day.' He was talking too much. He turned to face Becca and they stared at each other for a moment and then he popped the chocolate in his mouth. 'I'll get you that book,' he said through a

212

mouthful of chocolate, and went into the other room.

She went to the window and stared out at the lights of Broadcasting House, the flags flying outside the embassies, the long sweep of Portland Place leading all the way to Regent's Park, Primrose Hill and the secret giraffes.

And when Khan came back with the book in his hands, Becca was gone.

SIXTEEN

The lift doors opened and suddenly she was standing there.

JinJin looked from Bill's face to the suitcase in his hand, her all-conquering smile not wavering. She made no attempt to leave the lift. The doors began to close. Bill stuck out a foot and the doors clunked open again. JinJin stepped out, the doors closing behind her.

'I was bringing this for you,' she said, offering him a small square of plastic. There was a tiny DVD inside. 'The film we made,' she explained. 'It's very good, William.'

Bill smiled politely. 'I'll watch it when I get back,' he said, taking it with his free hand.

JinJin looked again at his suitcase. 'Holiday?' she asked him. 'Holiday in London?'

He slipped the DVD inside his jacket. 'Business trip,' he said. 'Excuse me.'

She stepped aside and he hit the down button. She looked disappointed but she was holding on to the smile. 'You are a good film maker,' she said.

'I look forward to seeing it,' he said, glancing at his watch. Tiger should be waiting for him downstairs. The lift came and they stepped inside together. 'When I've watched it I'll drop it in your mailbox,' he said as the lift began to descend.

'You can bring it to me,' she said. There was still some of the smile left. 'Bring it to me anytime you are free.' Her face brightened. 'We could watch it together!'

Bill nodded. 'I might just drop it in the mailbox,' he said.

They reached the ground floor. The lift doors opened and he saw that Tiger was there, the engine running and ready to drive him to the airport.

'As you wish,' said JinJin.

They stood there in awkward silence, the lift behind them and the glass doors to the courtyard in front of them. When they went through those doors they would go their separate ways.

'Where are you off to?' she said, and something about her choice of phrase made his heart feel like it was being squeezed. It sounded like something his mother would have said.

What a shame, he thought. What a shame we can only ever be friends.

'The Pearl River Delta,' he said. 'Shenzhen.'

She pulled a face and it was full of the northerner's instinctive distrust of southerners. 'Be careful,' she said. 'Many bad people down there.'

He laughed. 'I'll be all right,' he said. 'You be careful.' He found himself fumbling for the words. 'Drive safely and everything.'

He saw the sudden sting of tears in her eyes, like a child just told that their best friend is moving to a new school.

'Why are you crying?' he said.

She sniffed and wiped her eyes with the back of her hand. 'I'm not,' she insisted.

He looked out at Tiger. 'I have to go,' he said, reaching out to touch one of those long slim arms.

'I know you do,' she said, abruptly pulling away, and she stepped through the automatic glass doors with a swish of air.

He watched her walking across the courtyard of Paradise Mansions with that strange, awkward gait of hers, like a colt that was still getting used to the length of its legs, and she had one hand lifted to shield her face against the merciless morning sun, as though that was another one of the things that she had never really got used to.

*   *   *

Their car came to a halt, and beyond the stalled traffic ahead Bill could see the lorry on its side, its nearside wheels in a ditch.

The driver stood next to it, staring at his vehicle in bewilderment, as if he could not quite believe this betrayal. He was still holding the portable DVD player that he had been watching at the wheel when he went off the road.

It was a fruit lorry, and it blocked the road from Shenzhen to the factory of the Happy Trousers Trading Company. A garish avalanche was spread across the road, a vivid mass of apples, bananas, melons, plums, oranges, mangoes and lychees that had tipped out of their cardboard boxes but remained in their individual wrappers of cellophane and paper, as if tempting the palates of the bystanders who had gathered to gawp by the side of the road.

The accident must have happened just a few minutes ago, because there was no sign of the Public Security Bureau. Some of the crowd stirred into motion. While the men stood and watched, the women began stepping into the road and gathering up the fruit, working quickly, anxious to do their looting before the cops came. But there was such an abundance of fruit that for all they gathered up, they crushed even more underfoot.

Bill was sitting in the passenger seat, with Nancy Deng and Mad Mitch in the back. He turned to the driver impatiently. The man was staring blankly at the scene of fruity destruction. Bill missed Tiger.

'Is there another road, another way?' he said, and Nancy leaned forward, translating into Cantonese.

Mad Mitch placed a reassuring hand on Bill's shoulder. 'Slow down, Bill,' the firm's oldest associate lawyer advised him. 'We'll get there soon enough.'

Bill narrowed his eyes. Mitch shouldn't even be here. Shane should be fronting this trip. But Shane, still in a lot of pain, would not be flying to Shenzhen for a trip to the Happy Trousers Trading Company. So Mitch was here in his place, although Bill had seniority.

'Can't slow down, Mitch,' Bill said lightly. I might end up like you, he thought. I might end up like my father.

Then the PSB were suddenly on the scene, shooing the looters away and clearing a path for all the cars containing important foreigners on their way to do business in the free-trade zone.

216

Bill stared out at the blank faces of the looters, and at the fruit that still covered the road but was now reduced to a vivid pulp of red and gold, the colours of China.

The car began to move.

*   *   *

An ethical audit. That's what they called it. That's what they were there for.

One of the firm's clients had asked for an ethical audit of the Happy Trousers Trading Company, a moral accounting to weigh up the pros and cons of making cheap clothes for the West using factory workers wearing rags.

'It's an industrial revolution,' Devlin had told them, looking pained. 'And unfortunately you don't get too many paid vacations and tea breaks during an industrial revolution.'

So Nancy took notes as a podgy manager with a white nylon shirt and a paralysed grin gave them a guided tour of the factory.

They peered into a dead-aired dormitory where workers were sleeping twelve wooden boxes to a room, piled high in four triple-tier bunks. The sudden light produced snake-like stirring of lethargic flesh, and it made Bill shiver. He thought of slave ships, he thought of concentration camps. He looked at Nancy's face. It revealed nothing. They closed the door and moved on.

It's like something from another century, Bill thought, and tried to steel himself. He supposed he was going to have to get used to this kind of thing. Foreign companies who were under pressure from consumers in their own country to ensure that their factories were not breaching Chinese law, International Labour Organisation rules, and human decency were often requesting ethical audits now.

They saw the cold-water taps where the workers washed, displayed with grotesque pride by the grinning factory manager. They saw the gruel that the workers queued for in a stinking canteen. They saw the dull-eyed stare of men and women who had just pulled two shifts back-to-back. And Bill saw with a sinking feeling that the glittering malls of the Bund and the shining towers of Pudong and the whole PRC gold rush were built on these things.

But Bill also saw the girls in the canteen sharing a joke. He saw small pictures of well-scrubbed children pinned to the walls of the fetid, overcrowded dorms. And as the afternoon shift poured through the gates, he watched a boy and girl worker pair off and stand together by the factory wall, their hands entwined. And he thought that perhaps Devlin was right.

Although the factory conditions were like something from the nineteenth century he wondered if these workers would really have been better off staying in the villages. He just didn't know. He had no certainty left in him. And he could almost hear Devlin telling him that fifty years ago millions of them were starving thanks to the Great Leap Forward, and that now they were happy to have a full belly and a job to go to.

Bill wanted to believe him.

The manager grinned confidently at the lawyers from Shanghai. The man had done many ethical audits before, and in broken English he demonstrated that he knew his lines perfectly. He knew how to salve their troubled minds, Bill thought, he knew how to settle their weak Western stomachs. Bill suspected that these visits changed nothing much apart from the factory manager's ability to more fluently mouth any assurances the big-nosed pinkies wanted to hear. But without these visits it could have been even worse. Who knew?

They entered a room where hundreds of young women sat hunched behind weaving machines, their ponytailed heads half-hidden behind enormous reels of yellow cotton. The women looked grubby, badly fed, used up. Their hair, their teeth, their skin—it all looked worn out, although most of them were not out of their teens.

They were not like JinJin Li. They did not have the look. Not the look of the girls in Paradise Mansions, the look of the women in Shanghai. They had the other kind of look, the look that Chinese women more frequently had—the look of women who had grown old before they were ever really young. The look, Bill thought, of a piece of fruit with all the juice sucked out. The din their machines made was deafening, like being inside a giant dustbin that had been thrown from a cliff. Mad Mitch said something and Bill shook his head. Conversation was impossible. Even stringing two thoughts together was difficult in the midst of that noise.

Then they were in a room full of young men. Everybody was so young. Bill wondered—where were all the old people? Where were the towns and the villages and the farms that these young men had left behind? And what did they look like with all the young people gone?

The noise was even louder in here, if that was possible. Gigantic presses slammed down on pieces of moulded rubber as they made their steady journey down the assembly line.

Young men sorted and shifted trainers as they passed by, their eyes cast down, fussing over the world-famous brand name, lavishing them with their unbroken attention. There was a smell of burning rubber in the air. There was no talking or eye contact. There was just the endless rumble of the assembly line, and the slamming of the presses, which came down with a whoosh of compressed air, like some giant door being slammed shut in hell.

And then, piercing all the industrial clamour, there was the scream.

At first it did not seem human. At first it sounded as though it was a piece of malfunctioning machinery. High-pitched, whining, like metal grinding against metal. But then the assembly line ground to a halt, and all eyes were looking to the far side of the room where a young man was clutching his arm just above the elbow, his face deathly white and eyes wide with disbelief and dread.

He was being supported by two of his friends. They were both babbling—offering explanations, calling for help, Bill couldn't tell. One of them was crying. He looked up and saw that Nancy was already on her phone, calling an ambulance.

The injured man was eased to the floor and laid on his side. He was still clutching his arm. Below the elbow it was a mangled pulp of flesh and bone. The factory manager knelt by the man's side and a thick scrum of workers gathered around to offer advice and opinions but mostly just to watch. Then the paramedics were there and the man was taken away on a gurney. There was nothing else to see. Orders were given, and the assembly line jolted back to life. Bill saw that a woman was cleaning the press where the man had worked.

The factory manager escorted them to their car. His smile didn't falter as he assured them that working practices were even now being reviewed to ensure that such an accident could never happen again. And Bill just wanted to be gone.

This was a cruel, hard, grubby place and he could not stand the thought that he was a part of it. They were driven back to the hotel and Bill stood under the lukewarm shower for a long while. By the time Mad Mitch met him in the bar a few hours later he was halfway to drunk.

'He lost his arm,' Bill said. 'That boy in the factory. Nancy called the hospital. They had to amputate his arm.'

Mitch nodded. 'She told me.' There was a small forest of green Tsingtao bottles in front of Bill. Mitch sat on the stool next to him and signalled for two more.

'All for a pair of trainers,' Bill said. 'All for some cheap clobber to flog to the West.'

Mitch shook his head. 'There's no such thing as cheap clothes,' he said. 'The real price isn't paid by the people who buy the stuff, it's paid by the people who make it.' He took a sip of his beer. 'But we're not here for them, are we? We're here for our clients.'

Bill looked at him with despair. 'Then what do we tell the client?'

'Tell them what we saw,' Mad Mitch said. 'Tell them exactly what we saw. Tell them the Happy Trousers Factory resembles a nineteenth-century workhouse. Tell them that you would need to be Charles Dickens to do the place justice.'

'And what will that change?'

'Bugger all,' said Mad Mitch. 'The client likes the profit margins he gets out here. And his customers like rock-bottom prices. The West wants it both ways. Dirt-cheap products and a clean conscience. Nobody is going to stop doing business here. Why should they? We are not going to stop doing business here, are we?'

'But I don't see why that means the locals have to be on two dollars a day,' Bill said. 'I don't see why that means some kid has to lose an arm.' He drained his beer. 'Can't we do something?'

'Like what?' Mitch said. He hadn't touched his drink.

'You saw them in there,' Bill said. 'Peasants straight off the farm working fourteen hours a day. Doing double and triple shifts till they drop. Getting £50 a month with one day off. And that factory manager only gives a toss when he wants to keep our clients off his back. What can we do? Do him for a start.'

'Perhaps the West can't have it both ways,' Mad Mitch said. 'Perhaps you can't have dirt-cheap trainers and Chinese factories where the workers get treated like human beings. And perhaps our client only cares when he wants to keep the press off his back. Look—if the client gets too much bad publicity here, what do you think is going to happen? They'll just ship the factory to Vietnam. Or India.'

'But there are rules about working practices,' Bill said. 'There are regulations about safety. Every day of the year that place breaches International Labour Organisation rules, not to mention Chinese law. The boy who lost an arm should sue.' Bill nearly fell off his stool and steadied himself with a smile. 'Know any good lawyers, Mitch?'

The older man sipped his Tsingtao carefully.

'We're lawyers in a country with no rule of law,' Mad Mitch said. 'Where we come from, the courts are independent and have authority over all. Judges protect the freedoms of individuals against the state. Here it's just not like that. The PRC operates a Communist legal system. Nobody with any kind of power—financial, political or military—considers themselves bound by any court rulings they don't like. Where the rule of law doesn't apply, legal solutions are always going to be imperfect. That boy who lost an arm wouldn't stand a chance.'

Bill shook his head. 'Can I ask you something, Mitch?' he said.

'Go ahead.'

'Why did you never make partner? What happened there?' Bill laughed, trying to keep it light. 'You slow down once too often?'

Mitch laughed along with him. 'Up at the firm they say that I lacked the stamina for Hong Kong and the stomach for Shanghai. And I think that's probably a fair and reasonable assessment. But also, practising law is a service industry and I never really understood that. I thought it was about truth, justice, decency and all that old-fashioned stuff.' He raised his glass in a toast. 'And I was wrong.'

Nancy arrived in the bar and Bill carefully climbed off his bar stool. He knew it was going to take a supreme effort to avoid falling on his face.

'You coming in to dinner?' he asked Mitch.

Mitch shook his head, grimacing, and looked at the younger man with wonder.

'You can still eat?' Mitch said. 'After what we saw today?'

Bill nodded, surprised, and Mad Mitch gently patted his arm.

'Don't worry, Bill,' he said. 'There's no doubt about you making partner.'

*   *   *

The hotel's restaurant was empty apart from a group of drunken Russians eating their sweet-and-sour pork with knives and forks. Bill and Nancy turned around and were about to leave when he noticed the only other diner was Alice Greene. Bill went over to her table and she raised her chopsticks in salute.

'Butterfield, Hunt and West doing business in Shenzhen, the sweatshop of the world,' she said. 'Who would have thought it?'

Bill laughed. 'A hack chasing an ambulance,' he said. 'What are the odds of that? And isn't it the *workshop* of the world? What did you do? Fly down from Pudong this morning? I didn't see you on the flight.'

'I got the train from Hong Kong,' Alice said. 'I've been touching base with my paper. They sent me over when we heard about the accident. Any comment on the man who lost his arm?'

'It's obviously a tragic accident,' Bill said, aware

224

that anything he said could be used against him. He thought of the deep-frozen grin on the manager's face, and how it had never faltered. 'The factory have already launched an investigation.'

Alice nodded with approval. 'You're getting very good, Bill.' She carried on tucking into her honey-roast pork. 'Any comment from your clients?'

He had given her enough. 'I haven't had the chance to speak to our clients,' he said. 'I'm sure they'll be devastated.'

The journalist looked unconvinced. 'Well, I don't know if they'll be exactly *devastated*, Bill. A dozen workers a day lose a limb in the factories of Shenzhen. A dozen a day! And they're ten times more likely to die than their counterparts in Europe.'

It's so easy, he thought with a flash of anger. It's so easy when you are that certain. 'Would you like it better if they were all unemployed?' he said.

'I would prefer it if these poor bastards were treated like human beings,' she said.

Bill was aware of Nancy hovering awkwardly behind him. He introduced the two women and Alice smiled up at Nancy.

'Will you join our Russian friends and I for dinner?' she said, glancing over at the other occupied table. One of the Russians was entertaining his friends by pulling the waitress's ponytail as she attempted to pour their Tsingtaos. 'They're enormous fun. Just before you arrived one of them hit me on the back of the head with a spring roll.'

But Bill declined, and they left Alice and the Russians in the cavernous hotel restaurant and went out into the teeming streets of Shenzhen, a world of noise that smelled of diesel fumes and roast duck.

He looked at Nancy.

'That's a friend of the family,' he said apologetically. 'My wife's side.'

Nancy nodded. 'I saw your wife,' she said as they began to move through the evening crowd. 'I saw Mrs Holden.'

Bill nodded. 'That dinner on the Bund.' He remembered holding hands with Becca out on the deck, the skyline of Pudong shining like their shared vision of the future. It seemed like a long time ago.

'No, before that night,' Nancy said. 'She didn't remember me, but I remembered her.' She was speaking quickly now, relaying something that he could tell she had kept to herself for a long time. 'Just after you came over. In the museum. The museum on Huangpi Lu in Xintiandi. You know the one?'

Bill thought about it.

'Is that where the Party first met?' he said.

Nancy nodded. 'I think your wife is very kind,' she said, and Bill was again baffled by the weight the Chinese gave to certain words. They used words like *kind* and *love* in a way that seemed to change their meaning, or drain them of meaning altogether. But Nancy Deng nodded emphatically. She knew what she meant. 'Your wife must be very kind to be interested in that place.'

Bill nodded, feeling stupid. 'She's a sweetheart, all right,' he said. The crowds and the smell of roast meat and clogged traffic were starting to make him feel claustrophobic. They didn't seem to

226

trouble Nancy.

'I like that place very much,' she was saying happily. 'Not many people are so interested. That museum always empty. But I think—very interesting place. They want justice. People forget that now. That place—my high school took us there—it is why I became a lawyer.'

Bill thought of Mad Mitch and his belief in the essential goodness of the law.

'China not such a fair place then, and not such a fair place now,' Nancy said. 'You saw the factory.' She snorted with contempt, shaking her head. 'The dogs of the rich live better than the children of the poor.'

Bill stopped walking. 'Then why do they come to work at the factory?' It was a stupid question, and he already knew the answer.

'Because they all want to be part of the new China,' Nancy said. 'They have seen it on TV.'

He looked at her. Fifty years ago she would have joined the Party. Now she tried to make her country a better place by studying at the Tsinghua University Law School and going to work for Butterfield, Hunt and West.

'Is that why you became a lawyer?' he said. 'To change the world?'

'You are laughing at me,' she said.

He shook his head. 'I would never laugh at you,' Bill said.

They began moving with the crowds, following the smell of roast duck.

'My father thought that being a lawyer was a sacred profession,' she said. 'Like being a doctor. And not just—I don't know—a businessman.'

'Your father must be a good man.'

227

She shrugged with embarrassment. They had stopped at a line of food stalls. Nancy ordered for both of them. Some chicken dumplings, and what looked like slices of roast duck on rice.

'I have no big dreams,' Nancy said. 'I know I am unimportant. But I think perhaps my country's future is still to be decided. It doesn't matter what anyone says. Nothing is inevitable in China.'

'One thing I don't understand,' Bill said. 'Up in Yangdong, why don't the local government just give those farmers the compensation they have coming to them? Why cheat them?'

She had bought two plates of thin slices of roast duck on rice, and she handed one to Bill with a pair of plastic chopsticks.

'I blame Confucius,' Nancy smiled. 'Confucius emphasised loyalty to family above duty to society. That's very Chinese—perhaps hard for you to understand. Why give something to a stranger when you can keep it for your own people without fear of punishment? That's what they think. Someone like Chairman Sun. That's what he thinks.' She dug a heap of meat and rice on to her chopsticks and paused with it before her mouth. 'In China the important men hate everyone's corruption but their own.'

'I saw this couple when we were at the factory,' Bill said. 'A young man and woman, they looked like they had just come off work, and I wondered if their lives would have been better if they had stayed in whatever little place they come from. And I don't know.' He stared at her helplessly. 'I really don't know.'

Nancy Deng chewed thoughtfully. 'Then they never meet.'

He laughed. 'That's one way of looking at it.' He began to eat. It was the best duck he had ever tasted. 'This is good,' he said. He watched her order a plate of glossy green *choi sam*, slick with oyster sauce. 'But what's going to happen in China?' he said. 'Come on—you're a lawyer. What's your educated guess?'

Nancy nodded emphatically. 'The old men will die,' she said. 'That's the one certainty. The old men will die. But who knows when? Old men can live for a long time.'

Then they did not talk for a while, because they were both shovelling the piping hot food into their mouths. He smiled gratefully as Nancy passed him a plate of lychees. He felt better than he had all day.

Talking with Nancy Deng on that street corner in Shenzhen, hearing this young woman speak with careful optimism about her country's future, breathing the night air full of diesel and duck, eating what the people eat—here at last was the real China.

They walked back to their hotel and when Bill was alone in his room he took out the three photos that he carried everywhere.

Holly looking adorably dishevelled in her nursery school uniform a year ago. Becca and Holly on that beach in the Caribbean two years back, his daughter grinning under a pink Foreign Legion hat, and his wife in big shades and that orange shift thing, her hair pulled back and tucked into a chignon, looking like a movie star from the fifties. And Holly as a stern-faced, slightly damp baby, wrapped in a white towelling robe, glaring at the camera on bath night. He looked at the photos of

229

his family for a while and then he propped them up on his little hotel desk, like his own private barricade against the world that was out there beyond the window.

He thought of Becca's eyes, as blue as pieces of sky, and he knew that he would not see JinJin Li when he returned to Shanghai. Or rather, he would still see her—coming and going from Paradise Mansions, across a crowded restaurant on the Bund, walking through the ornate lobby of some new hotel—and he would be polite, but he would keep his distance. He would not see her smile, or the long lines of her body, or the way her eyes seemed to light up when she looked at him. He would harden his heart and he would not see these things and he would wait for his wife to return, and look at him once more with eyes so blue they looked like pieces of sky.

SEVENTEEN

The stomach cramps woke him, tight spasms of pain that dragged him from sleep and sent him staggering blindly towards the bathroom.

Bill knelt in front of the toilet and threw up until he was empty, shivering and bewildered with the sweat pouring from him, and then he left the bathroom, came straight back and tried to throw up some more, retching on an empty stomach until he was spitting up blood.

He shuffled back to the bedroom and flopped on to the bed. An alarm was ringing in his ears and it took him a few dazed seconds to realise that it was only the clock. Where was he? He was in Shanghai. It was Monday morning. It was time to go to work.

He went back to the bathroom and made an effort to shower and shave. He must have cut his face because when he was forced to sink back to his knees, his drained stomach straining to be free of him, a few beads of blood ran down his chin and stained the tiled floor.

He dressed with shaking hands and lay back on the bed, worn out and sweaty. The spare room revolved around him. He stood up and it stopped. Muttering encouragement, Bill let himself out of the apartment, light-headed and stomach aching.

In the lift he realised that his legs were not all they should be and propped himself up against the door until it opened on the ground floor. The day seemed over-lit and harsh. He stepped into the courtyard and took a few steps before he realised that he wasn't going to work.

He leaned against a new BMW that had been parked there overnight and tried to catch his breath. Annie came out of the opposite block, dressed for the gym, and regarded him warily with her hard little face. Bill raised his hand, a listless plea for help, but she was soon gone, moving quickly on her trainers, shooting him a disapproving look over her shoulder. He had not known that Louis Vuitton made trainers.

Time seemed to stop as he slumped against the car. He looked for the porter but there was no sign of him. He would call the office, that's what he would do. He fumbled in his jacket pocket for his phone, but he had left it in the flat.

Bill looked up at clouds scudding quickly across the sky, his mind grasping for a plan. He would go back to the flat, that's what he would have to do. He cursed, launched himself from the car, but before he could make it to the lift he felt himself pitch forward.

Someone did their best to catch him. He felt hands on his arms that almost broke his fall, and then the hands were dragging at the lapels of his suit jacket, hauling him off his knees, and there was another pair of hands helping him to his feet.

He opened his eyes to see Jenny One and Jenny Two on either side of him, conferring in Shanghainese as they guided him to the lift. They were both dressed in black. All black. But somehow he did not register that they were going to a funeral.

The two Jennys fumbled in his pockets and found the key to his apartment. They tried to lead him into the master bedroom but he pulled away and had soon resumed his prayer position in front of the toilet, with Jenny Two patting and stroking his back as he strained and groaned and sweated, with nothing left to come out.

Back in the master bedroom Jenny One had pulled the curtains. He was too tired to explain to them that this wasn't his room, that his room was the other one, the guest room, that the master bedroom was where his wife and daughter slept, or used to, but it was all too complicated and too much of an effort and so he said nothing and just did his best to help them as they undressed him down to his Calvins and eased him between the sheets. The sheets were cool and fresh. This was a great bed.

Then he must have slept for a while because JinJin was suddenly there, and then there was some conversation that he couldn't understand, and the door was closing as the Jennys went away. The bedroom tried to spin round but her face remained before him, the still centre of his universe.

'Sleep now,' she said.

'You deserve,' he said, reaching for her hand, trying to sit up. It was so small. How could anyone have such small hands? She pulled it away with an impatient scowl. He wanted to talk, there were things he had to say, but there was something wrong with his breathing, he was all clogged up, and it distracted him, and the thought of exactly what she deserved escaped him.

'Too much talk,' she said, shaking her head. She pulled him up, plumped his pillows meaninglessly, and then eased him back on the bed. He closed his eyes, which were stinging from the sweat, his guts felt empty and painful, and he was more tired than he'd known it was possible to feel.

He reached for her again and this time when he took her hand she didn't pull it away. A phone was ringing somewhere. They ignored it.

She stayed with him through the endless day, half-carrying him to the toilet when he needed to get on his knees and pray, and he later realised that she had seen him at a lower physical ebb than anyone had ever seen him in his life. She slept beside him, fully clothed on top of the sheets, a slender arm draped across his chest.

And in the morning, when a full twenty-four hours had gone by and he was still shivering and sweating as he slept in that wonderful bed with nothing but the stomach cramps inside him, she searched through his pockets for his wallet, trying to find someone to call.

* * *

'We talk about heart failure but the phrase is misleading,' said the cardiologist. 'In a medical sense, heart failure is a relative term. Failure implies that the heart is no longer pumping blood into the arteries and the patient is dead.' His thin lips moved to somewhere between a smile and a grimace. 'And this can of course happen.'

Becca, her father and Sara were in his office. Becca thought that the office was surprisingly small for such a coveted, expensive specialist. He was a ski-tanned fifty-five-year-old, looking forward to retirement, looking forward to dinner at the Ivy. Her father was his two o'clock appointment, but he was running late. They should have learned that by now, Becca thought. Get the early appointments and then there was less chance of sitting in the waiting room flicking through worn-out glossy magazines, wondering if the end result would be life or death. They should call it the wondering room, she thought.

The cardiologist's assistant, a fat nurse in a blue coat, was placing black medical plates on a light screen. It didn't look like her father. It didn't look like a heart.

Becca sat there between her father and her sister and wondered, *How many does he see every day?* There was a practised compassion about the cardiologist. He has seen it all before, Becca thought. The terror in the face of the patient, the weepy disbelief in the loved ones, the desperate hunger for a scrap of good news. How many death

234

sentences, how many reprieves? Too many to count, she thought. And we are only his two o'clock.

'Think of an unhealthy heart like an inefficient worker,' said the cardiologist. 'The inefficient worker works twice as hard as the efficient worker, but he doesn't get half as much done. The healthy heart—'

Becca's telephone began to ring inside her bag. The fat nurse looked at Becca as if she wanted to kill her. Becca released the hands of her father and sister and quickly pulled out her phone. She saw that the screen said UNKNOWN CALLER just as she switched it off.

'Sorry,' she said to everyone, but mostly to the fat nurse who wanted to kill her.

Then Becca felt the hands of her father and sister reclaim her own hands, their fingers digging into her palms, holding her for comfort and reassurance and as if to stop her getting away.

*   *   *

'You can pull your pants and trousers up,' Dr Khan told Shane. While Shane was getting dressed, Khan went to the bathroom and splashed cold water on his face. He looked exhausted. He was only hours off the flight from Heathrow and in the grip of the dazed, spaced-out dislocation of full-blown jet-lag. When he went back to his office, they were waiting for him.

Shane's wife sat beside him, but Shane felt completely alone. Somehow Rosalita's presence in the doctor's surgery made him feel more isolated than if he had been there without her.

235

They were here because the pain had not stopped. The pain down there in his trusty old meat and two veg, his faithful servants for so long and on so many adventures. They had betrayed him at last, for the pain down there had sometimes gone away but it had never gone very far. For a while now he had believed that there was something very wrong with him. Today he would find out.

It was a time when he wanted a friend, an ally, and a wife. Someone to tell him that it would be all right—whatever happened, he would get through it. They would get through it together. But instead he felt like the loneliest man in the world.

'It's not cancer and it's not a scrotal hernia,' Dr Khan said, but something about his tone prevented Shane from releasing a sigh of relief.

At least the examination had been mercifully swift. Shane on the couch, his pants and trousers pulled down but not pulled off. The fingers in the plastic gloves had located the source of the pain, dug expertly into him, and now Dr Khan was confidently announcing that it was not the thing that Shane had feared most. It was not cancer. The plastic gloves had moved away from the testicles, heading north, pressing against the top of the groin, and his abdomen, and then back down south of the border to the source of the pain. But it wasn't a hernia either. And the way that Dr Khan pronounced on these things, Shane knew that he had no doubt.

But there was something else.

'Unfortunately it could be torsion,' Dr Khan said, and Shane thought—torsion? It was a word, a fate, that he had never encountered, never dreamed of. Shane had spent weeks with medical encyclopaedias running through the things that could be wrong with him if it wasn't just the after-effects of a kick in the balls.

Cancer? Maybe. A scrotal hernia? Possibly, and although it would be nasty it would be infinitely preferable to the Big C. But torsion? He had never heard of torsion. Was torsion even listed in the *Concise Medical Dictionary*? Oh, definitely. But he had not looked it up. This is what will kill you, Shane thought.

Something you can't even name.

'Torsion is an abnormal twisting of a testicle,' Khan said. 'Imagine a ball being spun round.' Shane crossed his legs and then uncrossed them, opening them wider apart, imagining only too well.

Shane tried a brave smile, but there was too much that he didn't know, and too much he was scared of.

'Worse-case scenario?' he said, as lightly as he could.

Dr Khan stared at them. 'Well, if it's torsion, and if you've lost viability in that testicle—if there's no blood getting to it, if it is essentially dead—then it will have to be surgically removed as soon as possible.'

Then Shane was too numb to be afraid.

He was conscious of his breathing, and his heart in his chest, and he could see his life veering off in an insane, unexpected direction. Torsion! Now I've heard of it! Then his wife spoke, her voice cold and flat and hard.

'Will he still be able to have children?' she said, as though she had just suffered a gross personal insult.

Dr Khan chose to swerve around the question.

'We need to get you a scan immediately,' he said. 'There's a consultant radiologist who is the best in the city and I want you to go and sit outside his office until he can fit you in. I'm going to call him now, but as you don't have an appointment I'm afraid you will have to sit there until he can see you.'

Shane nodded, still in shock. Where else did he have to be? What else was there outside of this room? His wife was silent by his side. She didn't touch him, and he almost forgot that she was there.

The phone on Dr Khan's desk rang and he angrily snatched it up. 'No calls when I'm with a patient, you know that.'

His secretary was apologetic. 'It's emergency, Dr Khan,' she said, her English faltering under pressure. 'About Mr William Holden from JinJin Li. She say you know.'

Khan almost had to laugh. God, he was tired. 'JinJin Li?' he said. 'That narrows it down. There must be fifty million JinJin Lis in China.'

But he took the call, making an apologetic face at Shane and Rosalita. There was a click and then her voice came on the line.

'Dr Khan?' she said. 'You don't know me.'

*   *   *

In the big strange bed Bill drifted in and out of dreams. He shook and shivered under the sweat-stained sheets, listening to her moving around the flat, his exhausted mind racing.

What if the problem was not trying to meet someone great but that you would meet a lot of

238

great people? What if the problem was not finding someone worthy of love, but meeting an endless number of people who were worthy of love? What then? Was that a blueprint for a happy life? Or a recipe for disaster?

*   *   *

'You're a very lucky man,' said Dr Khan, leaning over Bill's bed.

He was in the International Family Hospital and Clinic with an IV drip inserted into his arm. It flowed through his veins like molten ice and he flinched with the pain. JinJin stood awkwardly in a corner of the hospital room, uncertain if she should stay or go.

'I don't know what you've been eating,' said Khan. 'But this is some kind of viral infection of the stomach and intestines. Looks like amoebic dysentery. We're going to keep you in for tests. And of course you are seriously dehydrated. That's what could have killed you.'

'Did someone call my wife?' Bill croaked.

'Someone from your office came by while you were sleeping. Miss Deng, is it?' Against the wall JinJin nodded but Khan did not see her. Bill realised the doctor was doing his best to not even acknowledge her presence. 'Your office is aware of the situation,' he said. 'Miss Deng said she would personally call Becca. Call your wife. You can call her yourself when you're up to it.'

'I'll do that,' Bill said, and Dr Khan nodded shortly, and looked away. When he had gone, nodding curtly at JinJin, she pulled a chair to the side of Bill's bed, watching his face. She placed the back of a hand on his forehead as if taking his temperature then gently pulled it across his temple, and down one cheek, and across his lips, and up the other cheek, removing a thin film of sweat.

'Thanks for saving my life,' Bill said, and she smiled her priceless smile, and it is possible that she may have replied, but by then he was sleeping.

*　　*　　*

He awoke not knowing where he was, disorientated by the dream-like sounds of a hospital at night.

Someone crying out in their sleep. Wheels rolling by his room. Nurses conferring in the corridor. A telephone ringing, and left unanswered.

The IV drip was by his side, but the little bag had been sucked half-dry, and he groaned as he felt that icy pain crawling up his arm.

Now he remembered.

Khan was gone. JinJin was gone. But in the shaft of light that seeped through the top of the door he could see Shane's familiar bulk sitting in the chair by the bed.

'You all right, mate?'

Bill closed his eyes and nodded and smiled, comforted by the rough Aussie burr.

'Touch of the running squirts, eh?' Shane said. 'Happens to the best of us.'

'I don't know what I ate,' Bill groaned. The last meal he remembered was some late-night Dan Dan noodles with Shane and the Germans on the Bund. But Shane had clearly survived the noodles. Bill closed his eyes. He had never felt so tired.

'Amoebic dysentery,' Shane shrugged. 'It's just as likely to be in the water as in the food. You probably got a bad ice cube. Stay away from the water, mate. Don't you Poms know anything?' He patted Bill's arm. 'Anyway—everyone sends their love. Take as long as you like, Devlin says.' Shane shifted awkwardly. 'Had a bit of a bastard day myself. Had warm jelly rubbed all over my crown jewels.' Bill opened his eyes and stared at his friend. Shane sighed at the memory, and couldn't quite manage a smile. 'Lot of people would pay good money for that, mate. When the doc said a scan, I thought that he meant one of those scans where they stick you inside that big machine—you know, the big machine like a coffin. What do you call that machine, mate?'

'MRI scan,' Bill said. 'It's called an MRI scan.'

'Yeah, MRI scan. But this scan was the kind that a woman has when she's got a bun in the oven. Where they rub jelly on her belly so you can see the little nipper inside her.'

Bill thought of the long-ago scans holding Becca's hand as they stared with wonder at their unborn daughter. That was the best time. No, when their daughter was born was the best time. No, when she was bigger, and she was walking and you could see the little girl she would be, that was the best time. No, he thought, maybe later, when we could talk to each other. That was the best time.

Shane was still talking about scans. 'The kind of scan when the woman's up the duff and there are lots of oohs and aahs,' he said. He moved uncomfortably in his seat. 'Well, there were plenty of oohs and aahs when they started rubbing this jelly on my Elgin marbles.'

Bill closed his eyes and laughed. He didn't want to laugh because it hurt too much, but he couldn't stop himself. The ice crawled up his veins and made him gasp with pain. 'Are you all right, Shane?'

The big Australian shifted in the darkness. He had not talked about any of this. He had kept it all locked up. 'The doc thought I might have to have a bollock lopped off. From our big night out in Pudong, remember?'

Bill looked at him, not laughing now. 'Jesus, Shane.' The secrets that we keep, he thought. 'I'm so sorry.' And he did feel sorry, and he felt responsible, and he knew that if he had never gone near JinJin Li then his friend would not have had to live through today.

'It was okay,' Shane said lightly. 'The radiologist said there was no torsion. Great guy. Lovely man. Just the effects of getting a good kicking, he reckoned. But your mind plays tricks, doesn't it? Your mind plays all sorts of tricks.'

'Then that's good, Shane,' Bill said, his voice a croak. Their voices were soft in the hospital night, as though there was some third party asleep in the room who they were trying not to disturb. 'Then that's great.'

'I remember when my grandmother died of breast cancer,' Shane said. 'Great old girl. And she did the most generous and bravest thing that I ever saw anyone do in my life. She took my mother's hand and made her feel the lump—made her know the thing that was killing her. And my grandmother said, "That's what you are always looking for, love, that is what you must guard against, sweetheart, and if you find it, you beat it. You spot it early and you get it cut out of you and you live." And when I thought it might be testicular cancer, I thought—fuck me, as much as I love him, there's no way I'm letting Bill Holden stick his hand down my trousers.'

Bill laughed again, harder now, as though some weight had been lifted from both of them, and he didn't care about the way that any kind of movement made the ice ache in his arm. 'It turned out all right,' he smiled. 'It turned out all right in the end.'

Shane nodded. 'But something like this—it shines a light on your life.' He rubbed his fingers across his eyes. 'It shines a light on your marriage. It really does. When something like this happens—when it looks like they are going to start cutting bits off you—well, you find out what you've got, and what you haven't got.' He turned his face away, although Bill couldn't see it in the darkness. 'She had her bags packed, Bill. I saw it. Not literally, but I would have been in this thing alone. If it had been anything bad, Rosalita would have been off.'

Bill thought of his friend looking at the woman who became his wife before she was even his girlfriend. He thought of how quickly it could all come apart. 'You don't know that,' Bill said, reaching for some reassuring cliché, and unable to believe in any of them. 'It might have brought out the best in her. It might have brought you closer.'

Shane snorted.

'Radical way to patch up your marriage, mate. Have a bit of surgery on the family heirlooms.' He shook his head. 'Sad fact is, she's not there for me the way a wife should be there. She's not my best friend.'

Bill closed his eyes. He wanted to help his friend. He wanted to comfort him. But he was so tired now. The only thing keeping him awake was the ice that crept through his blood, and made him wince from the pain.

'It's not like you and Becca,' Shane said. 'Me and Rosalita—it's just not like that. We're not partners. We're—I don't know what we are. Fuck buddies with wedding rings. That's all. And lately, since that night in Pudong, not even that.' Shane covered his face with his hands, and Bill could hear his friend breathing in the darkness. 'You've got the kind of marriage that every man dreams about,' Shane said, and Bill knew it was true.

But your mind plays tricks, he thought.

Your mind plays all sorts of tricks.

*   *   *

'I feel terrible,' Becca said. 'I feel awful. Really rotten.'

On the other side of the world, Bill laughed weakly. 'Snap,' he said, and in one word she could tell how bad it had been. Her husband sounded as though he had had the stuffing knocked out of him.

'I'm so sorry, baby,' she said.

'What are you sorry about?'

'Sorry that we had to come home. Sorry you had to get through this alone. I should have been there.'

'You can't help your dad getting sick.'

'I know, but—I just want us to have a happy life.

244

Really. That's all I want. I just want us to be together again.'

'Me too,' he said.

It was such a simple and obvious thing to wish for, and she couldn't quite remember why they had ever wished for anything more.

'How's he doing? Your dad?'

'No change,' she said. 'The tests were not conclusive. He has an irregular heartbeat but they don't seem to know what's wrong. I don't know. He suddenly seems like an old man, Bill.'

'And Holly,' he said, and she remembered their screaming row, and she wanted to avoid another one.

'She's well, Bill,' she said quickly. 'She's fine with Sara and her kids.' A beat. 'Please believe me, baby.' She deliberately did not mention the partner. She knew how the unknown partner touched a raw nerve. 'And I promise you it's just for a little while, until my dad can really take care of himself.'

'That's good,' he said, keeping it as neutral as possible.

'How are you? When are you going to be back at work?'

'I'm better. Really. Don't worry. Devlin's told me to stay away for a while. That's okay. There's plenty of stuff I can do from home.'

'Still, maybe I should come over,' she said. 'I'll talk to Dr Khan.'

'No,' Bill said. 'Please don't do that.'

It wasn't true that there was nothing she could have done about it, Becca thought as she hung up. She could have stayed with him. But there was no point in thinking about it now. The worst of it was over, she thought, as she went into the kitchen and made some pasta and salad for herself and her father. Her dad was dozing in front of the evening news and Becca woke him when the meal was ready. He made lots of delighted and appreciative noises, but he hardly touched a thing.

After dinner Becca called Sara's number to say goodnight to Holly. Then she watched a few hours' television with her father, changing channels to follow the news. Or rather Becca watched television while her father slipped back into his snoring slumber.

It was strange. He could not sleep during the night, and she would often hear him bumping around, but he had no trouble at all sleeping on the sofa, when it wasn't time to sleep.

Near midnight she woke him again and waited until she had heard him successfully negotiate the stairs, the bathroom and lights out before she turned in herself.

And Becca smiled wistfully to herself and thought how strange it was that now it was her turn to go to a spare room, and climb into a single bed, and go to sleep alone.

*   *   *

Tea was good for his recovery, JinJin said. And fresh air. And walking.

So when he had been home for a few days, and during one of those mornings when there was no ayi and no Tiger bringing him groceries and no Shane dropping in to see him or maybe just to delay going home from work, JinJin rang his bell and announced that she was taking him out. She

246

recommended the Old City and Yu Gardens and the teahouse on the lake.

They drove there in her red Mini and he could not decide if she was the worst driver in the world or just a typical Shanghai racer. But they arrived in one piece and she took his arm as they walked through the Old City until they came to the zigzag bridge leading to the teahouse. He felt her long body pressing against him and stopped to look at her. Her eyes drifted to the waters bubbling with golden fish beneath them, and then back to his face.

'Good father, good husband, good man,' she said, then nodded once, as if making an important decision. They looked at each other for a very long moment. 'Yes, I think so.'

When he kissed her it was a good fit. In fact their mouths fit together perfectly. There was usually something wrong with the way mouths fit together, he thought. Tongues too active or passive, lips too hard or wet, teeth that got in the way. Noses all over the place. But not with her.

'It's not going to happen,' he said, stepping back, feeling himself responding instantly to her, wanting to hold her and stepping away so that he could not. 'It's not going to happen because if it happens then I'm none of those things, am I? Good father, good husband, good man—it's all out the window, JinJin. I'm none of those things if we start.'

She nodded thoughtfully, as if agreeing with him. 'We can't go anywhere,' she said.

He didn't know if she meant that the relationship could go nowhere, or if she meant they could not go out for fear of being seen—the teahouse by the lake was a lot emptier during the week, there was not much chance of seeing someone from the firm today, but it was still a possibility—or if she meant that it was unthinkable, conducting an affair at either of their apartments.

Maybe she meant all those things.

'No, no, no,' he said, desperate now, backing away from the edge of a cliff. 'Nothing could ever happen. I can't take you to the place where my wife sleeps and my daughter plays. And we can't go to your place—your friend might walk in.' There was no keeping the jealous bile out of his voice. 'He has keys, doesn't he?'

JinJin confirmed this in her devastatingly matter-of-fact tone. 'He has keys, yes,' she said. 'He owns the apartment.' They began slowly walking towards the teahouse. She smiled as if at some good clean joke. 'No making love in William's apartment. No making love in JinJin's apartment.'

He could not smile back at her. This had gone too far already. The kiss had been a mistake. But she had been so kind, and she looked so good, and he had been so lonely for so long.

'How can we?' he said. 'I think you're terrific—you know I do—but how can we?'

Then they said nothing at all until the woman had brought them their tea and poured two cups. And while they were waiting for the boiling water to cool, JinJin opened her bag and silently gave him an envelope that contained two Dragon Air tickets with their names on. He looked more closely. Shanghai to Guilin. Leaving tomorrow morning. Impossible, he thought. No chance.

'No,' he said. 'I'm not going to—where is it?—Guilin. I'm going back to work.' He stared at the tickets, shaking his head. 'I've never even heard of Guilin.' He held out the tickets. She made no move to take them. She blew on her tea. He leaned forward. 'Listen to me. Look at me. I'm not free, JinJin. Three little words before it begins. *I'm not free.*'

'You'll like Guilin,' she said, giving him three little words of her own, and she lifted her cup, although gingerly, because it was almost too hot to hold.

Then they didn't talk until the red Mini with the Chinese flag on the roof was bombing east, back to New Gubei, and she was turning to chat to him in the fast lane of the freeway, telling him how her father came from Guilin, so she had a mother from the far north in Changchun and a father from the distant south, next door to Vietnam, and she was leaning on the horn just to announce her presence in this world, overtaking on the inside, tailgating, flashing her lights, showing absolutely no fear.

That was what scared him most. That total lack of fear, as if JinJin had no idea of how bad it could get.

EIGHTEEN

On a wooden bridge high above the river they huddled together under an umbrella bearing the hotel's name and watched a fisherman with his cormorant.

After dark there were boats that took the tourists out to watch the men fishing with their birds. Bill and JinJin had gone out on the first night in

Guilin, the searchlights from the boat illuminating the fishermen squatting at the back of their flat little punts, the cormorants facing them with a kerosene lamp between them, man and bird gathered around the lamp as though it was a camp fire.

When the birds were put to work they burst into the water and immediately exploded back out again, a miraculous fish in their beaks. The fishermen—ageless little men made of nothing but brown muscle and ropey sinew—threw most of the fish into a big wicker basket. But with every seventh catch they released the metal clasp around the bird's neck, allowing the cormorant to swallow the fish. At night, surrounded by the dumbstruck Chinese tourists, it had seemed like a clever circus trick. But during the day, when the men fished with the cormorants and there was no audience, and you could watch them fishing from the high wooden bridge for free, you knew that this was just the way they fished, it had nothing to do with tickling the tourists. Bill thought it looked like a vision from a thousand years ago.

Guilin was the China he had seen in paintings. Beyond the town he could see the limestone mountains stretching on for ever, self-consciously picturesque, some of them so triangular that they looked like the mountains in one of his daughter's drawings, and all the scene swathed in mist, as if posing, as if waiting to be captured for posterity.

It felt like the edge of China, and he almost suspected that it was the end of the world, even though he knew that Vietnam was on the far side of those mountains. But although it was the most ravishing country he had seen in his life, the postcard beauty of Guilin did not grip him like the sight of the fisherman and his bird.

'That's China for me,' he said. Far below them, on the glassy water of the River Li, the river that shared her name, the lone fisherman was releasing the metal clasp around his bird's neck. The fish in its beak was gobbled down in an instant. 'That fisherman,' he told her, 'that bird.'

JinJin shrugged. She smiled at Bill and squeezed his arm, but the light in her eyes hardly changed, as though the sight of the fisherman and the cormorant was nothing to make a fuss about, as though she was just humouring him. As though her country, and the world, was a far more simple place than he believed.

'Practical,' she said, as the bird plunged once more into the water, and came out with a fish that this time it would not be allowed to keep. 'Just practical.'

*   *   *

This was the time when he couldn't get enough of her.

In the day they walked around Guilin. In the late afternoon they put the sign on the door to make the maid and the world go away, and he moaned and loved her and slept in her arms.

It all made perfect sense, and it was also a kind of madness—because the world slipped away and being there in that room with her was all that mattered. He didn't know how, he had no idea how, but they would work it out. He would make their days in Guilin go on, back in the real world. He would make a holiday romance last for ever.

251

All he had to do was work out how.

At the same time the guilt was as real inside his body as the sickness had been—the crushing guilt and sense of shame, and it came to him like a baseball bat smacked against the back of the head as he lay awake and she slept. The guilt was as undeniable as the illness, and so was the terrible knowledge that if he had his chance to do it all over again, then he would do exactly the same thing, and take JinJin Li's hand, and drive to the airport, and catch the flight to Guilin, and watch the fishermen with their birds, and step right off the cliff.

*   *   *

He was amazed that she wanted to see her father.

On the first morning in Guilin, inspired by the proximity of her father's hometown, she had casually told him a string of horror stories about growing up with his violent rages, and Bill had assumed that she had severed all contact after her parents had divorced. But he was in a village in the countryside beyond Guilin, a brief taxi-ride away, reportedly in ill health, and to JinJin it was unremarkable that they should pay him a visit.

'A father like that,' Bill said, outraged on her behalf, 'in the West you wouldn't have anything to do with him.'

JinJin shrugged. 'But we are not in the West,' she reminded him.

So they caught a cab to his village, the limestone mountains and the glass-smooth river and the paddy fields drifting by outside the window as the horrors of her childhood at the other end of

252

the country came back to Bill. Her father rapping JinJin and her sister across the hand with chopsticks if they annoyed him at the dinner table. Her father dragging their mother off for a beating with the words, 'Say goodbye to the children—you will never see them again.' And her father eventually leaving but never leaving them alone, arguing in the street with JinJin when she was fifteen and he was forty, and the passers-by mistaking them for lovers.

He was a gambler. The violence came from the gambling. He worked, he gambled, and when he had lost everything he came home to blame his wife and two daughters, and to take it out on them.

His village sat in a valley between two stubby hills. The white stumps of trees that had been cut down years ago crept up the hills like the massed tombstones of some forgotten war. The village itself was part shantytown and part campsite. Shacks of wood and corrugated metal stood alongside grubby brown tents. Barefoot children came out of the tents to gawp at the arrival of the taxi. It was hardly a village at all, Bill thought.

'What happened in this place?' he said.

JinJin looked up at the hillsides. 'Flood,' she said. 'In the past, many trees were cut down around here.' She groped for the word. 'Soil? When typhoon comes, soil comes quickly down the hill without trees there.' She slowly raised one of her small hands, palm down. 'Rains come, river get big—you understand?'

He nodded.

'How long have these people been living in tents?' he asked her. 'When was the flood?'

She thought about it. 'Three years ago. Come on,

let's find my father.'

JinJin's father was at the bus depot where he worked. He had a Clark Gable moustache and he was as wide as he was tall. He was so physically different from his long lean daughter that Bill struggled to believe they shared the same blood. He grinned shyly at Bill as he chattered with JinJin, and perhaps because she was so apparently at ease with him, Bill could not find it in his heart to hate the man.

'I this girl father!' he announced, and Bill nodded, both of them smiling away at this shocking revelation. His two friends cackled with amusement at his mastery of a foreign language.

'He speaks no English whatsoever,' JinJin said dismissively.

Her father had not prospered in the years since leaving his family. The gambling and the violence had ruined two more little families, and now he lived alone in a wooden shack, troubled by his lungs and the damp, existing on a diet that JinJin said consisted of congee, roll-up cigarettes and whatever brand of tea had stained his teeth that dark brown colour.

There was a noodle shop next to the bus depot and Bill watched the pair of them as they noisily slurped their meal while he—suddenly wary of the local fare—ate nothing. Even locked out of their conversation by language, he could see that the balance of power between them had shifted. The father answered his daughter's questions almost bashfully, unable to maintain eye contact for very long. It was the daughter who called the shots.

'My father says the local government are very bad,' JinJin told Bill. 'After the flood, there was a relief fund set up for the village by the central government. But the village did not even know about it until they sent representatives to Beijing to protest.'

Her father grinned with embarrassment below his Clark Gable moustache.

'My father says he would like to invite you to his home,' JinJin said. 'But they are very poor here, and he is ashamed to invite you to such a low place.'

Bill lifted a hand in protest. 'Please, sir, there is no need to be ashamed, I am happy to meet you.'

They shook hands, enthusiastically, pointlessly, and before Bill knew what he was doing, he had taken out his wallet and was pushing a grubby wad of RMB into her father's hand. He made a token protest, but then waggled his eyebrows happily, staring at the money with disbelief.

'I this girl father!' he proclaimed, and JinJin looked away, as if she could not stand to look at either of them.

*   *   *

His parents had made it look easy. You find someone and then you stick with them forsaking all others until you are parted by the grave. You kept the big promises you had made in bed and in church and on all the days you would never forget. That's what you did, and your life was simple, and the future was clear. It did not seem impossible, unimaginable.

So why couldn't he do it?

What was wrong with him?

They had flown back from the shockingly

255

modern airport at Guilin and he was sick of it. Already sick of it. He didn't want an affair, and he didn't want to be the kind of man that kept a bit on the side. He did not want to be the Chinese man in the silver Porsche. He didn't want arrangements made, bargains struck, secrets shared. He wanted the one who would make him forget about all the others. That was what he wanted. That was all he had ever wanted.

You find the one that obliterates all the rest and it immediately solves all problems, it resolves everything and puts an end to all the wanting, because once you start the wanting, it's never enough until your heart stops beating, and there can be no rest and no peace and no real happiness. All you had to do was to find the one that would blind you to the rest of the world. That's all he wanted, the same as everyone else. It didn't seem too much to ask.

And this girl who had sat in the window seat next to him, frowning over the in-flight magazine—this fabulous girl—she filled his heart. But when he switched on his phone when he was alone in the apartment, it told him all the calls he had missed. MISSED CALL. HOME, it said. MISSED CALL. HOME.

His parents had made it look easy and perhaps in the end it was easy. As long as you kept the promises. If you broke the promises then suddenly everything else was breakable too.

*   *   *

He came home late from his first day back at work and saw that all the lights in her apartment were

256

out. He knew that she wasn't sleeping. He knew that the car had come for her.

He was angry and jealous and glad. Good, get it over with, end it now. Did he think that she was going to sit by the phone waiting for his call? Did he think that Guilin meant that there was nobody else who could make demands on her time? Did he expect her to sit at home, curl up those endless legs, and spend the evening with *Crossword Work-Out*? Yes, yes, yes—in his madness in their double-locked, do-not-disturb hotel room he had expected all of these things, even though he knew he could only be let down. JinJin was out for the night, the only place she could be, and he was glad about it— end the thing now—even though it was like being kicked in the stomach.

He was sitting on the stairs outside her apartment when she came home at midnight. He had thought about what might happen if the man came back with her. It would not be pleasant. But the Porsche decanted her back at her rented apartment, and then it left, and Bill was rising to his feet as she pulled out her key.

'I'm not doing this,' he said. 'I can't do it. I love my wife and our little girl. I'm not leaving them. And I don't want a woman on the side. A permanent girlfriend. That's not for me. I can't take it—you out with him and me waiting for you to come back. How does that work? How does that make me feel?' He was raising his voice now. A woman called out a protest in Chinese from behind a closed door. They both looked in the direction of the complaint, and then back at each other. 'How could it work?' Bill asked again. 'Do we get you on alternate nights?'

257

JinJin let herself into the flat, not looking at him. He followed her inside, grabbing her by the shoulder and pulling her round.

'Or are you going to see both of us the same night?' he said. He had never seen her look so sad. 'You know what that would make you, don't you?'

'I end it,' she said. She always slipped into the present tense when she was tired, or stressed, or hurt. 'I end it with that man.'

Bill stared at her. He didn't know what to say. He felt like he was always rushing to judge her, and always getting it wrong.

'Tonight I tell him,' she was saying, *'We can't go on.'* Now she looked at Bill. 'Because I don't want to go that way.' She shook her head. 'I don't want to go that way. And because I love you all the time.'

Then she was in his arms and his mouth was on her face, kissing away her tears, refusing to allow them, no more tears, and he was mad for her, starved for her, moaning his love and apologies, sorry again, endlessly sorry for everything, and endlessly grateful, and all his wise decisions obliterated by the touch of her mouth on his mouth, and everything tasting of salt.

I don't want to go that way.
I love you all the time.
He loved her all the time too.

*   *   *

Outside her window they could hear the unbroken buzz of the city going about its everyday business, but in JinJin's room he felt that the world had entered a different time.

Everything about her was a source of wonder. He

258

cupped her knees and ran his hands along the endless flanks of her legs and it seemed to take for ever. He wanted it to take forever.

'Measuring me again,' she laughed. There was a lot of laughter. The long afternoon felt light-hearted and deadly serious all at once. They were giddy with joy, punchdrunk with happiness. She pressed her mouth against his, her brown eyes alight, and then those eyes closing, and he could tell she felt it too. This hunger that was more than a hunger, this craving that could not be satisfied if they stayed in this room for the rest of their lives.

She rose naked from the floor where they had been lying and looked at herself in the mirror, her arms and legs long and gawky as she examined herself, her small hands cupped across even smaller breasts.

'Too small,' she said, pulling a face. 'Ugly me.'

'Yeah,' he smiled. 'Ugly old you.'

'Not even A cup,' she said, and when she arched her back he saw the ridges in her ribcage, and they made him ache with tenderness. It was just a ribcage—he knew that. But the ridges of her ribs against her skin tormented him, and he wanted to touch them, and no other man to ever touch them.

'Double A!' she cried, eyes wide, as if she had just discovered her bee-sting breasts. 'Yes, you are right—ugly old me.'

'Well, everyone has body issues,' he said, propping himself up on one elbow. He reached out a hand and idly stroked her foot, looking up at her. She stared down at him seriously, her hands falling away. It was true. Her breasts were very small. Even in this room, even now, he could see that she was not perfect—her bum was too flat, her breasts

259

were too small, her skin was too troubled for perfection to be considered.

But she was perfect for him.

He didn't want to change a thing about her. He loved the imperfections as much as he loved her greatest hits—those eyes, those legs and—why not?—those double-A cup breasts. That was her. That was who she was, and he revelled in it all.

'Take me, for example,' he said, sitting cross-legged and casting down his eyes. He hesitated. 'I don't know if I want to talk about it.' She knelt beside him, a consoling arm draped across his shoulder, encouraging him to go on. 'I—I worry that I'm just too big,' he said, looking up at her concerned brown eyes. 'You know. Down there. Too big for any woman . . .'

She stood up and slapped his shoulder. 'Hah,' she said. 'English joke!'

He rolled on his back, chuckling to himself. 'You wouldn't look right with large breasts, JinJin. Your legs are too long. You'd look top heavy—like Jessica Rabbit.'

She laughed shortly. 'Ah yes,' she said. 'Beatrix Potter.'

When he looked up at her she was smiling. That toothy, goofy grin that he could never get enough of. He nodded. 'Very good,' he said. 'Chinese joke.'

When the night came they did not leave the room but lay entwined and wrapped up in each other, as if they were closer than any couple in the world, and closer than anyone had ever been, as if they were one flesh now. He looked at her looking at him and he knew that nobody else in his life had ever looked at him in quite that way.

As if he was special.

As if he was—and he had to smile at this—exotic.

But it was true. He was a different kind of man and she was a different kind of woman. He explored her long, almost hairless body and it was like discovering another planet. She ran her fingers through the light covering of blond hair on his arms as if he was some strange new species.

'Very hairy,' she said. 'My goodness. Like a monkey. Help, help—there's a monkey in my room.'

'This isn't considered hairy where I come from,' he said, but he knew that she didn't really know anything about where he came from. She knew how to conjugate verbs and she knew about writers and she could use all the antique idioms, but that was all she knew. His eyes were an unremarkable shade of green and yet she looked into them as if they were Solomon's treasure.

And he knew that Becca did not and could not ever look at him with eyes like that. His wife loved him—he was sure of that—but she looked at him the way a sister would look at a brother, with a kind of amused familiarity, an affection that was unclouded by mystery.

But JinJin Li looked at him with new eyes, eyes so brown that they were almost black, eyes so large that they shone from her face, and he loved being looked at like that.

His first Asian woman. Her first Western man. And as the night moved on and the city slept, neither of them doubted that they would also be their last. What more could you want beyond this room?

She slept and he placed his hand on her stomach and it was as flat and hard as a table. He smiled to

261

himself. You could bounce ping-pong balls off that belly, he thought to himself. Instead he placed his lips softly against it, and kissed her as lightly as he could before putting his arms around her and snuggling up against her long, beloved body, and soon he was also in the bottomless sleep of happiness and exhaustion.

If he had gone to the window of JinJin's room then he would have been able to see across the courtyard of Paradise Mansions to his own apartment, and the windows of his other life. But he never did.

When he awoke in the milky Shanghai dawn he watched her sleeping, and he studied her skin, her limbs and her face until he knew them better than his own. He never went to the window.

And he got lost in her.

NINETEEN

'Granddad's going to die, isn't he?' Holly said.

'No, angel,' Bill said and he felt the distance between them throbbing like a fresh bruise. 'Your granddad's not going to die. He's still young. He's got some great doctors looking after him.'

'Martin said that everyone dies in the end.'

Martin was the oldest of the sister's children. Bill felt a sudden surge of hatred towards him, immediately followed by a twinge of guilt. Sara—he was trying hard to think of her as Sara, and not *the sister*—was going out of the way to accommodate his frequent phone calls to Holly, and always had her standing by the phone when he was scheduled to call, or not too far away.

'Listen to me, angel,' he said gently. 'Nothing lasts for ever. A flower doesn't last for ever, does it?'

Holly thought about it. He could hear her thinking. 'Penguins don't last for ever,' she said.

'That's true,' he said. 'I hadn't thought about that.'

'And dinosaurs didn't last for ever.'

'The dinosaurs. That's right.'

'There was a change in the earth's temperature that killed the dinosaurs.'

'Wow,' he said, genuinely impressed. 'Where did you learn that, Holly?'

'At school.'

'That's very good.'

'Grandparents don't last for ever,' she mused.

The philosophy was new. A year ago, at three, Holly's conversation had been an endless round of questions and orders, sentences that began either with, 'Why . . .' or 'You have to . . .' As in, 'Why does Tony the Tiger wear a bib if he's a grown-up?' and 'You have to be the prince now, Daddy.' But at four Holly was wrestling with the big issues, and he did not know what to tell her. The truth seemed too hard, and lying seemed wrong.

'We all die,' he said. 'But not for a long, long time.' A pause. 'Are you listening to me, angel?'

But her attention had been distracted. Bill could hear that the commercials had come on the TV that was playing in the background. There was a persuasive adult voice, followed by children squealing with excitement. Bill waited patiently. He could hear other noises. All the sounds of Sara's crowded, unknowable house. Children arguing. Doors slamming. Sara pleading at the dinner table, *Just one more . . . eat one more . . . just a little bit . . .* That was what he shared with Holly, he thought. It was different when you were an only child. You were not constantly surrounded by all the clamour and clatter of siblings. You were left alone with your thoughts.

'Are you going to die, Daddy?'

He stared out of his office window at the lights of Pudong, and heard the sounds of his side of the world. Shanghai had its own distinctive noise, he had realised, especially at night, an unbroken metallic hum that seemed to be made up of traffic on the road and the river, and the lives of twenty million other people.

'I'm going to die one day,' he said. 'But not for a long time. And you know what, angel? If it's possible for me to come back and be around you, then that's exactly what I am going to do, and I'll be there for ever. Everywhere you go. You'll be all grown up but I'll still be there. I'll be in the sunlight on your face, and I'll be in rain on your shoes, and I'll be in the wind in your hair. I'll be there when you wake up in the morning, and I'll be there when you go to sleep at night. And I'll keep watch by your bed all night, and you will feel me smiling at you, and you'll never be alone because I will be there, always and forever.' The telephone line crackled and then was silent. 'Do you hear me, angel?'

But Holly wasn't listening to him. She was watching the commercials.

*   *   *

264

There was something strange about JinJin's eyes. Those wide-set brown eyes—there was a mystery about them, something that he just could not work out, even though he had spent uncountable hours staring into them.

He saw now that there were no lines of black mascara drawn around her eyes. That wasn't it. He had been mistaken. She did not wear make-up, she never wore make-up, and yet somehow he felt that she was always wearing make-up. He didn't understand it. He was a married man and long accustomed to the rituals of a woman and her cosmetics and the ceremony of apply, repair and remove. He knew that his wife looked so totally different when she was or was not wearing whatever it was she put on her face. When they went out and Becca was wearing make-up, there was a polished, glossy beauty about her, and when she came home and took it off the beauty was still there but it was fresh-faced and unadorned and natural and pretty and lovely in quite another way.

It was not the same with JinJin.

He looked at her, and he looked at her some more, and he could not work it out, he didn't understand the thick black and totally unnecessary eyeliner that never needed replacing. The mystery was solved the moment he mentioned it.

'Permanent eyeliner,' she said, one night when they were stretched out on the sofa, facing each other, and he looked again, at those eyes that needed no help at all to look beautiful.

'Permanent?' he said, unable to fight the sinking feeling. 'What—you don't mean tattoos, do you?'

But that was exactly what she meant.

'I will change it,' she said, sensing his distaste,

jumping up from the sofa to confront herself in the mirror, her long slim body pale in the moonlight. 'I get removed.' The English was deteriorating the longer she looked. 'I take away.'

And he went after her, and held her from behind, pulling her away from the mirror, telling her that he didn't want her to go through with that, everything was fine, she was gorgeous, he was just surprised. He did not mention that he had never seen it before. On a girl in the West. Tattooed eyes. But JinJin Li wasn't a girl in the West, and he forgot that sometimes.

'I was young,' she said, and he thought that she sounded like an actress who has suddenly had a youthful photo session revealed. *I was young, I needed the work.* 'High school student. We didn't know about such things. And we could afford. And we want to look like the ladies in the magazines.'

'I'm sorry, it's okay,' he said, gently leading her back to the sofa, wishing he had never mentioned it, knowing that he would never mention it again for fear that he would one day find that she had had the permanent eyeliner surgically removed. The thought of it made his flesh crawl.

Still, he was sorry about the tattoos on the rims of her fabulous, wide-set eyes. She didn't need that crap, and now it would be with her forever. Anything as permanent as that was always going to be a mistake.

*   *   *

'Wives are like fires,' Tess Devlin told Bill. 'They go out when unattended.'

They were watching Rosalita weave her way

266

towards a band in a hotel bar eighty floors above the city. The band was Filippino, like most of the bands in Shanghai, but they showed scant signs of kinship as Rosalita approached them with a mojito in her hand and a wiggle in her hips.

The band's singer, a stick-thin beauty in a backless black dress, was no more than twenty. She stepped sideways as Rosalita turned abruptly to confer with the musicians, sending a splash of cocktail slopping from her glass. The boys in the band were nodding reluctantly, as if they knew this could only end in tears.

'Shane gives her plenty of attention,' Bill said. 'He doesn't neglect her. He really doesn't. He's crazy about her.'

His friend was on the other side of the table, talking to a London partner who was passing through on his way to Hong Kong, and currently blinking back the jet-lag. Shane didn't turn around even when his wife lurched into 'Right Here Waiting for You'. He had the look of a man who was steeling himself for something bad to happen.

Rosalita's voice was as sweet and pure as ever, but she shuffled backwards and forwards uncertainly, her old slick professionalism impaired by the lack of space and the potency of the mojitos. When she trod on the bass player's foot, impaling his instep on a Jimmy Choo spike and making him hop around, shrieking in protest, Shane still didn't turn around. If he heard the laughter in the bar, he gave no sign.

'Whatever he gives her,' Tess Devlin told Bill, 'it's clearly not enough.'

Devlin and Nancy were at opposite ends of the table, and they looked from Shane to his wife and then back again. Shane failed to react as Rosalita went into her second number. He was telling the London partner an interesting story about Bao Luo, the aircraft hangar of a restaurant where they had had dinner, and how it had started life as a noodle stand in a bicycle repair shop. Devlin got up and came quickly to Bill's side.

'Get him to control his wife, will you?' he muttered angrily.

Bill shrugged helplessly, but when he saw Nancy making her way to the tiny stage where Rosalita was now grinding her hips while crooning, 'I Will Always Love You'—the band appeared to be playing something else entirely—he got up to help her. The pair of them reached Rosalita just in time for a close-up of her falling on her bottom. Holding one arm each, they got her to her feet as sarcastic applause came from dark corners of the bar.

'Show's over, Rosalita,' Bill said lightly. 'Why don't we all get some coffee?'

'He never lets me have any fun,' Rosalita complained. They started leading her away, to the relief of the band. Unseen men were calling for an encore. Women were laughing. Rosalita's eyes were blazing with anger and self-pity. 'He is such a cheap guy,' she said. They had reached the table now and as the band struck up a polite version of 'The Girl from Ipanema', Rosalita shouted at the back of her husband's head, 'Such a cheap guy!' Shane flinched but did not turn around.

Bill and Nancy escorted Rosalita to the bar and ordered coffee. They were told there was no coffee in the bar. Only room service could get coffee. Bill impatiently threw a fistful of RMB on the counter and the bartender went off to get room service.

Rosalita laid her head on his shoulder and told Bill that he was a nice guy and that she had always liked him. Then she sang a wonky chorus of 'Yesterday Once More', wiped away a sentimental tear, put her head on her arms and fell asleep. The woman on the next stool glanced at her and then looked away with a snort of contempt.

'The Carpenters,' said Alice Greene. 'I always hated the fucking Carpenters.'

Bill turned as Shane's bulk parked itself on the stool beside him. The big man stared down at his sleeping wife and reached out a hand. It hovered over her mass of glossy black hair, not quite daring to touch her.

'She'll be okay,' Bill told him.

'It's true what they say,' Shane said sadly. 'You can take the girl out of the bar. But you can't take the bar out of the girl.'

'That's not what you did,' Bill said. 'You didn't take her out of a bar. She's a regular girl.'

Shane wanted to believe him. 'Yeah,' he said, eyeing his wife with a mixture of fear and longing. 'A regular girl.'

He nodded and turned away, slapping Bill once on the shoulder, not looking him in the eye. Alice was still talking to him.

'So,' she said. 'How's business at Butterfield, Hunt and West?'

'Better than yours,' he said. Bill had looked for her story online, the one about the man at the Happy Trousers Factory losing an arm, but it had never appeared. As far as he could tell, nothing with Alice's by-line had appeared for months.

She laughed. 'Yeah, well,' she said, and he

realised that he had never seen her looking embarrassed before. He felt a stirring of sympathy for her. 'My paper has got moral-outrage fatigue,' she said. 'I mean, how many stories can you do about land grabs or industrial pollution or some poor little sod in some miserable factory dropping dead from exhaustion?' She stared into her glass, as if it might contain a clue. 'Or losing a limb in machinery because nobody really, truly cares? I mean, how many times? In the end it's like a starving child in the Third World or a bomb going off in the Middle East. Everybody's heard it all before. And everybody's bored shitless with it.' She looked at Bill over the rim of her glass. 'Remember what I said to you? When Becca found that baby?'

Bill nodded. He remembered. *It's not news.*

Alice nodded too. 'Well, none of it is news. Not any more. They want journalists who are going to report the miracle. That's what these editors want. Booming China. Funky Shanghai. Tell the world that Beijing is Washington and Shanghai is New York. All that stuff. All that happy, shiny bullshit.' She raised her glass in mock salute. The bartender had returned with three cappuccinos.

'Black coffee,' Bill said. 'I ordered black coffee.'

The bartender looked sad. 'Only cappuccino,' he said. 'No more black coffee.'

On top of the foamed milk on each cup the chocolate was sprinkled into careful heart shapes.

'You won,' Alice said. 'Your lot. Cheers.'

'My lot?' Bill said, watching Nancy gently trying to wake Rosalita. He pushed his cappuccino away. 'They're not my lot.'

But Alice wasn't listening. 'I should have been born earlier,' she said, signalling the bartender for a refill. 'I should have been in Tiananmen Square.' She narrowed her eyes at Bill. 'The fourth of June 1989. That's where it started. All of this. The greed. The corruption. The poison at the core.'

Nancy stared at her but Alice didn't notice. There was a fresh drink in front of her. Rosalita was sipping the cappuccino that Nancy offered her. The heart-shaped chocolate broke and melted at the touch of her lips.

Alice jabbed a finger at Bill.

'You think it's a coincidence that the guy who sent the tanks into Tiananmen Square is the same guy behind the economic miracle?' she said. 'You think it's a coincidence that Deng Xiaoping is responsible for all of it? It's not a coincidence. Tiananmen Square was where they sent out the message to every man, woman and child in China—*Support us and we will make you rich, oppose us and we will crush you.*' Alice sipped her drink and shook her head. 'I should have been there.'

'Stick around,' Nancy said, and they all looked at her. Alice. Bill. And even Rosalita through her bleary, mojito-fogged eyes. There was a ring of chocolate around her mouth.

'Really, you should stick around,' Nancy said. On her lips the idiom sounded like something borrowed from a Berlitz guide. *Stick around.* 'You may have missed the last massacre,' Nancy told Alice, smiling pleasantly, 'but you will probably be just in time for the next one.'

*   *   *

Instead of going home, Bill walked down the Bund,

swerving between the tourists gawping at the lights and the beggars with their babies and the drunken businessmen and the off-duty bar girls and the fashionable young Chinese who were increasingly claiming the famous old street as their own. He was meeting JinJin in the bar of the Peace Hotel. And it wasn't until he was sitting at the crowded bar sipping his Tsingtao and the band were banging their way through 'I'll Be Seeing You' that he realised it was a rotten place to meet.

What was he thinking? The bar of the Peace Hotel was a great place to go if you were a man and wife out on some special occasion. What many people didn't realise about the band in the Peace Hotel was that the old boys were very happy to play requests. So you could sit there all night listening to them play your songs. It was a fine place for all that. But it was a lousy place for a liar.

The bar was full of out-of-towners, as always, but Bill was aware that someone he knew—anyone he knew—could walk in at any moment. Every expat with a relative in from the old country had to take a look at this bar. Every Pudong suit entertaining a client who was a Shanghai virgin had to have a drink in here. If his body clock suddenly shook him awake, it was even possible that the senior London partner himself could be brought here tonight by Devlin and Tess.

Bill watched the door, aware of his pounding heart, and drinking far too fast. He saw JinJin enter the bar, and watched her serious face as she scanned the crowd, not seeing him. He smiled because he loved this moment—when he could watch her without her knowing he was watching. He also loved the moment when she saw him and that perfect beauty was split by the toothy grin, and became something else, something better, something that he could claim as his own. The face of his girl.

JinJin moved through the crowd towards him.

It's not her fault, he thought with a rush of shame. She had no one to hide from. She had no reason to watch the door. He was the liar, not her.

She kissed him on the mouth and took the hand that was resting by his beer. The bartender asked her what she wanted to drink.

'We've got to go,' Bill said, still holding her small hand, and squeezing it tight, but keeping it off the bar and out of sight.

*   *   *

They sat at a table at the back of Suzy Too and as JinJin urgently conferred with the two Jennys and Sugar and Annie, Bill watched the dance floor.

There was something—a trick, a knack, a skill—that all the working girls had in Suzy Too. They would approach a man with a look of such tenderness and generosity that he couldn't help but feel singled out and special and chosen. As though this loud, smoky dive on Tong Ren Lu could provide him with everything that he was missing at home, as though he might find someone who really wanted him in here. If the man declined the offer of company, the Suzy Too girls would move away with a smile of regret, as if enduring a tiny death—that was the magic trick, Bill thought, their ability to stay in character even after rejection. But if the man was interested, and responded with some crucial gesture—a drink,

273

a dance, bodily contact—then the expression changed in the woman's eyes, and although the painted smile never faltered, the softness was replaced by a look of cold, hard professionalism that took your breath away. Bill wondered what happened to those men who mistook commerce for affection, or desire, or love. What happened to them?

He saw that what was sold in Suzy Too was not sex but dreams, and he guessed that beyond the cold hard commerce that filled the air as much as the smoke and beer and the greatest hits of Eminem, the dream on sale was coveted by a surprising number of the men in here. The dream of the great unmet lover, the dream that you might meet someone who truly cared about you, the dream that in the morning you would wake up in the arms of someone as beautiful and untouched and unchanging as JinJin Li.

His eyes stung from the smoke. His ears were ringing from 'The Way I Am' and 'Lose Yourself' and many songs that he didn't know. They should have just gone back to JinJin's apartment and closed the door—he never took her to his own apartment, and without discussing it they both knew that he never would—but Spring Festival was coming and JinJin wanted to see her friends before they all went home for the duration of China's great holiday. It would soon be time to strike camp. Soon the entire country would be on the move.

The conversation at their table seemed never-ending and complex. He could not even guess the subject. JinJin and Jenny One were arguing with Annie, who seemed to be tearfully protesting her innocence. Bill had never seen Annie show any emotion before, beyond her default frosty haughtiness. Jenny Two and Sugar nodded thoughtfully and held her hands, but Annie broke free of them and rolled up her sleeve, her tears streaming.

Bill saw with a jolt that there was a fresh tattoo on her right arm, inch-high capital letters that spelled out a name in Chinese characters. Under the lights of Suzy Too the brand on her smooth pale flesh looked like fluorescent ink.

'He became very angry when he saw it,' JinJin said in English, including Bill in the story, and Bill didn't have to ask who *he* might be.

'And he said she must go away,' Jenny Two said. 'But she did this for him. Only for him!'

'And he refused her,' Jenny One said. This is what they said when someone was dumped. *He refused her.* Annie stared at her ruined skin, her disastrous stab at commitment to the man who had brought her to Paradise Mansions, and they all looked at Bill with pleading eyes as if he might explain the strangeness and mystery and fickle nature of a man's heart.

He shook his head apologetically.

'We've got to go,' he said.

*   *   *

Back in her apartment he told her to put her feet up while he made some tea.

As the sound of a young woman reading the news drifted out to the kitchen, Bill opened doors until he found cups and tea. He pushed the packet to one side and dug deeper inside the cupboard

275

because, although it felt like he drank it every day of his life, he was no great fan of Chinese tea.

Chinese tea was one of those things, like jazz or cricket, that he had tried very hard to like but could never really see the point of. He thought that Chinese tea was never much more than okay. So he was delighted when he found an unopened packet of English breakfast tea, something exotic that JinJin had picked up at the local Carrefour supermarket and then never used. Her kitchen was full of these odd souvenirs. A dusty bottle of Perrier. A jar of decaffeinated instant coffee. A forgotten packet of muesli. A six-pack of Coca-Cola. They were like messages in a bottle washed up from some foreign shore that she had only read about in magazines.

He came into the living room carrying a tray with two steaming cups of English breakfast tea, a carton of milk and a bowl of raw cane sugar that she sometimes used for cooking. She was staring hungrily at the young female newsreader on the TV. She looked at him and recoiled.

'English tea,' he said. 'Just for a change.'

She raised her eyebrows. 'Tea with milk?'

'Just try it,' he smiled. 'Please.' He carefully placed the tray on the table before her. Then he hesitated. 'JinJin?'

JinJin had turned her face back to the young woman reading the news. He knew what she was thinking. I could do that. 'What is it, William?'

'You're still in the flat,' he said, pointing out the obvious, finally broaching something that had confused him for a long time. 'This flat, I mean. You're still living in it.'

She turned to look at him, the young woman with

the autocue forgotten. 'Yes.'

'How come?' Bill said, sitting down beside her. 'I mean—it's not your flat. You don't own the flat.' She stared at him, waiting. 'He owns the flat. The man. Your old boyfriend.' He could not bring himself to say *husband*. Never that. 'I was wondering—why didn't he throw you out when you ended it?'

She looked shocked. 'He's not such a one,' she said. 'Perhaps he always knew that I would meet someone. That such a day would come.' She sipped her tea, and grimaced. 'I can't stay here for ever. I know that. But he would never—' she reached for Bill's brutal phrase '— throw me out.'

Bill placed his hands around his cup, and then took them away. 'He must have loved you very much,' he said.

'He cares about me,' JinJin said.

She doesn't call it love, Bill thought. What she had with him. She never calls it love.

'Are you all right for money?' he said.

'I have enough,' she said. 'For now.'

'How's the tea?' he said.

She pulled a face. 'Tea with milk. Horrible!'

He laughed and reached for the sugar bowl. 'Some people need a little sweetness,' he said, heaping in a spoonful of the raw cane sugar and stirring it for her.

JinJin sipped it carefully.

'Better?' he asked.

She nodded. 'A little sweetness,' she said.

*   *   *

Early next morning Bill came into the courtyard

where Tiger was sitting at the wheel of the car, his new laptop resting on his thighs, fingers flashing across the keyboard. Tiger was so lost in the images passing before his eyes that he did not see Bill approach the car, bundled up inside his new Armani coat against the freezing January morning, and he did not see him try the handle on the passenger's side. Tiger only saw Bill when he rapped his knuckles against the windscreen.

'You can do that on your own time,' Bill told him, sliding into the car. He nodded at the laptop that Tiger was attempting to deposit on to the back seat. 'What's so fascinating anyway?'

'It's nothing, boss,' Tiger said, flushing with embarrassment. Bill shook his head, eased the laptop from Tiger's hand and flipped open the lid. He was expecting naked girls or new cars but instead he found himself looking at a colour photograph of a chair that was the size and shape of a phone box. It was a red chair, some sort of old-fashioned Chinese chair made of lacquered hardwood with elaborate carvings down one side and calligraphy running down another. There were barefoot children standing around the chair and a caption in English. *Hong Kong, 1963*, it said. *Young relatives try to peek at a bride as she is carried to her wedding.*

'What is this?' Bill said.

'This is my business, boss,' Tiger said. He smiled uncertainly. 'This is my website. Can I show?'

Bill smiled encouragement and Tiger took the laptop from him. His fingers danced across the keys, and images of furniture that looked like sculpture flashed before their eyes. Black lacquer bedside cabinets. Travel trunks and hand-painted

278

screens and hardwood coffee tables and pillow boxes and a canopy-covered bed. Red lanterns that could have been from a Gong Li movie. There was an austere beauty about it all.

'This is how I will get rich,' Tiger said, smiling shyly. 'This is my way. I have contacts in Hong Kong and Taiwan. And there are factories down south. Many factories, boss.'

'Big market for this stuff, Tiger?'

'Booming market, boss. During the past bad times, lot of traditional Chinese furniture was smashed up. Now many rich people in China. Don't want Western furniture. Not interested. Want Chinese furniture.' Tiger looked at him with pleading eyes. 'Bad idea, boss?'

Bill shook his head. He was impressed, and a little sad, because sooner or later he would lose Tiger. But that was Shanghai. Everybody wanted to make their fortune.

'It's a good idea, Tiger,' he said. 'It's a great idea. And I wish you well. Is this stuff real or fake?'

'Do both classic and contemporary,' Tiger said, nodding emphatically. 'Many masterpieces from the Ming and Qing dynasties. I have good people can do restoration. But also genuine replicas from factories down south.'

As always, Bill thought, the line was blurred between what was real and what was fake. It largely depended on what you wanted to believe, and how much you were prepared to pay. Things could be found, or they could be restored, or they could be copied. But as the images of hand-carved, hand-painted black and red hardwood furniture flowed in front of them, Bill saw that none of this stuff was easy to copy. It took a kind of genius to

279

fake something so brilliantly that you never really knew when you had the real thing.

*   *   *

He could hear her banging about in the tiny kitchen. He had been ordered to remain on the sofa and watch BBC World while she prepared his treat. But he wasn't interested in BBC World.

'May I help?' he called.

More banging and crashing. 'Your help is not required,' she said, just before he heard something drop and shatter. 'Oh my goodness,' she muttered.

If he craned his neck, he could see what she was doing. She had boiled the water long ago, ages before she started her search for the tea bags. That had held proceedings up for a while, but now the water was being poured into his cup. She splashed in a small waterfall of milk and then heaped in three spoonfuls of raw cane sugar. Then she proudly carried the cup the few steps to the living room and placed it before him.

'English breakfast tea,' she announced. 'Like the Queen drinks.'

'You're not joining me, JinJin?'

She shook her head and grimaced. 'I'll make some proper tea for myself.'

She watched his face as he carefully lifted the cup and sipped his tea. It was a tepid, milky concoction, so sweet that it made his eyes water.

'Mmm,' he said, and her smile came out like the sun. 'Delicious.'

TWENTY

The airport was clogged with people. It felt like everyone in China was returning home, as if the entire country was on the move, wrapped up against the sub-zero temperatures, carrying overstuffed suitcases. Everywhere he looked there were red lanterns celebrating Spring Festival.

The black snow of February was piled up by the side of the roads. Changchun was a hard, ugly place and the people at the airport looked different from the confident citizens of Shanghai. In Changchun they were noticeably shabbier, less worldly, part of the old China, gawping at Bill and JinJin and revealing teeth like vandalised tombstones.

Bill had a room at the Trader's Hotel in downtown Changchun, and JinJin came with him to check in. She would be staying with her family in their flat on the outskirts of the city. She said her mother would not approve of her staying with Bill at the hotel, and somehow this made him happy. He wanted her to be cherished. He wanted her to be protected.

She left him alone for a few hours and when she came back to collect him she was dressed in a bright red sweater, her cheeks flushed with the cold. The grey city was turning red for Spring Festival.

Downstairs there was a palpable excitement in the lobby of the hotel, and in the long queue for a cab and on the streets of the city. It felt like Christmas and New Year and the first day of the summer holidays all rolled into one. JinJin's face shone with excitement and when the mist from their breath mingled and formed a small white cloud in the back of the cab, she ran a gloved hand through it, laughing with delight.

The taxi took them out of the centre and they passed boxes of grey flats that went on forever. It looked like a Communist city, a city that had been built without a passing thought for the individual man, woman or child, but a red lantern shone in every single window of those hideous flats, scarlet splashes of colour everywhere among the bleak state housing.

As Changchun drifted by, he held JinJin's hand and wondered about her growing up here. He saw her as a child in the faces of the children on the street, bundled up like little Eskimos, their faces rosy with cold and celebration as they walked home with their parents. But perhaps she was nothing like those children. Perhaps it had been much harder for her. He had some idea of how poor her family had been. He had learned in those moments when he had wanted to know every inch of her and commit it all to memory. He had seen it in her toes.

The small toe on each foot was not the size it should have been. Her small toes were stunted, loomed over by their normal-sized neighbours. She was proud of her strange small toes, glad to cite this minor disfigurement, always happy to cheerfully deny his assertion that she was beautiful. She told him she had been born that way, that she came out of her mother with those runty small toes, and he knew it was not true. Being poor made her toes like that.

Her shoes had not been changed often enough when she was growing up. Outgrown, undersized footwear had blunted the growth of her feet. They were a mark of her family's poverty. All that new money in China, Bill thought, and none of it had reached her childhood. She could not even have a new pair of shoes when she needed them.

They reached the block of flats where she had grown up. Here, as everywhere else, a cheery red lantern glowed in every window, but when they entered the flats he could see that they were little more than giant matchboxes made from tons of concrete, miserable Soviet-style houses for the unloved masses who toiled in Changchun's factories in the days when the state still had some use for the masses, in the years when Changchun still had factories working around the clock.

Inside the flats it was filthier than anywhere he had ever seen, and he tried to hide his shock. The grey walls, the stone steps, the dripping ceiling— everything was coated with a black grime from decades of industrial filth puked out by the factories. With a gentle formality that broke his heart, JinJin took his hand and led him up to her family's home. There was no lift, and he felt ridiculous for expecting one.

Her family were waiting for him. Her mother, plump and happy, a little buck-toothed Buddha in tight leggings with a bottle of Tsingtao in her hand, all smiles. And JinJin's younger sister, Ling-Yuan—shy and curious, angelically pretty but not long and lean like JinJin, more short and stubby like their mother.

And as they fussed around him, bringing him tea, talking to him confidently in Mandarin—the

mother—and bashfully in fragments of English—
the sister—Bill sensed how hard it had been for
them, for these three women. Ling-Yuan was born
just after the one-child policy of 1978, making two
daughters and no son and then no hope of a son.
How had their father taken that?

Their father had been one of the *xiagang*, the
country's millions of laid-off state workers.
Changchun was full of them, and when he had
walked out for the last time when JinJin was
thirteen, the mother had raised her two girls alone,
working at three jobs just to survive, her youngest
child often left in the care of her big sister. In this
clean, tiny flat the mother had slept on the sofa,
and JinJin shared a bed with Ling-Yuan. Even
now, years later, Bill could almost taste the
money-starved past.

The mother spoke no English. The sister spoke a
little, and she falteringly explained the rituals of
Spring Festival to Bill while the mother poured
him a Tsingtao. They made him feel at home, and
their generosity and grace touched his heart.

Did they know he was a married man? Did they
know about Becca and Holly? JinJin did not say,
and he did not ask. It was enough that he was here,
tonight, helping them to make *jiaozi* dumplings,
meat and fish and vegetable, money inserted inside
one dumpling for good fortune the way Bill's
mother used to put a fifty-pence piece inside a
Christmas pudding.

Then he heard the baby crying.

Ling-Yuan went into the bedroom and came
back with a wailing child in her arms, around two
years old, Bill guessed, with hair like Elvis in his
prime. He was wearing a light blue Babygro

covered in dark blue hearts, and that's how Bill knew that it was a boy, and the family had its son at last. Ling-Yuan rocked him and soothed him, and his tears subsided to a few sniffles. Then, wide-eyed and unsmiling, the baby considered Bill and promptly burst into tears. Everyone laughed, and Ling-Yuan handed the baby to JinJin.

'ChoCho,' she said, bouncing him close. 'Don't cry, little ChoCho. This big-nosed pinky is a nice man. He likes babies and children very much.'

It was a good night, a wonderful night, with little ChoCho crawling between them as they made their dumplings, and everyone taking turns to hold him and play with him, even Bill, whom he slowly warmed to, despite the strangeness of his appearance.

At midnight the fireworks suddenly erupted and they went to the soot-blackened landing to watch the lights and explosions, all wrapped up against the freezing night, the baby's head peeking out of Ling-Yuan's fake-fur coat, eyes closed and whimpering from the bitter cold. The mother was in an old green army coat that was a few sizes too big for her. JinJin wore a quilted yellow ski jacket, the collar pulled up and the hood pulled down, with only her large brown eyes showing as she held Bill's hand.

When it became too cold for the baby they went back inside and ate their dumplings and wished each other happy new year. And as the last of the fireworks went off outside it really did feel like a new year to Bill, even though it was the middle of February.

JinJin wanted to escort him back to the Trader's Hotel but he told her to stay with her family. If she came back to the hotel with him then he would want her to stay and he knew that was impossible.

So he said goodbye to her mother and the kid sister and little ChoCho. JinJin put on her yellow coat and walked him to the landing where he banged his knee hard against a bicycle that had been dumped at the top of the stairs. She made sure he had a card with his hotel's name in Chinese to show the driver. He unzipped the top of her yellow ski jacket so he could slip his arms inside as he kissed her goodnight. Their bodies trembled against each other. The last of the fireworks were exploding.

'It's cold,' he said. 'Go back inside. I'll see you in the morning.'

'Okay, William,' she said, lifting her eyes to him.

She kissed him for a long moment and then she let him go and he walked down to the street, trying not to fall and break his neck in the pitch-black stairwell, attempting to avoid the soiled walls and the prehistoric bicycles that were parked on every floor.

Bill stood in the shadow of the concrete blocks, his breath billowing clouds of mist in the night, and on the wide road there were no cabs to be had. He looked up at the landing where JinJin's coat was a smudge of bright yellow in the darkness. She waved and he waved back. He wished she would go inside. The square black blocks of flats stretched off in every direction, as far as he could see.

He had never been around such poverty. He had never known it existed. But in every window of every flat of those ugly concrete blocks a red lantern was shining for Spring Festival, and the birth of another lunar year.

The moon was behind the clouds as he started walking in the direction of downtown, and as he looked up at the countless flats with all those unknowable lives he could see none of the grime and the poverty and the concrete.

All Bill could see were the pretty red lights.

* * *

He fell asleep in his hotel bed thinking about the baby.

There was a dark line on her hard flat belly and it ran from her navel to the sparse tuft of pubic hair. It had been another tale of mystery on her body like the toes, like the black-rimmed eyes, like the scars on her knees from a childhood of climbing walls and falling off walls and making her own entertainment—but the dark line on her belly was the one puzzle that he did not want to solve, because he already knew what it meant.

The line meant that she had been pregnant.

The vertical line on her belly was not like the stunted small toes or the scars on her knees—he did not want to know where it came from; he was not interested, because whatever the answer was he knew it would hurt.

He had thought it meant a terminated pregnancy. After tonight, it seemed he had been wrong. He had taken it for granted that the child he knew she had carried had never been born. The father would have been some boy in Changchun, or the man in Shanghai, or someone else, some unimaginable other man, and he did not want to know. It did not matter.

This was a country where abortion was freely and

casually available. What had Dr Khan said? It was easier than having a tooth out.

How wrong he had been. The baby explained why she'd had to give up work as a teacher. She had an entire family to support—mother, sister, and child—and bills that could never be met on what they paid a teacher in Number 251 Middle School. The line on her belly said it all—why she'd left the schoolchildren she loved, and why she lived in Paradise Mansions, and why she had to be practical.

He knew about the line. He even knew what the line was called—linea alba, white line, when you could not see it, and linea nigra, dark line, when you could.

He had seen that line before, in another bed, in another time, on another woman.

He had seen that dark line on the hard snow-white belly of his wife, and in close-up as he had gently brushed his lips across skin pulled as tight as a drum, his head reeling at the wonder of it all.

*   *   *

JinJin met him at the hotel with a pair of cashmere long johns. Her mother was worried about how he would deal with the cold. They walked through the empty streets and just before they came to the park she stopped, and held him, and told him about the married man who had fathered her child.

He had guessed a childhood sweetheart, a poor boyfriend her own age, and he had been wrong about that too. She told Bill how she had loved the man with all her heart, and how her mother had turned up at the bank where the man worked,

288

screaming that he was abusing her daughter. The relationship ended, and the man never did leave his wife. But she kept the baby.

Bay-bee, was how she pronounced it, and it held his heart. 'I always knew I would keep my baby.'

In the early days in Paradise Mansions, when she was still the girl who was picked up by the man in the silver Porsche, he had asked himself—is a woman like that capable of love?

But it wasn't what he thought, what the world thought. What the men who had beaten him and Shane would have thought. It was not sex for money, it was never sex for money.

It was sex for survival, perhaps, and a relationship with a man because there were mouths to feed. It was practical. She came from a place with no expectations and no hope. She was practical because there was no other way.

They had reached the park. There were food stalls just inside the gate. JinJin bought something that looked like a toffee apple on a stick.

Inside the park there was a frozen lake where people were skidding around on wooden boxes, steering themselves with what looked like a pair of sawn-off skis. It was like the roller-skating rink in Shanghai, one of those antique entertainments that had somehow survived into the new century.

They rented a couple of ragged old boxes and set off, and when he looked over his shoulder at JinJin, he fell in love with her, he fell in love with her at exactly that moment in Changchun. He saw her yellow coat against the frozen whiteness all around, her laughing face, her huge brown eyes shining, and he could do nothing but fall in love. He kept looking over his shoulder at her, committing it all to memory, because he had to set it down perfectly, exactly as it was, so that he could remember it in the time to come when he thought about all the things that had made his life worth living.

'Watch where you're going, William!'

He turned just in time to avoid a head-on collision with a pair of teenage boys. He swerved and skidded off the rink on to the rock-hard grass, and felt JinJin clatter into the back of him, her laugh turning to a gasp of pain as one of Bill's sawn-off skis pierced the back of her hand.

Mortified, he pulled off her glove and placed his mouth over the bead of red. He felt the salt taste of her blood on his lips. She was still smiling, telling him it was nothing, and he could not imagine a day when she would ever be out of his life. He loved her, you see.

They returned to the hotel and when JinJin had gone home, Bill turned on his phone.

You have twelve missed calls . . .

He had been expecting the call—the sudden collapse of health, the rush to the hospital, the doctor's verdict. But it was not Becca's father who was dying.

It was his own.

He listened to the messages, and then he listened to them again, and it took him some long, confused minutes to accept the reality. The old man's lungs. There was something terribly wrong with the old man's lungs, and it looked like it had been wrong for a long time. And Becca had been calling him— while he was with JinJin. Becca had been looking after his family and trying to reach him all that time, all the time that he dared not turn on his

290

phone because if he did he would have to lie.

He packed his bags and called JinJin on the way to the airport, so she didn't have the chance to accompany him back to Shanghai. He didn't want to spoil her Spring Festival. Because he was starting to believe that he spoiled everything for anyone who ever came anywhere near him.

And in the cab to the airport he listened to the messages yet again. The tone of his wife's voice made something inside him shatter. Her voice was patient, exasperated, choked up with feeling—the voice of a woman who knew him too well, and loved him far, far more than he deserved.

* * *

Fly out of Asia into Europe and time runs backwards. You crase the present, you hurtle towards the past, and your old life rushes towards you. You just can't stop it.

Bill spent the night in Changchun's freezing airport trying to get a flight, any flight, back to Shanghai, and in the morning he was on a bumpy Dragon Air ride south, the first flight out, every seat in the cabin taken, and then three more hours spent in the lounge at Pudong, waiting for his flight to Heathrow.

In the lounge at Pudong a girl brought him a cup of English breakfast tea. Fifteen minutes later, she brought him a saucer. It was the only time he smiled in the twenty-four hours it took him to get from where he was to where he had to be.

But no matter how many hours were squandered and wished gone, Asia was always ahead of Europe, and it would always be that way, and the long flight back to where he had begun never made up the difference.

* * *

Becca and Holly are waiting for him at the arrivals gate and when he sees their faces and sees them both wearing their pink Juicy T-shirts under their North Face ski jackets and their green combat trousers, like two girl soldiers, a big one and a little one, he chokes up and tries to hide it and wishes with all his heart that he had died and been burned and scattered to the wind before he had ever loved anyone but them, his wife and daughter.

Things had been simple and good and he had made them complicated and toxic and impossible, he sees all that now, understands it in a heartbeat, at long last understands the blindingly obvious. He holds Becca and Holly and longs for that old simplicity and a time when he could leave his phone turned on, and love without lying, and look at the two faces before him without feeling ashamed.

Then, with his wife holding his hand and his daughter on his lap, the little girl laughing with delight at her father's sudden presence, her small teeth even and white and perfect, they catch a black London cab to the hospital, and what Bill Holden can only think of as his punishment.

PART THREE:

HOME CALLING

TWENTY-ONE

Bill pulled back the curtain and there was his father in his hospital bed. He went quickly to the bedside, and kissed the old man on the cheek, trying to mask his shock.

The old man, Bill thought, fighting back the tears, afraid he was going to disgrace himself. What had happened to the old man?

His father looked unkempt for the first time in his life. The face was unshaven, his sparse hair too long, the eyes rheumy with drugs and bewilderment. He did not look like Picasso now. The brief peck on that patchy grey beard was like brushing his lips against sandpaper. It was like kissing death itself.

In just a few short months something had eaten up the old man, eaten him away. He looked like a husk of his former self, the shell of the strong, proud man he had always been.

The broad-shouldered boxer's body looked drained of all strength and energy and purpose, and as a young Filippina nurse propped him up on pillows to receive his latest visitors, the oxygen tank standing like a black sentinel by his bedside, the old man looked like a sick child—weak, passive, heartbreakingly unable to perform this simple act by himself.

Bill hugged him, straightened up and their eyes met. As Becca and Holly embraced the old man, something passed between the son and the father, something unspeakable and unsayable, but then it was gone, replaced by all the strained jollity of the hospital ward.

'What have we here?' Bill said, peering into the bags he carried.

'Presents!' Holly cried.

On the bedside table Bill placed a box of sweets with a picture of the Pudong skyline and a duty-free bag holding a portable DVD player and a stack of DVDs, and he was as creakingly jovial as a department store Santa on Christmas Eve.

'Your favourites, Dad,' Bill said. 'Liquorice Allsorts and cowboy films.' For want of anything better to do, Bill began pulling DVDs out of the duty-free bag. 'Let's see—you've got *The Wild Bunch . . . Shane . . . The Man Who Shot Liberty Valance . . . True Grit . . . High Noon . . .*'

The old man examined his box of sweets.

'Gary Cooper and Bertie Bassett,' he said wryly, his voice a rasping wheeze, like something with a puncture. 'Who could ask for anything more?' His old voice had gone. He had a new voice now. He turned to the nurse. 'This is my son,' he said. 'He's a big-shot lawyer.'

The nurse gave Bill a big white grin. 'He gets more visitors than anyone,' she said, and then, to the old man, raising her voice as though he were deaf or simple or both, 'He's very popular.'

'They don't know me, darling,' the old man said.

The nurse was a good woman, Bill could see that, but there was something about her tone, combining condescension and kindness in equal measure, that Bill resented, because it made him realise that the old man's illness had set him apart from the rest of the world.

Becca and Holly sat on the bed, Holly enthusiastically relaying the latest gossip from her ballet class, the old man and Becca smiling at her as she prattled away. Bill tried to busy himself by unloading his presents, and throwing out old flowers, and going to fetch tea.

When he came back two elderly neighbours had arrived, bringing petrol station flowers and banter about the old man being looked after by all these attractive young nurses. And when the old man suddenly found it impossible to take another breath, they all watched in silence as he placed an oxygen mask over his mouth and nose and struggled to fill his exhausted lungs with just one more mouthful of air.

Becca took Holly off to the toilet. When the old man was finished he flopped back, the mask in one hand, shaking his head. Then Becca came back with Holly and the grey, stubbled face was all smiles.

The nurse was right. There were many visitors. They kept coming, bringing grapes to the cancer ward, and soon the little curtained-off space was crowded. Bill thought how foolish he had been to think that his father might die alone. There was no chance of that. Too many people loved the old man to let him die alone.

It had been a small family for such a long time, just Bill and his old man, such a small family that Bill grew up and went away and started his own family wondering if they had ever really qualified as a family at all. No mother, no wife, no woman. Just a father and his son.

But the old man had his own family behind him, the brothers who were still alive, and the widows of the ones who were not, and Bill saw that there were many people who loved the old man because of who he was, and without the obligation of blood. They all came, and there was a sad grandeur to these final days in the hospital, as if all the friends and neighbours and work mates of a lifetime had to be gathered here, in this special place, to show they cared and to say goodbye.

And Bill thought, *Who will be there to mourn me?* Perhaps that was what had troubled his sleep on the long flight back—not the thought that his father might slip away with nobody by his bedside, but Bill's fear that when it was his own turn, he surely would.

When it was time for Becca and Holly to leave they kissed his father goodbye and Bill walked them to the lobby. Just beyond the glass doors an old man in stripy pyjamas and carpet slippers was smoking a cigarette. Becca picked up Holly and Bill wrapped his arms around them.

'You're out on your feet,' Becca said. 'Come home, Bill.'

But their old home was being rented out to the family of a lawyer from New York to pay the mortgage, and Becca was staying at her sister's place with Holly now that her father was feeling stronger. And Bill wanted to stay.

'I can't leave him, Bec,' he said, and she didn't argue with him.

He kissed them and let them go. Then he went back to the crowds around his father's bed. The little curtained-off space had taken on a festive air. There were people he had not seen in years, people he had never met. Introductions were made, hands shaken, cheeks kissed.

But in the end everybody left the old man except Bill, for it was getting late, and you can't stand by a hospital bed forever. There is no timetable for these things, Bill realised. He attempted to make the mental leap to the brutal fact that this was it, there was only one ending, and although the doctor said weeks rather than months they did not really know. Bill could not truly believe it, he could totally not comprehend that the world could keep turning without his old man.

It was late now and he watched the nurse, a different one, a tall young Czech, hold the oxygen mask over his father's mouth. He and his father held each other's stare for a moment and the old man closed his eyes. He was scared, Bill saw, and somehow that surprised him, although he thought—who wouldn't be?

'My son,' the old man said when the nurse took the oxygen away. 'A handsome devil, isn't he?'

He had never heard his father boast about him before and it seemed ludicrous, fake, completely out of character.

The nurse tucked in the blankets. There was a rubber sheet under the old man's bed, like the kind Holly had had when she was very small. 'I come back later for to give wash,' the nurse said.

'We've got a lot of catching up to do,' the old man said, fighting for breath again, shaking with the effort, and for a moment Bill wondered if the oxygen tank was empty.

The nurse left them alone. The lights went out. They could hear the sound of a hospital ward at night. That echoing sound that never quite managed silence. Distant voices, restless sleep.

The two men smiled at each other and Bill took the old man's hand and it seemed completely natural although he hadn't held his father's hand since he was five years old.

Those old builder's hands. The hands of a tough man, a man who worked with his body not his head, a physically capable man.

'Don't die, Dad,' Bill said, and the tears came with the words, burning his eyes. 'Please don't die.'

They had a lot of catching up to do.

*   *   *

The old man woke up in the night, writhing in his bed, and Bill was suddenly awake, rising out of the chair and hitting the button that called for help. There was too much pain, he couldn't stand it. Bill stood by the bed as a black nurse he had not seen before came and calmly gave the old man a little white pill in a plastic container. The nurse tucked in his sheets, gave Bill a weary smile and then left them. In the next bed a man cried out a woman's name in his sleep. Bill stroked his father's hand as the old man lay back, eyes closed, mouth open, and every breath another battle.

'I wish it had been better between us,' Bill said after a while, very quietly, almost to himself, and the feelings he had held back for so long came tumbling out. 'You were always my hero. I always admired you. I always thought you were the most decent man I ever knew.' He patted his father's hand, so lightly that it seemed as if he hardly touched it. 'I always wanted whatever it was that you and Mum had.' Bill was silent for a bit. The ward was very still now, but he could sense all those bodies in the darkness beyond the curtain. He took a breath. 'And I always loved you, Dad,' he said. 'It might not have seemed that way, but I

300

never stopped loving you.'

His father was sleeping.

*   *   *

A few hours later the ward was stirring. There were voices, the smell of food, gathering light. A breakfast tray lay untouched in front of the old man.

'How long have you known?' Bill asked him.

'A while,' the old man said. 'Didn't want to worry you.' He pushed the breakfast tray a bit further away. 'Got enough on your plate.' Bill could hear the breath in the ravaged lungs. 'Tell me about your life,' the old man said, closing his eyes. 'I want to hear about it. Tell me how it's going out there.'

'Sure.' Bill pulled his chair closer to the bed. 'It's going well, Dad. When you feel better, you'll come out again. When Becca and Holly are back. I'll fly you out. I will. First class this time, Dad.'

He thought of all the times his father had bored him or made him impatient and ashamed and he wanted to make up for all that, he wanted to take it all back, and now it was too late, now it would always be too late.

'We'll meet you at the airport and it will be great. You'll stay with us, Dad,' Bill said, and the tears came again, because he knew he might as well be promising a round trip to the moon. 'You'll stay with me, Dad, you'll stay with us, and it will all be good.'

And the old man gently touched Bill's hand, as though his young son was the one in need of comforting.

301

During the day they could not talk, not with all the visitors around, not with all the chitchat and sympathy. At night, if the old man was not too distracted by the pain and not too numbed by the drugs they gave him to obliterate the pain, then they could do their catching up.

'And are you all right? You and Becca?'

Bill wished he had the stomach to lie. But he was sick of it. That's why he would never make a truly accomplished liar. Because it ate him up. It took something from him that he would never get back.

'I don't know,' he said.

The old man looked at him with hooded eyes, and Bill felt some of the old scared feeling that he always felt when he had displeased his father.

'Got somebody else, have you?' the old man said, guessing it all, and Bill wondered how this one-woman man knew so much about the frailty of modern relationships.

Bill thought about lying, his last chance to lie, and then nodded. He waited for more questions, but the old man said nothing.

Bill looked up at him. 'You and Mum stayed together. If she hadn't died then you'd be together now. How do you do that? How do you stay with someone for a lifetime?'

The old man winced with pain. He exhaled once, and seemed to writhe against the pillows. Bill jumped up but his father motioned for him to sit down.

'We weren't perfect,' he said. 'Children always think their parents are made of different stuff to them. But we were no different. We had our moments.'

Bill tried to place his mum and dad in their moments, and in the modern world, he tried to put them into somewhere like Paradise Mansions, into the mess he had made of his own life. But it was beyond his imagination.

'But you stayed together,' he said. 'Whatever happened, you stayed together.'

The pain was strong now. You could see it written all over the old man's face. Bill was standing again. The old man held the metal box with the red button, but he didn't press it, as if unsure if he should call the nurse now or try to wait a while.

'Because you don't leave your child for a woman,' the old man told him, and he gave Bill a look as though he knew nothing. 'Nobody's that good in bed.'

*   *   *

The old man liked bragging to the nurses. It was as if he had to impress the last young women he would ever know. Anything would do.

'Look at this,' he said, fondling his portable DVD player as the Czech nurse looked at his chart. 'One of the latest gadgets. My dad bought me this.'

Bill laughed with disbelief. His dad bought him that? He couldn't let the old man get away with that. It meant he was slipping off the edge of sanity. And it frightened Bill. He touched his father's arm, covered in black-and-yellow bruises from all the needles for the blood tests and the IV drip and the injections for the pain.

'It was me,' Bill said, with a smile to ease the way. 'Remember? I got it for you.'

Unexpected tears sprang into the old man's eyes, confused and humiliated at this casual contradiction.

'But my dad *was* here,' he said with real anger. 'I saw him.'

The Czech nurse glanced at Bill and on her impassive face he saw the message loud and clear. *Their minds go, you know. All the chemicals. By this stage they're in their own little dream world.*

'You want shave?' said the nurse, raising her voice. 'You want nice I give little shave?'

'I'll do it,' Bill said.

*　　　*　　　*

On the seventh day Bill could no longer keep his eyes open. He slumped forward in the chair by the bed, his head lolling, unable to believe that he could be so tired.

'Go home,' the old man wheezed. 'Go home and get a good night's kip.'

Bill was used to his father's new voice by now. He had almost forgotten what the old voice sounded like. This was normal—the croaking voice, the lungs with no air, the unbearable pain of inhaling and exhaling. All normal now. Bill could hear every pitiful breath, every one of them as undeniable as a scar. But although Bill was fighting to keep his eyes open, his father seemed more awake than he had been for a long time. The pain had retreated for now, and with it the doses of morphine. The old man almost seemed restored to his former self. Giving his son orders, knowing what was best for him, and not willing to discuss it.

'I mean it,' the old man commanded. 'Go get some kip.'

Bill stood up, stretched his back. 'I might do that,' he said. 'I might get some kip, Dad. Come back in the morning.'

'Good idea.' His father was sitting up in bed. But then he was always sitting up, even when he was sleeping. The old man nodded encouragement, not so stern now. Just wanting what was best for his son.

'Just for a few hours,' Bill said, and he looked at his father's freshly shaven face, smooth as a baby, and he suddenly remembered what he had to tell him. 'Dad?'

The old man had sunk back into his pillow. There was no sign of the pain that seemed to suddenly paralyse every muscle in his face. He seemed peaceful. As though he were about to close his eyes and get some kip too. 'What?'

It was so simple. And so obvious. And so necessary. 'I love you, Dad,' Bill said. And then he laughed with embarrassment.

The old man opened his eyes and smiled. 'Yeah. I know you do. And I love you too. You know I do.'

Bill hung his head. 'I'm so sorry, Dad.'

'What for?'

'That I never told you before.'

The old man smiled at his grown-up son.

'Once is plenty.'

*   *   *

They called him in the morning to tell him that his father had died.

305

He knew what it was before he answered his mobile in the spare room of Sara's house. He already knew.

A world without his father in it.

It was a one-minute phone call from someone he had never met and who he would never meet. They were as sympathetic as they could possibly be, under the circumstances. Bill sat on the edge of the bed and stared at his phone. It was the most natural thing in the world, and the most momentous. The end of the old man's life. It felt both ordinary and epic.

Bill went to the room's small window, stared out at the suburban street and tried to feel something. But nothing came. He couldn't even cry. All he could feel was a bleak relief that all that pain was over, and a nagging guilt that he had not been there at the end, and a gratitude that the old man had been his father.

He went downstairs to where he could hear voices. He didn't feel like company but Sara was there with Becca in the kitchen. Becca looked at Bill and stood up and she knew, just got it straight away, and he went to her arms and let her hold him before breaking away with an apologetic smile. Sara touched his arm and slipped out of the room.

Becca pulled him close and he leaned against her, her blonde hair in his face, his mouth against her skin, and he revelled in his wife, he inhaled her, he wanted to get lost in her.

'He was a lovely man,' she said. 'I'm so sorry, Bill.' She looked at his face. 'You should sleep on for a bit.'

'But there's so much to do, Bec.' Feeling giddy with the thought of it.

He had to collect his father's things from the hospital. He had to arrange a funeral. He had to tell everyone who knew and loved the old man that he was gone. He had to register the death. All the banal admin of death. He had to do all of that. And he had no idea how to do any of these things.

'It can all wait a while,' Becca told him, and she stroked his back as he held her. 'I know,' she said. 'I know, Bill. But you've still got us.'

He nodded, turning away from her, hiding his face. In the hallway he bumped into Sara, rounding up her children. To get them out of the house, Bill thought. To give us space. They were girls of six and eight and a boy of ten. And then he was in Sara's arms and he was touched by her tears, the tears that he couldn't cry himself.

Sara was an older, sportier version of Becca, wearing a T-shirt advertising her Pilates class, and her cropped, dyed red hair was the only sign of any other life beyond the one she had now.

Becca had been right about Sara and Bill had been wrong. Sara had been through her adventures, and her changes, and come out the other side as a real sister to Becca, and a loving aunt to Holly, and a friend to Bill's family, even though he had not known it until now.

Sara's partner came down the stairs. He shook Bill's hand, offered his condolences and told Sara's children they were going to the park. He was a tall, quiet man in a track suit, some sort of personal trainer. Bill had been wrong about him too.

Here was the little family that had looked after Holly when Becca was nursing her own father, and they were clearly all such decent people, and so smitten with Holly, and so sorry to hear of the death of Bill's dad, that Bill felt a flush of shame. Not only for what he had thought of them, but what he had thought of his wife. How could he have believed that Becca would ever leave Holly somewhere she wasn't safe and loved? How could he have imagined that? What was wrong with him?

'Thank you,' Bill said to them. 'For everything. I'll go to see Holly.'

She was watching a Wonder Pets DVD in the living room. He picked her up but she squirmed out of his arms, her eyes not leaving the TV screen.

'I want to watch this,' she said.

The room was cool and dark and the only light came from the screen where the Wonder Pets were rescuing some sort of egg.

'But when are they going to have the happy ending?' Holly asked him.

He smiled. 'I'm sure they'll get there in the end,' he said, standing up and lifting his daughter with him. Heavy, he thought. Heavier all the time. But always his baby girl. She peeped at the DVD over his shoulder. He wanted to get it out of the way. He wanted to be beyond this moment.

'Darling, your granddad's in heaven now.' He didn't know what to say to her. He didn't know how to explain death to a four-year-old. He didn't know where to begin. 'He loved you so much. Just so much. And he will always be looking down on you, and he will never stop loving you.'

'I know,' she said, turning her blue eyes from the television to her father. 'Granddad was here.'

'Yes, Granddad Joe is always here for you, and he loves you too,' Bill said. 'I'm not talking about Mummy's daddy. I'm not talking about Granddad

Joe.'

Holly shook her head impatiently. 'Me neither. Not Granddad Joe. My other Granddad. The one that died.' She looked at him now and did not turn away her clear, unwavering gaze. 'Your daddy. He was here. And he smiled at me.' Holly nodded once, as if it was all settled. 'It's true, you know.'

He looked at her for a moment and then he held her tighter than he had ever held her before. Winter sunshine was pouring into the room, the windows of the suburban London house turning to blocks of blazing gold, and Bill had to close his eyes against it.

'I know it's true,' he whispered to his daughter, and his heart was full of love and grief and an edge of fear that he could not deny.

*   *   *

The key turned in the lock and Bill had to press hard against the door to move all the junk mail.

Becca followed him into the darkness and stale air of his father's house, watching his face as he paused and looked around, as if seeing the place where he had grown up for the first time.

She found a switch and turned on some lights.

'You okay?' she said, touching his arm.

He nodded. 'You can't breathe in here,' he said.

'I'll open some windows,' she said.

She looked around for a key to the back door and found it under the mat that said *Our Home* in florid, faded letters. She threw open the back door and looked out at the scrubby patch of neglected garden, filling her lungs with air that didn't taste of tobacco and illness.

Bill was in the living room, peering at the bookcase. Under one arm he carried a stack of flat-packed cardboard boxes and in the other hand he had a thick black roll of rubbish bags. That was their job today. To decide what went to Oxfam and what was thrown away.

'Remember this?' he said, and she was glad to see him smile.

He was looking at a photograph of Holly. She was three years old, holding a thick pink crayon like a miniature javelin and grinning at the tiny black girl standing next to her.

'First day of nursery,' Becca said. Their eyes scanned the bookcase. It was a bookcase that contained no books, just a few ragged copies of *Reader's Digest* and *National Geographic*, some souvenirs of foreign holidays—Spanish castanets, a Chinese doll—and shelf after shelf of family photographs.

Bill's parents on their wedding day. Bill as a baby in the arms of his mother. Bill as a crop-haired toddler with his father down on one knee beside him, the boy standing on his father's thigh. Bill and Becca on their wedding day. And Holly everywhere, from birth to now. If Becca looked quickly along the shelves, it was like watching her daughter grow up before her eyes.

'He was lonely,' Bill said.

'He had a lot of people who loved him,' she said. 'You saw that at the funeral.'

Bill picked up a *TV Guide* on the coffee table, still open at the day his father had been rushed to hospital. His finger traced the favourite programmes ringed in red ink. Cop shows, hospital dramas, sport.

310

'Shall we make a start?' Becca said. 'Or do you want to do it some other time?'

He shook his head.

After she had filled a few rubbish sacks with the contents of the kitchen cupboards, much of it with a use-by date from the last century, Becca went upstairs. Bill was in the bedroom, sitting on the bed with a green box file on his lap. She sat down next to him. He was holding a photograph clipped from a magazine, a picture of Bill in black tie with Becca in an evening gown by his side. They held champagne flutes and each other, smiling uncertainly.

'Our first Burns night at the firm. We look so young.'

He nodded but said nothing, and she saw that the box on his lap was full of cuttings from trade papers. Bill made no move to touch them so, very carefully, Becca began to leaf through them, as if afraid they might disintegrate in her hands.

'Look,' she said, showing Bill a torn and sellotaped certificate with his name on it that said, LEGAL WEEK AWARDS—SECOND RUNNER UP—HIGHLY COMMENDED.

'All the crap he kept,' Bill said. He shook his head and covered his face with his hands. 'I just wanted to make him proud of me.'

Becca put her arm around his shoulders. 'Look around,' she said. 'You did.'

He kept his hands over his face. 'Don't give up on me, Bec,' he said.

She laughed at the thought.

'Why would I do that?' she said.

*   *   *

The three of them stood at the foot of the hill, waiting. The only sounds were the distant buzz of the late-afternoon traffic, the voices of small children playing in the park, and the wind whipping through the bare branches of the trees up on Primrose Hill.

Holly yawned. Bill looked at Becca.

'It's not going to happen,' he said. 'Let's go.'

Becca shook her head.

'Wait. Let's wait just a little bit longer.'

Holly sighed elaborately. 'Oh, come *on*, Mummy,' she said, her shoulders slumping theatrically to convey her exhaustion. *'Please.'*

'One more minute,' Becca said, not budging. She felt her husband and her daughter exchange exasperated looks, and ignored them. She had faith.

Then she saw it. While Bill and Holly were still fidgeting with irritation and looking elsewhere, Becca saw the giraffe suddenly sway into view above the tree line, looking at the three of them out of the corner of its eye, ruminatively chewing a mouthful of leaves, and before she could cry out there was another, and then another, all of them gazing down on the little family with quizzical disdain.

'Look, look, look!' Becca was crying, afraid that her grumpy companions would miss them, but by then Bill and Holly were laughing too, squinting up into the pale winter sunshine and applauding wildly at the sight of the secret giraffes.

*   *   *

Bill wanted them to check into a hotel, but Sara would not hear of it.

Holly was in with the two girls and Becca and Bill were in the guest room. Becca knew it was not what he wanted. Bill was anxious to be alone with his family again, and to close the door on the rest of the world. On his last night, he watched her as she came towards the bed in just her panties and a T-shirt, and she knew that look. She stood by the side of the bed, smiling at him.

'Bill, I'll be back in Shanghai next week,' she said. 'And these walls are really, really thin.'

He shrugged. 'We could just have a cuddle.'

'Yeah, right. I know your cuddles.' She slid into bed beside him and he wrapped his arms around her as if he had been waiting for a long time. He whispered her name, and then said it again.

'We would have to be really, really quiet,' she said, stifling a laugh. 'I mean it, Bill.'

He nodded, ready to promise anything, pushing up her T-shirt. 'I'll put on my silencer,' he said, and she felt his mouth on her lips, and on her face, and on her ribs, and she could feel how much he wanted her, and it felt familiar and new all at once.

Later he lay on his back and she lay on her side in his arms, the pair of them drifting away to sleep, the way they always used to.

Becca wondered—when had they stopped sleeping like this? After they were married? After Holly was born? When had sleeping in his arms become something that she no longer did?

'Come back with me,' he whispered. 'In the morning. The pair of you. I can get you on my flight. It's not too late, Bec.'

'Soon,' she said, patting his chest. 'Very soon.'

313

He seemed desperate.

'Why not now?'

'Holly's school. My dad. Our house. These people we've been renting to have made a bloody mess of it, Bill. I have a million things to do. Just give me a few days. Next week, okay?'

In the morning he flew back alone.

TWENTY-TWO

From the back seat of the car Ling-Yuan watched the factory workers stream out of the gates, her pretty face trying to hide the fear as her big sister sat in the driver's seat talking to her quietly in Mandarin. Encouraging her, Bill thought. Taking care of her even as she prepares to let her go.

A bell was ringing to signal the end of the shift. The workers were mostly young and female and many of them were still in the light blue coats that they wore at their workstations. Some of them were eating as they walked, their chopsticks shovelling noodles from plastic bowls held just a few inches from the mouth. They looked worn out, ravenous, like refugees in their own land.

'What do they make?' JinJin said, turning to him.

'They make Christmas decorations,' Bill said. The sisters looked at him blankly. 'Santas and reindeers. Angels and silver bells. You know—the stuff they hang on a Christmas tree.'

They didn't know. Not really. All the Christmas trees they had ever seen were in shopping malls—giant merry monsters strung with strobe lights, although both of them had vague memories of seeing the more domestic Yuletide tree in half-watched Hollywood movies. But they got the point. 'Like a toy factory,' JinJin concluded. It didn't really matter what they made here. The factories were all the same in the end.

Ling-Yuan said something and her big sister barked back at her. Bill looked at JinJin.

'She's talking about modelling again,' she told him, then directed a stream of angry advice at Ling-Yuan. 'I tell her—forget about modelling for now.'

Ling-Yuan wanted to be a model. One of those new Chinese dreams, Bill thought. And she was young enough and pretty enough. But even Bill could see that she was too short and too heavy to do much more than hand over the money that JinJin had given her for a one-month modelling course in Shenyang. The course had been completed, a certificate awarded, but no modelling offers had materialised. So now they sat outside the factory gates as the workers flowed around them and JinJin said something to her sister, more softly now, and Ling-Yuan leaned towards him, her face pale with worry.

'Thank you, William,' she said.

He shook his head. He wished he could have done more, he wished he could have found her a better job. But there were no economic miracles for an untrained young woman. 'Shall I come in with you?' he said.

JinJin shook her head. 'I have the name,' she said, studying a scrap of paper. They got out of the car and started walking towards the factory gates, one sister so tall and lean, the other so small and round. Ling-Yuan was carrying a small Hello Kitty

315

bag. In the West she would be going to the gym, Bill thought. Here she's going off to a new life. No wonder she's terrified.

He wished he could speak to the little sister in her own language and tell her that he knew what it was like to be that scared, to be that petrified of change. But she's a kid, he thought. Just a kid. She's too young to feel like that.

The sisters disappeared inside the factory gates, and Bill sat watching the shattered faces of the workers until JinJin came back out alone.

*   *   *

They made love in the new apartment, the one she had rented with the money he had transferred to her account, and he needed her and he loved her and he was so ashamed of her, so ashamed that she had quit her old life as a school teacher for the other man, the man before him, the man who had paid for the flat in Gubei and everything in it, including her, and Bill was so ashamed of himself, and even as they lost themselves in the big new bed in the beautiful unfurnished apartment, he knew that they would never have a happy ending, not in a million years, no matter how much they loved each other, because the shame would see to that.

'This is *our* flat,' she said firmly, and her innocent optimism broke his heart. It was not their flat. The lease was in her name. It was the least he could do, and the most he could do. Because he already had a home.

They were happy. That was the funny thing. That was the madness. They laughed at nothing, they laughed at everything. They were always happy

316

when they were together. But then came the moment when he had to get out of bed and get dressed and go home. She buried her face in the pillow, the black hair tumbling over her eyes, and she never confronted him, she never issued ultimatums, and that made it worse.

'I can't stay,' he said, preparing to go back to the real world. 'You know that.'

She knew that. She was ready to sleep. Like a normal person. And he was tired too. But it was time to get dressed and step out into the night. It had been a long day—the drive out of the city to the factory in the northern suburbs, saying goodbye to the sister, coming back to Shanghai, making love, holding each other, the clock running.

Any normal person would be ready for sleep.

And as Bill looked in on his daughter tucked up in dreams in his old room, and then went into the master bedroom and slid into bed next to his sleeping wife, he knew that he would never feel like a normal person again.

*   *   *

She had knocked on his door.

After Holly and Becca had come back, and she had known they were there, JinJin had done the unthinkable and crossed the courtyard and knocked on his door with a smile on her face. That was the thing that shook him when he opened the door and saw her standing there—she was smiling.

'Denial,' Shane said later. 'That's what they call big-time denial, mate.'

Bill did not know if it was denial. How does

317

anyone deny a wife and a child? But he could not believe it was an act of malice. Despite all she had seen of the world, there was an innocence about JinJin. She probably just wanted to see him. It was as simple as that. She followed her heart. And she just wasn't being practical.

'But JinJin,' he said, genuinely not understanding what she was doing there, wondering what would have happened if Becca had opened the door, what would have happened if his wife and daughter had not been sleeping off their jet-lag, 'you can't come in here.'

And she didn't. She went away. Then she cried for a few days. It was all crazy. What did she expect? And when he finally went to her new flat he had to hold her and tell her as gently as he could what he had told her long ago and what she could not have forgotten—*I'm not free*—and just hold her some more and let her break her heart in his arms until she was ready to let him lead her to the bed.

'Who was that at the door?' Becca had said.

'Nobody,' he had said.

His friend was right. They call it denial.

*   *   *

Then he did not see her for a month.

His family were back and he was sick of secrets and in the remnants of the week when he was not at work he was with Becca and Holly, watching the dolphins in Aquaria 21 at Changfeng Park on Saturday afternoons, and on Sunday mornings going on the slides and rides at Fun Dazzle in Zhongshan Park, and then eating brunch together

318

at the Four Seasons or the Ritz-Carlton or M on the Bund. One time he thought he saw her. But there were a million girls who looked like her. And none of them were her.

In the end he found himself back in the rented apartment, hating himself for leaving her alone for so many nights, flinching at the sight of her crossword puzzles, knowing that on any of those nights he could have gone from the office to her flat before going home, and as they ate the noodles she had prepared, he plotted how to steal a tiny piece of time.

The city was suddenly different. There were places that were safe and there were places that were not safe and there were places where you took your chances but you just didn't know.

New Gubei was off limits. The Bund was out of bounds. Hongqiao, where they had rented her apartment, was reassuringly foreign ground, but he soon tired of the local restaurants because they were full of wealthy men who had installed their sleek mistresses in the lush anonymity of the Hongqiao apartment blocks. It wasn't the girls who appalled him. It was the men. Bill couldn't stand being around those men. He could not stand the thought that he was one of them.

Trips were best. There was much less chance of being seen together on a trip. When they started to feel the pressure of being confined to her bland new neighbourhood, JinJin suggested a short boat trip down the Chang Jiang, the Long River, the Chinese term for what Westerners knew as the Yangtze.

It was believable, both at home and in the office, that he could have pressing business in Chongqing,

319

the big ugly capital of southwest China, and their departure point for a trip down the Yangtze. After they flew to the filthy old port, Bill even had a brief meeting with Chinese clients at a freight company while JinJin bought their boat tickets for their trip down the Yangtze.

The best lies were the ones that stayed closest to the truth, Bill realised, the lies that you could almost believe yourself.

Or were they the worst lies?

*   *   *

Outside their cabin window the rain lashed down on the green limestone cliffs.

There were white man-made markings high up on the cliffs, even higher than the wispy clouds of mist that clung to the rock face, and these white markings indicated where the water would rise to when the Three Gorges dam was completed. Bill found it hard to believe, but in a few years all this impossible beauty would be gone forever, and it would be as if it had never existed. It was like concreting over the Grand Canyon to turn it into the world's biggest parking lot. Yet somehow the Chinese expected you to be impressed. The boat's PA system was a constant tinny blare boasting in Mandarin about the march of progress. And it wasn't just the land they were destroying. Two million people were being moved from their homes. Entire communities would be under water. It made him feel physically sick, it made him feel a long way from home.

Their Yangtze trip was wrong from the start.

'I don't know why you can't go back to teaching,'

he said, pacing the tiny cabin. 'You were good at it. Your students loved you.'

JinJin was sitting on one of the cabin's single beds studying the smiling face of a CCTV presenter. 'A good horse eats going forward,' she said, not looking up.

'I don't know what that means,' he said, though he knew exactly what it meant. It meant you can't go back. 'What's that? Another wise old Chinese saying?'

'Yes,' she said, in that clear, quiet voice she used when they were about to argue. 'Another wise old Chinese saying. It is true there are so many.'

He turned and looked at the sheer green tower outside his window. All this useless beauty, he thought. What good does it do anyone? They will only kill it, cover it with concrete and tons of water and the dumb bastards will still want to take their photographs.

The boat was horrible. Like a floating block of council flats, Bill thought. MS Kongling *is a deluxe cruise ship of the most up to date facilities, perfect functions and a great variety of amusements of almost all kinds*, said the leaflet that JinJin had proudly presented to him as they waited to board. *The Three Gorges are celebrated for their majestic steep crags, secluded beauty, dangerous shoals and magnificent stones and sceneries. When the Three Gorges Project completed, these treasures will be covered by water, so please to be welcome to the unspoiled pristine Three Gorges, a natural landscape gallery of unique beauty, peril and serenity, where you will escape from the worldliness and remain fresh and healthy in Nature and Beauty.*

But they were rarely fresh and healthy in Nature

321

and Beauty on that floating eyesore full of tourists, and in the dining room at every meal they had to share their table with two silent Taiwanese men who shovelled in food held an inch from their faces while staring at Bill and JinJin as though they had never seen such a sight.

There were a few game old American tourists in baseball caps and khaki shorts, and on the first night one of them borrowed JinJin's camera to take a picture of Bill and JinJin dancing. A patch of deck in the restaurant had been designated a dance floor and as Faye Wong sang a love song Bill held JinJin in what he imagined was the old-fashioned style, the way his father would have held his mother. As the kind old American took their picture, they could not stop smiling. That was the best time.

Apart from Bill and the elderly Americans, everyone else on board was Chinese, and he knew that this was the real problem with the good ship *MS Kongling*. This was a luxury ship only if you were Chinese. If you were not Chinese, then it was like a prison, but with poorer food and more rules and regulations.

A bell rang signalling lunch and above their heads they could hear the tourists scrambling to be fed. Bill's heart sank at the thought of the Taiwanese eating with their mouths open. JinJin tossed her TV magazine to one side and crossed her legs. She was wearing a white mini-skirt, boots and a black roll-neck sweater. Her hair was pulled back in a ponytail, and he liked it that way, because it meant you could see her face. No matter how simply she dressed, she always looked great. They looked at each other and she smiled at him and they both knew they would not be going up for lunch.

The boat drifted by the Three Gorges in the rain and he knew that this was the biggest problem of all. His head said forget it, but his heart said that he could never forget it.

Not when the Three Gorges was as lost as Atlantis, not when the waters rose and the mountains fell, not in a thousand years.

*   *   *

There was one Chinese character that had lodged in his mind and that he always recognised and it was the character for her family name. He could read *Li* when he saw it written in Chinese. So when they came through domestic arrivals at Pudong airport and he saw one of the hordes of drivers holding a sign with her name on it he pulled her arm and nodded at the sign and they both laughed with pleasure.

Then he saw Tiger.

He was idling at the end of the line, watching the other exit door, and while JinJin laughed as a middle-aged businessman approached the driver holding up her name—'Look, William, it's Mr Li!'—Bill searched the crowd, wondering who Tiger was waiting for.

And then he saw them.

The boys came out first, those three wild blond monkeys, the small one fiddling with his iPod while the two big ones bickered and slapped each other, and then their parents—Devlin pushing the trolley loaded with luggage, raising a hand to Tiger, and Tess beside him, giving instructions to the boys, and carrying a carrier bag that said *Chek Lap Kok Airport*.

Back from a long weekend in Hong Kong, Bill registered, just as Mrs Devlin turned her head and stared straight at him.

Then Bill was gone—quickly but far too slow to avoid being seen.

He turned away and headed in the other direction and got lost in the crowd, with JinJin still holding on to him but struggling to keep up, aware that something was very wrong, and he hated the wild panic inside him, it made him burn with shame, but he still didn't stop or slow down until they were out of the airport and at the end of a mercifully short taxi queue.

'What's wrong?' she said, not getting it, and really wanting to know. 'Tell me.'

'Nothing,' he said, not looking at her, not daring to look at anything, wishing the queue away, wanting to be safely hidden in the back of a cab, and all the while waiting for the moment when he would hear an English voice right behind him say his name.

But the queue moved, and they got into the back of an old Santana taxi, and JinJin let him be. She knew him well enough for that. And she was smart enough to guess.

*   *   *

'William, why don't you tell me what's wrong? Perhaps I can help.'

JinJin was sitting up in bed in a T-shirt and panties, thumbing through a book of crossword puzzles. This was the exotic for them, he realised, this was a special treat. Hanging around the apartment like a normal couple, as though they had all the normal time in the normal world. As though Bill was a good man with no other place to be.

'I told you,' he said, his voice thin and tight. He didn't want to take it out on her, not her, she did not deserve it, but he could not stop himself. 'Nothing's wrong, okay?'

'Was it the woman at the airport? The one who was looking at us? It was the woman from the teahouse, wasn't it?'

Jesus Christ, he thought. *What happens now?*

He was standing at the window looking down at the traffic on Zhongshan Xilu and the lights of the Shanghai stadium, and not seeing any of it.

He shouldn't be here. He should have gone home. Change the cover story. Change his life. Because his daughter was waiting for him. Because Tess Devlin had seen him. And now everyone would know. Now his dirty little secret would be released into the world.

The things that had once made him glad to be alive now made him wish he were dead. It wasn't worth it. To feel this way—it just wasn't worth it. He felt like he was being torn in two.

'William?' He heard her setting down the crossword puzzle.

He didn't move from the window. 'What is it?'

'Are you cross with me?' she said.

He turned to look at her. 'Am I cross with you? You do realise—or perhaps you don't—that nobody talks like that in England? Outside of—I don't know—Enid Blyton novels. Nobody says— are you cross with me?' He turned back to the window, hating himself. 'Your text books were fifty years out of date.'

'Please don't be cross with me,' she said, and he covered his eyes with one hand. He shook his head, almost laughing. Her voice was soft and understanding. She would forgive him anything. She loved him and he knew it. 'Why don't you just come to bed?' she said.

He met her eyes. 'And why don't you get out of my fucking life?'

He went into the bathroom, for want of anywhere better to go, slamming the door behind him. He stared at his face in the mirror and he was ashamed of taking it out on her when she had done nothing wrong. He cursed, threw cold water on his face. It was him. It was all him. He was the one who had done everything wrong. He went back into the bedroom so that he could hold her and tell her that he was sorry and let her see that he meant it.

But by then JinJin Li had got up, got dressed and got out of his life.

TWENTY-THREE

'You should see this,' Becca said.

She was standing at the window, looking down at the courtyard of Paradise Mansions. Bill went across to her, remembering when she had said the same thing on that first night. Looking down at the girls getting into the cars. That first night, when he saw JinJin for the first time, all dolled up for Saturday night and the man in the silver Porsche.

326

There was the same note of amused disbelief in his wife's voice now. *You should see this.* Then she turned to look at him and he saw the concern on her face.

'You all right?' she said, her fingertips on his day-old stubble. 'God, Bill—you look beat.'

'I'm all right.'

Bill joined Becca at the window and his wife slipped her arm around his waist. There were raised voices in the courtyard. A Chinese woman in her fifties was screaming abuse as she threw things from a window in the opposite block. Dresses, underwear, bed sheets were tossed out and fell and floated to the ground. Annie was down in the courtyard, desperately gathering up her belongings, weeping bitterly.

'The wife found out,' Becca said, indicating the woman at the window. 'That's what happened. She just found out.'

'Well, maybe,' Bill said, turning away from the window. He couldn't stand watching all that raw grief. 'Or maybe she knew all along but the time came for a crackdown.'

Becca's smile grew wider. 'Listen to you. You sound like an expert.'

He grimaced. 'I don't know anything about it,' he said.

There were loud thuds in the courtyard. Annie's wailing went up a pitch, registering fear as well as misery. The wife had found a store of Louis Vuitton bags. They hit the courtyard like small rocks and as each one fell it brought cries of real anguish from Annie.

Bill remembered the tattoo on Annie's arm, the beginning of the end. He wondered if the man had

327

confessed to his wife, shopped Annie and himself, and let the wife do the dirty work of evicting her, or if she had found out some other way. He hated this man he had never met.

'I wonder why they do it,' Becca said, turning away from the window. 'These girls, I mean.'

Bill stayed at the window, wanting to help Annie and knowing he could do nothing. 'They just want to better themselves,' he said. 'That's what we all want, isn't it?'

Becca shook her head, sinking into the sofa. She picked up a glossy catalogue.

'A woman has to have something missing to get involved with a married man,' Becca said. 'It takes a lack of imagination, or a lack of heart, or—I don't know—some kind of mad optimism.'

She flicked past images of chairs, tables and wine glasses embossed with Chinese symbols. Down in the courtyard Annie gathered up her beloved bags. A light wind had lifted one of the sheets and wrapped it around her legs. The woman in the window was pointing down and laughing. Faces were appearing at other windows, and calling to their spouses to come and see.

'It's just so bloody cruel,' Becca said.

'Well,' Bill said. 'I guess she's really angry. It can't be easy. Finding out something like that.'

Becca looked at him strangely.

'I'm not talking about the wife, Bill,' she said. 'I'm talking about the silly bitch who has been running around with a married man. Can't you see? She's the cruel one.'

* * *

328

They went shopping. Suddenly Holly's expanding social schedule allowed these pockets of time for just the two of them. Perhaps it would carry on like this all through her childhood, Bill thought, and in the end they would not be needed at all.

'What about these?' Becca said, picking up a wine glass with a tastefully embossed Chinese symbol. 'Do you like this, Bill?'

He nodded. 'Very nice,' he said. 'You know, Bec, Devlin said we should take Holly to the Natural Wild Insect Kingdom on Fenghe Lu,' he said. 'It's aimed at kids. They can hold big hairy spiders. The boys love it, apparently.'

'I bet they do,' she said, holding the glass up to the light. 'Those little horrors. But I'm not sure it's really Holly's thing. She'd run a mile if she was presented with a tarantula.' She touched his arm. 'You know, we don't always have to do something.'

He looked bewildered.

'I know you've been trying really hard since we came back,' she said. 'Dolphins, bumper cars, creepy crawlies . . .' She smiled. 'But sometimes we can just take her out on her bike to the park. Try and get her off the stabilisers. Or we can stay home. She loves drawing and crayoning and all that stuff.' She touched her husband's face. 'Sometimes we can just be together.' Becca put down the wine glass and glanced at her watch. 'We're going to have to pick her up from ballet soon,' she said.

'I'll get her,' he said.

'You don't mind?' Becca said, running her hand over the lacquered wood of a red Chinese lamp. 'I could spend all day in here.' She picked up the wine glass again and slowly twirled it. The Chinese symbol looked like it had been drawn in frost. 'Do you have any idea what this means?' she asked.

'Double Fortune,' Bill said. 'It means a happy ending for both of you.'

* * *

'Full moon,' said the ballet teacher, and the class raised both their hands above their heads. Bill watched Holly, her pale face frowning with concentration, and imagined her on stage for the Royal Ballet, hugging a bouquet to her chest as she took a standing ovation, her proud father wiping a tear from his eye in the stalls.

'Half-moon,' said the teacher, and all the little girls in their pink tutus—and one weird curly-haired boy in white shorts and vest—dropped their right hands to their side, apart from Holly, who dropped her left hand.

Bill smiled as she did a double take at her friends, and corrected herself.

'No moon,' said the teacher, and the class dropped the other hand to their sides, and Bill was amazed how the frail little girl Holly had been a year ago was turning into a bundle of endless energy.

She was still thin and pale and slighter than her contemporaries, but the asthma attacks were further apart, and less severe, and she no longer looked as though a strong wind would carry her away.

As the class began running around in circles, their faces beaming with delight, flapping their hands close to their sides—'Small wings,' the teacher had commanded—Bill thought she was

330

growing into the person she was meant to be. She was becoming herself.

After the class he helped her out of her pink leotard, pink tutu and pink slippers and into combat trousers, T-shirt and trainers.

'I can do it by *myself*, Daddy,' she said impatiently, as if he was the biggest idiot in the world. He watched her as she attempted to force her left foot into her right shoe.

They were meeting Becca in a coffee shop across the street from the Gubei International School.

'I need my pens, Daddy,' Holly said as he scanned the place for a table.

'I've got your pens and some paper, angel,' he said, and he held her hand as they moved quickly to the one spare table. The tabletop was covered in the crumbs of half-eaten muffins and the sticky circles of stained empty cups. Bill cleaned the table, then got out the crayons and sketchbook from her rucksack.

'Okay?' he said.

'Okay,' she said, not looking at him, yanking the top off of a felt-tip and already immersed in the act of creation.

He went to get their drinks. When he came back she said, 'Look at this, Daddy,' and held up a picture of a stick creature with a lopsided smile, wild yellow hair and a pink dress. Her drawing was getting better. She still drew straight lines to represent arms and legs, but her faces were getting more expressive, the eyes and mouths of the round blob heads conveying real emotion. Perhaps she would be a painter. Perhaps she would be another Matisse. Perhaps his daughter would be the greatest painter who ever lived.

'It's brilliant, angel,' he said, unwrapping a straw and placing it in her orange juice. 'But what is it?'

Holly looked outraged. 'It's me,' she said, amazed that he was so stupid that he hadn't got it immediately. 'Can't you see?'

'Now you point it out,' he said.

They were sitting at the end of a line of booths. In the one closest to them, two white boys in suits were arguing.

'But you can't compare Bangkok and Manila,' one of them said. 'It's like comparing a team of battle-hardened professionals with a bunch of happy amateurs.'

'Well, that's my point exactly, dickweed,' said the other suit. Bill realised they were both Brits, although he couldn't quite place the accents. They were not quite Londoners.

'The thing about Manila,' one of them said, 'is that they will fuck you blind for nothing. Whereas in Bangkok you have to give them a credit-card number before they even look at your knob.'

'Look at this, Daddy,' Holly smiled, holding up her drawing. There was a large stick man with a foolish grin in the corner. 'That's you,' said Holly. 'You're waiting for me.'

Becca walked into the Coffee Planet and came over to them, all smiles, kissing them both and saying, 'So how was it?' as she pulled up a chair. And then, to Bill, looking at his clenched face, 'What's wrong?'

'But Bangkok and Manila can't compare to Hong Kong in the old days,' said one of the suits in the adjacent booth. They were loud enough to hear every word. Holly kept drawing. Becca looked at Bill and Bill stared off at nothing. 'My granddad,

332

right, my granddad Pete, he was in Hong Kong at the end of the war and he got a blow-job through the wire.'

The suits laughed. 'What?' said the other suit, not quite believing. 'He actually had his knob—'

'I'm telling you—my granddad Pete was on the Hong Kong side, patrolling the border, keeping out the mainland wetbacks, and he had his knob through the wire and was sucked off through the wire. Cost him a shilling.'

'A shilling?' said the other suit. 'What's a shilling?'

'Bill?' Becca said, but he was gone, stumbling over the Simply Life bag that he had placed between his feet.

Then both the suits looked up to see Bill standing over them, leaning into the booth, his knuckles resting on their table.

'You want to keep it down?' he said. He was trying to stop his voice from shaking, but it was no good. His voice was shaking all over the place. 'I've got a little girl here.'

The two suits looked at Bill and then at each other. They smiled uncertainly. They were accustomed to doing what they liked. Then one of them laughed.

'It's a free country,' he said, and they both had a real chuckle at that, and they kept laughing until Bill picked up a large glass sugar shaker and hurled it at the wall between them. The suits sprang to their feet, glass and sugar dusting their jackets and shirts, scrambling out of the booth.

For a long moment he thought he might have to fight them. And that was a horrible prospect, the idea of rolling around on the floor of a Coffee

Planet with a couple of his fellow countrymen, but it was fine too. He would beat them or, more likely, they would beat him. He didn't much care. All he cared about was that it ended. The talk that his daughter should not have to listen to. But they did not want to fight him and Bill turned to watch them go. He was aware that the crowded coffee shop was completely silent. His wife was holding his daughter and they were both staring at him as if they had never seen him before.

'Jesus Christ,' one of the suits shouted on his way to the door. 'De-caf for Dad from now on.'

Bill sat down with Becca and Holly and tried to pick up his coffee. But his hands were trembling harder than ever. He put the cup down. He didn't speak, and he did not touch anything. He was too shaky. So he just stared at the table, waiting for his breathing to come back. He hoped that Becca might say, *Thanks for standing up for us, Bill, thanks for being a man.* But he knew there was no real chance of that happening.

'Do you know what you do with idiots like that, Bill?' Becca said.

Bill looked up at her, and swallowed hard when he saw Holly burying her face into her mother's chest, hiding behind her hair, watching him through the blonde veil. 'Why don't you tell me?' he said.

'You ignore them,' she said. 'Because they are *nothing.* And if you get down to their level, then you make yourself nothing too.'

He wiped his eyes. He was so tired. He wanted to curl up in the booth and sleep. Then he realised that he had kicked Becca's shopping across the floor when he jumped out of the booth.

He reached for it, picked it up and placed it on the table like an offering for his wife and daughter, and he watched Becca flinch as she heard the soft shifting jingle of broken glass.

* * *

He had looked for her for most of the night. He had to look for her. How could he not look for her?

He had looked for her on Mao Ming Nan Lu and on Tong Ren Lu, pushing his way through the hard-core crowds that refused to go home. He thought he saw her face across the mobbed dance floor of Real Love, silhouetted against the red neon heart that throbbed on the wall. Then he thought he saw her again in a beer-stained red leather booth at BB's, a Chinese girl with a ponytail, her face covered by the cropped blond head of a Westerner. He pressed his face close, blood pumping, and then the kissing couple broke and as the man raised a fist, Bill realised with a gasp of relief that it wasn't her.

And he saw her in his head, in the blackest parts of his imagination—beaten in the back of a car, raped in an alley, murdered behind locked doors. Dumped in the street. Or back in the arms of her married Chinese man, tired of the endless drama with her Englishman, happy to be back between familiar sheets, murmuring sweet nothings and second chances in her own language, and moaning with pleasure.

Oh, he saw that all right.

He had no trouble seeing that.

But he looked for her and did not find her.

335

He went to the police station on Renmin Square to report her missing. Nobody on the front desk spoke English. Nobody even came close to understanding him.

Men who looked like migrant workers were being dragged down to the cells. A ten-year-old beggar boy sat weeping and wiping his bloody, broken nose on his sleeve. A taxi driver and his passenger screamed at each other and had to be held apart by laughing cops. Bill went away, suddenly knowing where she would be.

At the roller-skating rink he thought he saw her face—the hair flying, the lovely face with its goofy grin of pleasure, long legs in faded denim expertly balanced on ancient skates—but it was not her, it was just someone with the look, and the city was full of them.

At the edge of the rink a girl, no more than fifteen, pulled at his sleeve. He turned to her with the hope flooding through him. Was it one of her ex-students? She had the red-cheeked face that you saw on the migrant workers.

'You looking for girl, boss?'

'Yes,' Bill nodded. 'Li JinJin—do you know her? She was a teacher—'

The girl was nodding emphatically. 'You take me with you, boss. I'm a nice girl.'

Then there was another one, talking to him in Mandarin, and another one with just a few jagged shards of English, and another one that could only say, *Nice girl, boss*, as though she had learned it in night class. Prostitution for Beginners, Module One, he thought, as grubby hands slipped into his pockets to explore whatever was in there, until he pushed his way through them, feeling as if he was

336

suffocating.

Outside there was a sign in English plastered across the side of the ugly concrete building that housed the roller-skating rink. ACQUIRED FOR DEVELOPMENT, it said. LUXURY SPACE TO RENT.

And then he realised that there were signs all along the ramshackle buildings of the little backstreet. CONDEMNED, they said, as he slowly walked past them down the unlit street. CONDEMNED. CONDEMNED. CONDEMNED.

TWENTY-FOUR

Some nights he would go to the flat in Hongqiao and let himself in with the spare set of keys and then he would wait for her, he would wait for her until around midnight and when she still had not come he would go back to Paradise Mansions at the time he would be expected home, even though he knew they would be sleeping.

On the first night he wandered the apartment, tormented by the signs and souvenirs of who she was—the Sony Handycam bought to launch her TV career, the stacks of crossword puzzles, the selections that had been made from the piles of CDs and DVDs—a live Faye Wong CD, an obscure Zhang Ziyi film—and the photographs on her bedside table.

The framed picture of the pair of them in the rain on the bridge in Guilin, another picture of him at his desk in the London office, white shirt sleeves and a tie and so much younger, something he had

337

given her when they started, and a third picture of JinJin on graduation day flanked by her mother and her sister, that family of women.

But after the first time he no longer saw these things, the puzzles and the pictures, and they no longer hurt him. By the second time he had stopped calling her mobile, which was always off, and stopped leaving messages. And on the third time he was standing by one of her overflowing wardrobes, holding a green *qipao* in his hands, burying his face in it, feeling ridiculous but doing it anyway, trying to drown in the memory of her in that dress, when he suddenly looked up, hearing the key in the lock.

She came into the apartment with little ChoCho in her arms. They both seemed surprised to see him. He went to her and wrapped his arms around the pair of them.

She smiled, nodded, and jiggled little ChoCho on her hip. 'I had to go back home,' she explained. 'My sister is working. My mother is sick. In the hospital.'

'What's wrong with your mum?'

She clenched her fist. 'Stiff,' she said. 'All stiff. Pain.'

'Arthritis?' he said. 'Rheumatoid arthritis?'

JinJin grimaced. 'Getting old,' she said. 'Getting old lady.'

'Sorry,' he said. 'I'm so sorry I said those things.'

He squeezed her tight. She laughed and kissed him. ChoCho slowly stared from one to the other with his huge solemn eyes. Then a young man walked into the apartment carrying a folded stroller and a battered suitcase.

'Ah, thank you, Brad,' she said, all polite

formality and gratitude.

Brad? Who the fuck was Brad?

Bill watched him carry her things inside. He was not the typical Shanghai suit. He was in T-shirt and Levi's, pumped up and wearing glasses. He had that Liam Neeson speccy-hunk thing going on. The glasses made him look vaguely sensitive, but the muscles stopped him looking like a nerd. Maybe one of those wasters who teach English as a foreign language instead of working for a living, Bill thought, narrowing his eyes at Brad—fucking Brad—and then JinJin.

'Brad—this is my boyfriend Bill,' JinJin said, smiling from one to the other. The two men shook hands and Bill's features froze into civil indifference. *I don't care*, his face tried to say. *You mean nothing to me.*

'I live upstairs,' Brad said. Australian accent. No, a bit more clipped than the Aussies. A kiwi, Bill guessed. 'I was coming back from the gym when I saw the pair of them getting out of the cab.' He had the nerve to stroke ChoCho's cheek with a hairy finger. 'Well, I'll let you crack on,' he said, beaming at JinJin. Bill knew what he wanted to do to her, and it wasn't just carry her luggage. Fucking Brad . . .

When he had gone, Bill took ChoCho and watched JinJin busying herself in the flat. Relief had been replaced by suspicion. As she crashed about in the kitchen, he rocked the child and went over the encounter in minute detail. The way that Brad had smiled at JinJin as he kindly carried her things into the flat. The way she had touched his arm when introducing him to Bill. The way she had called Bill *my boyfriend*—what was that? Goading

339

the nice man upstairs? Letting him know that she was in demand? Letting him know that the good ones are always, *always* taken.

JinJin smiled at the sight of him holding her son and he smiled back, knowing that there would be plenty of opportunities for the nice New Zealander upstairs to knock on her door when the boyfriend was not around, and knowing that he could not trust her, this man who knew that he could not be trusted, this man who knew he would betray her in the end.

For there was a part of Bill that could not help believing that JinJin Li was just like him.

*   *   *

'We were up at Yangdong and it's going to be so beautiful,' Tess Devlin said, lifting her voice above the restaurant din. 'It's incredible what they've done up there—these magnificent houses rising out of goat farms, or whatever they were . . .' She glanced at her husband. 'And we're thinking of buying one, aren't we? If next year's bonus is as big as we all hope.' She lifted her glass to Shane and Bill. 'Got to work hard, boys.'

Bill and Shane laughed dutifully. 'We're doing our best,' Shane said.

'Is the air better up there?' Becca said. 'The air must be better.'

'And it's so good to get out of the city for the weekend,' Tess nodded, signalling for the waiter to bring another bottle of champagne. 'Give the boys somewhere to run wild.'

'Indeed,' Devlin said, stiff with dignity. He was drunk. They were all drunk. The dinner was to

340

celebrate the return of one wife, and to begin the search for a new one, but it had gone on for a few bottles too long, as dinner on the Bund always did. 'Let the little buggers wear themselves out,' Devlin chuckled.

There were six of them. Bill and Becca. Tess and Devlin. And Shane placed next to a blonde South African woman, somebody Tess Devlin had found in her Pilates class, one of the new fashion people that had suddenly washed up in Shanghai—a stylist, she told them, as if any of them had any idea what that meant. Well, maybe Becca and Tess did. But Shane and the South African had not hit it off—he was too much the straight macho suit for her tastes, and Shane was still in mourning for his wild young bride. He looked sullen, shy, closed up in the presence of all this domestic chitchat. But by the time the table was littered with bottles, the stylist was starting to look better.

'Any chance of a shag tonight?' Shane asked.

'Every chance of a shag,' said the South African, staring straight ahead. 'But not with you.'

'Saw some of the locals,' Tess was saying to Becca. 'Talk about the great unwashed. The children look like little chimney sweeps. Like urchins out of Dickens, you know? The Artful bloody Dodger or something. And they just gawp at you with their little black faces. They just stand there and *gawp*. Gawping—it's the only word for it.'

The South African turned to Tess. 'I've seen some of those migrant workers selling fake watches outside Plaza 66,' she said, suddenly animated. 'They're filthy. I nearly puked.'

Bill smiled, shook his head. 'But, Tess,' he said

341

gently, 'those kids—half of them never see the inside of a school. That's why they're so dirty—they're in the fields all day. You know what the schools out there spend half their budgets on? Wining and dining school inspectors. They can't tell those important men there's nothing for dinner . . .'

'Oh Bill,' Tess laughed, shaking her head, as if he were pulling her leg.

'It's true!' he insisted, wanting her to believe him. But he had drunk too much. He knew that. He shouldn't have started with this. But he thought of the boy he had seen being beaten at Yangdong, and he could not keep his mouth shut. 'The kids of those farmers up at Yangdong have been left behind, and they'll always be left behind. There's no difference between them and some laid-off state factory worker in the Dongbei. China doesn't need them.'

Becca got up to go to the rest room. Bill noticed her catch his eye and tap her watch with her index finger. They had to get back to Holly and relieve the ayi.

'It's true there are certain inequalities that have to be addressed,' Devlin said. He lifted his glass to his lips but it was empty. He did a double take. What had happened to his drink?

'I agree,' the South African stylist said, not quite grasping Devlin's point. 'Those migrant workers for a start—the police should do something about them.'

Bill felt his wife's hand lightly touch the back of his head as she drifted away from the table.

'Certain inequalities?' he said to Devlin, ignoring the fashion airhead.

342

'Have another drink, mate,' Shane said, holding out a fresh bottle, attempting to fill his glass, trying to distract his friend.

Bill ignored him. 'But the whole thing is built on inequality,' he said. 'By the middle of the century China will have a bigger economy than America. And they'll still have five hundred million people living on two dollars a day. They're meant to be Communists, for fuck's sake.'

'They haven't been Communists for a long time,' Devlin said with irritation. 'You know that.'

'And anyway—whose side are you on, Bill?' Tess laughed.

'But you would expect at least a token nod towards equality, wouldn't you?' Bill said, really wanting Devlin to understand. He drained his glass. 'Even if it was just going through the motions, a nod towards fighting injustice, or giving a damn about the poor. Like those kids from the farms in Yangdong. But they don't want equality here. Equality wouldn't work here.'

Devlin looked pained. Shane looked for a waiter and waved for another bottle.

'Without the millions of poor buggers who will work for a bowl of noodles,' Bill said, 'and can be cheated out of even that, this place loses its attraction. China gets rich as long as most of its people stay poor.' He looked up at Shane impatiently. 'Where's that drink?'

'Oh, Bill,' Tess laughed. 'Bill, Bill, Bill . . .'

Shane refilled their glasses. Bill sipped his champagne. He was tired of champagne. Something about the enforced jollity of the drink was wearing him down. 'Oh what, Tess?' he said. 'What, what, what?'

343

She leaned across the table, as if it was just the two of them now. 'Without all that horrible inequality, Bill,' she said, in not much more than a whisper, 'you would lose everything.'

He leaned towards her with a faint smile. 'How's that, Tess?'

She shook her head, suddenly disgusted. 'Spare me your tears for the great unwashed, Bill. Everything we have is built on things being exactly the way they are—everything you have right now, everything you will have when you make partner— and everything you've *had*.'

'What do you mean?'

The table was silent now.

He knew exactly what she meant.

'Without the great unwashed—that big supply of desperate humanity who are anxious to work, anxious to spread their legs, anxious to clean our toilets, anxious to eat—we would not have our nice lifestyles, our second homes, our bonus,' she said, and then she seemed to hesitate, then decide something, and plough on. 'All of the things we currently enjoy. And *you* would have missed out on your great little adventure.'

He waited.

Daring her to spell it out.

They stared at each other for a long moment.

'Is that the time?' Shane said. He barked at the nearest waiter in Mandarin. Devlin laid a hand on his wife's arm. She didn't seem to notice.

'I don't know what you're talking about, Tess,' Bill said, but beyond the comfortably numb feeling of the booze, he felt the panic rise.

'Can't you see, Bill?' Tess said. 'Don't cry for the great unwashed, because it's all fake. Everything they sell.'

'Those watches are definitely fake,' said the South African. 'I was going to get one for my brother in Durban but I said to him, I said, Peter, they look so cheap.'

Tess Devlin let the contempt show. 'Fake DVDs and fake software and fake watches. Fake orgasms, no doubt. Fake love? Certainly.' She drained her glass, banged it down empty on the table and held his stare. 'Love with Chinese characteristics.'

'You don't know what you're talking about,' Bill said. 'You haven't got a clue. I doubt if you ever really knew one Chinese.'

'In the Biblical sense, you mean?' Tess said.

'Oh, go home,' Bill said.

'Steady on, Holden,' Devlin said. 'That's my wife you're talking to.'

Shane was on his feet, clapping his hands. 'Come on, mate, let's get you home,' he said to Bill. 'Tiger's waiting.'

'Can someone call me a cab?' said the South African stylist. 'The Bund is crawling with beggars.'

Bill stayed where he was and Tess Devlin jabbed a finger at him across the table. 'I warned you when you started,' she said. 'I warned you when you started with your little Manchu slut and you would *not* listen, Bill. I told you that it ends one of two ways—you either leave your wife or you don't. I told you—*I fucking told you, Bill,* and you would *not* listen—it ends one of two ways and it always ends badly.'

Then she looked up and so did Bill and they saw Becca standing at the end of the table, the blood draining from her face, finally understanding everything.

Somewhere a champagne glass broke and there was laughter and Shane was shouting in Chinese.

'*Qing bang wo jiezhang, hao ma?*' he said, snapping his thumb and index finger together.

Time for the bill.

* * *

Tiger had seen it all before.

He drove them back to Gubei, glancing at them in the rear-view mirror, and wondered why he'd ever thought that these two would be different. But few marriages were ever improved by Shanghai.

What was different about the boss and the lady was that they said nothing. There were none of the flashes of pain and rage, no words spat out as if they tasted bad.

The boss and the lady sat in complete silence all the way home, as if the words they had to say to each other were too terrible to speak, and too terrible to be heard.

* * *

Like a normal married couple they let themselves into the apartment and they were both friendly and polite to the ayi, and she told them that Holly hadn't been sleeping very well, and when the ayi had gone Becca went to the second bedroom and from the master bedroom Bill could hear his wife soothing their daughter.

'It's all right, darling, it's all right, darling, I'm here now, it's all right, darling.'

Bill was sitting on the bed when Becca appeared in the doorway.

He looked up at her and he couldn't bear it.

'Who is she?' Becca said, all business-like, stepping into the room and pushing the hair off her face. 'Is she one of the whores who live here or is she one of the whores at Suzy Too?' She smiled bitterly at the look on his face. 'Oh yes—I know all about that place. You think the wives don't know all about that place? So what is she? One of the whores from there or one of the whores from here?'

He muttered something and she took a step closer to the bed. 'What?' She had a hand cupped to her ear. 'Can't hear you.'

He raised his eyes. 'I said,' he said quietly, 'she's not a whore, Becca.'

She hit his face with a flurry of furious blows. 'Stupid . . . stupid . . . stupid . . .'

Left right, left right, hitting his mouth his eyes his nose. He lowered his head but did not try to cover up. He felt her ring finger catch the side of his nose and bring tears to his eyes.

'Oh fuck you and fuck her too,' Becca said, dismissing it all. 'You're welcome to each other. You deserve each other. What did you tell her?' Slipping into a mocking sing-song voice, a grotesque parody of romantic sweet nothings. '*My wife doesn't understand me . . . we haven't got along in years . . . it will not always be this way, baby . . . trust me, baby, we can work it out . . . you're the best thing that ever happened to me . . .*'

And perhaps that's what it was, he thought, and what it would always be. A grotesque parody of the real thing. She sat next to him on the bed and covered her face with her hands.

'You broke my heart,' she said, her voice choked.

'You broke my bloody heart, Bill.'

'I'm sorry,' he said, putting one hand on her shoulder. 'I'm so sorry.' He said her name. He said it again, and he made her name sound like a question. 'Please don't stop loving me,' he said.

'Don't touch me,' she said, and he took his hand away. She took a deep breath, stopped crying, wiped her nose, suddenly all icy calm. 'Don't touch me when you've been touching her,' she said. It was like a new rule for their new life. 'And don't kiss Holly with a mouth that's been on that dirty Third World whore.'

'Don't kiss my daughter?'

Becca nodded. 'You stay right away from her.' She narrowed her eyes to thin slits of loathing. 'You stay right away from my daughter, you fucking bastard.'

He stared at his hands, and weakly muttered something that she didn't get, although it made her look up at him with eyes blazing, snot and tears on her face. 'What?'

'I said—she's my daughter too.'

She bared her teeth at that. 'Well, maybe you should have thought more about that before you started. How does it work, Bill? Do you have exclusive fucking rights? Or have you got her on a time share?' Becca shook her head. 'Are you going now or in the morning?'

He hung his head. 'Never.'

'What?' She was up now, pacing around the master bedroom, her arms folded across her chest.

'I'm not going.' There was no blood in his voice. All the blood had gone. He said the words but he didn't sound convinced. It was as if his wife had all the power now. 'I'm never going.'

348

Her voice was perfectly reasonable, but a little impatient, as if she was explaining something obvious to the village idiot.

'But, Bill—we don't want you here.'

'You mean *you* don't want me here.'

'That's right. I don't want you here.'

'But I don't want to go.'

'Why not, Bill?'

'Because I love you.'

'That's a fucking laugh.'

'And I love my daughter.'

He thought that it was the one thing she could never deny or refute. But she did. Even that. She stood in front of him, happy to explain why he had to leave.

'You love your daughter but you would break up her home—and break her heart—and give her a wound to carry for a lifetime for some dirty Third World whore. You don't know, Bill. Your parents didn't divorce. Your mother died. It's easy when one of them dies. All you feel is sad. When someone dies, you feel sad. But when one of them goes—when one of them walks out—then you feel so worthless. You just feel so worthless, and I don't think you ever get over it. I think a part of you always feels worthless, as if you deserved it, as if you made it happen, as if it happened because you were bad.'

'Then let me stay. Let me stay for Holly, if not for you.'

'But you've made staying impossible. Can't you see that?' She dissolved before him. Something seemed to crumple inside her. 'How could you be so cruel? To us, Bill. How could you be so cruel to the two people who loved you more than—oh fuck,' she said, and she sat on the bed, racked with grief, and he didn't dare touch her again. She pulled herself together, wiped at her eyes with the back of her hand. 'Let me ask you a question, Bill.'

'What is it?' he said, and swallowed, afraid of what she would say, afraid of what was ahead.

'Was it worth it?' Becca said.

He knew she hated him now. He knew that he had ruined it with Becca and he knew that it was likely that his daughter's life would be changed forever by what he had done. And he knew that no matter how many times he talked about how much he loved them, and begged to stay, their little family could never be the same again.

'Nothing is worth this,' he said, and he believed it with all his heart. She looked into his face, trying to understand him, not getting him, completely mystified by the man she had married.

'Did we mean so little, Bill? I mean you and me. Our marriage. Don't you get it? Marriage is time. Marriage is trust. Marriage—I don't know what it is, but I know you don't get it from somebody you pick up in a bar. You think you're smart. Sneaking around behind my back, keeping it hidden. You think you're so smart.'

He shook his head. 'No, I don't think I'm smart.'

'But you're stupid,' she continued, not hearing him, her voice breaking. She breathed hard, struggling to hold herself in one piece. She had things to tell him before she came apart. 'Oh you're so stupid, Bill, oh you're such a fucking cliché. Now Holly is going to grow up with one parent, she's going to be one of those poor little kids that only has one parent because the other one was fucking around and it will scar her and it

will hurt her forever and she will never get over it.'
He thought she was going to hit him again but she
shook her head, sadder than he would have
believed possible, and that was so much worse.
'And it will all be your fault,' she said, and he knew
she was right. 'And you betrayed me. I loved you
and I trusted you and you chucked it all away. You
treated it like it was nothing. All our time
together—nothing. All the things we went
through—nothing. You've spoilt everything that
was good in my life.'

She hung her head.

'Bec?' he said. 'Oh, Bec, don't cry.'

But she cried and cried. He tried to hold her but
she lifted her hands, forbidding it. 'She's not the
love of your life, Bill. Is that what you think? She's
just your dirty little secret. And it's not passion—
you think it's passion? It's the opposite. All the
lies, all the planning—it takes a very cold heart to
do all that. You must be a very cold-hearted
bastard, Bill.' She covered her face again, but she
had stopped crying. 'Oh fuck. Why did I choose
you? Why did I choose a cold-hearted bastard like
you? When I think of all the places I could have
been.'

'I'll make it up to you, Becca, I swear.' His voice
was desperate now. 'I'll make it up to you.'

She frowned, shook her head. 'But you could
never make it up to me,' she said. She stood up and
walked wearily to the door. 'I'll sleep with Holly. I
can't stand to be around you. I loved you so much
and now I can't stand to be around you. How did
you manage that, Bill?'

'Bring Holly in here with you,' he said. 'I'll go in
the other room.'

But she had had enough.

'Oh just get out of my life,' she said quietly. Dead on her feet, as if the strongest feeling of all was exhaustion. 'Just pack your bags and go. I'm sick of looking at you.'

He stood up, but made no move towards her. 'I'm so sorry, Becca.'

She exhaled wearily. 'How many times are you going to say that?'

'Until you believe me.'

Then she seemed so sad and exhausted, leaning in the doorway of their bedroom, as if she was already in mourning for the marriage, as if it had been a beloved living thing that had died.

'Oh, it's too late to be sorry,' she said.

Then she left him and he heard her getting into bed with Holly and after a while he took off his clothes and got into bed and stared at the ceiling, listening to them stir in the other room from time to time. It was Holly that always started it—he could hear the distressed waking from dreams, and then Becca's soft, reassuring words, followed by the long silence of sleep, or at least the attempt to find sleep.

Bill did not sleep, but he must have been close to it because at some point in the night he realised that she was suddenly standing over his bed.

She had been awake too, and she had been thinking, and she wanted some answers.

'Who is it?' she said, her voice hoarse from the crying. 'Is it one of the girls here?'

He nodded. 'But she's gone. She doesn't live here any more.'

He had visions of Becca at the window of JinJin's flat, tipping her possessions into the street,

352

although he knew that would never happen in a million years. She had too much pride, too much class. Becca would just cut him out of her life and would never treat JinJin as a rival. Nobody had stolen her husband. He had given himself away.

'What one?' Becca said. Her eyes were bloodshot and puffed up with all the hurt and anger of the night, but her voice was controlled now. She just wanted to know. 'Don't tell me,' she said, as if it was some sort of game. 'I can guess. The one with the red Mini and the legs. Is that the one?' She looked at his face and she nodded, not even needing a reply. 'Oh, Bill—she's nothing special. She's not a world-beater. There are younger and better out there.' She saw the look on his face. Of course there were younger and better out there. That was the world. There was always younger and better out there. But that didn't mean you wanted them.

'I don't care what you do, but keep her away from Holly, keep your whore away from my daughter,' Becca said, her question answered, the fury coming on like a fever, the anger tightening her throat, her face. 'You think you're a good parent, don't you, Bill?'

He shook his head. 'I wouldn't claim that for myself.'

'But you will never be a good parent until you put your child before and above everything, Bill,' she said, as if he had not spoken. 'Including the woman you want to spend your life with. Including the woman you want to fuck. You know—your Chinese whore.'

She walked to the door, pulling at her wedding ring, struggling to get it over the big first knuckle,

353

and she threw it at him from the doorway. It clattered against the wall and he could hear it spinning on the floor.

He had thought on their wedding day that the rings they exchanged would last them a lifetime. Now he saw that wedding rings get lost, they get stolen, they get thrown in anger. Now he saw that you might get through any number of wedding rings in a marriage. Now he found it difficult to believe that he had ever been as young as he was on their wedding day, young enough to believe that you only need one wedding ring.

*   *   *

She came to him in the morning, wrapped up in a robe and shivering as though she was freezing, and she watched him packing a suitcase.

'I love you so much,' he said, not looking at her, not looking up from what he was doing. 'You're the best friend I ever had. You don't deserve this.' He was crying now, but a restrained sort of crying, the sort of crying where you clench your teeth and tighten your jaw because you fear that if you let it all out you will just unravel. 'I'm sorry I hurt you. I know you're sick of hearing it, but I am.'

She sat down on the bed, next to his suitcase. Her eyes were almost closed now from all the crying. She placed one of her bare feet on the edge of his suitcase. 'How do I forgive you, Bill?'

He shrugged, shook his head. 'I don't know,' he said. 'I don't see how you can.'

'Truth is, I can't.' Her face was lovely, even streaked with tears and puffed up with grief, and he thought of all the men that had been after her,

354

and he wondered it too—*Why choose me?*

'And I can't trust you,' she said. 'Even if we—how can I ever trust you? But this marriage is not just about us any more, is it? It's about that child asleep in the next room.'

He looked at her, and he realised what she was saying. What she was offering. She raised a hand, telling him not to get carried away. 'You've ruined it, Bill. You're ruined it forever.' Her mouth twisted with resentment at his stupidity, and at all he had inflicted upon her, all that real, unendurable physical pain. 'Because *you fucked around,*' she said, and wiped her eyes. 'I can find a better husband than you.' She nodded. It wasn't open to debate. She knew this to be true. 'A better man than you. I know I can get a better man than you. You think you're anything special? But . . .' She laughed, shook her head and dragged her hands across her face. 'But I don't know that I can find someone who is a better father than you. I don't know if I can get a better dad for my daughter. Someone who loves her as much as you do. I don't know if I can find a man who will love Holly as much as you do, Bill. And a man who my daughter will love as much as she loves you. I don't think so. I don't think I can.' She shook her head. 'Which is a bloody shame, isn't it? For all of us.'

'Don't stop loving me,' he begged her. 'Please don't stop loving me.'

'Maybe it just wears out,' she said. 'You and me. Everybody. Maybe you just use it up, wear it out. I didn't feel that we were worn out. You and me, Bill. I loved you. You were the man I wanted to spend my life with. That's corny, isn't it? That's stupid.'

He shook his head.

'But maybe it just changes so much that we all end up married to strangers,' she said. 'Total strangers. And if you're lucky, you like them. Even love them. But you can't pretend that it's the same person you married.'

He touched her arm and said her name but she gave no sign of noticing. He felt like he had killed her.

'Marriage starts off as a love match and ends up as—I don't know what it is—an economic partnership,' she said. 'A home. A place to raise children. It starts as a love affair and ends up as a family.' She looked at him quickly, as if she was afraid he would miss the point. 'That doesn't mean I stopped loving you. But I love our daughter in a different way, in a bigger way, and I am letting you stay because of her. I loved her from her first breath and I will love her to her last breath. And I let you stay because of her. Am I being rational? Am I being mature? Am I thinking about my daughter? Well, fuck you. I feel like teaching you what it feels like. Shall I do that, Bill? Shall I find someone and teach you how it feels?' She looked at him as if something had suddenly occurred to her. 'Why did you stop loving me?'

'I never stopped loving you.'

'What's really funny about you, about all you men, is that you think you're the only one,' she said. 'The only one with choices.'

What *was she talking about? Who was she talking about? But Becca didn't say and he didn't ask. He was too afraid of what the answer might be. She was letting him stay. That was enough, and all that mattered.

He lowered his head and she took him in her arms, but she did not hold him tightly, and her body was tense and trembling, as fragile as a Double Fortune wine glass. They lay down on the bed, and they cried together at how the familiar body beside them had suddenly been changed for all time.

He knew that this was not the end. He knew that this night would always be with them, although he had no idea how bad the scar would be, or if they would be able to live with it. One day soon there would be questions—terrible questions, heartbreaking questions, all the questions you ask of a divided heart. But right now, as Becca got up to leave and the new day streamed in and they heard their child stirring in the next room, she had only one question.

'Is it over?' his wife said.

TWENTY-FIVE

The helicopter flew straight up and they were suddenly amid the skyline of Hong Kong, not looking at it but hanging in it, hovering like some giant insect by the steel-and-glass cliff face of the Bank of China, with the serried ranks of tower blocks marching up mid-levels to Victoria Peak, a green summit jabbing out of a drifting necklace of pearly mist, the eagles circling above.

There was nothing corny about the Hong Kong skyline. It was not like Shanghai where you always knew that the grand old buildings on the Bund were really just the beautiful leftovers of a colonial dream. This was a place that had been untouched by any ideology, a city that had never worshipped any god but money. Even now, reclaimed by the motherland, Hong Kong was all that the great cities of the mainland aspired to be.

There were seven of them bound for Macau. Bill and Shane together in the back seat of the helicopter with Mitch and Nancy in front of them, leaning into a laptop. Then Wolfgang and Jurgen from DeutscherMonde, looking more alike these days as the old rocker and the weekend golfer both acquired that ripe, over-watered look of the suit who has seen too many Asian nights. And then, Chairman Sun, sitting up front next to the Australian pilot, and staring down at Hong Kong with a proprietorial air from behind his mirrored shades. The pilot said something on the radio and it crackled in Bill's ear, completely indecipherable, and the helicopter dipped its nose, pointed west and buzzed out across the harbour, a frenetic patch of water crowded with tiny wooden junks and a giant cruise ship and the green-and-white Star Ferries that shuttled between Kowloon and Hong Kong island.

Soon they were skimming low over the South China Sea, the water rushing beneath them, and ancient fishing boats suddenly coming out of the fog like ghost ships and then abruptly disappearing.

The waxy yellow earplugs did little to keep out the drone of the engine, and the noise hammered them into silence, and left Bill alone with his thoughts. These days he really only had one thought—the thought that woke him in the middle of the night, his wife asleep beside him, the same thought that kept him from sleeping in the lazy, dreamy hour after making love when JinJin lay in his arms until it was time for him to go.

Was it over?

It was over because he saw now that he could never leave his wife and child. Becca could throw him out, that was always a possibility, but he could never just walk away from his wife and child. *Was it over?*

He thought that it would not be over until he stopped caring about the red lights of that Spring Festival and her face on the ice rink and how she looked in her yellow coat. It would not be over while he remembered these things, and he was sure that these were among the things that he would remember on the day that he died.

Was it over? He could never see her again in his life and it would not be over. *Was it over?* She could marry someone else and have his child and then another child and it would not be over. *Was it over?*

Not until he could harden his heart and stop seeing her, not until she stopped loving him as if there was something special about him, not until she stopped loving him as if he was a good man.

Not until she stopped loving him all the time. Not until he knew that she would be just fine without him. Not until he could think about what was going to happen to her without being worried sick.

It would never be over until then.

*   *   *

Last night Bill had come home from the office past midnight and found Becca awake and waiting for him, curled up on the sofa with a book, dressed in a robe and slippers. Her face was pale and drawn and when she looked up at him as he came into the apartment, she seemed to shudder. She clutched at the neck of her robe and the gesture made him think of sickness and hospitals.

He wanted to hold her and he knew he did not dare.

'You didn't have to wait up for me,' he said, hating the strained formality that was suddenly between them.

She laughed and shook her head. 'Oh, but I did, Bill,' she said. 'Oh, but I did because I don't know where you are, do I? And I don't know who you're with, do I?'

There was no real accusation in the words. It was a statement of brutal fact, quietly spoken. But he could feel the rawness of her feelings, and he could understand why it made sleep impossible. She did not trust him and perhaps she would never trust him again and he didn't see how they could live like this.

'It's all this Yangdong stuff,' he said, taking cover in the mundane chores of work. 'There's so much to do before they open.' He looked her in the eyes and shrugged helplessly. 'I was at the office, Bec.'

She laughed and wiped at her eyes with the back of her hand. 'I know,' she said. 'I know it, but I don't really believe it.'

He sat down on the sofa and she stood up, her book in one hand and the other at the neck of her robe.

'I'm so sorry,' he said, ready to say it a million times, to say it until she believed it.

She nodded and sighed. 'But sorry's not enough.'

Before she turned away he saw the book in her hand and realised that he recognised the thin green paperback. It was something he remembered from school. *Leaves of Grass* by Walt Whitman.

He never knew his wife liked poetry.

*   *   *

He had gone to JinJin and told her that it was over and they held each other and he could feel the tears on their faces and he knew that they belonged to both of them.

'Don't you see?' he said. 'This could go on for another five years, another ten years, and then where would we be? You want to grow old waiting for something that's never going to happen? Is that what you want?'

And she thought about it. She wiped her eyes and thought about it. For the first time, he believed. She saw herself as someone's forty-year-old mistress. Childless, sleeping alone, and a few years beyond any chance of a happy ending.

'I don't want to hurt your family,' she said. She pulled off a piece of kitchen towel and dried her face. 'Your little girl. Your wife. She has never done anything bad to me. I don't want to steal you.'

'You can't steal people,' he said, unwilling to let her claim responsibility for everything. 'People can't be stolen.'

They talked and they cried until they were both exhausted. Then he finally got up to go, but she took his hand and placed it against her face, her neck, her thigh.

He shook his head and tried to pull away. Not

that. Not now.

And that was when she placed his hand against her breast and he shook his head more violently now and tried to pull away again but she held his palm there until he felt it. It was on the right side of her breast.

A lump the size of a golf ball, a lump as hard as the real world.

*   *   *

The helicopter came out of the mist and suddenly there was the neon glow of Macau, with its Portuguese architecture looking like toy forts in a Victorian nursery and dominating it all, the blazing lights of the giant casinos.

Macau was the very tip of the Chinese peninsula, the end of China, or perhaps the beginning, and the neon sign that identified the Hotel Lisboa, the gaudiest casino of them all, shone like a beacon in the grey twilight, temple to a religion that meant more to the Chinese people than Communism or capitalism ever could, summoning the masses to prayer.

'One day there will be gambling in China,' Devlin had said. 'Perhaps not for a long time. Perhaps not until the Party has gone. Perhaps not until after Taiwan.'

Among the senior suits of Shanghai, this was the most popular theory of how the Communist Party of China would eventually disappear—the old men in Beijing would finally wage their long-promised patriotic war on Taiwan and they would fail miserably. Their planes would be shot down, their missiles would miss or be intercepted, the PLA would never get off the beaches. Then the old men in Beijing would fall, and fall forever—taking their rotten ideology and statues of Chairman Mao with them—with the abruptness and permanence of the Berlin Wall suddenly becoming a pile of bricks.

'The Chinese love gambling, it's in their DNA,' Devlin told them before they left. 'One day there will be casinos on the mainland and they will make Las Vegas and Atlantic City look like a few slot machines stuck on the end of an English seaside pier,' Devlin said. 'Until then—there's Macau.'

And Bill thought of JinJin's father, his factory wages gone again on mah-jong, coming home to his wife and two daughters with the loser's rage inside him, his face like thunder at the breakfast table, slowly taking off his belt.

She never had a chance, he thought.

                    *   *   *

The mamma-san brought the girls to them six at a time. Now only the five of them were left, Bill and Shane sitting on the cracked leather sofas with their clients and Chairman Sun, a fresh round of drinks before them, looking up at the girls. Nancy had gone back to the hotel immediately after dinner. Mitch had disappeared somewhere between the restaurant and karaoke bar. The night was nearing its punchline, and for the first time Bill understood the presence of Chairman Sun. He was here to collect his bonus.

The girls were all in their late teens and early twenties, too young to hide their true feelings. They tried to mask those feelings with a practised blankness, but they couldn't quite pull it off.

363

They were in turn bored, contemptuous, tired, amused, scared and sweet—though Bill knew it was the kind of sweetness that could curdle into a hard-boiled professionalism the moment a deal was struck.

He looked away from their faces to the giant plasma television. On the screen two lovers walked down a beach with ugly tower blocks in the distance as the Chinese characters of the lyrics were illuminated on the grubby sand. A sugary melody accompanied the couple. Bill didn't know the song. He did not know any of the songs in here. He was not meant to know the song. This place wasn't built for white boys.

'You have to be the one who cares least,' Shane was saying. 'That's the mistake I made. I always cared more than she did—I always cared more than my wife. Big mistake. Remember this always, mate—the one who cares the least has all the power.'

The karaoke bar was there to service an exclusively Chinese clientele—winning gamblers spilling out of the casino that occupied the floor below or licking their wounds on their way back to the hotel four storeys above.

The sell here was far harder than anything Bill had seen in Shanghai. The girls were more beautiful than any women he had ever seen, but the karaoke bar made him feel that sex with one of them would be like buying a slice of pizza. He murmured his feelings to Shane.

'But what's wrong with pizza?' Shane said.

In the small sealed room the girls stood waiting while the men sat watching and the giant TV screen waited with two microphones on top, ready for some more wobbly love songs, and they looked at the girls and the girls looked back at them.

Shane spoke to the mamma-san in Cantonese and she conferred with him through a rictus grin of yellow, tea-stained teeth. She must have been a beauty once, but her face was marked with old chickenpox scars, and Bill thought that she had the eyes of a corpse. For all the practised good manners of the seasoned mamma-san, she was not comfortable with the presence of so many Westerners.

Only Shane's fluent Chinese, and the fact that he had been here before and spent big, plus the Chairman's lordly demeanour, made their presence tolerable. But she was getting impatient.

The way the karaoke bar worked was that five girls were wheeled in, one for each customer, and they stayed for a drink and a bit of a sing-song, and then the mamma-san came back and took the girls out of the room. Next the mamma-san faced the men alone, as she did now, grinning in hideous conspiracy, waiting for them to decide which girls could come back and which girls must be replaced, and which of the girls they wanted sent up to their hotel rooms.

On a busy night—and with the Chinese suddenly transformed into the world's greatest travellers, they were all busy nights now—the supply of girls was not endless. The karaoke bar was a labyrinth of small airless rooms, and they all needed a steady supply of young female flesh. Beyond the frozen smile, Bill could see that the mamma-san was becoming increasingly frustrated. When were they going to decide which girls they would take home for the night?

'You going to stick with the one you've got?' Shane asked Bill, and he nodded.

Bill had spent the last hour sitting with a young woman from Zhuhai, just across the border. Most of the girls in here spoke no English at all, in this karaoke bar with only two neon Chinese characters above the door and no corny English name for them to sneer at, but Shane and the mamma-san had managed to find Bill one who was new, and nice, and quietly terrified, and who had even taken a few English classes.

Bill had showed her the pictures of Holly that he carried in his wallet, and the girl made impressed noises as she sipped her orange juice. He would never know her name, although he tried to say it a few times, but it was just too difficult for him to get, and although she said her bar name was Lovely, he could not bring himself to call her that.

They gave them such ridiculous names.

She generously tried to find him a song he knew in the thick menu—'Elvis,' Bill told her, 'try to find something by Elvis'—but she had never heard of Elvis and besides, there were no songs for his kind in this place. They were being tolerated. But they were not needed. It felt like someone else's century now. The big-nosed pinkies, deferred to for so long, were no longer needed.

The girl had enough English words for Bill to understand that she was studying to be a beautician and that her younger brother was shelling out good money to become an actor. Before she had left the room he discreetly slipped her a wad of Hong Kong dollars. He felt sorry for the kid.

'You want to pay her bar fine?' Shane asked,

366

already knowing the answer but urged on by the leering mamma-san. Her eyes glittered at Bill as he turned away, shaking his head. Sex with a stranger. Just what he needed. Along with a hole in the head.

The evening was winding down. Bill could smell the cigarette smoke of a dozen casinos on his suit, and he could feel the effects of too much Tsingtao. The drinks were insultingly expensive, but the mamma-san did not want them sitting here all night. She wanted them to buy a few rounds, bar fine the girls and get an early night.

Shane conferred with the mamma-san. One of the Germans, Jurgen, the one who looked as though he spent his weekends practising his golf swing, had made his selection. The other one, Wolfgang, the forty-year-old in a leather jacket, said he would have one more drink but he was going back to the hotel alone, as he always did. Like Mad Mitch a few hours earlier, Wolfgang had that slight air of sheepishness that the virtuous always displayed in these places.

Shane was with a girl he knew from a previous trip, and he was going to have her sent over to the hotel, although the thought seemed to give him no pleasure.

Chairman Sun had been entertaining the same girl all night, impressing her with sugary Mandarin power ballads sung with the voice of a dead bullfrog, but she had poured him a glass of red wine without leaving room for the Sprite, and now in a fit of pique he suddenly wanted to exchange her. He was very drunk.

Holding his hands out in front of his chest, his nicotine fingers spread wide to signify giant breasts, he described the qualities he was looking for to the mamma-san, like a wine connoisseur consulting the sommelier.

'One more round then,' Shane said, and the mamma-san went out and came back with all the girls they had been sitting with minus the Chairman's companion. Bill stared at her replacement. He could not stop staring at her. And after a stunned moment he felt the sickening shock of recognition.

The mamma-san grinned and held out her hands, like a magician's assistant at the conclusion of a trick. The girl was short and rather stubby but she had a pretty face and, requested as specifically as a vegetarian meal, large breasts.

The Chairman's eyes narrowed knowingly, an indication of pleasure, and Bill was still looking at the girl, who was wearing the same artfully torn tutu that they all wore, tottering uncertainly on her ill-fitting high heels, like ballerinas in a knocking shop, and he kept staring, and then he was out of his squashy sofa and pulling her to the door.

Because she was Li Ling-Yuan.

Because the new girl was JinJin's sister.

'What are you doing here?' he said, and even as he was asking his stupid question, he was aware of the mamma-san's angry protest, and the Chairman roaring with displeasure behind him.

Ling-Yuan looked at him and she finally saw it was Bill and her surprise turned to sullenness in a second and his presence didn't seem to scare her as much as he felt it should. In fact it didn't seem to scare her at all. This wasn't his place.

'What are you doing?' He angrily shook her. 'Answer me, Ling-Yuan.'

Then Shane had a hand on his shoulder and was saying his name over and over, trying to get him to calm down, but he still had hold of Ling-Yuan, and wouldn't let her go. She was trying to pull away from him but he had her by the wrist now, and he was turning to them, trying to explain, aware he had to clear something up. 'I know this girl,' he said, as if that said it all. 'I know this girl.'

'She name Cherry,' the mamma-san said. 'She good girl.'

'Her name's not fucking Cherry,' Bill said angrily. 'I know this girl.'

The Chairman snapped his fingers twice and Ling-Yuan made a move towards him. Bill held up his arm, stopping her. The Chairman was shouting at Shane in Mandarin, the mamma-san was barking in Cantonese, and Ling-Yuan joined the chorus, her voice the self-pitying whine of a spoilt teenager who has been unfairly grounded.

'We're leaving,' Bill said to Ling-Yuan, and he turned to Shane. 'I'm not arguing about it. This is JinJin's sister. He's not fucking her, okay?' He looked at the mamma-san. 'Nobody is fucking this girl tonight. She quits.' He raised his voice at the Chairman. 'Find somebody else.'

'But she can't just quit,' Shane said quietly, looking pained. 'It doesn't work like that.'

'Then pay her bar fine,' Bill said. 'I don't care. But she's leaving with me now. I mean it, Shane. She's going to get changed and we are walking out of here right now.'

Two bouncers were standing in the doorway. Shane was talking to the Chairman, placating him, and haggling with the mamma-san. Neither seemed impressed. The Chairman shook his head

369

furiously, his eyes never leaving Ling-Yuan's breasts. The mamma-san took a step back and stood between the two bouncers. The tea-stained rictus grin had gone.

'What are you doing here?' Bill said to Ling-Yuan, as if it was just the two of them.

'Working,' she said, rolling her eyes at the dumbness of his interrogation. He expected her to say, *And what are* you *doing here?* But she didn't. She didn't say anything else. As if it was all too obvious to need saying.

Shane consulted the mamma-san and an agreement was reached. 'You can pay her bar fine,' he told Bill. 'But it's the same deal as for the rest of the girls.' He held up a hand as Bill started to protest. 'Sorry, mate. We give the mamma-san the money. We also give her the name of our hotel, a room number and a time. Then she knocks on your door.'

'But this is—'

Shane shook his head, finally losing patience with him. 'You pay her bar fine and agree to see her later or you let her go back to work,' he said. 'Your choice.' Then he softened, and smiled, as Bill let go of Ling-Yuan's wrist. She stared at him like a defiant child. Shane wrapped his arms around his friend, and looked at him with infinite sadness.

'You see, it's different now,' Shane said gently. 'We play by their rules. Or we don't play at all.'

*   *   *

He could see China from his hotel window.

It wasn't much of a view. Just the coastal road

370

to the nearest mainland city, Zhuhai, with its scattering of whitewashed villas, most of them dark and abandoned, and the wild palms swaying under a string of yellow lights as the winds built in fury. Every once in a while lightning cracked across the sky and illuminated the scene. Rain began to fall.

He thought about calling JinJin. He thought about calling Becca. But in the end he called no one, and he stood waiting for Ling-Yuan to come, watching the late-night traffic on the road to Zhuhai, and checking his watch.

Then he thought *perhaps she will not come*. The more he thought about it, the more sense it made. Why should she come at all? Failing to show wasn't going to get her the sack. Why come to his room to be shouted at by her sister's boyfriend? He was sure she would not come.

And that's when she knocked on his door.

She looked like someone else. The tart drag and make-up had gone. She wore a black T-shirt and trainers and jeans that, as she came into his room, he saw said Juicy on the back. Like something her big sister would wear. Perhaps even an old pair of JinJin's jeans. No, they were nowhere near the same size. She was buying her own clothes now. No more hand-me-downs from her big sister. She had her own money. She came into the room and as she walked past him he saw there was a line of flesh and a slither of thong showing between the bottom of her T-shirt and the top of her jeans. She turned in the centre of the room to face him, and he shook his head.

'I don't believe you,' he said. 'What would your mother say? What would your sister say?'

But she was prepared. Now he understood why

she had to come to his room. To justify herself.

'My sister have someone,' she said furiously. She had that Chinese ability to suddenly flare up, to go from placid blankness to self-righteous rage in one swift move. 'My sister *always* have someone to take care her. The man, the Shanghai man. Now you. Rich foreigner. But I have no one to take care.'

He shook his head. It wasn't enough of a reason. Nothing could ever be enough of a reason.

'Ling-Yuan, if you needed money, I could have given it to you. Your sister could have given it to you.' His voice was soft. He still thought he could save her. 'Not this way, Ling-Yuan—this is not the way to go. You must know that.'

Her small white teeth were bared in defiance.

'That factory you take me *no good*,' she said. 'Just enough money *to eat*. The boss a *bad man*. He do *bad things* to girl. The money *not enough* to send home. You understand? My mother *sick*. Do *you* understand?'

'I know your mother's sick.'

She held up her fingers and waggled them. 'Karaoke money—four time, five time better than that factory. *Ten time* better. Good night.'

'Selling yourself—is that what you want? I can't believe that's what you want.'

'Factory very bad,' she said, turning away from him and going over to the window. He watched her staring out at the rain and the lights of the distant road. The wind whipped and screamed through the palms. It was raining harder now. Something was moving down the road. At first he took it for some kind of large runaway vehicle, a truck with the brakes gone, but it was a billboard that had been ripped from its moorings. It featured the face of a smiling girl holding a pink mobile phone and she seemed to smile up at Bill as the billboard rose and twisted and disappeared into the darkness, on the road to China, its movement as graceful as a giant kite.

'Typhoon season starting,' Ling-Yuan said, like a lethargic weather girl. 'Start of June. Always the same. Typhoon coming in June, July, August. This year very bad. Maybe many typhoon.'

He came and stood next to her, not knowing what to say. He felt as though the damage had been done. Even though the real damage hadn't even started yet.

'That's the road to Zhuhai,' he said quietly. 'You can see the mainland from here.'

'I know,' she said, surprising him, and then shocking him, and clearly loving it. 'I been this hotel before.' She looked around, as if searching for something she might have left behind. 'Maybe even this room . . .' She smiled at the look on his face. 'I been Macau one month—already know every hotel.' Childishly counting with her fingers again. 'Know Hotel Lisboa, Tin Tin Villa, Fortuna, Mandarin Oriental . . .'

The list of hotels filled him with despair. 'Get about, don't you?' he said.

She nodded proudly. 'Very popular girl. The mamma-san says, "You good girl, Cherry. You best girl in bar."'

He held up a hand. 'Please. Do me a favour, okay? Your name is not Cherry.'

She looked genuinely indignant. 'It beautiful name. Cherry *American* name.'

He flared up. 'It's a stupid name. Nobody is called Cherry in the West. Nobody is called Cherry

373

in the real world. Mothers just don't call their babies *Cherry*. It's the name of a bar girl in Asia, it's what some old mamma-san calls a silly little girl like you. Listen to me, will you?' He took her hands, really wanting her to understand. But he faltered because she looked a bit like her sister. A younger, chubbier version of JinJin.

In many ways the two sisters were physical opposites—one so long and lean and small breasted, and the other so small and round, so round that she looked like a collection of curves. One like a dancer, the other like a milkmaid, or perhaps a barmaid. But he looked at the younger sister as he took her hands and he could not deny that he saw the ghost of the girl he had loved.

'Your name is Li Ling-Yuan,' he said, reminding her, reminding all the men in all the hotel rooms, reminding himself.

She flashed those small white teeth again. Part smile, part grimace. 'Ah, but in that place, in this new life, my name *Cherry*.'

He shook his head. 'I don't know what I'm going to do with you,' he said, aware of the coolness of her hands, chubby hands, different hands, and he was suddenly conscious of a tightness in his throat. She raised an over-plucked eyebrow and smiled, more widely now, as if what he said was not strictly true. He dropped her hands and stepped away from her. But they kept looking at each other, as if for the first time.

Then she stopped smiling and they were silent and when she finally spoke her voice was barely audible above the drone of the air conditioning.

'Enjoy your good time,' she said, giving an emphatic little nod, and it was all so clear and so

374

matter-of-fact that it was like being hit by a hammer.

Then there was only the moment and perhaps the moment was all there had ever been and all there ever is and all his thoughts of love and forever was just some pre-packaged Western fantasy.

There was just the moment and the girl and the shadows of the hotel room and what you wanted. He took her in his arms and felt the heat rising and she was slowly walking backwards, leading him to the bed.

Then suddenly Bill was pushing her away and pulling her to the door by her elbow and shoving her out into the hotel corridor before he had the chance to change his mind.

'Go home to your mother,' he said angrily, and she raised her almost non-existent eyebrows and laughed at him as if he was joking, or a fool, or as if she would never go home again.

He slammed the door on her and went over to the window and watched the storm building over the mainland as he tried to control his heart and his breathing. Electrical flashes split the night and seemed to illuminate every last drop of rain. He pushed a button on the bedside table. The curtains started to close and he was glad.

He was sick of looking at China.

TWENTY-SIX

The rains came and they did not stop.

For three weeks it was all you heard. The rivers

375

that had broken their banks in eastern and southern China. The million people displaced from their homes in Zhejiang, Fujian, Jiangxi, Hunan and Guangxi. From south of Shanghai all the way down to the border of Vietnam, the wind and the rains came and there seemed to be no end.

It was all you heard. The flooding and the landslides, the farmland submerged, the homes destroyed. Military helicopters dropping bottled water and instant noodles to the displaced. A case of typhoid reported in Hunan. The latest figures of the missing and the dead.

Shane sat in the car park beneath his apartment block, an overnight bag on the seat next to him, his suit still soaked after his brief dash from short-stay parking into the airport terminal.

He was meant to be flying down to Hong Kong again with the Germans but there was nothing in or out of Pudong. Come back tomorrow, said the girl on the desk at Dragon Air. It might be better tomorrow.

So he sat in his car in his ruined suit, putting off the moment when he would have to go up to the apartment, afraid that his wife might be there, and afraid that she might be somewhere else.

*   *   *

Bill pressed his face against the glass of the maternity ward.

The babies came in many colours at the International Family Hospital and Clinic but they were all swaddled tightly in the Chinese style, wrapped up like little white packages, tiny arms pinned to their sides. Yet his eyes kept returning to

376

one baby.

A girl. He was certain it was a girl, even though he could not possibly know for sure. Half Chinese, half European. Neither asleep nor really awake, its little bud-like mouth moving with some unnameable complaint. The sleeping infant made him smile. There was something about mixed blood that made for strikingly beautiful babies, he thought. He could see all the beauty of the world in that sleeping baby girl.

Glancing at his watch, he turned away from the glass wall of the maternity ward just as Sarfraz Khan was emerging from the lift. Khan walked past Bill with his head down, studying some papers, making it easy for both of them.

JinJin was in her room, sitting on the bed, her bags packed, almost ready to go home. Her face was still pale from the general anaesthetic. He kissed her on the cheek.

'Just waiting for my prescription,' she told him. 'They're giving me antibiotics and painkillers and then I'll be discharged.'

He sat on the bed holding her hand. It was a whole new vocabulary, he thought. The lexicon of ill health. The realisation that one day your body would betray you.

At the Chinese hospital she had first gone to, they told her that the lump was benign and that she should just learn to live with it. That was old China. Putting up with things that you did not have to put up with. Bill persuaded her to go to the International Family Hospital and Clinic where she had a minor operation to remove the lump, and told her that the scar would be so small that she would hardly know it was there. But the need for surgery had been a shock to both of them. It felt as if the real world was coming to claim them.

Now Bill put his arms around her, very gently, because he knew she was still in a lot of pain, and she was still nauseous from the general anaesthetic. Not the embrace of a lover, he thought. No, not like a lover at all. They had gone beyond all of that.

He kissed her cheek again, and he thought that it was not really the kiss of a lover. It was more like the kiss of a best friend, more like the kiss of a man and woman who had stuck together in sickness and in health, a couple who were married, and who had been married for a very long time.

*   *   *

They saw the neighbour on the stairs. The guy from the flat above. Brad.

'You all right, JinJin?' he said, all concerned, as if you could just walk into someone's life and pretend that you cared. As if the bonds could be there in an instant, Bill thought, as if they didn't take time. Brad had the nerve to take her hands. 'Did it go okay?' he said.

So she had told him. They were close enough for that. Now he stood on the stairs, on his way out, and acted like he gave a damn, pressing his back against the wall as JinJin smiled and nodded and took her hands away. Bill squeezed past him with a bag in each hand.

'She's fine,' Bill said, not breaking his stride.

Then they were in the flat and as she showered he stood in the doorway watching her trying to avoid the dressing on her left breast, a black dot of congealed blood showing through the gauze, and when it was done they got into bed and lay side by side.

He couldn't stay. Not even tonight, when she was just home from the hospital. That was the unvoiced sadness between them. They both understood that there would come the moment round midnight when he got up and left her and went back home. He wanted to show her that he would do anything for her. He wanted to not just say it, but to prove it with his deeds. But in the end he couldn't even stay the night, and what he wanted meant nothing. He lay there by her side and listened to her voice, her lovely voice soft in the night, as if she was thinking aloud.

'You tell yourself you are going with an unmarried man,' she said. 'But then you see he keeps looking at his watch. Then you see he always checks the mirror to worry about if there is any lipstick showing. And you realise that he can't take your birthday and Christmas gifts home, or that he must hide them if he does. And you wonder how many gifts he has thrown away, gifts that you spent a long time choosing because they said how much you love him. And when you are together, and it is good, it feels so . . . beautiful. Really. That's the word. Beautiful. I know sometimes I get the wrong word. But that's the right word. It just feels beautiful and right. And then when you sit there by yourself—after he has gone, and on all the nights you are alone—it all looks so ugly. And that is the right word too.' She turned her face towards him. 'What am I going to do now, Bill? What's going to happen to me?'

He turned on his side, and put an arm across her

belly, and he held her, and he could say nothing. There was a limit to the lies he could tell. He saw that now.

'I have to go,' he said, sliding out of bed.

'But before you go,' she said, and he knew that she had planned this all along, 'I want to show you some pictures.'

They were photographs of her sister with her new boyfriend. A large grinning German with his arm around a smiling Ling-Yuan, who since he had last seen her in Macau had piled on the pounds and an engagement ring.

'He's very handsome,' JinJin said of this spectacularly ordinary man. 'Don't you think he's very handsome?'

'He's bloody gorgeous,' Bill said, and then he hesitated. 'But what about when she was away?' They looked at each other. 'What about that time?' he said.

JinJin shook her head, quickly leafing through the stack of photos like a croupier with a new deck of cards.

'Nobody talks about that,' she said. 'It's not important any more.' She studied the photographs thoughtfully. 'But I think I have been a better sister to her than she has been to me.'

He reached out for her and she didn't pull away. She didn't flinch under his touch the way he had expected her to. That was where they were so different, that was where they were worlds apart. She could not let go as easily as he could.

'I want one thing,' she said. 'I wish I could have our baby. I don't care about you staying with your wife.' She corrected herself. 'I care but I say nothing.' She paused. 'But I want our baby.'

Bay-bee, she said. *Bay-bee*. 'That's what I want.'

And a part of him wanted it too. Even now. For it would have been a beautiful baby. But it would kill him. The start of that new life would mean the end of his own. Because it would mean he finally had two homes, and two wives, and two lives, and those two lives would tear him apart. Bill liked to believe that he would do anything for JinJin. He liked to tell himself that. But in the end, he could do nothing. Because he already had a wife and a child and they filled his heart. And if his wife no longer wanted him, then they would still fill his heart. He had run out of time.

'I have to go,' he said, and JinJin nodded, the tears starting up, because now there was no way forward and no way back and nothing to talk about, and it wasn't until he was at the door that her voice stopped him.

'I saw on TV—they said that men never marry the woman they really love,' said JinJin Li. 'Do you think that's true?'

Bill shook his head. 'No, I don't think it's true,' he said sadly. 'But isn't it lovely to think so?'

*   *   *

There was music on in the flat. Shane heard it before his key was out of the lock. It was not his music. It was not Eddie and the Hot Rods. It was not Thin Lizzy. It was one of those singers his wife liked. Some singer with a shaved head, chains, tattoos. Making seduction sound like a threat of physical violence. It was not '96 Tears' by Eddie and the Hot Rods. It was not 'Do Anything You Wanna Do'. Rosalita and her special friend were not playing Shane's song. They were playing one of the new songs. They were playing their own song.

Shane didn't recognise the man in bed with his wife. And then he did. One of the bar owners from Mao Ming Nan Lu. From a place a few doors down from Suzy Too, one of the places with live music. That surprised Shane because he would have bet money on the bass player. He had always suspected the bass player who from the very start had looked at him with such hatred, as if Shane had come along and spoiled everything. And he was right. Everything had been spoiled, and nothing could ever be good again.

The sheets were half pulled back and the club owner was lounging on a stack of pillows with Rosalita kneeling in front of him with her head between the man's legs.

Her skin was so brown against his pallid European flesh. What was he? French? German? The French and Germans were all over Shanghai. This wasn't Hong Kong. The other European nations had staked their claim here. She had him in her mouth, the mouth that kissed Shane on their wedding day, the mouth that he had once believed was a perfect match for his own.

The music was loud and it had masked his entry, but then they had seen him and they were cursing, pulling apart, and the man looked so angry that Shane thought he would have to fight him, felt his fists tightening, knew he could take him, even with the man's blood at boiling point.

But the man, this bar owner from one of the places where they had live music on Mao Ming Nan Lu, was angry with Rosalita, he was angry with Shane's wife, not Shane, because after all she shouldn't have brought a man back if the dumb husband was not safely installed at the office or packed off on a business trip.

'You stupid cow,' the man muttered, sliding out of bed as Rosalita pointlessly covered her breasts with a fistful of crumpled sheet, and somehow the insult to his wife was the thing that moved Shane's own blood.

More than the deceit, more than the sight of her beloved brown skin against that soft white flesh, more than what she was doing with her cheating mouth, more than coming home to someone else's music on his sound system. The insult did it. *You stupid cow.*

He should watch his mouth, Shane thought.

Then the man and Rosalita were arguing with each other while Shane went to the living room, pulled back the *Mona Lisa*, and tapped in the code: his wife's birthday. He came back into the bedroom with the Makarov in his hand.

They stared at him. And they stared at the cheap Russian gun. Shane sighed. Silence at last. Apart from the sound of someone else's song.

This music is so hateful, Shane thought. So full of real hatred. He felt very calm, although he was aware that he did not seem to be breathing.

Then the bar owner laughed at Shane. He had been here before.

'You're not going to shoot me,' he said confidently, pulling on his trousers and zipping up. 'Rosalita's your friend and she's my friend too, so you're not going to shoot me,' he said.

And that's when Shane shot him in the stomach, shot him with one tiny flex of his right index finger, which produced the sudden crack of sound and the spectacle of the man knocked backwards with his hands clutching with wonder at a gut wound that would kill him, but not immediately, not that Shane had planned it that way, and the man cursed once and loudly in disbelief, clawing at himself as he sank forward on his knees, his head bowed as if in shame, shame at last, the blood spreading on the white sheets.

But Shane didn't see any of that because he was watching his wife, who was screaming for help, *Someone, help, he's going to kill me*, in that curious Spanish accent that Tagalog speakers bring to the English language, as she crawled across the bed and then on to the floor, and he felt his finger on the trigger again, flesh and bone squeezing on a sliver of cheap black metal. And then he felt it pause.

Her hair was down, not tied and tossed across one shoulder as usual, but hanging loose, as it only did when she was in bed, or she was sleeping, or when she was making love. And with her hair hanging down like that he could see it clearly, he could see the ink stain on her neck.

There it was, for the very last time, the birthmark that Rosalita tried to hide for almost every waking moment of her life. Shane knew then that he loved her and that he was glad he had married her, he would do it all again in an instant.

Shane saw Rosalita's birthmark and knew that the sun rose and set with her. So he lowered the gun, then lifted it and pressed the barrel against his own pulsing temple and finally squeezed the trigger.

And in the moment before oblivion he thought of how she had looked the first time he saw her, so full of life, you never saw anyone so full of life, and he was grateful for it, all of it, and he remembered further back, one long-forgotten dawn in his youth in Australia, the sun coming up as he waded out to sea, the board in his fists, the water so cool from the waist down that it made him gasp even as he felt the sun on his face and his shoulders, and he remembered one of his first nights in Asia, in Hong Kong it must have been, Kowloon side, he didn't even know enough to be on Hong Kong island, but it was great, with the first Peking duck and hoysin sauce he had ever tasted and also the first Tsingtao, and who had ever tasted duck like that or drunk beer like that, or even knew they existed, the plum sauce on his disbelieving tongue, the skyline across the harbour shining like the stars, and he was grateful for it all, and then he was paddling further out to sea and up on the board and the water on his skin was already drying and the sun was coming up, almost blinding him now.

It was only the last micro moment of his life, but he was aware of all the good things he had known, and how fleeting it had all been, and how could he feel anything but the stab of sadness you get when you know that something so sweet and strange and wonderful will never come again.

PART FOUR:

SEE YOU AROUND

TWENTY-SEVEN

They had told him it was a village, but it was not quite that—just a jumbled collection of shacks surrounded by rain-lashed paddy fields on one side and a broad, rising river on the other. There was a thick red slime on the banks of the river. That was the reason Nancy Deng was here.

The car bumped down a dirt-track road and the firm's new driver, the driver who wasn't Tiger, an older man who was less likely to rush off to join the gold rush, clung to the wheel and tried to avoid an old woman wheeling her bicycle, her bare feet sloshing through the mud. There were no other cars here.

'I can see her,' Bill said. 'Pull over.'

He could see Nancy out in the fields. She was surrounded by a group of villagers, small figures in transparent plastic macs, looking like ghosts against the lush green landscape. Bill got out of the car and took one of the paths that weaved through the paddy fields, his umbrella buckling in the wind. There were streams running through the fields. They were the colour of rust. He said her name and she looked up.

'I'm so sorry about . . . Shane,' she said, saying his first name for the first time.

Bill nodded. The villagers began to drift away, their heads bowed in the rain. They moved in single file down the path between the paddy fields towards their homes, and he thought it looked like a funeral procession. He stared down at the orange-coloured water beneath their feet.

'That's it, isn't it?' he said. 'From the factories.'

Nancy pointed down river. 'I have a scientist who helps me. Pro bono.' She took off her glasses and wiped them with her fingers. 'He has found traces of heavy metals in the water from the factories.' She put her glasses back on. 'They dump their waste in the river and nobody can stop them.'

The rusty water was soaking through his shoes. 'What do they make?'

'Pesticides. Insecticides. Fluorides. Plastics. The villagers rely on the river for their rice crop, for their drinking water. The rice crops have failed because of the poisoned water. Babies are being born with birth defects. This place has a population of a few thousand, and hundreds of them have died.'

Bill looked at the pitiful little shacks. A cancer village. That's what they called it. 'But what can you do, Nancy?' he said.

'Stop them,' she said. 'Establish the link between the factories and the sickness. Force the government to apply its own laws. Prove that the factories upstream have poisoned these people. Protect the living. Compensate the bereaved. Care for the sick. There are children here with no parents. There are mothers and fathers who are dying. Everybody has let them down. They have nobody. Not the party. Not the government. Nobody to fight for them.'

'Well,' he said. 'They do now.'

She shook her head. 'I'm nothing. I know that. But there are others like me. At legal aid centres. Running hotlines. Working within universities. All over the country.'

He had always felt hope for the future when he

looked at Nancy. He knew that there were countless villages like this one, but he also knew there were young Chinese lawyers like her, offering their services for nothing, or a pittance, sometimes holding down jobs in commercial law firms to fund their pro bono work, or until they could afford to quit and do work that meant something beyond a fat salary and a glittering future. And Bill guessed that's exactly what Nancy had been doing in all her years at Butterfield, Hunt and West. Saving up for the day when she knew she would have to work for nothing.

'What I want,' she told him, 'what I want is for the poorest people in the land to have access to the law of the land.' She looked down at the rust-coloured water on her boots. 'You will miss him so much,' she said. 'Your good friend.'

Bill looked away. 'I miss him, we all miss him.' He looked back at her. 'That's why I'm here. Devlin sent me. We've got more work than we can handle. There are new guys coming in from London, but it's not going to be enough. The firm wants you to come back. We need you.'

She shook her head, and indicated the plastic-coated ghosts disappearing into their modest homes. 'They need me more,' she said.

He did not push it. He had known that she would never come back. He had told Devlin that she would never come back. And in his heart he did not want her to come back. He wanted her to stay here and fight for these people. He did not want her to be like him.

'You need to be careful, Nancy,' he said. He had heard what could happen to idealistic young lawyers who did pro bono work for the poor.

'You're dealing with people who get away with murder.'

'I'll be all right,' she said, sounding as if she believed nothing could touch her, and he knew she was wrong. 'It doesn't matter how rich we get. China will always be a Third World country until the courts are willing to protect the little man. Until we have the rule of law, we will be a nation of peasants.'

'You sound like Mad Mitch,' he said.

'He was the one who talked to me about the rule of law. Did you notice? He talked about it all the time. *The rule of law means that the law applies to everyone in equal measure. Where the rule of law does not apply, legal solutions are imperfect. The rule of law is the root and branch of democracy.* Mitch believes that what we do is a sacred profession. Like a doctor, you know? He's a good lawyer.'

'But all wrong for this place,' Bill said. 'There's not a lot of the sacred in the PRC.'

'And how are you?' Nancy asked him.

He seemed almost embarrassed. 'They're making me a partner.'

She congratulated him, smiling for the first time, really pleased for him, because she knew it was what he wanted, and why he was here, and everything he had worked for.

Bill thanked her, and they stood under his umbrella watching the rain on the paddy fields and the red-etched river beyond, and he knew that he would be long gone from this place before it ever broke its banks, but that she would still be here.

*   *   *

392

Shane's parents were old and bewildered and dumbstruck with grief.

Bill accompanied them to the Australian consulate on the twenty-second floor of CITIC Square and gently steered them through the paperwork required by two nations for the release and transportation of their son's body.

They were staying almost next door to their consulate, at the Portman Ritz-Carlton in the Shanghai Centre, but Bill had decided that in this rain it would be best to make the short trip by car. This was a mistake. The traffic was not moving on Nanjing Xilu and while Shane's parents sat in stunned, red-eyed silence in the back of the firm's car, Bill sat up front and stared out at the crowds. And that was when he saw them. His wife and the man. They were at a window seat in the Long Bar.

Becca and Dr Sarfraz Khan.

Bill's first thought was Holly. They were talking about Holly and her asthma. But it might not have been asthma. Or it might have been Holly and other things. He did not know. They were sitting on opposite sides of the table, leaning across, Khan talking urgently and Becca listening, his wife just listening.

And he knew that she was right—there are always options, there are always options for all of us. And for the first time Bill saw that it wasn't the seeking and straying and coming apart that was touched by magic, but the staying together.

*   *   *

They stood on the tarmac at Pudong and watched the men loading the coffin on to the plane.

Shane's parents huddled together under an umbrella bearing the name of their hotel. You should not have to do this, Bill thought. You should not have to bury your child. Nobody should have to do what you are doing. He could not imagine life beyond losing your child. What life could there be after that?

Bill stood on one side of Shane's parents and on the other was a man from the Australian consulate. He must have been one of the junior staff, still in his twenties, but his presence gave the act a ceremonial feel.

As the coffin was loaded into the plane, on the same slow-motion conveyor belt they used for the luggage, the young man stood very erect, stiff with decency and respect. Bill was glad he was here, although as the coffin slid into the hold he could almost hear Shane's mocking laughter. *Any chance of an upgrade, mate? They've got me in with the bloody suitcases.*

The mother, a large grey-haired old lady, seemed to shudder as her son's coffin disappeared into the plane, and Bill felt like hugging her. The father— shorter and smaller than his wife, and determined to keep a grip on his feelings—was harder to warm to. But then in Bill's experience, fathers always were.

The coffin disappeared into the plane. They watched the hold close. It was the last act before flying. The young man from the consulate glanced at his watch. Shane's mother turned to Bill and put her arms around him, clinging to him as if he was holding her up. Then she abruptly pulled away.

'You come and see us,' she said. 'In Melbourne. With your wife and little girl.'

'I'll do that.' Bill nodded, knowing it was unlikely that they would ever meet again. There was a battered leather holdall at her feet. Shane's overnight bag. He had seen it a hundred times. Tossed into the boot of Tiger's car. In the back of the helicopter to Macau. Sitting on Shane's desk in the office, about to accompany its owner on a trip around the country or the continent. The mother picked up the bag and held it out to Bill.

'They found this in the car,' she said. 'Mostly work things.'

'We don't want it,' the father said.

The bag was partially open, as if it had been rifled and found uninteresting. Bill could see files, a print-out of an unused e-ticket in a plastic envelope, Shane's laptop. Clothes and a toilet bag. A thick green paperback. *The Rise and Fall of the British Empire* by Lawrence James.

'I'll take care of it,' he said.

The father stuck out his hand and Bill shook it. Although he was a small man—all of Shane's bulk came from his mother—the father had one of those old-fashioned handshakes where they think you are effeminate if you don't at least try to break a few bones. Or perhaps it's just the grief, Bill thought. Perhaps he doesn't realise what he is doing.

'How could this happen?' asked the old man, his voice trembling at last, baring his teeth with the hard physical effort of not coming apart. 'That's what I don't understand.'

Bill shook his head. He had no answers. The death itself was the only answer. 'Shane was lonely,' Bill said. 'I just think he was very lonely.'

The old man exploded. 'Rubbish!' he said with

such anger that Bill stepped back. 'How could he be lonely?' demanded Shane's father. 'He was married, wasn't he?'

*   *   *

He was sitting on the bed watching their daughter sleeping when he heard Becca's key in the lock. Holly kicked back the duvet and he gently covered her again. She had her fists lifted above her head like a weightlifter.

He heard Becca come quietly into the room but he didn't look at her. Her hand touched his shoulder. He reached out and brushed a swathe of blonde hair from Holly's forehead.

'What happened to the ayi?' she said, her voice very soft in the sleeping child's room.

'I sent her home,' he said quietly.

'She could have put Holly to bed.'

He still hadn't looked at her. 'I like doing it,' he said.

She put her arms around his neck. He felt her face close to his cheek. Her hair falling, her breath in his ear. He could smell her perfume and wine. The smell of someone else's cigarettes.

'I'm so sorry, Bill,' she whispered.

He was silent for a long moment. 'What are you sorry about?' he said.

'Shane,' she said, straightening up, sounding surprised. 'I'm sorry about Shane. It's a terrible thing. His parents—I can't imagine what his parents are going through.'

Holly moaned in her sleep and Bill reached out and stroked her shoulder. 'There's nothing anyone could have done,' he said. He looked up at his wife as she stood above him and he wondered what life would be like after she had left him. 'Something bad was always going to happen to Shane. I loved him, but the way he lived, it was inevitable.'

She dragged her fingers through her hair, pulling it off her face. And she shook her head.

'No,' she said. 'It's this city. It's Shanghai.' She turned and left him watching the sleeping child alone. 'It brings out the worst in people,' she said as she went out the door.

*   *   *

And then he went to see her again.

He went to see her again because he didn't know what else to do. He went to see her again because he couldn't stay away from her. He could see no reason why the spell would ever be broken. That's how stupid he was back then.

But she was gone. JinJin was gone and nobody knew where. The old Paradise Mansions girls were in her apartment, making dumplings the way they had the first night he had really met them.

At first he felt as if they were stalling him, the difficult ex-boyfriend, the obsessive got-it-bad schmuck who doesn't know when it is time to move on.

But as they took his wet coat and gave him a few pieces of kitchen towel to dry his hair and as he turned down their offer of a plate of dumplings, he realised that it seemed to be true. They really didn't know where she had gone. She had packed her bags and called Jenny Two, leaving a message on her phone saying that she was leaving the keys under the mat and that they were welcome to use

397

the place in her absence.

'There's a neighbour,' Bill said, glancing at the ceiling. 'A guy upstairs she was friendly with. Brad. He might know. She might have said something to him.'

They looked at each other and it took him a few seconds to understand, but he was there before the words came blurting out of Jenny Two. How stupid men are, he thought. And how stupid I am. How could I not have seen this coming? How could I have believed that her heart would never change?

'They left together, William,' Jenny Two said, and she squinted at his face, as if it hurt her too. There was no way back from this moment, and it was not a good moment. 'I'm so sorry.'

He nodded, and smiled like a happy idiot, smiled as if he had heard nothing but good news all day long, and sat down between Annie and Sugar, facing the two Jennys, swallowing the sob of grief that rose in his throat. So this is how it ends, he thought. She goes off with the first guy who comes along. It was almost funny.

Asked again, he accepted their offer of a plate of dumplings, and he realised that he did not want to run away from them and hide his feelings. The taste and smell and sound of the frying dumplings brought back her voice, and the pride she had taken in being a *Dongbei ho. 'Jiaozi dumpling from Shenyang. Like ravioli. You know?'*

They told him their stories. Annie had returned to the bars after being run out of Paradise Mansions but had met another American boy who was taking her back to Hawaii. 'I shall drive a Mustang and surf,' she said proudly. 'You watch. I post on YouTube.'

Jenny Two had been left enough money in her old boyfriend's will to start her own business. She was wavering between a food stall and an Internet café. 'I shall be part of my country's economic miracle,' she said. Bill suddenly realised that she was no longer wearing glasses and gestured at her eyes.

'Laser surgery,' she said. 'In shopping mall.'

Jenny One's Frenchman had come back. Bill could see how it might yet work out for her, he could understand how a lonely married man in Paris might wake up one night and believe that the woman he thought was his bit on the side was actually the love of his life. He could see how that might happen.

Sugar was working in one of the new bars on Mao Ming Nan Lu, but the thought did not seem to depress her, perhaps because she alone had never expected to be rescued.

And from Sugar he learned that the bars were changing. After the best part of a hundred years, the old anarchy of the Shanghai night was passing into history as the freelance girls finally came under control of the bars where they worked. The boomtown was not exactly getting respectable, but it was becoming increasingly regulated.

'And I got a promotion,' Sugar told him. 'I was a Customer Care Agent but now I am a Guest Relations Officer.'

They were all happy endings, of sorts, and he was grateful for them because he had reached the stage of his life when he was struggling to believe in happy endings. But then they were in Shanghai, where the act of survival was a happy ending.

Then it was time to go. They gathered around

him at the door.

'See you around,' Jenny Two said, and it sounded like a phrase recently mastered in a language class.

'Yes,' Bill smiled, and he kissed each of them on the cheek, and they hugged him like they cared, and as if they were so sorry that it had ended with him and JinJin, and as if he—soon to be a partner at Butterfield, Hunt and West—was the one to be pitied. 'See you around, girls.'

And he left, knowing that he now had his reason to never go back, to never see her again, and to finally get her out of his blood, and out of his life. In the end it was so obvious. He should have expected it all along.

A new man. Of course. What else?

He wondered how he could ever have been so dumb, how he could ever have believed that she was really any different to him.

She was just another girl. She was just another woman. How could it possibly end any other way? She had met some new guy. Right. Of course. He almost laughed. But somehow the banality of it all was impossible to grasp. A new man? JinJin with a new man? Yes, we all have our options. There was a part of him that still found it incredible.

A new man, when she had told him that there would never be another man, and that she would love him until the day she died. All that stuff that they put in the songs. All the lies they tell you and you are so eager to believe.

Only you, for ever and ever, like one of the old songs. That's what she had told him, that's what had come out of the mouth he knew so well, and he had believed her, and it made his life impossible because it meant he could never give her up. It meant that one day and someday and somehow they would be together, because there was no escaping the other. They were bound together like two mountaineers. But now she had broken the bond.

He stepped back out into the pounding rain and he didn't see it, he didn't feel it. In his face, in his shoes, drenching his suit. It didn't really touch him. Because he saw her in the arms of the new unknown lover and it was more real to him than the rain soaking him to the bones. He saw it all. It was as if he was in the room with them. He could almost smell her, almost hear her. Her face, her legs, her sighs and moans, the scar on the left breast. Her long thin arms wrapped around the new man's neck. Fine, he thought. Great. If that's the way it has to be. Get him to take you to the hospital next time, he thought. Get him to find you a flat. Get him to turn his life inside out and destroy all the people he loves. Get him to listen to your lies. Get him to tear his heart in half.

Bill began walking, briskly but without direction or purpose. The rain blinded him.

He can have you, he thought.

He can fucking have you.

TWENTY-EIGHT

Bill stood at the window watching the rain come down on the courtyard of Paradise Mansions.

He could hear the sound of water running and laughter. The ayi was giving Holly her bath. And in the master bedroom, the voice of his wife was an indistinct murmur that came and went, as if she was pacing as she talked on her phone, as if she could not keep still. Probably her old man, he thought. And then again, maybe not.

He could feel the keys to JinJin's flat pressing into his flesh. Bill took the keys out and put them back in his pocket. He thought about throwing them away but immediately dismissed the idea. He thought about putting them in an envelope and leaving them with her porter but that almost seemed like an act of cowardice, and she had meant too much to him for that. He could go back and give them to the girls. But he did not want the girls to see how he felt.

Bill knew exactly what he had to do. It was so clear. He had to give them to her. He had to place the keys in her hand and set her free, and set himself free.

Becca looked up as he came into the master bedroom with his overnight bag. She was sitting on the bed now, the mobile phone still in her hand, but the connection broken.

'I have to go,' he said.

He began opening drawers and throwing things into his bag. A change of shirt, socks, pants. His shaving kit. His British passport for ID. Not much. Just enough for one night. This wouldn't take long.

'You have to go? Go where?'

'Changchun. It's up north. Near the border with North Korea.'

'I know where bloody Changchun is,' she said.

She stood up and folded her arms across her chest as she watched him packing. 'You can't get a flight,' she said.

'The airport's open,' he said, zipping the bag

402

shut, and placing it on the bed. 'And I'll be flying away from the weather. Going north. The trouble is all in the south.'

'Daddy, look,' Holly said, padding into the room in her pyjamas, her golden hair damp and tangled. She was holding a picture of a red panda. The ayi came after her with a hair dryer in her hand.

'That's beautiful, darling,' he said, scooping up his daughter, kissing her face. He turned to his wife. 'There are no typhoons up there,' he said. 'Too far north. One night. That's all I need.'

He kissed his daughter again, and she ran off holding her picture with the ayi struggling to keep up.

'You're not going,' Becca said. She unzipped his bag and began pulling out his clothes.

'One night and it's done,' he said. He reached for her and she pulled away. 'Please, Becca.'

'Don't go,' she said. 'I don't want you to go. I don't want you to go to that Third World whore and talk things over or whatever bullshit you have in your head.'

She held the bag upside down and shook out what was left inside. Bill slowly began to repack.

'I'm sorry,' he said.

'You're always sorry,' she said, and punched her fist hard against his chest. 'Do we have a life here or not? I want you to read Holly a story. I want you to draw with her. I want you to sleep with me tonight. I want us to be normal, Bill. Or I want us to be nothing. Do you understand all that?'

'I have to do this one last thing.'

'Why?'

'So that it's over.'

She smiled with contempt. 'And do you honestly

expect us to be here when you get back?' she said, and she shook her head and dismissed him with a wave of her hand, as if giving up on him at last.

*   *   *

The plane banked for landing and he saw the mountains beneath him, conical and black, satanic remakes of the green limestone mountains of Guilin.

As the plane turned towards its destination, the mountains reared up on either side and he saw that they were not mountains at all. There were no conical mountains here. These were mountains that had been made by men. What he had seen were giant slag heaps of coal, and he saw now that there were people on them, bent double, tearing at the surface for usable chunks of fuel.

Then the black peaks were gone and the plane was coming down through fluffy white clouds, but then he saw that they were not clouds at all, but the emissions rising from the smokestacks of the remaining iron and steel mills. Then the plane was out of the man-made clouds and below them and rising up beneath him were the abandoned factories sitting in scrappy fields like wasted muscles on the arms of a dying man.

The plane hit the runway with a screech and he was back in her hometown of Changchun, the jagged metal in his pocket still pressing into his flesh, wondering how he had ever seen romance in this wretched place.

*   *   *

He stood outside the ugly grey apartment block looking up at the windows that had been hung with red lanterns during Spring Festival. The windows were empty now. The sky was a flat grey. He had travelled beyond the rains.

He climbed the blackened stairwell, coated with the filth of long-dead factories, preparing himself for the moment when he would see her face, and see the new man, and give her the keys.

JinJin's mother opened the door to the little flat and she was all smiles, and as Bill stepped into the apartment, he saw that she was quite alone.

She ushered him inside, and as she made them tea she spoke rapidly in Mandarin interspersed with one-word stabs of English.

'Father. Sick. Guangxi.'

'Guangxi?' But that was all the way down south. That was the other end of the country. Near Hong Kong. Even nearer to Vietnam. Guilin was in Guangxi. JinJin's father was in Guangxi. Bill brought the teacup to his mouth and it scalded his lips. He struggled to understand, the map of China reeling in his mind. Guangxi? That was the province where the limestone mountains looked across at Vietnam, and where they had watched the fishermen with their birds from the bridge in Guilin. That was where they had seen her father, and Bill had given the man money, and JinJin had looked away.

'Guangxi!' her mother said. 'Guangxi!'

She had a newspaper and she showed it to him. There was a map of the country on the front page, giving the latest on the typhoons and the flooding, and although it was a Chinese newspaper and he could not read a word of it, he understood everything.

Because the page one headline was nothing but a number. 20,000,000, it said. Twenty million. The number of the displaced.

Zhejiang, Fujian, Jiangxi, Hunan, Guangdong, Guangxi. No part of southern or eastern China was untouched. It was impossible to comprehend. It was a bigger landmass than Western Europe.

Her mother tapped a stubby finger on the bottom end of the map, tittering with glee. Then he saw that her laughter was that peculiar Chinese response to disaster. She was terrified.

'Here! Here!'

And finally Bill got it. JinJin was at the other end of the country. She was as far away as she could be, down in Guangxi with her father and the new man.

She was down among the floods.

The old woman grinned, baring her brown, tea-stained teeth. It had once maddened him, this habit of responding to disaster with delight. But now he understood. They wrapped their pain in a smile. Their laughter in the face of disaster was like a bandage on a wound. He touched the old woman's arm, and nodded. They wrapped their pain in a smile. That was what she was doing. That's what they all did.

He understood at last.

*   *   *

It took him three flights to get to Guilin.

From Changchun he flew south and west to Xi'an and then on to Chongqing. In Chongqing he waited with tourists who had been down the Yangtze River, and then the tourists left on flights to Beijing and Bill slept overnight in the terminal. In the morning he woke up and there were two old women sitting opposite him. His eyes were drawn to their abnormally small feet. He looked away, appalled, and looked again.

The old women were small but their feet belonged to dolls, to toys, to another age. He knew they had been bound even before one of them absent-mindedly tugged off her blue canvas slipper and massaged her wilfully deformed foot, the end of it flapping like a door in the wind. She pulled her slipper back on and stared straight through Bill.

Suddenly their flight was called and the old women stood up and hobbled off quickly to their gate, their boarding passes in their hand. He watched them go. Their feet had not been bound but crushed. The process was more like having their limbs put in a vice than wrapped in a scarf. The bare foot he had seen was a memento of old China. But to the old woman it was just a foot. It had been just a foot for years, decades, for a lifetime. That was the strange thing. The normality of it all.

He had thought that he could not survive losing her, and he had been wrong. He would get over it. It would hurt and he would live, and she would live too. Bill watched the old women limp through the boarding gate.

You could get used to anything.

*   *   *

He was the only passenger on the flight to Guilin. The stewardess strapped herself in beside him

407

and clutched his hand as the pilot brought the plane down. They hit the runway, lifted off, hit the tarmac again and went into what felt like a wall of spray. Bill could feel the water on the runway dragging at the undercarriage, trying to pull the plane sideways, trying to turn them over.

But the pilot braked in a screech of rubber and the wall of spray subsided. As they taxied to the terminal, the stewardess vomited quietly into a paper bag. Bill pressed his face against the window. Outside, the rains came down as if they would never end.

There was chaos at the airport. It felt like the entire city was trying to leave. The green uniforms of the Public Security Bureau were everywhere, holding back the crowds. Bill pushed his way through the mob, moving in the opposite direction.

The car-hire desks were abandoned so he went outside to the taxi rank. It was deserted and he stood there listening to the wind, uncertain what to do next. The wind was like a warning, a lament. He had never heard wind like it. An old red Santana taxi pulled up and began to unload a family laden with suitcases. When they had paid the driver, Bill stuck his head in the window.

'I need to get to a village,' Bill said. 'A village on the road to Yangshuo.' He realised he did not even know the name of the place where her father lived. Perhaps it did not have a name. But he could remember the road. He could get them there.

'No Yangshuo,' said the driver. 'Road all closed Yangshuo.'

Bill took out his wallet and pulled out all the money he had and stuffed it into the hands of the taxi driver, closing the man's fist around the notes.

The driver examined the grubby RMB notes and bared his yellow tombstone teeth. His breath was foul.

'Road still closed,' he said apologetically, although he made no attempt to return the money.

'As close as you can,' Bill said, getting into the car.

The driver stared straight ahead, muttering to himself, as the wind blew the rain sideways against the windscreen. Sideways rain, Bill thought. How do you get sideways rain? A steady stream of traffic and pedestrians were coming in the opposite direction, making for the airport. Everywhere there were suitcases that had been dropped or dumped or blown off of roof racks. Everywhere there were bits of trees and billboards. The trees and billboards were the first things to go in a typhoon, he realised, and as he stared out of the window it was as if he had never been to Guilin, as if he had dreamed the time they had spent here.

The limestone peaks of the mountains were smothered in mist but it was the river that made it seem like somewhere he had never been.

The river had broken its banks and changed everything. The paddy fields were now lakes, and they looked as though they had been lakes for a thousand years. On the river where they had watched the fishermen with their cormorants, a giant barge loaded with what looked like sand seemed to be abandoned and drifting. As Bill watched, it split clean in two with a crack like lightning. He strained to see some sign of the crew fleeing for their lives. Nobody appeared and the two halves of the broken barge began to slide beneath the water. Then they were gone, and it was as if it had never been, or he had imagined it all.

There were no PSB police this far from the airport. Here it was all PLA soldiers. He watched a group fish something from the river and lay it on a tarpaulin by the side of the road. It was the body of another soldier.

'No road Yangshuo!' shouted the driver, recoiling at the sight of the bloated body.

'Just drive,' Bill shouted back at him, and he drove, and Bill felt bad that he had raised his voice at the man, because he knew he could not get to her without him.

Bill was sure they were going to make it. But then they were at a roadblock, soldiers everywhere, their lorry parked at an angle across the road, blocking everything, and a soldier was flagging them down. He stuck his head in the window and Bill could see they were being told to turn back. Beyond the soldiers Bill could see the road ahead buried under a mudslide. It looked like a congealed brown river that had slid down the hill. The driver was moaning to himself.

'Is there another way?' Bill said. 'Is there another road to Yangshuo?'

'*This* way Yangshuo,' the driver said, banging his steering wheel as the PLA began shouting at him, gesturing more fiercely. The driver began to turn the taxi around. 'Fuck you, man, okay?' he told Bill in an American accent.

Bill pulled off his watch. 'This is a good watch, okay? Worth a lot of money. A lot of money, okay? You take this watch and find another road.'

The driver showed Bill his wrist. He already had a watch. It was even a Rolex. It might not have been the real thing, but it was a Rolex of sorts and he clearly did not want another one. Bill took out his empty wallet and offered the driver his black American Express card. The driver looked away.

Bill got out of the car leaving his bag on the back seat and began walking towards the soldiers. Someone grabbed his arm. A young red-haired woman with an Irish accent. Some kind of aid worker.

'You can't go down there,' she told him. 'There's disease in there now. Typhoid. Dengue fever. Malaria.'

He nodded politely and kept walking. The woman shouted something but the wind was too loud and he did not catch it. He had reached the soldiers now. They were very young. They had rifles slung over their shoulders. They were looking at the mudslide. He walked past them. A child's arm was sticking out of the sludge. Bill felt his flesh crawl with horror, but he kept walking, leaning forward, pressing against the wind. The wind dropped for a second and he heard the raised voices in Chinese behind him and, further back, the Irish woman repeating that he couldn't go down there. He kept going. Then he felt fingers digging into his arm, and he turned and placed his hands on the young soldier's chest, and with no more force than was necessary, shoved him away. The soldier stumbled two steps backwards and then lurched forward, and in one smooth movement swung the rifle off his shoulder and rammed the butt as hard as he could into Bill's face.

He didn't fall over but his legs went, and he staggered around drunkenly with red and yellow

411

flashing lights the only thing he could see. He had been struck on the right side of his face, and he could feel the blow still, it was as if he was still being hit. The feeling ran for about six inches from just above his eyebrow to just below his cheekbone. The pain filled his head, a balloon of pain that was expanding by the second, but the damage was all in his eye. His right eye. His eyebrow and cheekbone had absorbed most of the blow but he had also been hit in his right eye, and when the reds and yellows faded there were black stars floating in his foggy vision.

Bill gave the soldier a sick, wonky smile and turned and walked obediently back down the road. The soldier watched him go, his rifle held like a club in case he came back. The taxi had gone but the Irish woman was standing in the same place. 'It's from the stagnant water,' she said, as if their conversation had not been interrupted. 'The disease. The mosquitoes and the stagnant water.'

He didn't know what she was talking about. He had already forgotten about the disease. The right side of his face was throbbing. The black stars dived and swooped, as if blown by the wind.

'Is there another road to Yangshuo?' he said, gently dabbing his cheekbone. It came away smeared with blood, but there wasn't much of it. He blinked repeatedly, trying to clear his eyes. The black stars continued to float across his vision, distracting him and scaring him. He closed his right eye. The other one was fine. 'I really have to get to a village on the way to Yangshuo.'

The Irish woman looked sympathetic. 'Have you got family there?' she said, and he didn't know how to answer that.

He walked down the hill and below the mudslide. The soldiers were on the road above him. He could see the stumps of trees when they had been chopped down, and the frozen brown river that had slid across the road. The hill looked as though it had collapsed. Black stars lazily drifted across the scene. But his eye was closing now and the black stars were not so bad.

The ground was slick with wet mud. As he descended the slope he fell over almost immediately, pitching forward on to his hands and knees. He got up slowly, holding on to a stunted tree for support, his palms and trousers covered in mud. He kept going down the hill, but treading more carefully, walking sideways, digging his shoes into the churned earth.

When he was beyond the mudslide he walked back up to the road and among the stalled traffic. He could hear a helicopter above him. He kept walking. He felt he knew this road but when he came to her father's village he almost walked through it before he recognised the place.

The river was a broad brown flood. There were no tents. There were no fields. The fields and the tents were all gone. A mountain of mud had slid to the very edge of the village, burying the school, and wiping the place clean of any distinguishing features. He stared around, completely disorientated.

The small, carefully divided paddy fields that he remembered were now a glassy lake. He heard a noise and could not place it. It was like a growl coming from the centre of the earth. It was like underground thunder. He was very scared. But this was the place, even if everything had changed.

He could not find her father's house. He looked around at the world of mud that had invaded this place. Then he saw it. Propped up with thick logs. The house next door was gone. Just gone. He heard the noise again and this time understood. The mud was rumbling in its core.

Something landed on his hand and he slapped it dead. A mosquito with black and white stripes. There were helicopters in the sky, as if watching him. He went inside her father's house. JinJin was sitting on the side of a single bed, holding ChoCho. Her father lay on the bed, shivering uncontrollably. Bill took a few steps forward. There was a rash on his face. Bill stared at them with wonder. He would never have guessed that she would come to her father. He thought the years of violence had killed her sense of duty towards the old man. But nothing would kill it.

'William,' she said, as if expecting him. 'Your face.'

There was a cracked shaving mirror on the wall. He looked into it and saw his right eye was buried under gorged black-and-purple bruising. He turned away and didn't look at it any more. The black stars had gone for now, and he was glad of that. He saw that the rash on her father's face was also on the baby.

'What's wrong with them?' he said.

'Sick from the mosquito,' she said. 'From the bad water.'

Dengue fever. The Irish woman was right. He put his arm around JinJin and outside he could

414

hear the tons of mud growl and move. Or perhaps he imagined it. The mud was what he was frightened of. It had not scared him on the road but it did now. There it was. The noise from outside again. Louder now. It was real. They could all die today. 'We have to get out of here,' he said, jumping up, ready to be gone. 'We have to go, JinJin.'

'The soldiers will come for us,' she said, indicating the ceiling. You could still hear them up there. 'The helicopters.'

'Nobody's coming,' Bill said. He looked around the shack. Something was missing. He stared at her, trying to concentrate. 'Listen to me,' he said, kneeling beside her, feeling the sickness in this place. The child scared him. The child wasn't crying. 'Nobody's coming,' he said. 'The helicopters are not coming. You know why? Because they can't land.' He realised that he saw it all with perfect clarity. The hovering helicopters and the ground transformed to shifting mud. They could look but they couldn't touch. 'They want to help us but they can't, so we have to help ourselves.'

JinJin smiled weakly. 'The soldiers are so great,' she said. She was a real Chinese patriot, a true believer. Perhaps they all were.

'The soldiers are so great but they can't help us,' he said, standing up. 'The roads have gone. Everyone is stuck. We have to help ourselves. We have to go now or we will die.' He looked around the room. 'Where's your friend?'

'He went back to Guilin,' she said, as the wind picked up outside. 'There's only you, William.'

She still didn't move. They could hear the old

man breathing, the rain beating against the corrugated roof, the moaning wind, and he could almost feel the great mass of sludge outside, waiting to bury them all.

JinJin remained where she was and Bill saw for the first time that she was paralysed with exhaustion. How many nights had she gone without sleep, caring for her father and her son? Bill took ChoCho from her arms and wrapped him in all the blankets he could find. Then he helped her father from the bed. If he could stand up then he could walk, and if he could walk then he could live. They could all live.

'I this girl father,' he told Bill, leaning against him, and Bill nodded, taking the man's weight. The rash on his face was a splatter of red welts.

'Listen to me. I can't carry both of them. I can't carry everybody. I can't do it.' Bill held out the listless child. 'You understand?' The old man took his grandson.

Bill got JinJin to her feet and she reached for her son. Then she was on her knees and Bill was crouching beside her, his arms around her, holding her, whispering to her until she nodded once, acknowledging that carrying her child was impossible. She looked at him and wiped her eyes with her fingers.

'Bad mother,' she said.

'No,' he said.

Bill scooped her up in his arms and carried her out of the shack. The old man trailed behind them, carrying the boy. Bill carried her through the mud with the half-buried and three-quarters- buried bodies and the wrecked homes and ruined lives, cursing the heavens and then saying, *Please God,*

416

Please God, until he was too tired to do even that.

They reached the highway. The old man was dropping behind. But he was still there. ChoCho was still in his arms. Bill sat down on a tree stump, JinJin beside him, leaning against him, almost sleeping now, or something like sleep, and they let the old man catch up and rest, and they kept resting until Bill thought he heard a sound. From the hill above them, from the ground below. Mixed in with the terrible wind, the sound of something underground, about to appear and devour them. Then he stood up and they kept going. The old man was soon trailing behind. Bill shouted at him to keep going, and JinJin held him with her arms around his neck, and he felt her breath on his face, and it was as if they were still lovers.

They got to the roadblock and it was only then that his legs gave out. Bill collapsed into the arms of a PLA soldier and he could feel arms lifting JinJin from him, and someone holding him close, and not letting him go, as if the human touch would heal everything.

*   *   *

At the shelter they wrapped him in a blanket and gave him a bottle of water and a bowl of instant noodles.

There were no dry clothes to be had, but he felt warmer inside his blanket and gulped the noodles down, far too fast at first, making him giddy with nausea, and then more slowly, like a child learning to eat, and then he licked the plastic bowl clean when the food was gone, trying to get the last bit of goodness.

JinJin had gone to the hospital with her child and her father. Bill was still dumbfounded that he had found her here. This was the part of her that he had never imagined. Despite everything, she was still her father's daughter and she did not hesitate to go to him in his need. He had thought that he knew her better than anyone in the world. But perhaps he knew nothing at all.

Bill realised that his hands were shaking and he stared at them with his good eye, willing them to be still. But they kept trembling with shock and cold and relief.

He looked up at the sky. There was something wrong with the sky. It was different. He realised that the rain had stopped and the wind had fallen silent. And it was only then that he remembered the keys.

He felt in his pocket, then shoved in his hand. Nothing. Lost in the mud somewhere. On the hill. At the roadblock. In the back of the taxi. Left in a plastic security tray at an airport he would never see again. It didn't matter. It didn't matter. He had not really come thousands of miles to return her keys. He saw that now.

He had told himself that he was coming to return the keys, but now he understood that he was coming to tell JinJin Li that he had loved her, and to tell her that his heart did not change so easily, and to tell her goodbye.

*　　　*　　　*

The apartment was empty when he got home.

It was late afternoon on the next day. They should have been here. It was a school day, a

418

Monday, and whatever they had been doing, it should have been over by now.

Bill took off his mud-caked clothes and looked at the laundry basket and then put them in a rubbish bag. Everything. It was all ruined. Then he went to the shower and stood under the hottest water he could stand until the black stars were swarming over his damaged eye and he thought he was going to faint.

He came out of the shower and found a T-shirt and jeans and went to the window. The weather was finally lifting. Mountainous clouds rolled across the sky, the dying sunshine struggling behind them. The courtyard of Paradise Mansions was deserted. It was as if his wife and daughter had disappeared. He tried calling Becca's mobile and there was only the voicemail. He said that he was back, and his cracked voice sounded weak and strange in the empty flat.

Dinnertime came and went and still there was no sign. He ate nothing, and felt as if he was floating. Even the pale sunlight from the window seemed dazzling. He sat on the sofa and massaged his temples, but the pounding would not stop. He was lost, he realised. He had never felt so lost in his life. He closed his eyes and he must have slept because he awoke with a jolt when he heard the key in the lock. Then his daughter was standing in front of him. She was holding a pink balloon with Shanghai Zoo printed on it.

'What happened to your eye?' she said.

He self-consciously touched his face. 'I hurt it, angel.'

Holly pulled a face. 'It looks really gross.'

'It will be better tomorrow,' he said.

She tapped the balloon against his legs.

'We saw the red panda,' she told him. 'And the golden monkeys.'

He smiled. 'You sure it wasn't the other way round?' he said.

She looked confused. 'What?'

'You're sure it wasn't a red monkey and a golden panda?'

Holly shook her head, wise to his tricks. 'Daddy,' she sighed. 'You're going to have to stop being so dumb.'

Becca had gone into the kitchen and he did not see her face. She was at the fridge, pulling out drinks. They must have eaten out.

Holly went off to her room. He heard the sound of her playing. No, he realised. She was reading. She was already reading. He had missed so much. He stood up and it felt like every muscle in his body was aching. His legs, his arms, his back. There was an old man's stiffness in them, and he knew that he had asked them to do too much. He walked over to his wife and watched her face in the light of the fridge.

'I thought you were gone,' he said, and she turned to look at him. There were three cartons in her hands. Orange juice for Holly, cranberry juice for herself and milk for his tea. A drink for each of them.

She shook her head. 'I'm not gone,' Becca said simply. 'We're not gone.' She put down the drinks and stood in front of him. She reached out and lightly touched his broken face and he held her hand there and he would not let it go.

He remembered.

TWENTY-NINE

'This is Suzy Too,' Bill told the two new guys. 'Everyone comes to Suzy Too.'

Business was good. The cake was getting bigger. The firm couldn't cope with the work. So Devlin had flown to London and a little over a month later a pair of lawyers arrived with two-year contracts and dreams of early retirement.

On their first night in Shanghai, Devlin and Bill took them for dinner on the Bund and then Bill took them out for drinks on Mao Ming Nan Lu.

Jet-lagged and drunk and free at last from the chains of home, they stared with disbelief at their first sight of Suzy Too. The girls at the bar. The girls on the dance floor. The girls everywhere. They had never known there were so many women in the world.

Their very first night in this city, Bill thought, envying them as he signalled for Tsingtao all round. He blinked up at the strobe lights. The black stars had almost gone but the lights all had an aura, like a misty halo. He looked away, remembering his own first night in Shanghai.

Jenny One walked by, suddenly looking a lot older. She took Bill's hand and placed a chaste kiss on one cheek and then the other. She smiled sadly and kept walking. Bill wanted to ask—*But what about the Frenchman?*

The new guys were covered in girls. Hanging on their arms, asking them where they came from, swaying their hips, and trying to encourage the new guys to dance, because then there would be no need to talk to them.

'Bill—these girls?' said one of the new guys. Somehow it was a question, although Bill did not know exactly what the man was asking. There was a tall, haughty woman behind him with her long arms around his waist, and two smaller ones by his side, one of them doll-like and pretty, the other one chubby but proudly large-breasted. Bill did not recognise them. It felt like Suzy Too was full of newcomers. The women were holding the guy's hands and trying to encourage him to shuffle his brogues to Eminem's 'Shake That'. Bill guessed that Elgar was more his thing. The guy was one of those old-fashioned Englishmen—all Adam's apple and glasses and an accent that told Bill he had been educated privately and among boys. Harry something. He looked as if he had struggled to meet girls all his life. But even Harry something wouldn't struggle in Shanghai, Bill thought. In six months Harry something would think he was Errol Flynn. In six months he would be the cock of the Bund. But for now there was a thin film of nervous mist on his spectacles.

'I'll tell you about these girls,' said the other new guy. Fresh off the flight from Heathrow, he fancied himself as something of an expert. Bill looked him up and down. Blond, cropped, fit in a Sunday-morning-football sort of way. Nigel somebody. He was not so obviously overwhelmed as Harry something. Probably been on a two-week package tour to Thailand, Bill thought. Probably had a hand-job in Patpong and thought that made him Marco Polo.

'These girls are whores,' Nigel said confidently. He reached out and squeezed a small breast too hard. The girl flinched, pulled away with a grimace of pain and distaste.

Bill took a breath, and held his temper.

'Don't call them that,' he said. 'Please don't ever call them that.'

The man looked at Bill with surly belligerence, but said nothing. Bill was about to become a partner. He was billing more hours than anyone in the firm. Soon Bill would be their boss. He could make their lives very hard.

'Then what are they?' said Harry something. His little eyes had completely disappeared behind his steamed-up glasses. The chubby girl with large breasts had a hand in his trouser pocket and she was laughingly telling the other one that she could not find anything. This is not a deferential society, Bill thought. 'If not whores,' asked Harry something, 'then what are they?'

Bill took a long pull on his Tsingtao. He was going to start cutting back on the beer. He was going to stop coming to Suzy Too. He wasn't a tourist guide. Let them find their own fun. A shower of black stars fell across his vision and was gone.

'They're just practical,' he said.

*   *   *

He had been told that they did not feel love in the way that he felt love, that they responded to acts of kindness and generosity with all of their body and heart, but that was not love, they told him, not in the Western sense of the one true one, the partner for life, the unmet lover found at last. Not love like that, like love back home, the way that it was

423

meant to be, they said. Not real love the way it was made in the West.

They were just so practical when it came to love, they told him until he believed it, until he could see what they meant, and he could see that we in the West were not practical at all—we simply fell, we just took the giddy step over the cliff and landed where our wayward hearts took us.

The East was practical. The East could not afford to love. The West was romantic. Because the West could afford to love.

But he came to believe that somehow he and JinJin Li had traded places. He came to believe that she had somehow stopped being practical and become infected with the Western concept of love—loving him even when common sense told her to bail out, loving him even when her head told her to find someone else, loving him when every instinct in her soul told her *to be practical*—she still loved him, she loved him through all the hurt and betrayal and sadness, and she kept on loving him even when it was not wise, and even when it brought her no happiness.

And Bill changed too. He had started out believing that he was different from the married man in the silver Porsche who had brought her to Paradise Mansions. Bill thought that he was better than that man because his heart was good, because he cared for her in a deeper, truer sense than that man, and that his love for her was real. But even back then, when he thought he loved her well and true, he could not deny that he felt that he had a claim on JinJin Li.

He had invested so much of everything he had to give, and he had risked losing all the things he

424

loved, and he told himself that—unlike the man in the silver Porsche—he expected nothing in return. That was not true. What he expected in return was that she would love him and that she would keep on loving him as if he owned the lease on her heart. They would both be disappointed.

Was he any better than the man who had kept her in Paradise Mansions? No, Bill saw now that he was far worse, because he had dressed it all up as love. But when JinJin Li finally remembered to be practical and walk away, when the contract between them was finally broken, he'd felt totally and utterly betrayed, and responded with a bitterness that he thought might choke him.

Bill, you're behaving like a romantic Western fool, he told himself. You're acting like she has the power to rip out your heart.

And he knew that just wasn't practical.

*   *   *

The office was dark now.

The only light came from the twinkling jewel box of Pudong in the early hours beyond the window, and from the glow of the screen of Shane's laptop. It shone on the face of Alice Greene as she copied the files, and Bill wondered what she was seeing. Corruption and justice, he thought, scoops and awards. It was all mixed up with her, he thought. The wish for a better world, the need for a better life. Greed and conscience. Perhaps it was all mixed up with everyone.

'Why did he keep all this stuff?' she said, not looking away from the screen. 'I mean—even if this Chairman Sun character needed paying off by these Germans, why keep a record of it?'

'Because he was a good lawyer,' Bill said. 'And a good man.'

She snorted. 'That's an oxymoron, isn't it?' She looked over her shoulder and smiled. 'Just kidding.'

'Are you almost done?' He wanted her to take what she needed and get out of here. There was something else he had to do tonight.

'Finished,' she said. There were perhaps a dozen disks on Bill's desk. She straightened them like a card dealer with a new deck, and slipped them into her shoulder bag. Bill walked her to the lift.

'Thanks,' she said. 'I mean it, Bill. You did the right thing.'

'First time for everything,' he said.

When he was alone he unlocked his desk and took out a shoebox. He opened it and leafed through the evidence of their time together in Guilin, Changchun, Shanghai. On the boat, going down the Yangtze, the Three Gorges outside their cabin window. All their photographs. The box was stuffed full. So many photographs. And now he had to destroy them. He carried the box across the office to the shredding machine.

There were too many. She had had a fanatical need to record their happiness. Were they all like that? Or was it just JinJin? He never really knew what was typically Chinese and what was typically JinJin Li. Now he would never know. It didn't matter. He began to feed his memories into the shredder. In the end there were only two that he could not destroy.

The passport photograph taken the summer before he had met her. The only passport

426

photograph that anyone ever looked beautiful in. The cool wide eyes staring back at the camera, lips wet, mouth closed, beauty intact, goofy charm successfully concealed. Then there was the second photograph that he could not bring himself to destroy. The picture of them dancing, taken by the elderly American after dinner on the boat down the Yangtze. It had almost been a joke to them, Bill and JinJin dancing to Chinese pop music on the ship's tiny dance floor. But the lovely old tourist had told them that they looked so happy, and so perfect together, and he'd insisted that JinJin hand over her camera so that he could record the moment. They were both grateful and touched, although Bill could not tell if the old American was a saint or a crazy person. Maybe a bit of both. And anyway, the old American had been wrong about them. Because so soon after that picture was taken it was all over forever. Perhaps that was the perfect reason for taking the picture. Perhaps the old tourist on that dreadful cruise ship knew that it could never last.

Bill slipped the two surviving photographs into his wallet, and then he stood there staring at the shredding machine, and the pile of glossy paper beneath it, wondering what had hit him.

It was never meant to be this way. He had thought that he could somehow stand back from the thing they shared, as if what he thought of as the real part of his life—Becca and Holly, family and home, wife and child—could remain untouched by his feelings for JinJin Li.

He had been wrong.

Now the evidence had been reduced to the two surviving photographs. The passport photo. The picture of them dancing on the boat. He wasn't going to keep them forever, just for a little while, and when they were gone there would be nothing to show that they had ever met, apart from what they carried inside.

Perhaps the thing that killed his father would one day come for him. In fifty years, or next week. It did not matter. He would still have time to destroy the two photographs. What did they call it? Oh yes. Putting your affairs in order.

He would do it. He would put his affairs in order. One day. But he couldn't do it yet. Not yet. He couldn't do it yet.

Bill walked to the lift and pressed the call button. The lift came and he stood there staring at it. The doors closed as he turned and went back into his office, where he fed the last two photographs into the shredding machine.

You have to remember the bad times, he thought. That's the only way to get through it. That's the only way to go on. You don't remember the good times. You deny them. You forget them. That's how you get over it. That's how you carry on with your life.

The passport photo. Gone. The dancing picture. Gone. Every trace of her and them was now destroyed. It was the only way.

Remember the bad times, Bill thought.

*   *   *

From page one of the *South China Morning Post*, 1st June 200-:

SHANGHAI GRAFT PROBE SPREADS

Government plans to curb illegal land grabs
by Song Tiping and Alice Greene

The Communist Party's top disciplinary watchdog is expanding its Shanghai corruption probe to the city's leading property developers, state media said yesterday.

Following this newspaper's exposé of the Yangdong land grab, senior local government official Chairman Sun Yong was arrested at the grand opening of the Green Acres luxury development and charged with 'loose morals, economic crimes and decadent living'.

Plainclothes secret police accompanied by officers from the Public Security Bureau ushered Chairman Sun from the cocktail party in handcuffs, protesting his innocence and still clutching a champagne flute.

Rather pre-empting the verdict of Sun's trial, the state news agency commented, 'His punishment of a lengthy jail term will fully demonstrate the central committee's resolution to build a clean party and to fight corruption.'

Now more cases of illegal authorisation of land for property development are expected to be uncovered, leading to investigations of more government officials and businessmen.

Dong Fan, a property industry professor at Beijing Normal University, said most corruption cases occurred during the land acquisition stage.

'Land is owned by state and local governments and the whole development *operation is run in a murky, non-transparent environment,' Mr Dong said.*

In a speech to more than 800 guests at the city's National Day banquet, in what appeared to be a manoeuvre to boost the city's reputation, Shanghai mayor and acting party chief Han Zheng yesterday expressed optimism in Shanghai's future development and commitment to the battle against corruption.

New urgency as heads roll—A4

Devlin tossed the paper on to his desk. Then he put his feet up, the heels of his Church's brogues resting on the cover of the *South China Morning Post*.

'The thing is,' Devlin said, 'when they crack down on corruption, it has actually got bugger all to do with justice and truth, and everything to do with political manoeuvring. The things that poor old Sun stands accused of—cutting in his family, feathering his nest, grabbing as many sweeties as he could cram into his greedy old cakehole—are equally true of any local or government official in the country.'

Devlin did not ask Bill to sit down.

'Okay, Sun was a fool,' Devlin continued, with a small sigh of regret. 'He didn't have enough friends in high places. Should have cut in some friends in Beijing—or their families. They always crack down sooner or later. They have to. That's the funny thing—they would have got him anyway.' And finally the flash of anger in the eyes, at last the murderous rage of the betrayed. 'Without you

430

selling me out,' he told Bill, 'and without this hack from Hong Kong.'

The firm's senior partner looked at Bill with a mixture of hurt and loathing. Above his head the red light of a CCTV camera gleamed like an ember of hell. Of course, you couldn't take a leak in this building without someone watching you. But Bill had known that, hadn't he?

'So you think you're better than the rest of us, Holden,' Devlin said. It wasn't a question. His mouth twisted with mockery. 'Purer. More noble.'

Bill shook his head. 'I never thought that.'

'But you couldn't close your eyes to the rottenness,' Devlin said. He got a sly look about him. 'Just because some Chinese bitch fucked you blind.'

'Watch your mouth,' Bill said quietly.

Devlin looked frightened for a moment. But it was just a moment. He was the one with the power here. He jabbed a finger at Bill.

'More people are climbing out of poverty in this country than anywhere at any time in human history,' he said. 'In human history! Think about it! And assholes like you are fighting against it. So, you tell me—who's the idiot here, Bill? Who's the villain? You or me?'

Bill said nothing.

'And what's your wife going to say when she learns you chucked a partnership away?' Devlin said. 'What's your daughter going to say, Bill, when she finds out her daddy is a self-righteous loser who doesn't have a job?'

Bill shrugged. 'I don't know. Becca will be disappointed. But my daughter's a bit too young to understand.' He smiled at a memory. 'She just wants me to pretend to be a prince all the time.'

Devlin snorted. 'Well, you're good at that, if nothing else. Pretending to be a prince. But you're no different to everyone else in this country, Bill. You hate everyone's corruption except your own.'

There were two Chinese security guards in the doorway. One was holding a cardboard box containing what Bill recognised as his personal possessions. The other had his briefcase and jacket.

'Get him out of my sight,' Devlin said.

Bill's briefcase slapped hard against his stomach. He was handed his jacket. And then the open cardboard box was placed in his arms. He stared down at the detritus on his desk.

Time to leave.

The office stopped to watch him go. No Shane. No Nancy. But Mad Mitch was still there, standing up as Bill passed his desk, and shaking his hand. Then the new guys, their faces masks of shock and delight. Harry looked as though he thought he might get Bill's office by lunchtime. Nigel something had a love bite on his neck that was not quite covered by the white collar of his Brooks Brothers shirt. You can never go back to the Home Counties, Bill thought. You are Mr Charisma now. You are Brad Pitt. You are Errol Flynn. The city did that to you. It made you feel you were special.

And as the Chinese security guards escorted Bill from the building, he thought about a young man who'd been convinced that the world was his for the taking, and who never dreamed he could fall flat, or let his family down, he thought about a young man who had wrongly believed he was special, and he wondered what had ever happened to him.

*   *   *

There was the smell of paint in the apartment. Fresh paint and some sort of paste. The smell of things being changed, and life moving on.

Bill dropped his empty briefcase by the door and went into Holly's room. Becca was putting up wallpaper while Holly sat on the floor leafing through a book. Disney princesses smiled down from the walls. Snow White. The Little Mermaid. Cinderella. Sleeping Beauty. Pocahontas. Mulan. Belle from *Beauty and the Beast*. Holly smiled at him too.

'Daddy will know,' Becca said. 'Go on, ask him.'

'What do you call a baby penguin?' Holly said.

Bill's mind was blank.

'Baby horses have a special name,' Holly said, frowning impatiently. 'And baby cows. And baby sheep. But what about baby penguins?' she sighed elaborately. 'I don't know what's this.'

'I don't know what it is,' Becca corrected her.

'Me neither,' Holly said, and Becca laughed.

He picked up his daughter and held her in his arms. Heavier still. Definitely heavier. More robust and substantial. Staking her claim in the world.

'I'll think about it,' he said. 'The penguin thing. I'll give it some thought, angel.'

'Get back to me.'

'I'll do that.' He put her back on the floor and turned to Becca. 'Can we talk?'

'First I want to show you something,' she said, and there was an awkwardness about her, and he wondered if it would always be there now. Becca took him to the computer in the living room and she sat down in front of it.

'Look,' she said.

On the screen there were pictures of properties she had been looking at. A shortlist of new lives in new luxury homes. Homes fit for the family of a partner at Butterfield, Hunt and West.

He looked over her shoulder as she scrolled through the options. WESTWOOD GREEN—NEW LAKE-VIEW TOWNHOUSES TO BE RELEASED SOON—A HOME FOR THE HEART. This one was apparently an international community with a commitment to natural living. CALIFORNIA DREAMING AT RANCHO SANTA FE—ELEGANTLY FURNISHED SPANISH-STYLE VILLAS WITH PRIVATE GARDENS, 30 MINUTES TO HONG QIAO AIRPORT.

'I don't want to live here any more,' she said. A statement of cold fact. 'I'm not going to live here any more.'

He said her name and she looked up at him and it was a new way of looking at him, a look that buried bitterness and wariness and hurt, as if she carried a wound that was far from healed.

'The new house—becoming a partner—it's not going to happen,' he said. He hung his head, the sour taste of humiliation in his mouth. He was so ashamed. 'I lost my job.'

'Is that it?' She turned back to the screen, shaking her head. 'I thought—something else.'

He stared at her and then he understood. She had thought he was leaving. But he knew now that he would never leave. She would have to do the leaving.

434

Her fingers moved deftly across the keyboard. 'But they were going to make you a partner,' she said flatly. There was no disappointment in her voice. It was as if they hardly knew each other.

He shook his head. 'I'm sorry, Bec. I let you down. I let you down in every way I could.'

She was busy deleting files. Clicking on the dream homes with the mouse and dragging them to the icon of a wastepaper basket at the bottom of the screen. She turned to look at him. 'It's just a job, Bill. You'll get another one.'

He hung his head with despair. She didn't understand what this meant. 'We're going to have to go back. That life we wanted . . .'

'Someone will give you a job. You work hard. You're good at what you do.'

He shook his head. 'They fired me. I'm out. They cleared my desk and walked me to the door.' There was a shocked silence before he spoke again. 'And Holly—she loves her little friends here . . .'

'She's five years old,' said Becca, flaring up at last, glad for the chance to be openly angry with him. 'She'll make new friends. And that's what she will have to do all her life, the same as everyone else.' Then she softened, and put the palm of her hand on his heart. 'Look—we'll be okay. Our home—it's not the place in London, and it's not here. We take it with us wherever we go. It's you and me and Holly. That's our home. It's the three of us. I see that now.' She touched his face. 'Oh Bill—don't you know it yet?'

He blinked against the shameful sting of tears.

'I think you have to keep falling in love with each other,' Becca told him, dry eyed and calm. 'A man and a woman. A husband and wife. I think that's what you have to do. And if you can't do that, if you can't keep falling in love with each other, then I don't think you've got much of a chance.'

And later, when their daughter was sleeping in her room, and the light had been turned out on the Disney princesses, Bill went to the master bedroom and sat on the bed as Becca got undressed. But they didn't talk about what had happened that day or how it would work back in London. They were both a bit sick of talking. They both felt that they had talked enough for now.

She just took off her clothes and came quickly to him, as he sat there still dressed and watching her, and they said nothing. Not like a married couple at all. More like lovers.

My wife, thought Bill.

THIRTY

He saw her one last time.

He was on the Bund, in front of the Peace Hotel, on his way home after closing down his bank account, one of a hundred chores he had to do before they left the next day, and that was when JinJin Li walked past him with her new man.

It was a dazzling day in early July and he did a double take, snapping out of his reverie. She looked familiar, but he didn't think it could possibly be her, because it was only a passing resemblance, no more than that, and if it was her, if it was that special one, then surely he would recognise her in an instant? How could he mistake her for anyone else? How could she ever look like a mere imitation of the girl he had loved?

She looked too ordinary to be JinJin Li. Surely an ordinary woman could not have been the cause of all that wild happiness, of all that misery and upheaval and pain in so many hearts? Surely it would have to be someone very special to do all that?

But as he stood on the Bund, staring after her, the woman looked over her shoulder at him, and the man looked at him too, placing a protective arm around her shoulder as if to say, *Don't worry, darling, I will protect you from that bad man.*

And so it was really her.

It was JinJin Li. And they had walked past each other like total strangers. Bill almost laughed out loud at the absurdity of it all. So much spent emotion and then he almost failed to recognise her.

JinJin and the man kept walking.

Bill turned and followed them, with no idea of what he was going to do or say. But he knew that he objected to that man's arm around her shoulder. He objected to the idea that JinJin Li would ever need protection from him.

And as Bill increased his pace, gaining on them now, suddenly knowing it was her, he understood why she would never be a TV presenter. He had always suspected that one day he would turn on CCTV and there she would be, reading the autocue and staring straight at him, looking like the passport photograph taken the year before she had met him. But like so many of their plans, he saw that it was not going to happen.

The glow had gone, or the glossiness of youth, or

the magic, or whatever it had been. Maybe it had never been there in the first place, only in his eyes. Perhaps it was only there, that magic light of love, because he wanted and needed it to be. But now he saw her with the light extinguished and she was an attractive Chinese woman in her thirties, no more and no less, and she was getting older, and none of it was very complicated.

And here was the funny thing—as he saw her ordinariness, as he registered that she was just another human being trying to make her way in the world, trying her best to look nice for her new man and for herself, Bill Holden still loved her—or at least he still carried the love that remains when love has died, and he always would.

But she was not for him and he was not for her.

The happy couple had stopped walking. The man was buying a newspaper. He was a Westerner, maybe a bit younger than Bill. He didn't look like anything special. He looked like the first guy who had come along. He looked like someone she had met in a bar or a gym or wherever it was that normal people met.

Bill realised that she had not stopped smiling since she had seen him, a strained and defensive smile, as if he were amusing, or as if she was trying to convince herself that all of this was funny.

And perhaps I am funny, Bill thought. Perhaps I am a barrel of laughs. Or perhaps her smile was just another bandage on another wound. He did not know.

Bill and JinJin stared at each other—they were both wearing dark glasses, and Bill was grateful for that, he could not stand to have her look in his eyes again—and the man, the first man who had come along, the man from the gym or the bar, put his arm around her again—*Don't worry, I'll protect you from this bad man, darling.* You know nothing, Bill thought. Oh, you have no idea.

And suddenly Bill found that he had started mouthing banalities. 'Nice to see you, nice to see you,' he said, while he stood there shaking everybody's hand like the sporting captain of a losing side. The man's hand. JinJin's hand.

That's the role he chose to play, the only one he could think of—the good loser. Three cheers for the guy from the gym or the bar or wherever it was. Had he ever shaken JinJin's hand before? He didn't think so. He was told the name of the new guy and immediately forgot it as he kept saying, 'Nice to meet you, nice to meet you.' Nice. So nice. Everything was so nice that it almost suffocated him.

Then he turned away, but her voice called him back, even as he kept moving.

'My mum's in town!' she said, a happy exclamation unveiled as if it should mean something to him. He kept walking.

'Then give her my love,' he said over his shoulder, and he meant it. And perhaps she said it because she felt it too—the terrible finality of the ending, of letting it go, and she wanted him to stay for just a few more seconds, because they both knew they would never see each other again after today, and all they would ever share now was the past and whatever photographs that JinJin Li had been unable to destroy.

She was not innocent. She was not that. She was from a far harder world than he could ever imagine, a world that he had only glimpsed. But if

439

she was not innocent, then there was still an innocence and purity about her, part of her that could never be touched or spoiled or owned—not by her father, not by the man who put her up in Paradise Mansions, and not by Bill. There was a part of her that was untouchable, and he envied and loved her for it.

He got to the end of the street, that famous street, old colonial Shanghai staring across the river at the future, and he hailed a cab, and as the taxi turned and drove back down the Bund he saw them sitting outside a café.

The man was reading a newspaper while JinJin sat opposite him, staring off into the middle distance, being ignored by her boyfriend, not even an attempt at a smile on her face now.

Bill had to laugh. They were arguing about him, or they had argued about him, and what she had said—*My mum's in town!*—and what she had meant by what she had said, and did perhaps JinJin want him to call, and all of that, and it felt like the most pointless argument in the world—to argue about him, as something as dead and over and finished as Bill.

The smile was gone and JinJin Li looked quite ordinary and they were just a man and a woman sitting at a café trying to make sense of being together, and making no sense at all right now, and Bill had to grin because he felt like it was some higher power's gift to him, a consolation prize to the man who would never stop believing that he had loved her first and best and then lost her. He raised a hand in salute and farewell and, sitting across from the grumpy new boyfriend reading his newspaper, JinJin waved back.

Bill knew that somewhere down the line she would smile again, and he could not begrudge her that, he could even be happy about it, even if she would not be smiling it for him, the world-famous smile of JinJin Li.

*   *   *

The plan was that Tiger would drive them to the airport in his new BMW. But the BMW was reclaimed by the loan company when Tiger's business collapsed, and so the plan changed.

Down in the courtyard of Paradise Mansions, Holly adjusted herself in her father's arms as she contemplated Tiger emerging from an old red VW Santana.

'Is Tiger a taxi driver now?' she said, gesturing with the yellow plastic pony she held in her fist.

Tiger laughed with embarrassment, looking from Bill to Becca, and then down at his shoes. 'Too many people with same idea,' he said, turning to Bill. 'Now too much Chinese furniture in China.' He looked shyly at Holly. 'Yes, old Tiger a taxi driver now.'

'It was still a good idea,' Becca said.

Bill placed a hand on his shoulder. 'You'll think of something else.'

Tiger cast a mournful eye at the red Santana. 'But should be a better car. Should be a limo, boss. Like the one you came in on.'

Bill placed Holly on the ground and hefted the first of the suitcases. 'We're grateful for the lift,' he said.

'And limos are overrated,' Becca said, getting into the passenger seat. The phone in her bag rang

441

once and then again and it was ringing for a third time as she turned it off.

Bill sat in the back of the cab with Holly on his lap and as the city slipped away from them the child slept. He turned his head to look at the Bund, and a single black star seemed to fall across the sky. As they crossed the river his daughter stirred in his arms.

'Are we home yet?' she said sleepily, and in the front of the car Becca laughed, turned to look at her, and at her husband. One day their beautiful daughter would stop saying these things, he thought. But not for a while.

Bill pulled his daughter close, his arms wrapped around her, her head nodding against his chest. She was still gripping the yellow plastic pony. The old VW turned on to the highway and the last lights of Shanghai were lost to him.

'Just rest your eyes,' he said, so quietly that only his daughter would hear. 'That's the big secret. You just rest your eyes and then you're home before you know it.'

CHIVERS
LARGE
PRINT
–direct–

If you have enjoyed this Large Print book and would like to build up your own collection of Large Print books, please contact

Chivers Large Print Direct

Chivers Large Print Direct offers you a full service:

• Prompt mail order service

• Easy-to-read type

• The very best authors

• Special low prices

For further details either call Customer Services on (01225) 336552 or write to us at Chivers Large Print Direct, **FREEPOST**, Bath BA1 3ZZ

Telephone Orders: **FREEPHONE** 08081 72 74 75